YORICK
AND
BÖNES

JEREMY TANKARD
AND HERMIONE TANKARD

HARPER
alley

An Imprint of HarperCollinsPublishers

HarperAlley is an imprint of HarperCollins Publishers.

Yorick and Bones
 For information address HarperCollins Children's Books, a division of HarperCollins Publishers, 195 Broadway, New York, NY 10007.
www.harperalley.com
Library of Congress Control Number: 2019939423
ISBN 978-0-06-285430-8 — ISBN 978-0-06-285431-5 (paperback)
The artist used Clip Studio to create the digital illustrations for this book.
Typography by Chris Dickey
20 21 22 23 24 SCP 10 9 8 7 6 5 4 3 2 1
❖
First Edition

Jeremy: For Hermione, of course!

Hermione: For my mom and dad, and for my friends.
You guys make nerdiness cool!

ACT ONE:
LOVE BITES

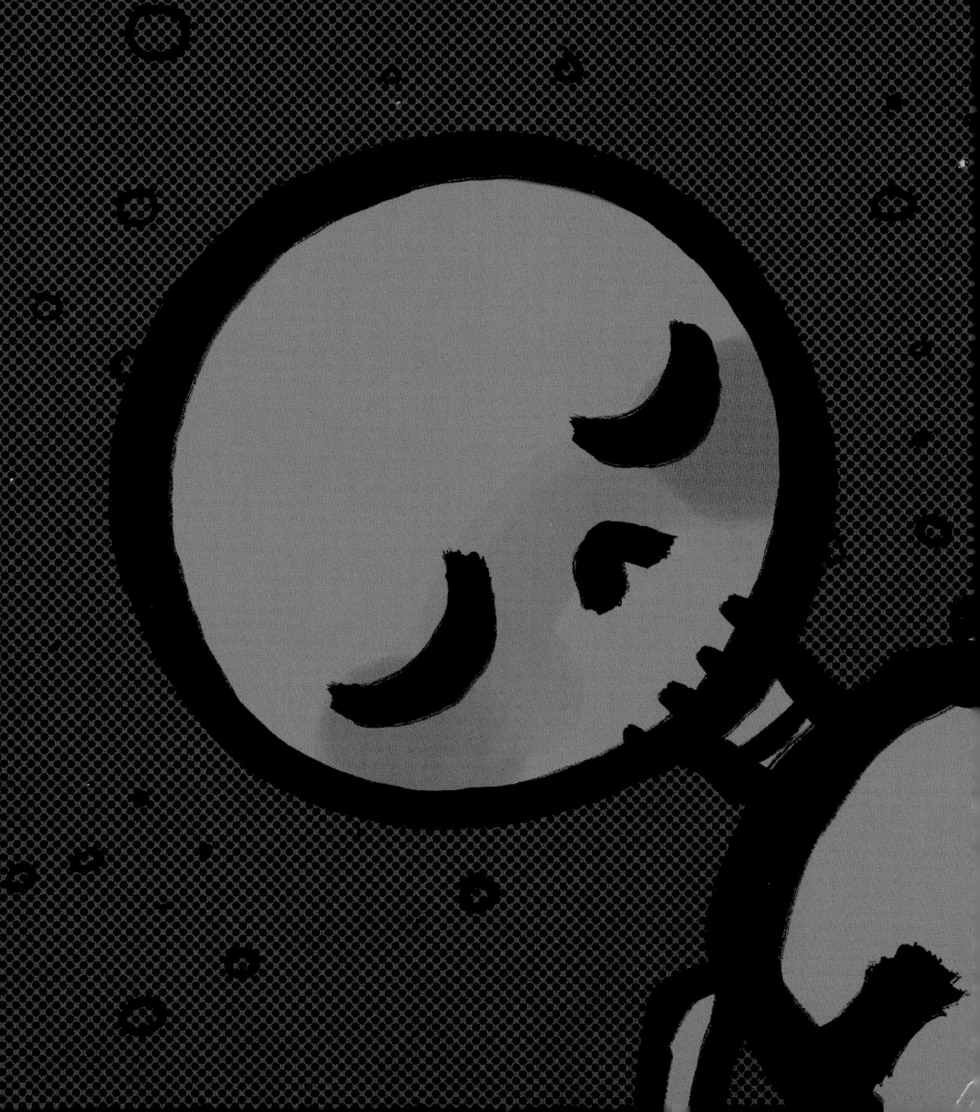

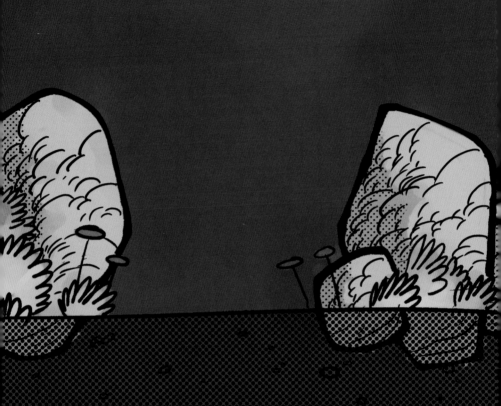

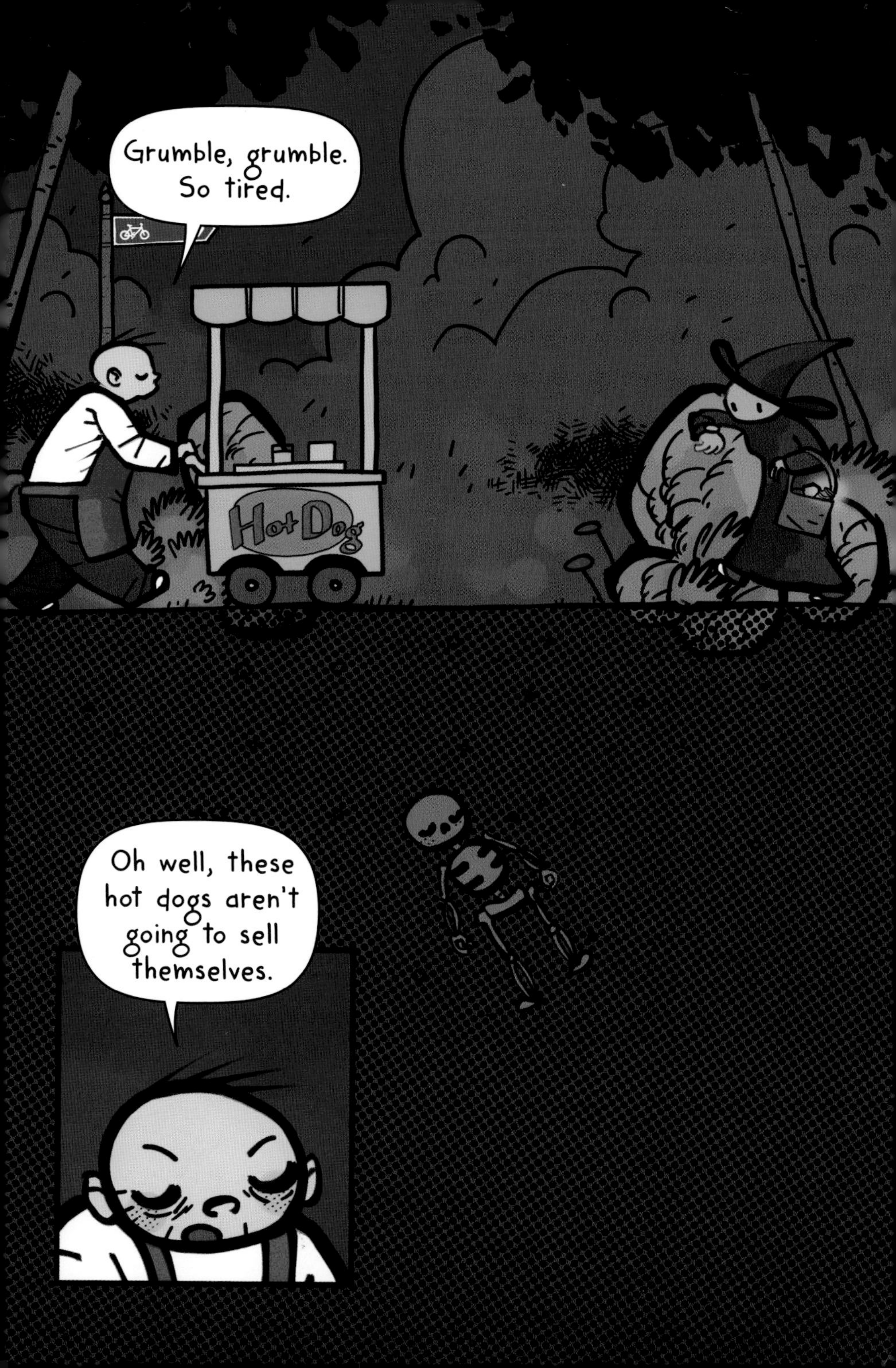
Grumble, grumble. So tired.
Hot Dog
Oh well, these hot dogs aren't going to sell themselves.

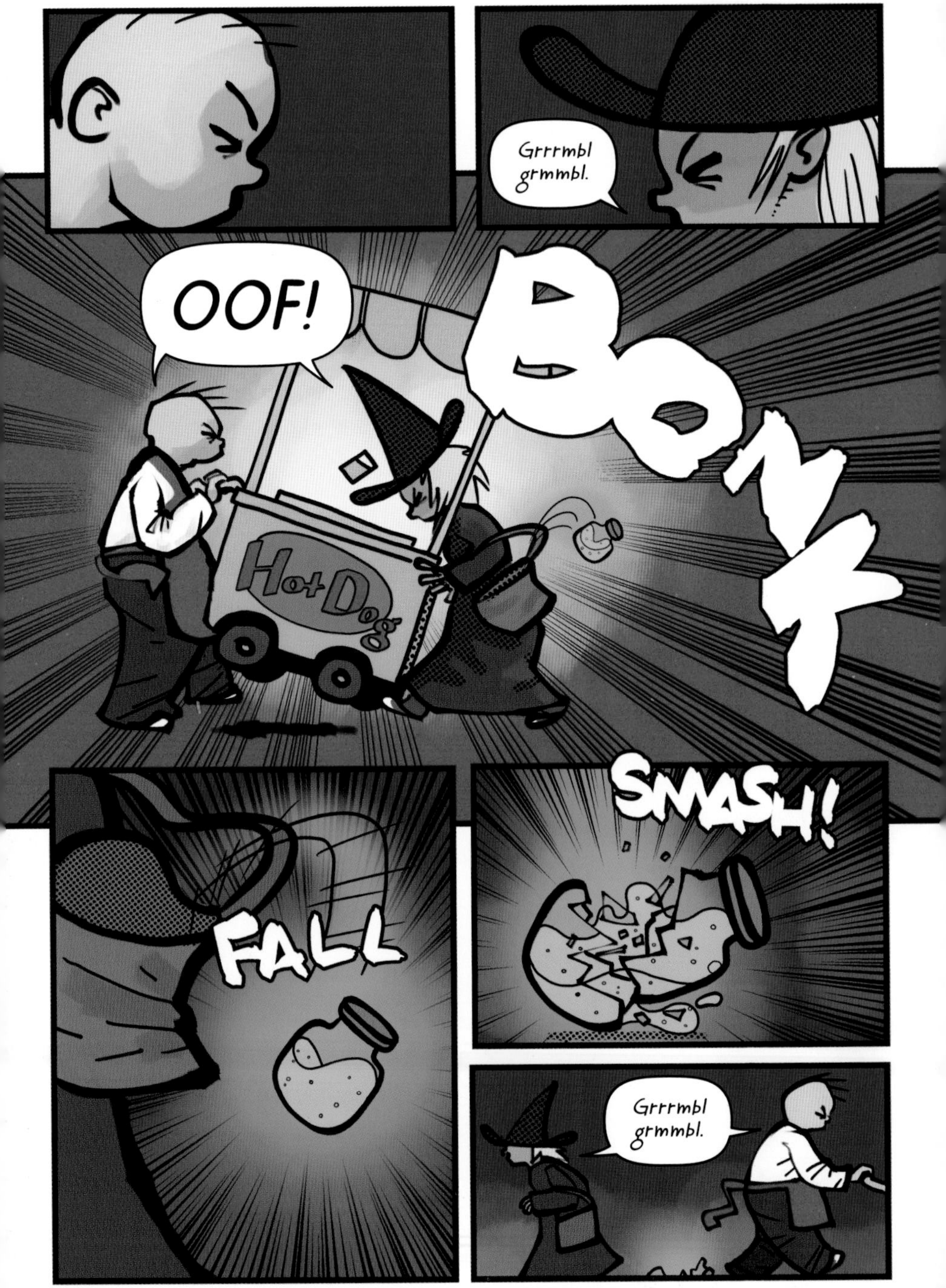
Grrrmbl grmmbl.
OOF!
BONK
FALL
SMASH!
Grrrmbl grmmbl.

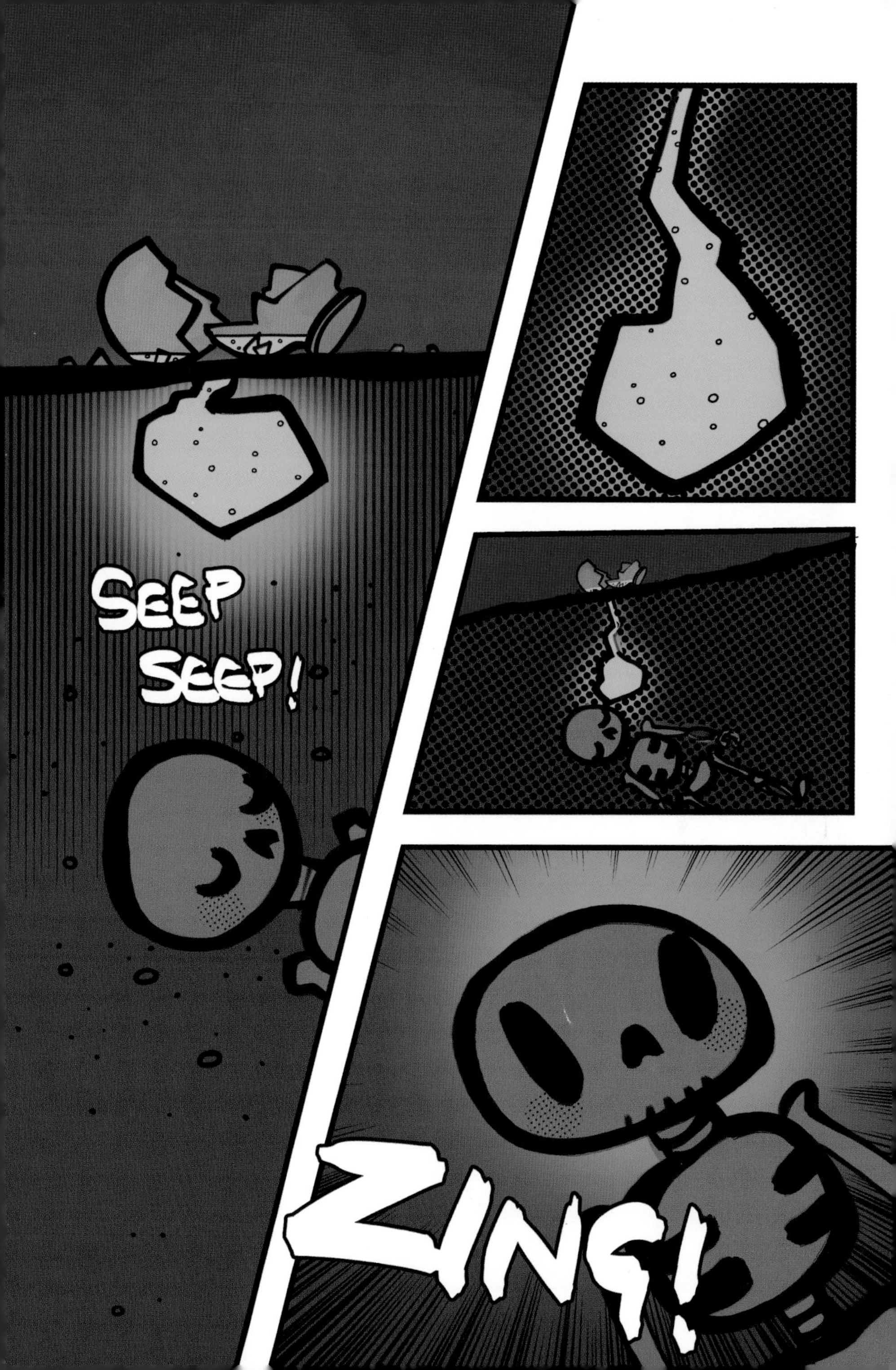
SEEP
SEEP!
ZING!

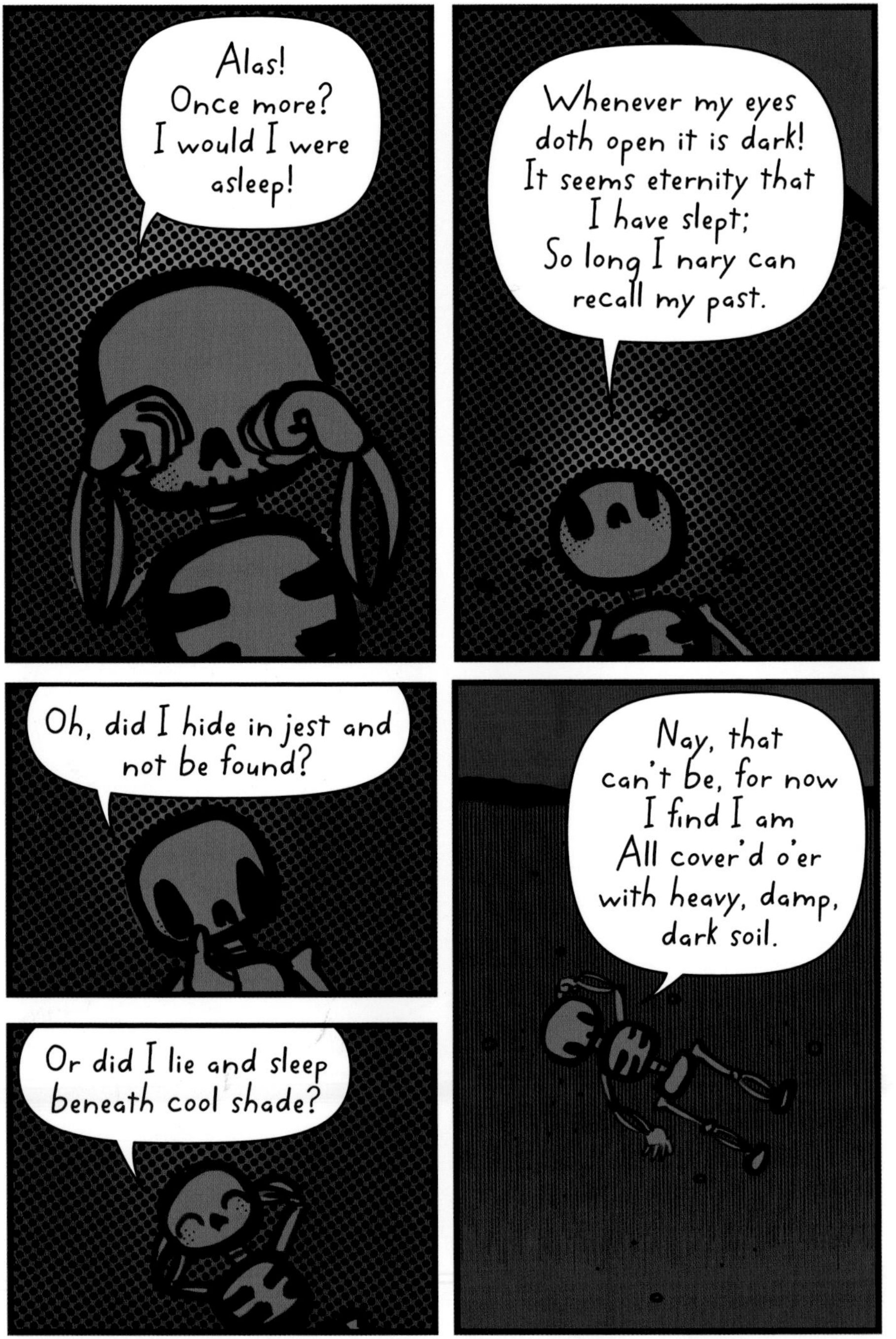
Alas! Once more? I would I were asleep!
Whenever my eyes doth open it is dark! It seems eternity that I have slept; So long I nary can recall my past.
Oh, did I hide in jest and not be found?
Or did I lie and sleep beneath cool shade?
Nay, that can't be, for now I find I am All cover'd o'er with heavy, damp, dark soil.

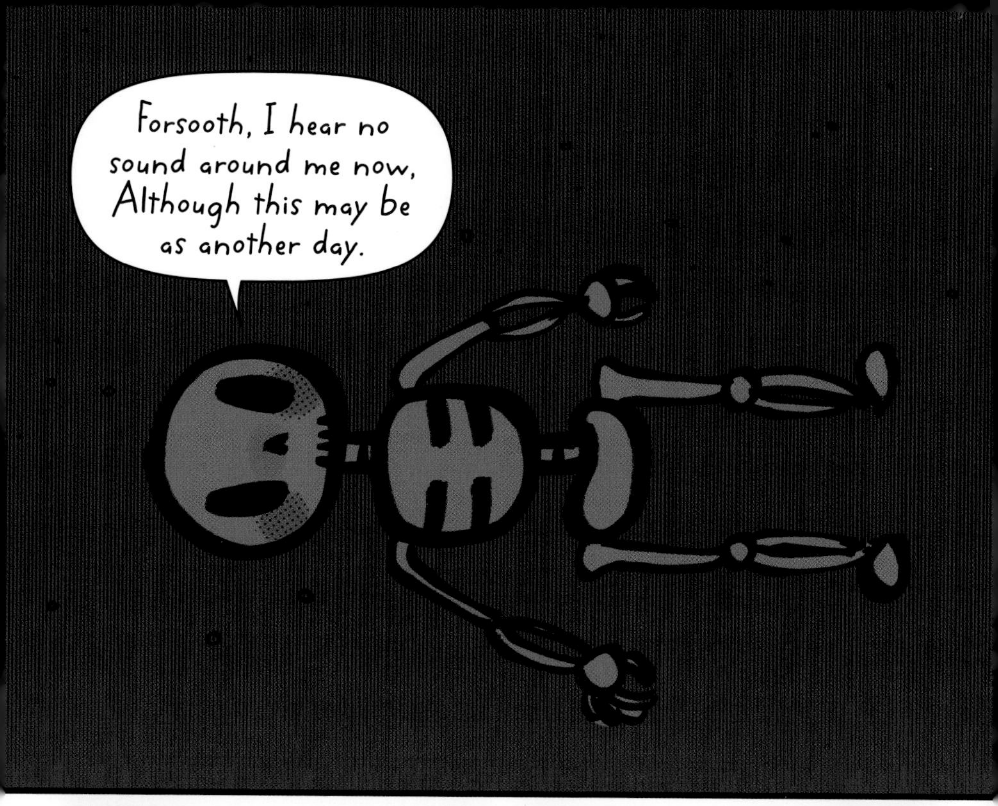
Forsooth, I hear no sound around me now, Although this may be as another day.

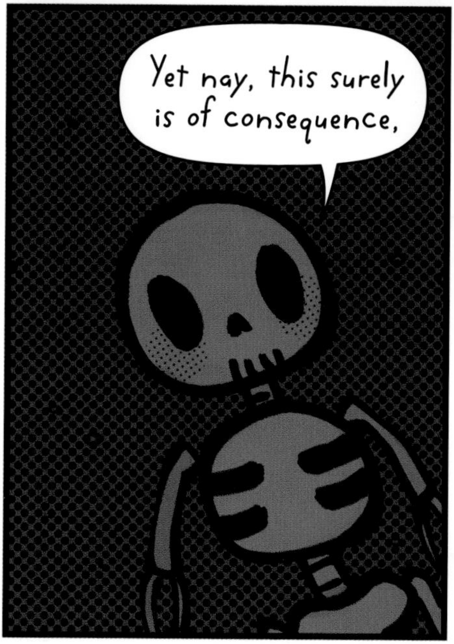
Yet nay, this surely is of consequence,

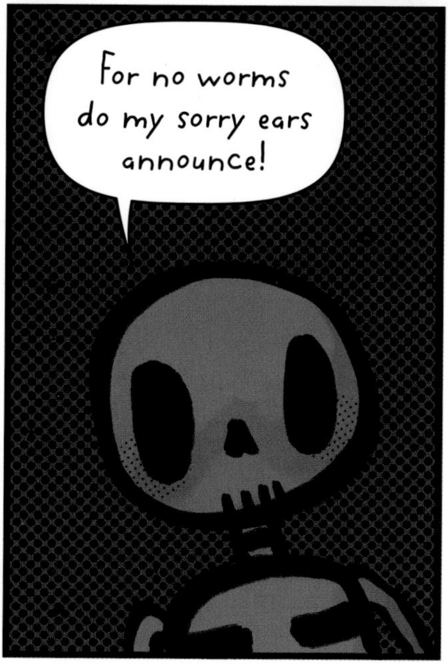
For no worms do my sorry ears announce!

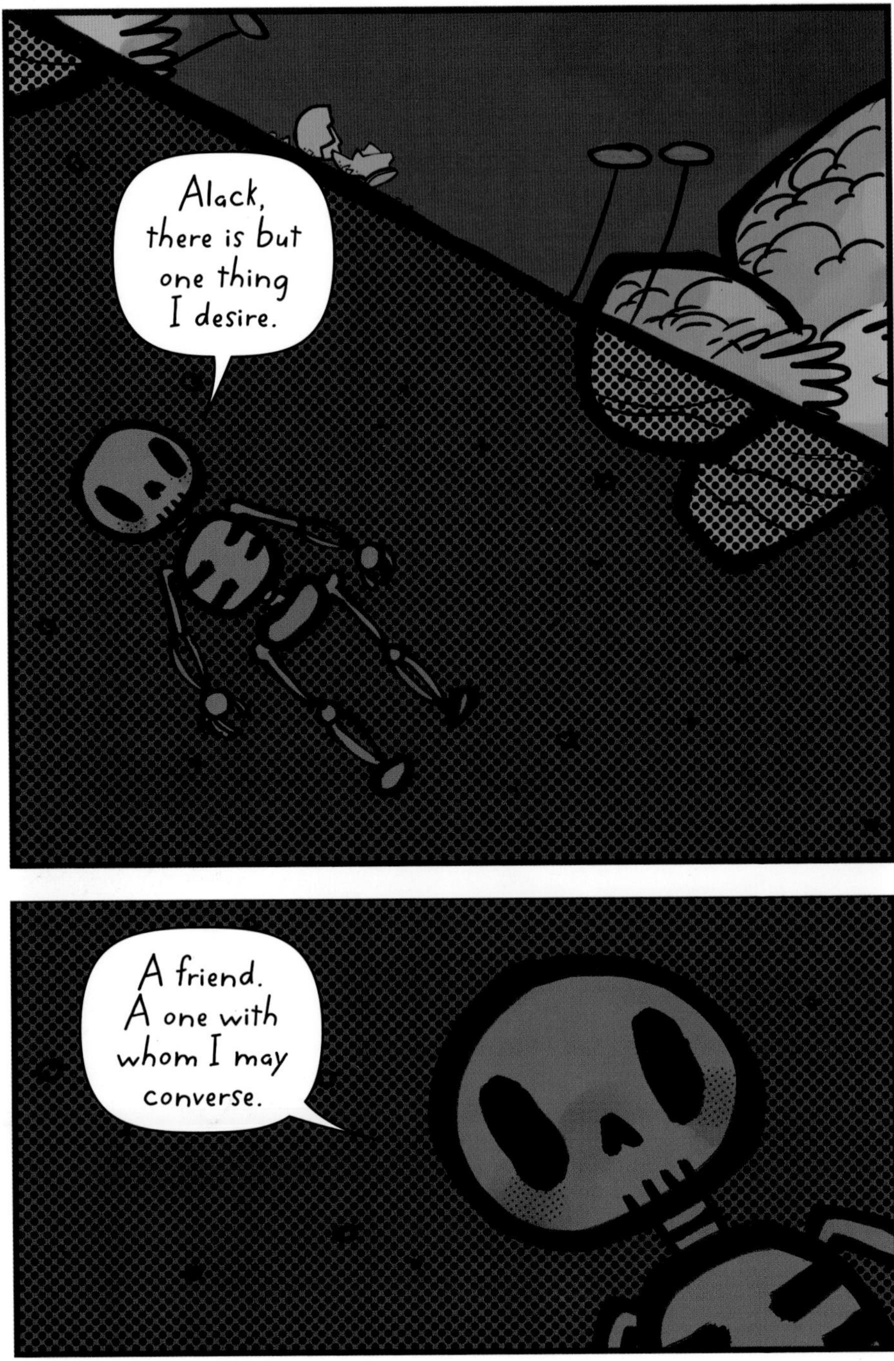
Alack, there is but one thing I desire.
A friend. A one with whom I may converse.

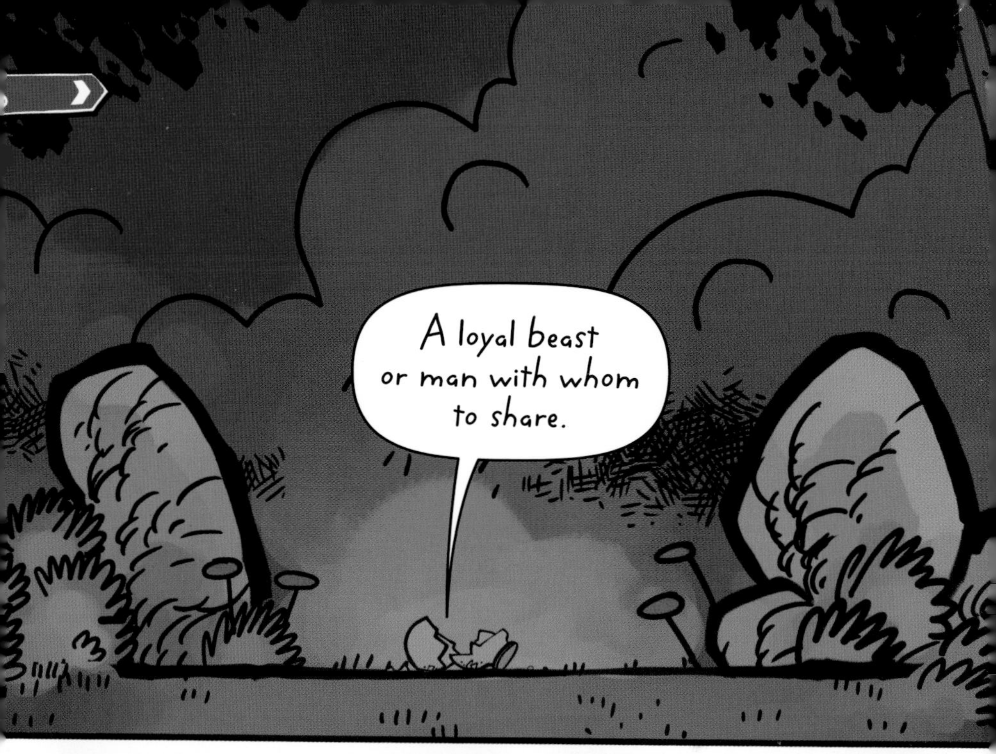
A loyal beast or man with whom to share.

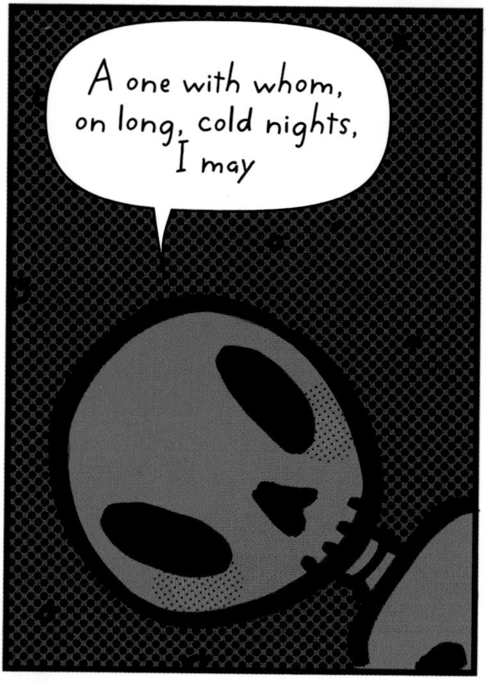
A one with whom, on long, cold nights, I may

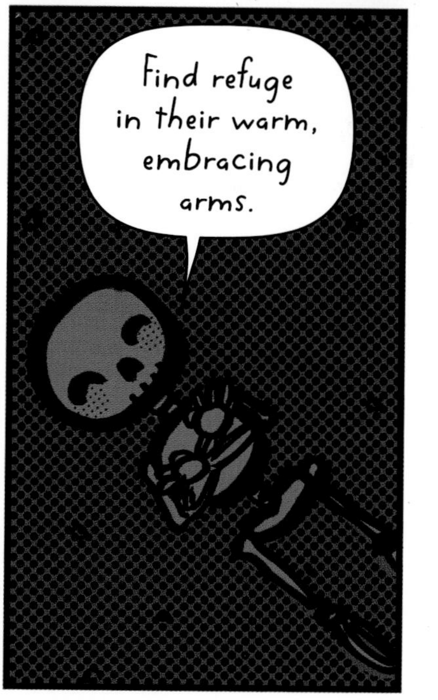
Find refuge in their warm, embracing arms.

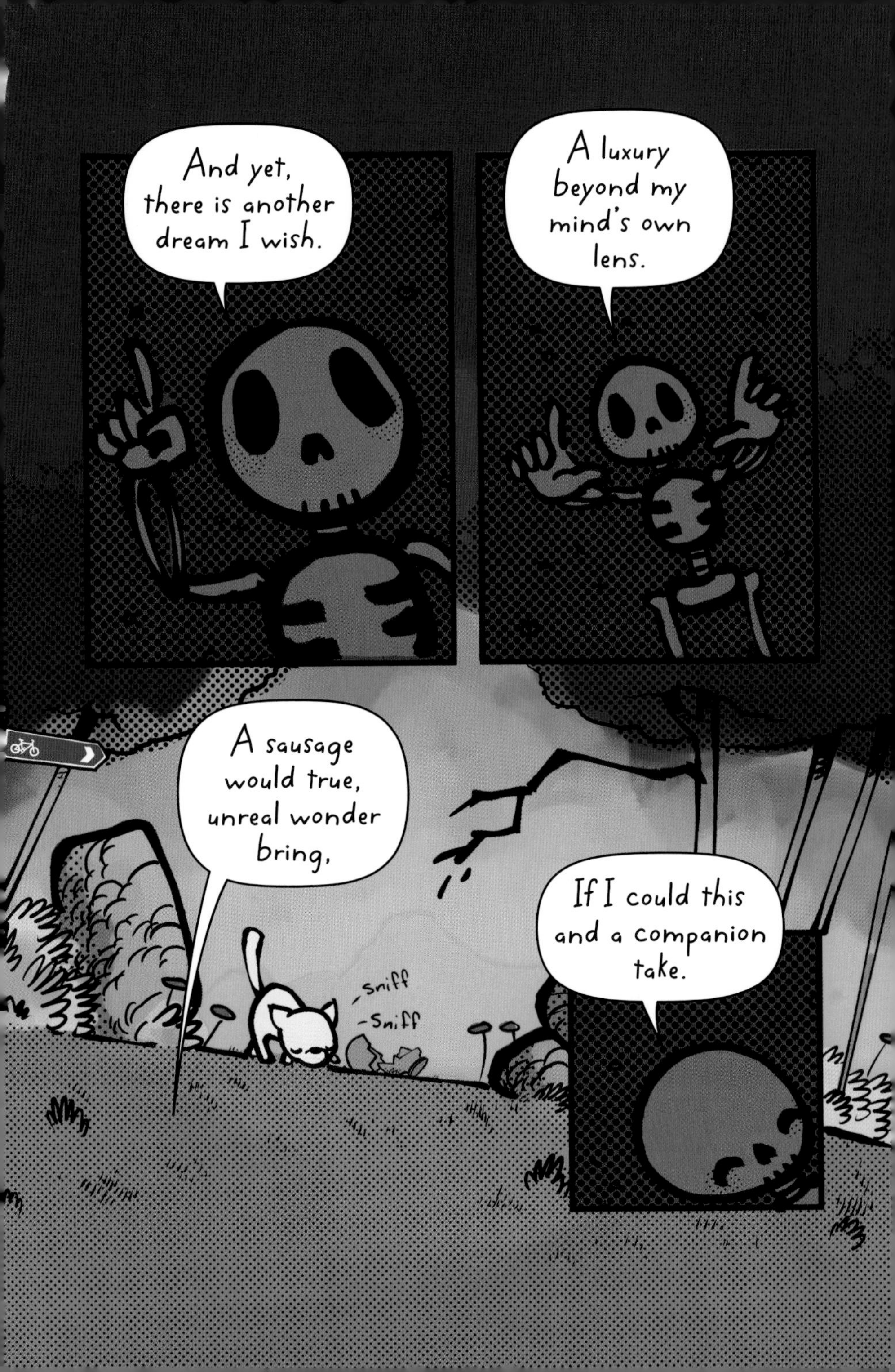
And yet, there is another dream I wish.
A luxury beyond my mind's own lens.
A sausage would true, unreal wonder bring,
-Sniff
-Sniff
If I could this and a companion take.

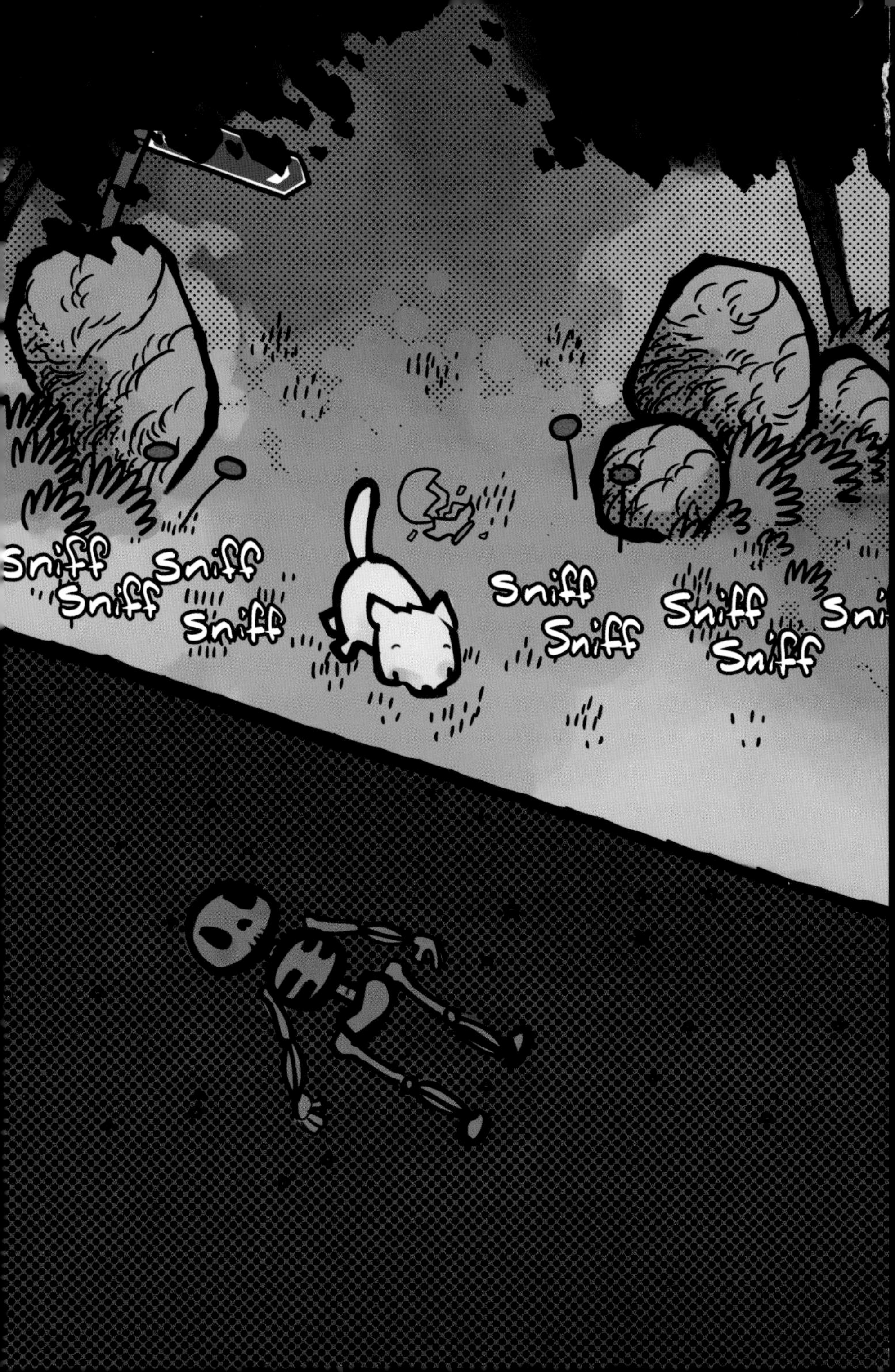
Sniff
Sniff
Sniff
Sniff
Sniff
Sniff
Sniff
Sniff

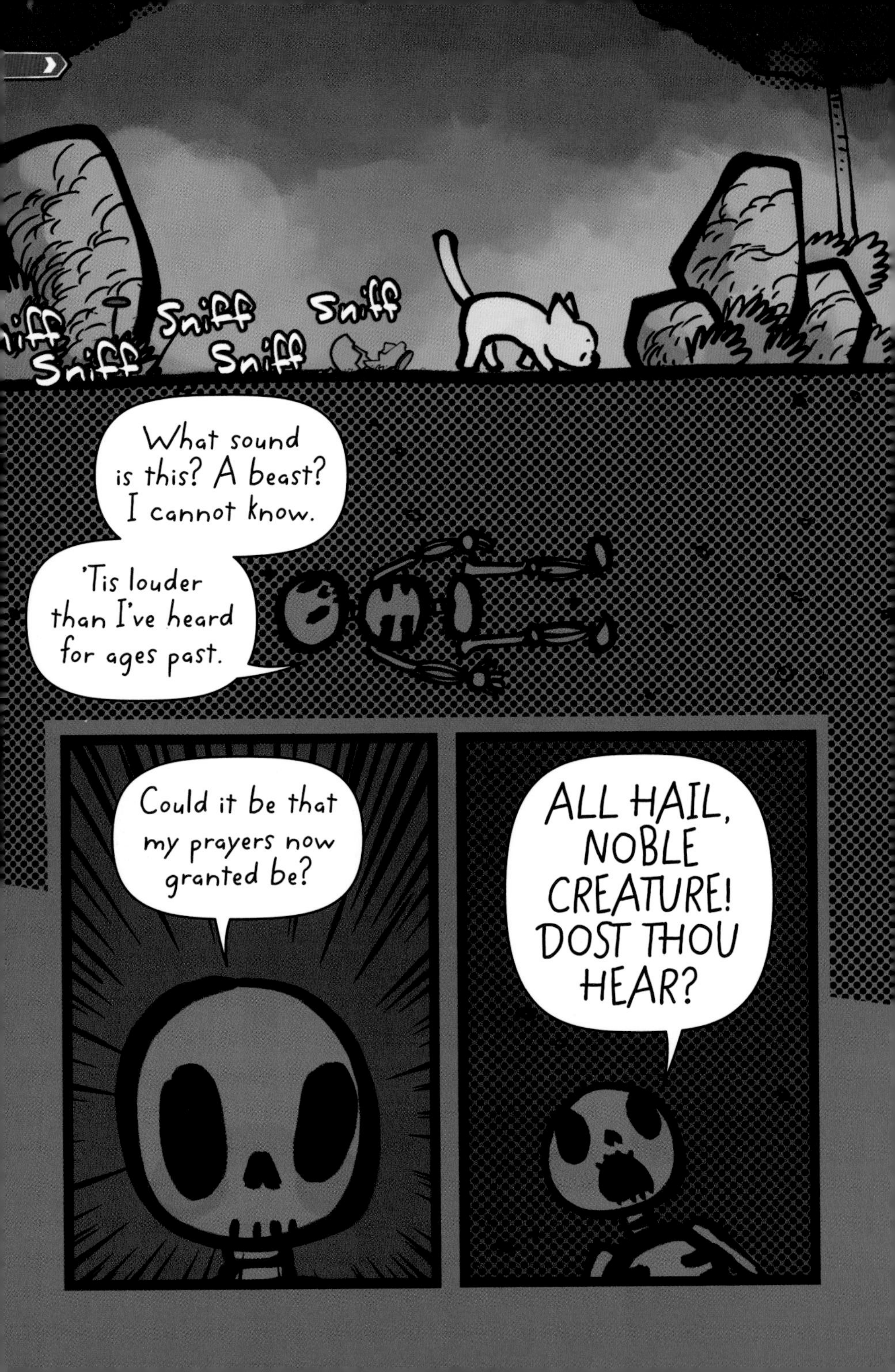

Sniff
Sniff
Sniff
Sniff
Sniff
What sound is this? A beast? I cannot know.
'Tis louder than I've heard for ages past.
Could it be that my prayers now granted be?
ALL HAIL, NOBLE CREATURE! DOST THOU HEAR?

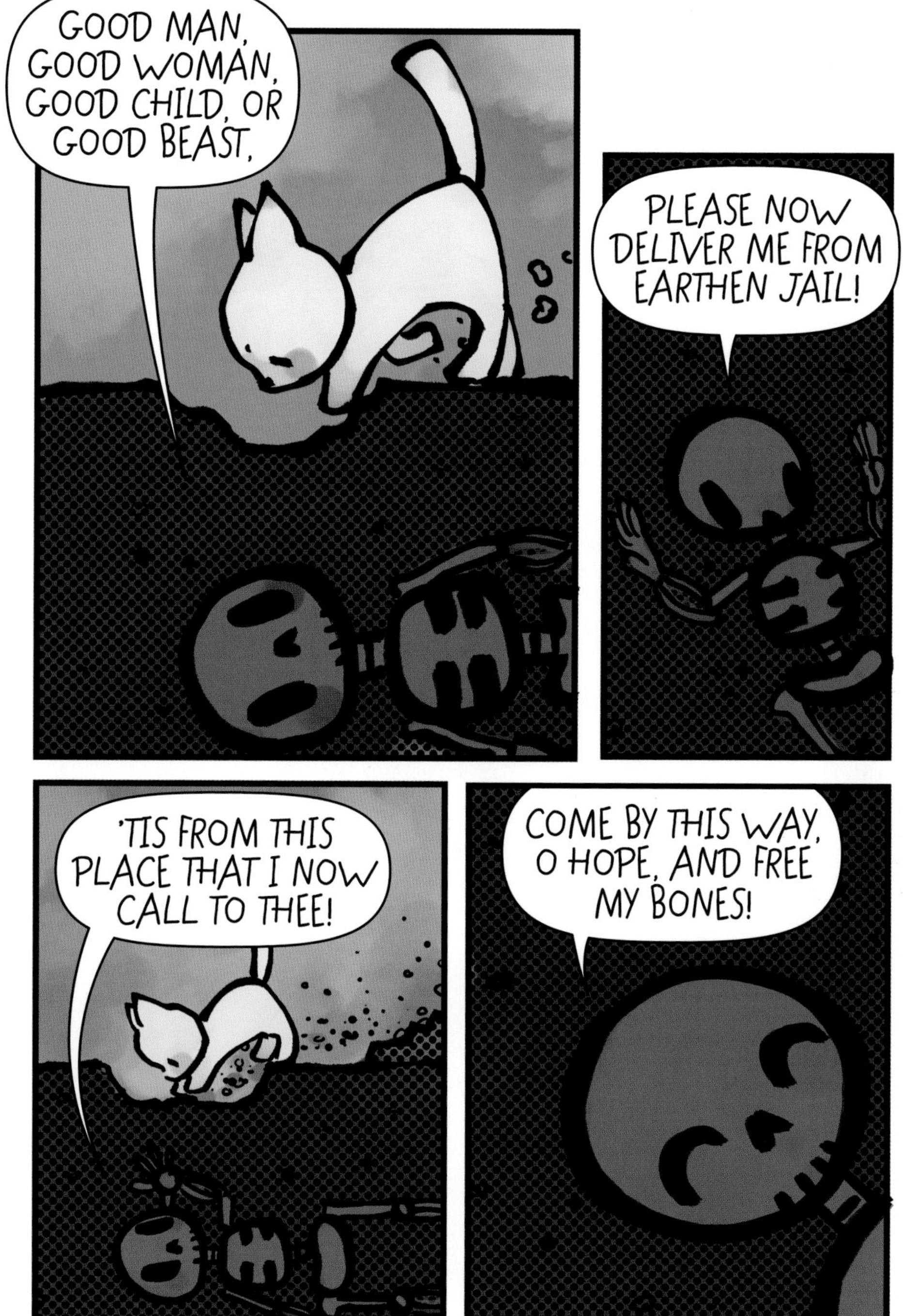
GOOD MAN, GOOD WOMAN, GOOD CHILD, OR GOOD BEAST,
PLEASE NOW DELIVER ME FROM EARTHEN JAIL!
'TIS FROM THIS PLACE THAT I NOW CALL TO THEE!
COME BY THIS WAY, O HOPE, AND FREE MY BONES!

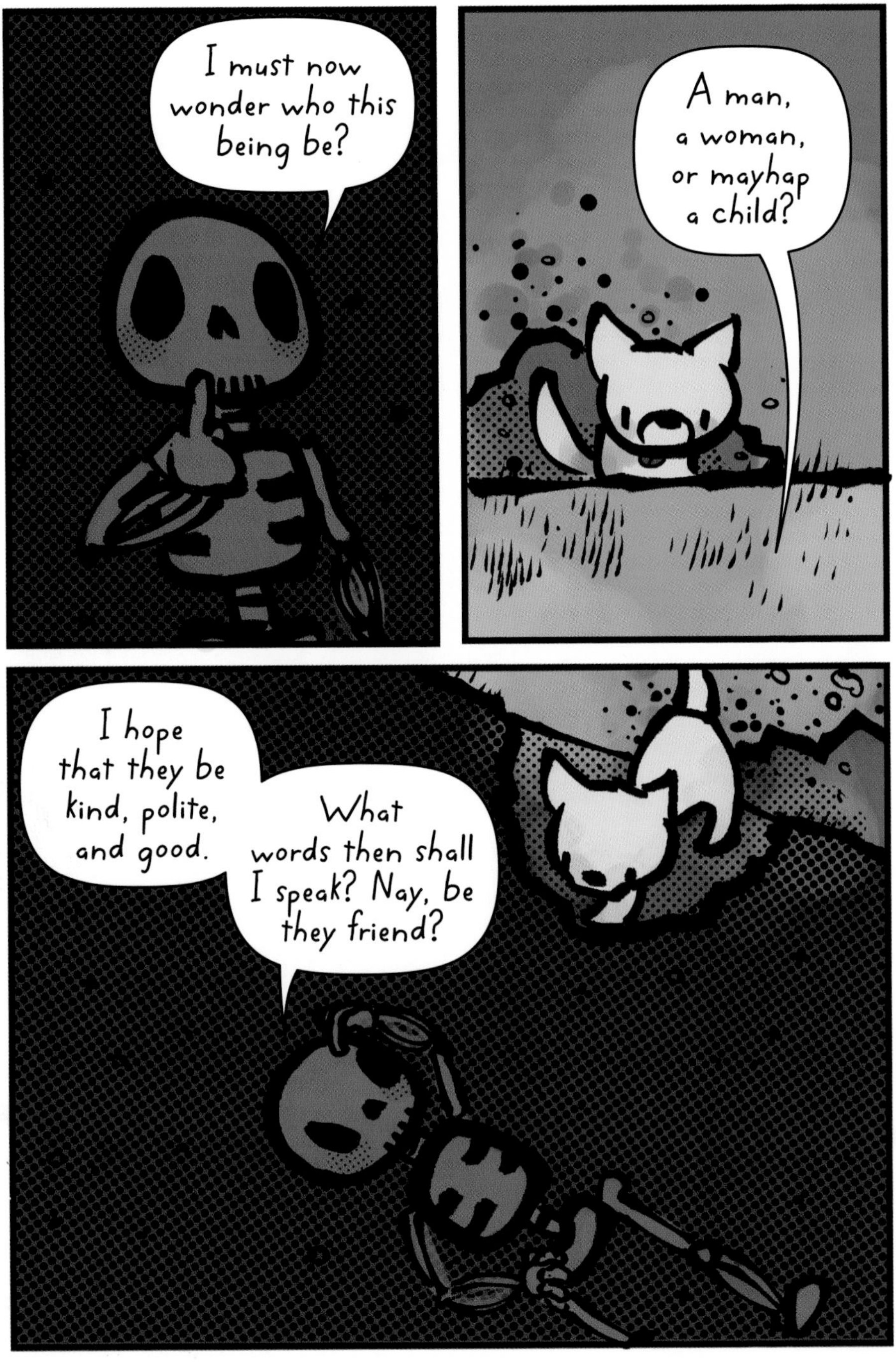
I must now wonder who this being be?
A man, a woman, or mayhap a child?
I hope that they be kind, polite, and good.
What words then shall I speak? Nay, be they friend?

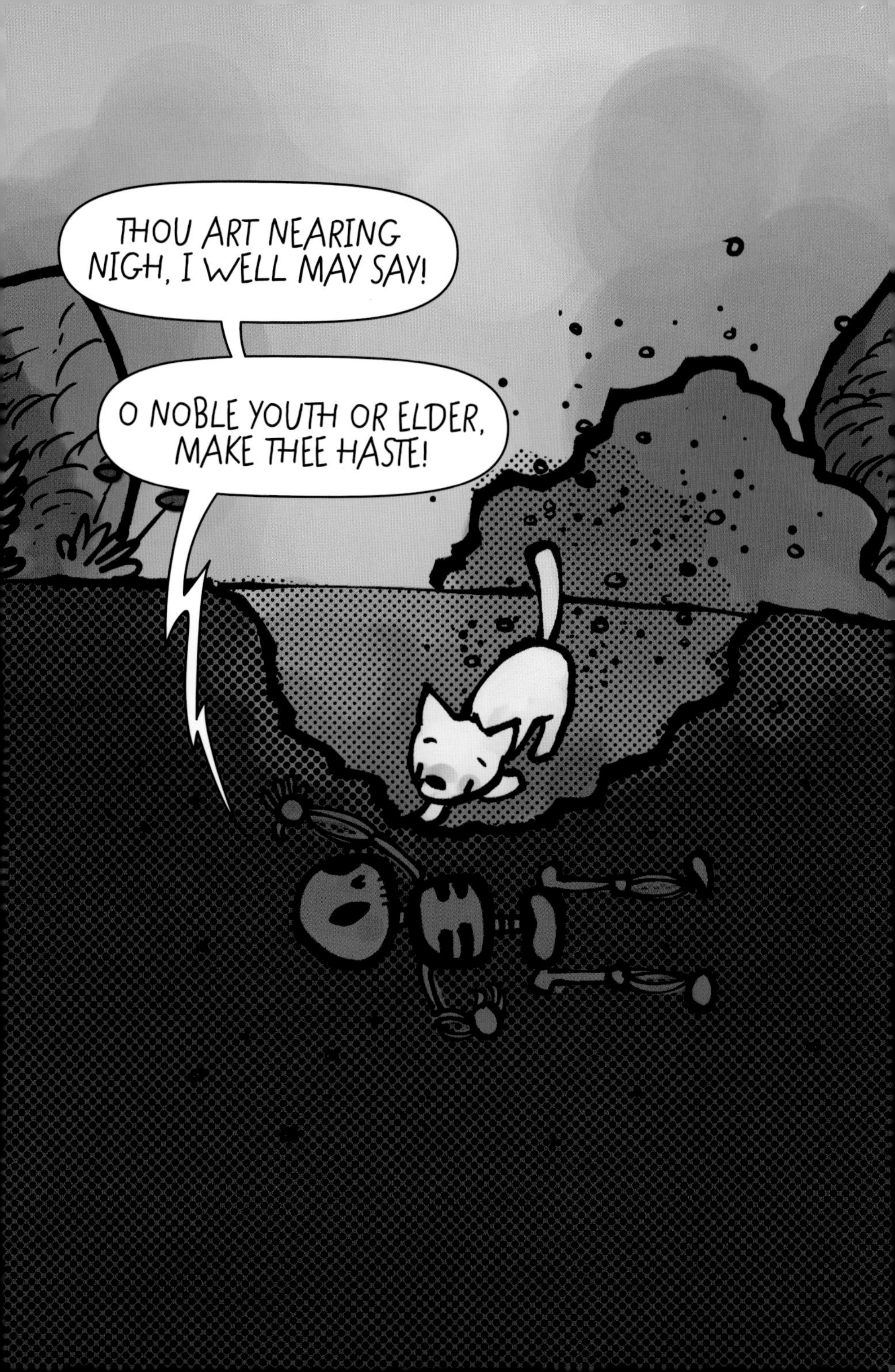
THOU ART NEARING NIGH, I WELL MAY SAY!
O NOBLE YOUTH OR ELDER, MAKE THEE HASTE!

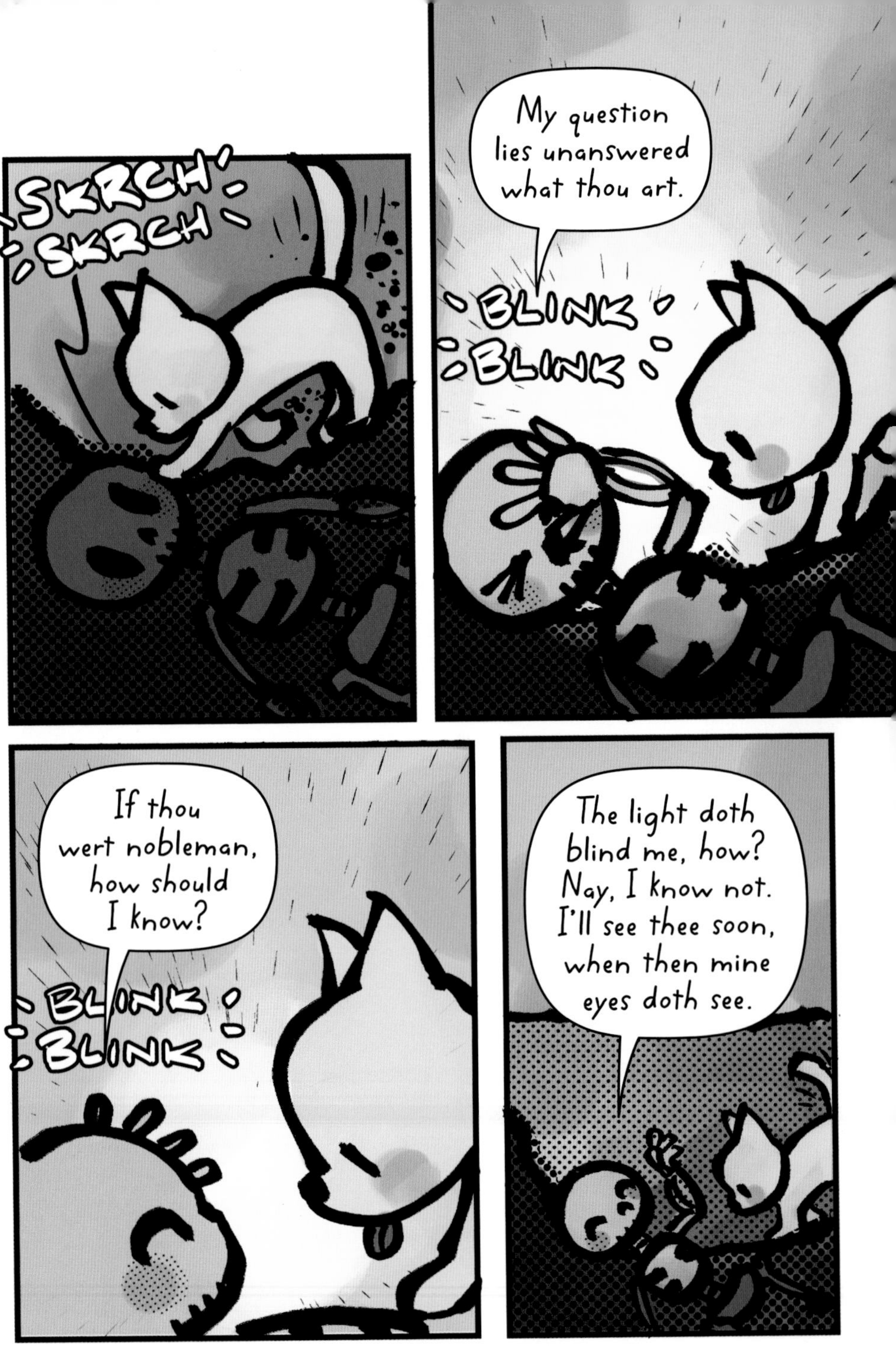
SKRCH SKRCH
My question lies unanswered what thou art.
BLINK BLINK
If thou wert nobleman, how should I know?
BLINK BLINK
The light doth blind me, how? Nay, I know not. I'll see thee soon, when then mine eyes doth see.

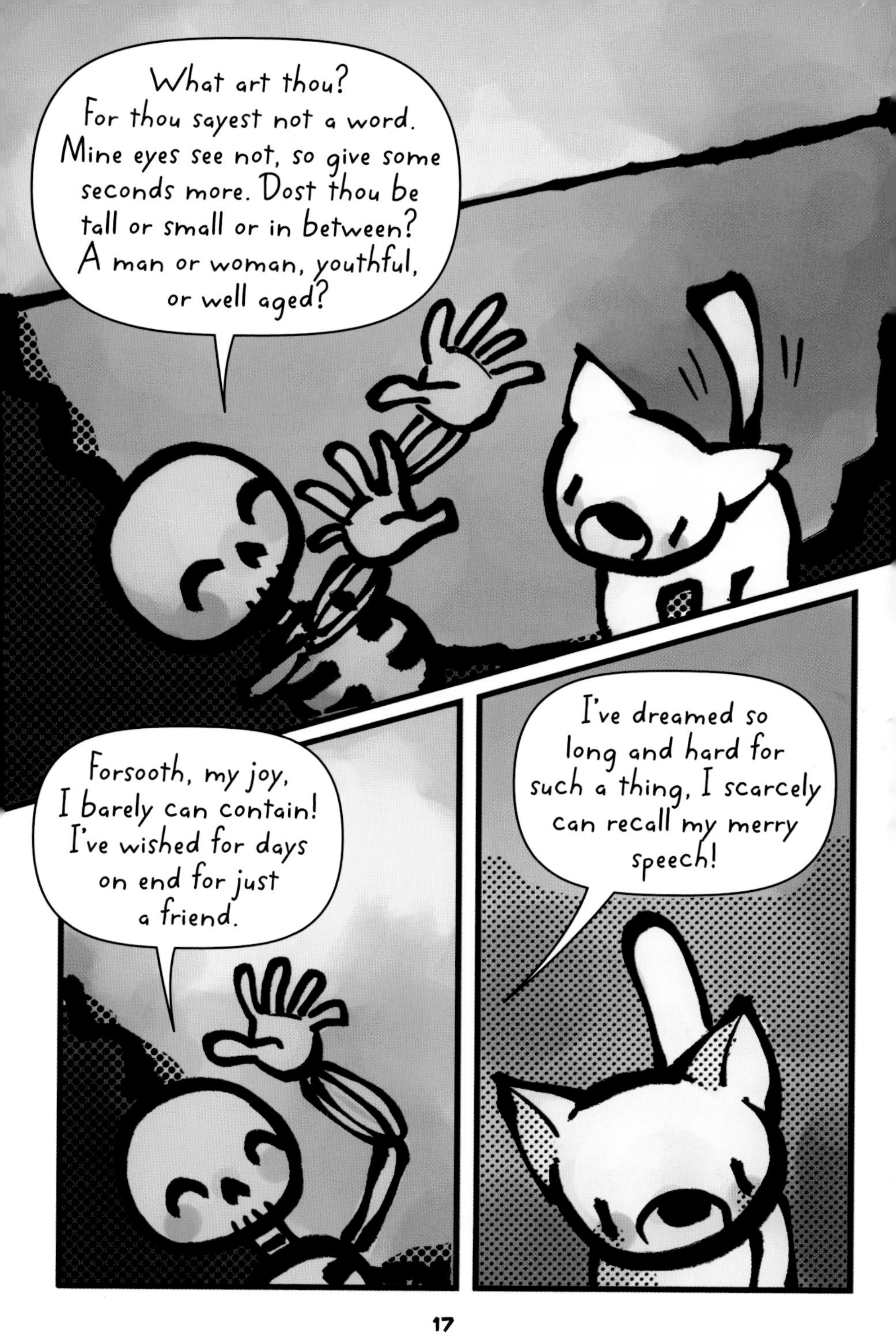
What art thou? For thou sayest not a word. Mine eyes see not, so give some seconds more. Dost thou be tall or small or in between? A man or woman, youthful, or well aged?
Forsooth, my joy, I barely can contain! I've wished for days on end for just a friend.
I've dreamed so long and hard for such a thing, I scarcely can recall my merry speech!

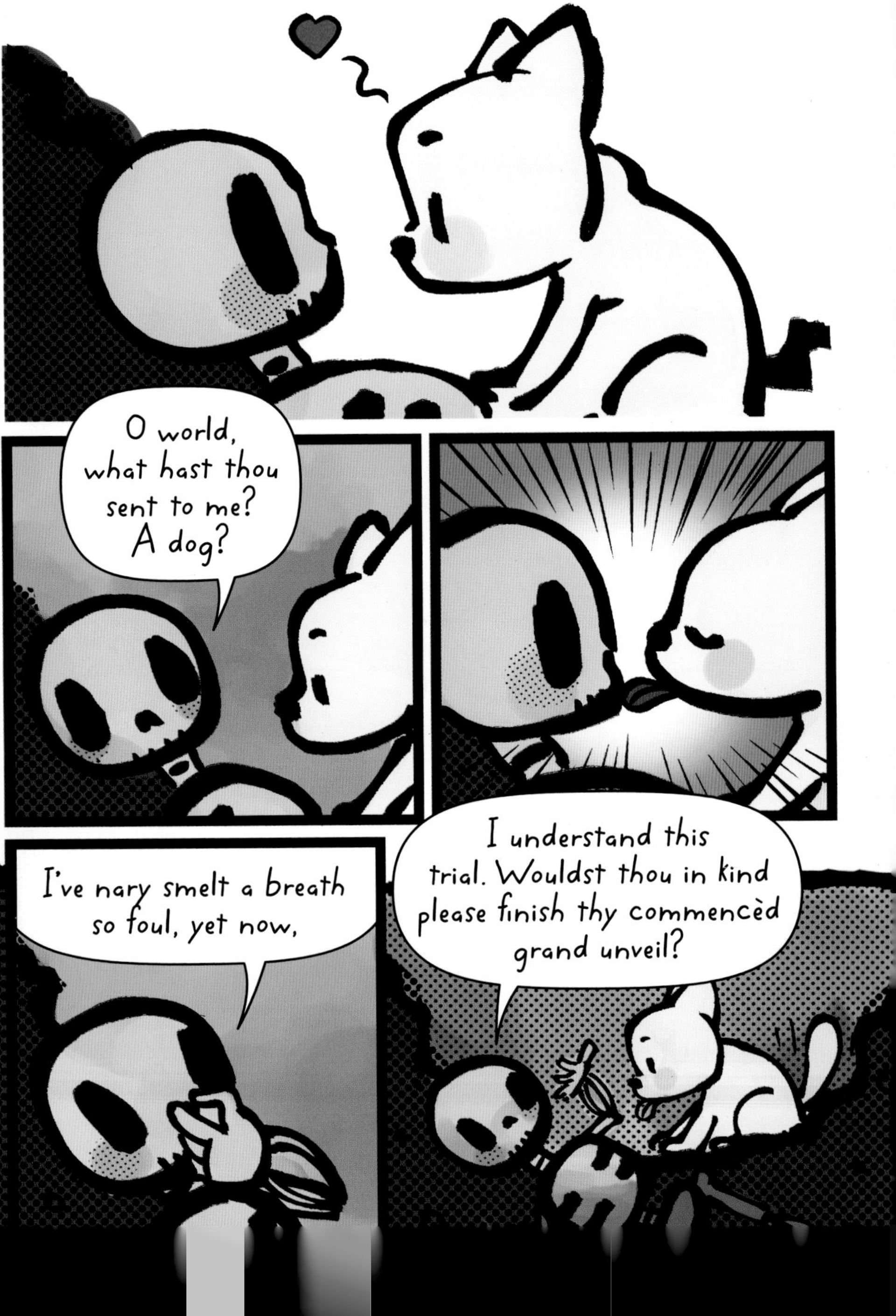
O world, what hast thou sent to me? A dog?
I've nary smelt a breath so foul, yet now,
I understand this trial. Wouldst thou in kind please finish thy commencèd grand unveil?

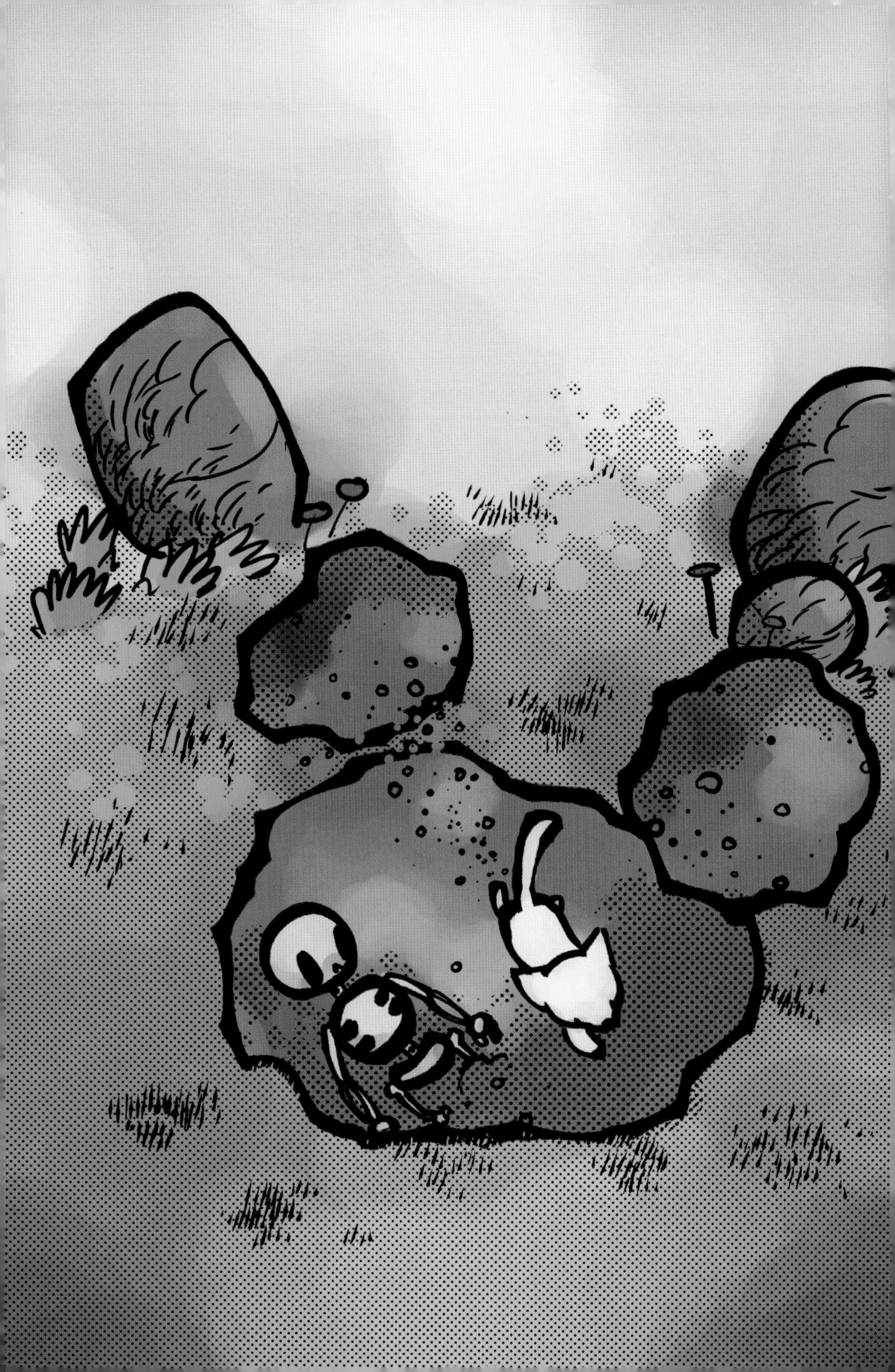

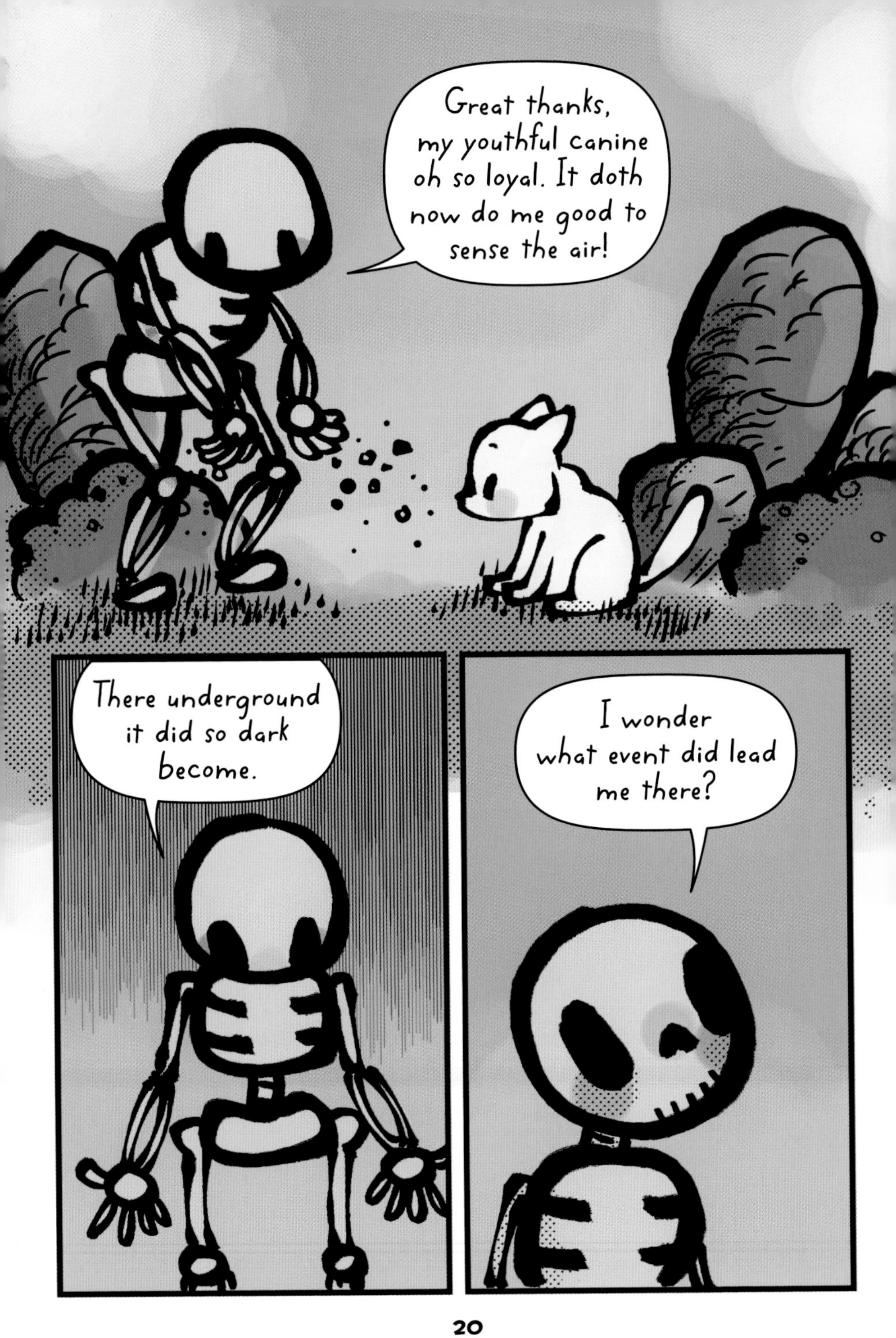
Great thanks, my youthful canine oh so loyal. It doth now do me good to sense the air!
There underground it did so dark become.
I wonder what event did lead me there?

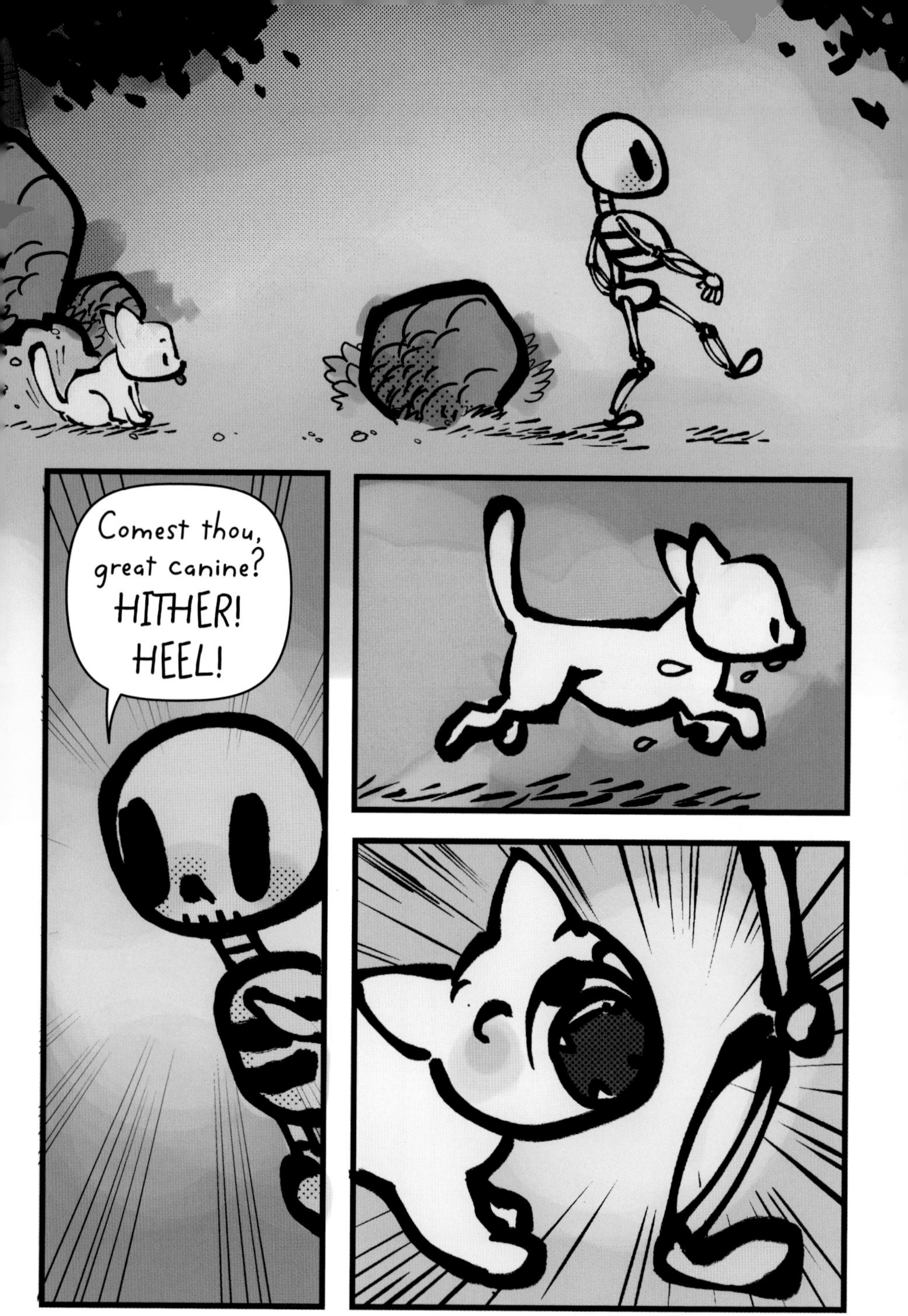
Comest thou, great canine? HITHER! HEEL!

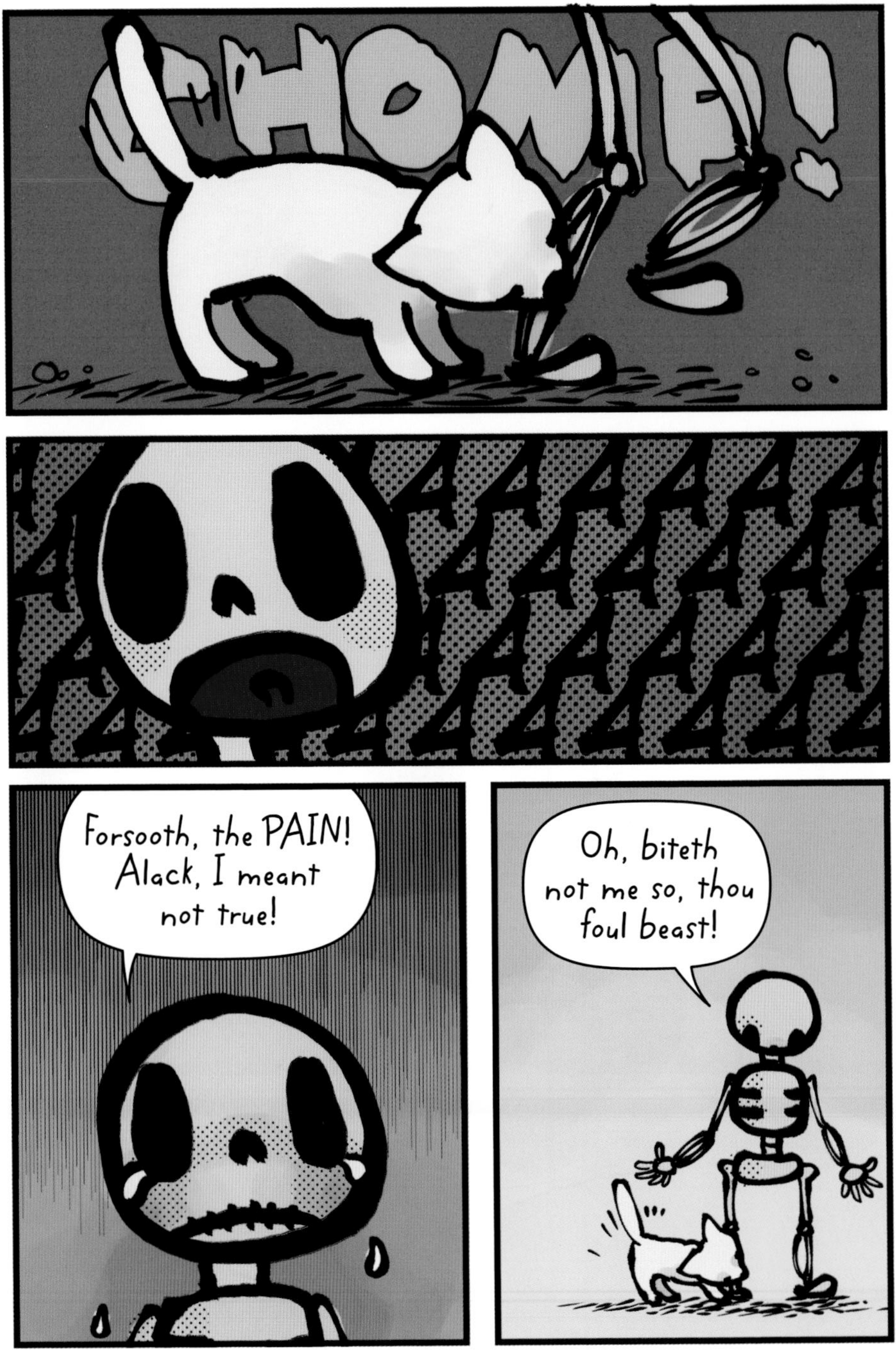
Forsooth, the PAIN! Alack, I meant not true!
Oh, biteth not me so, thou foul beast!

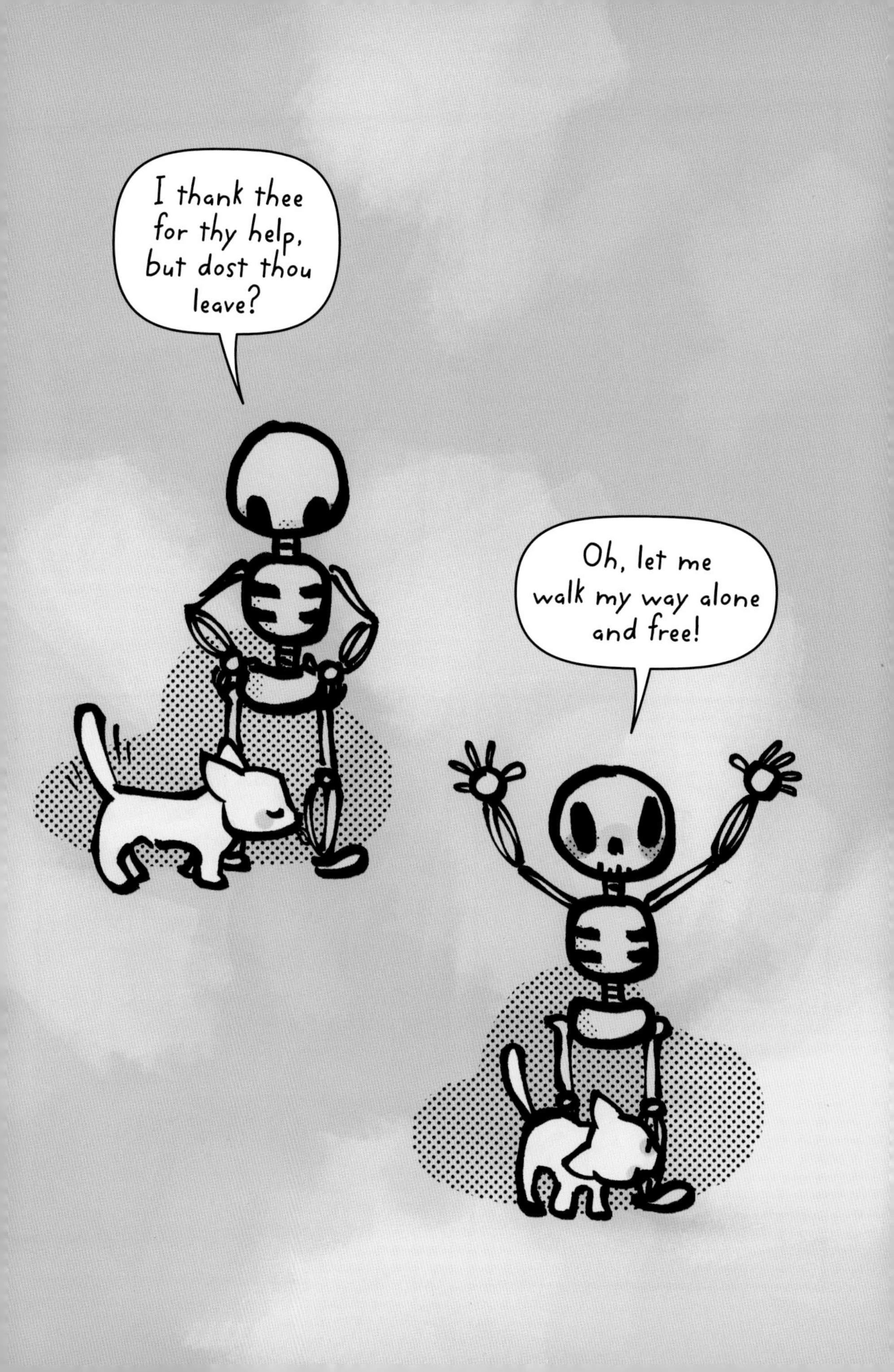
I thank thee for thy help, but dost thou leave?
Oh, let me walk my way alone and free!

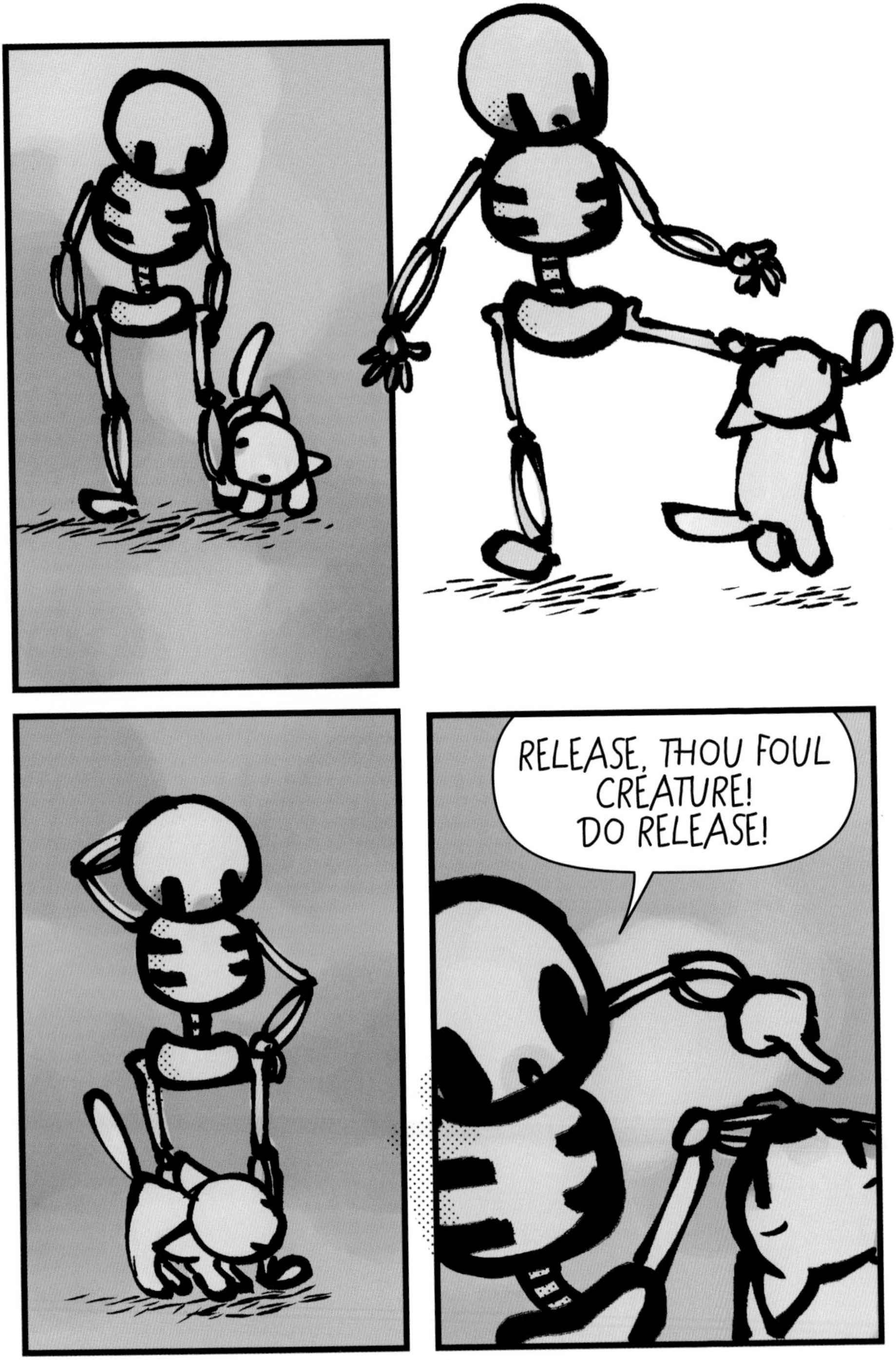
RELEASE, THOU FOUL CREATURE! DO RELEASE!

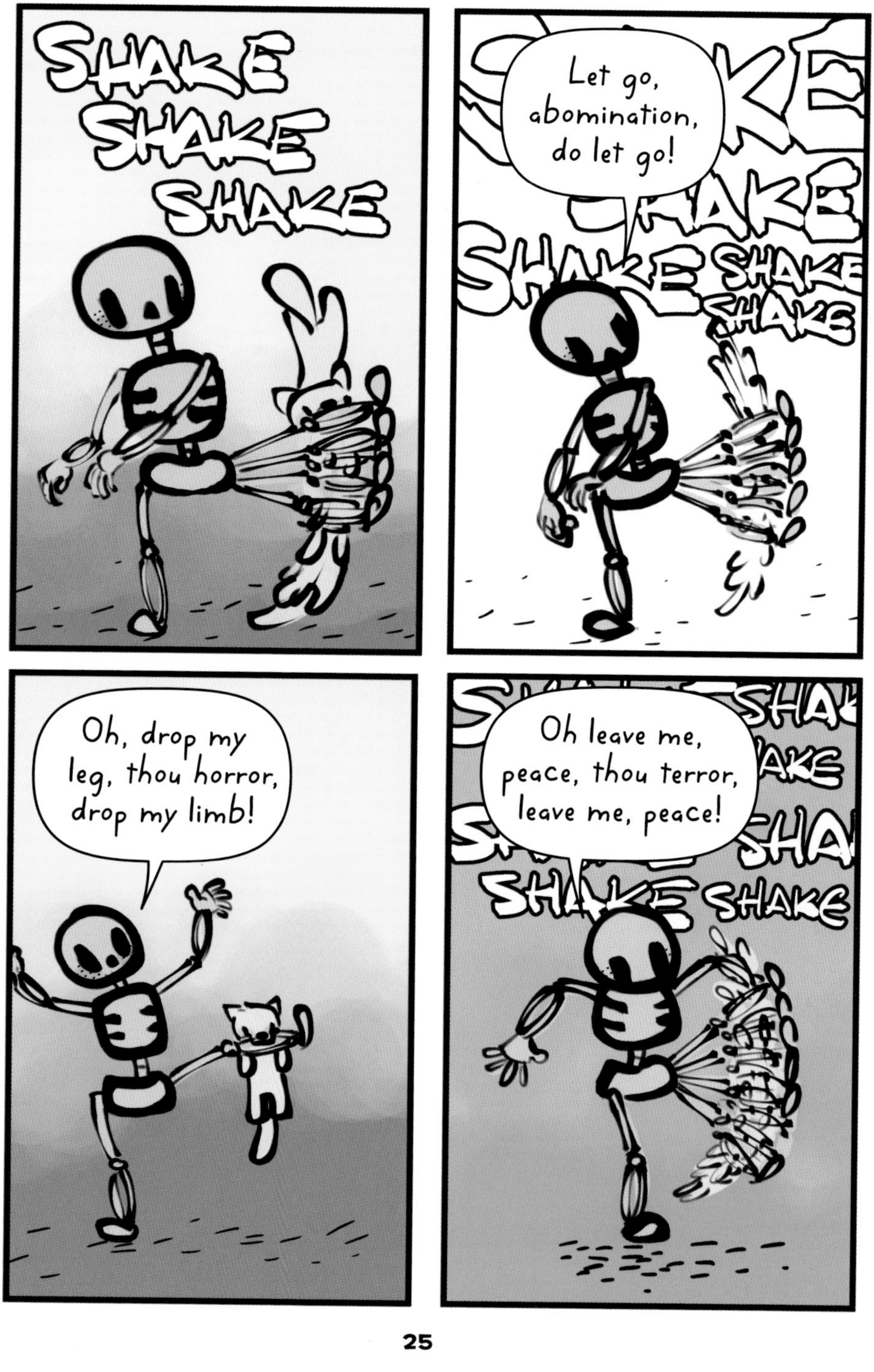
SHAKE
SHAKE
SHAKE
Let go, abomination, do let go!
SHAKE SHAKE
SHAKE
Oh, drop my leg, thou horror, drop my limb!
Oh leave me, peace, thou terror, leave me, peace!
SHAKE SHAKE

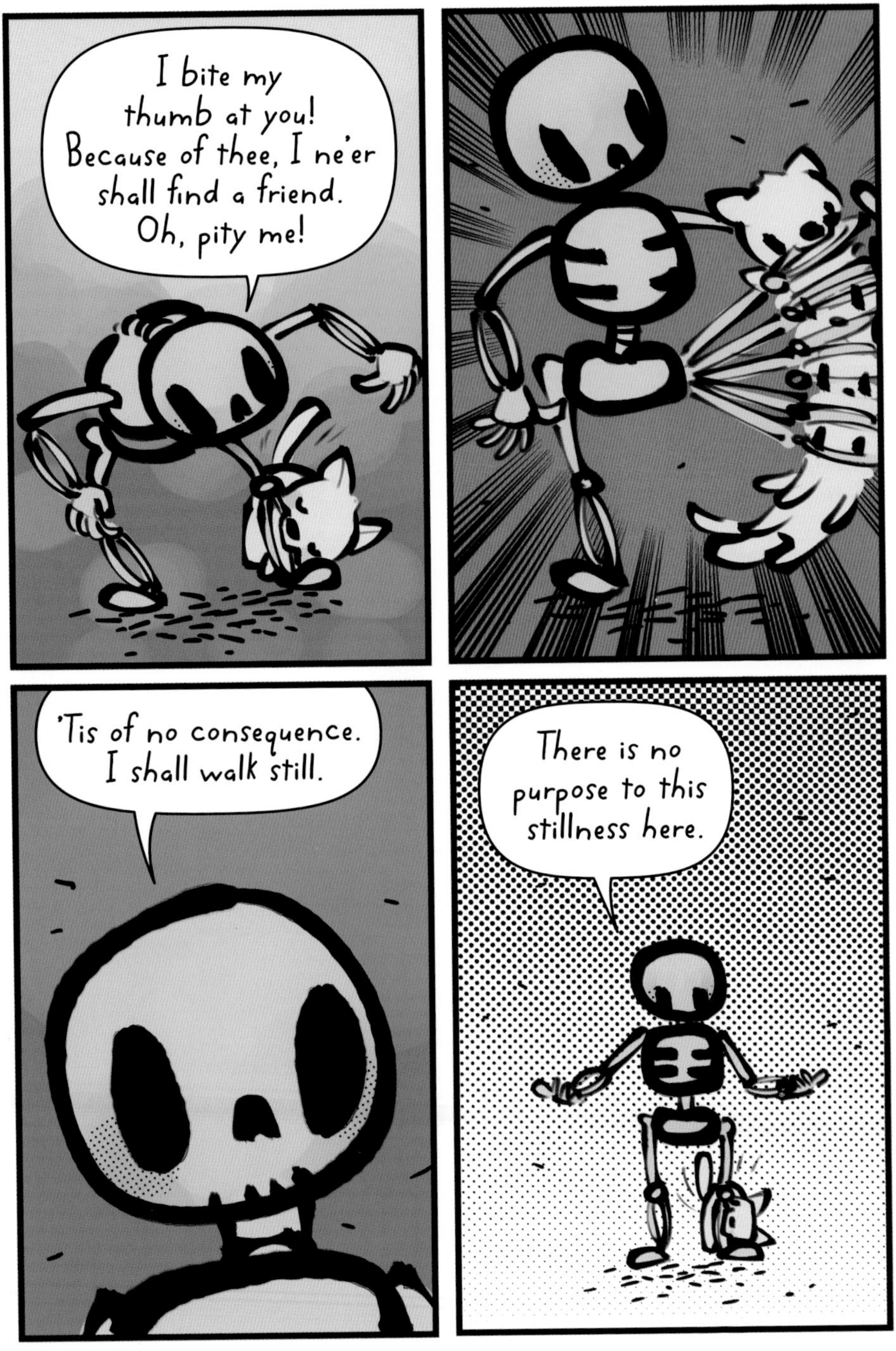
I bite my thumb at you! Because of thee, I ne'er shall find a friend. Oh, pity me!
'Tis of no consequence. I shall walk still.
There is no purpose to this stillness here.

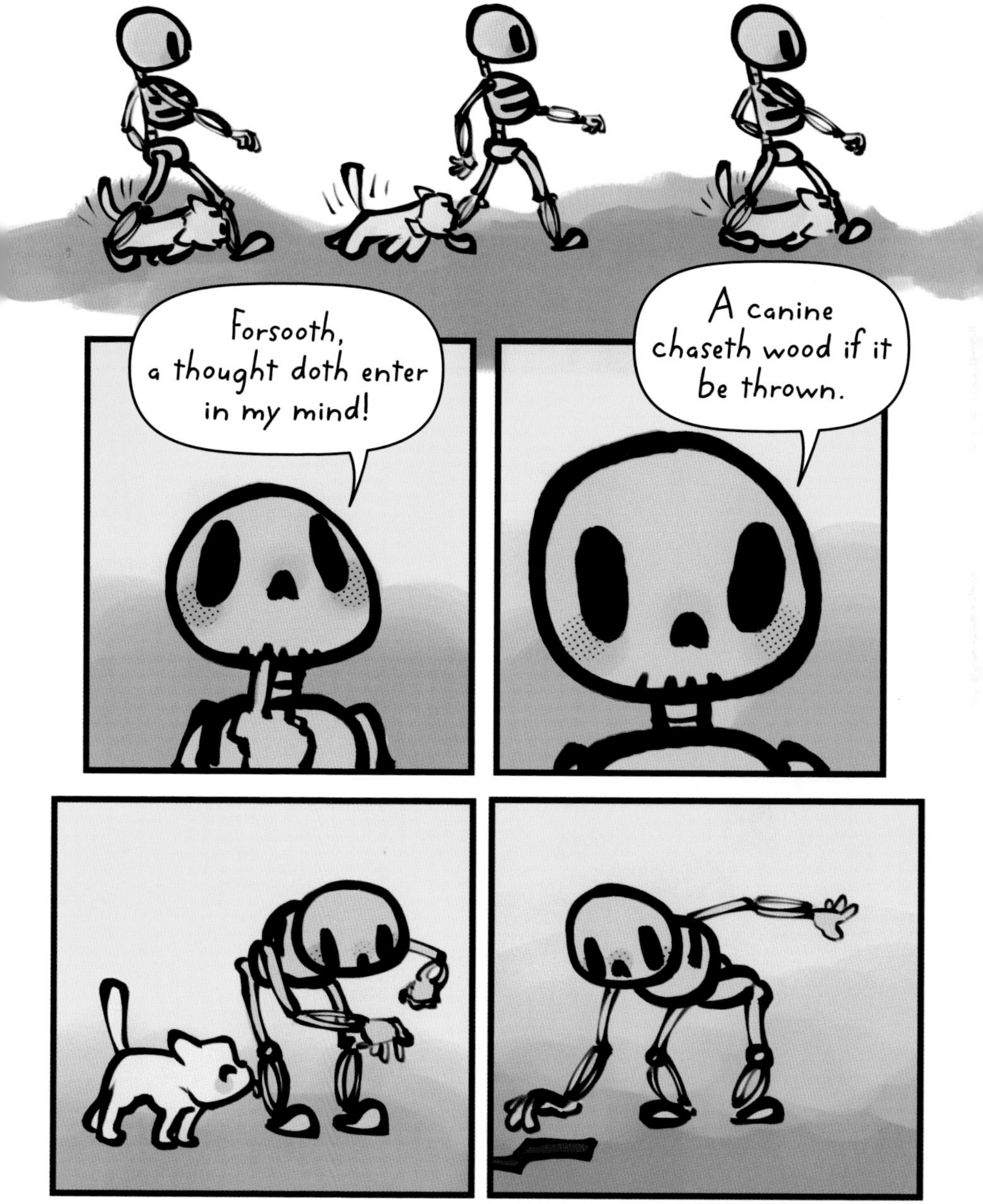
Forsooth, a thought doth enter in my mind!
A canine chaseth wood if it be thrown.

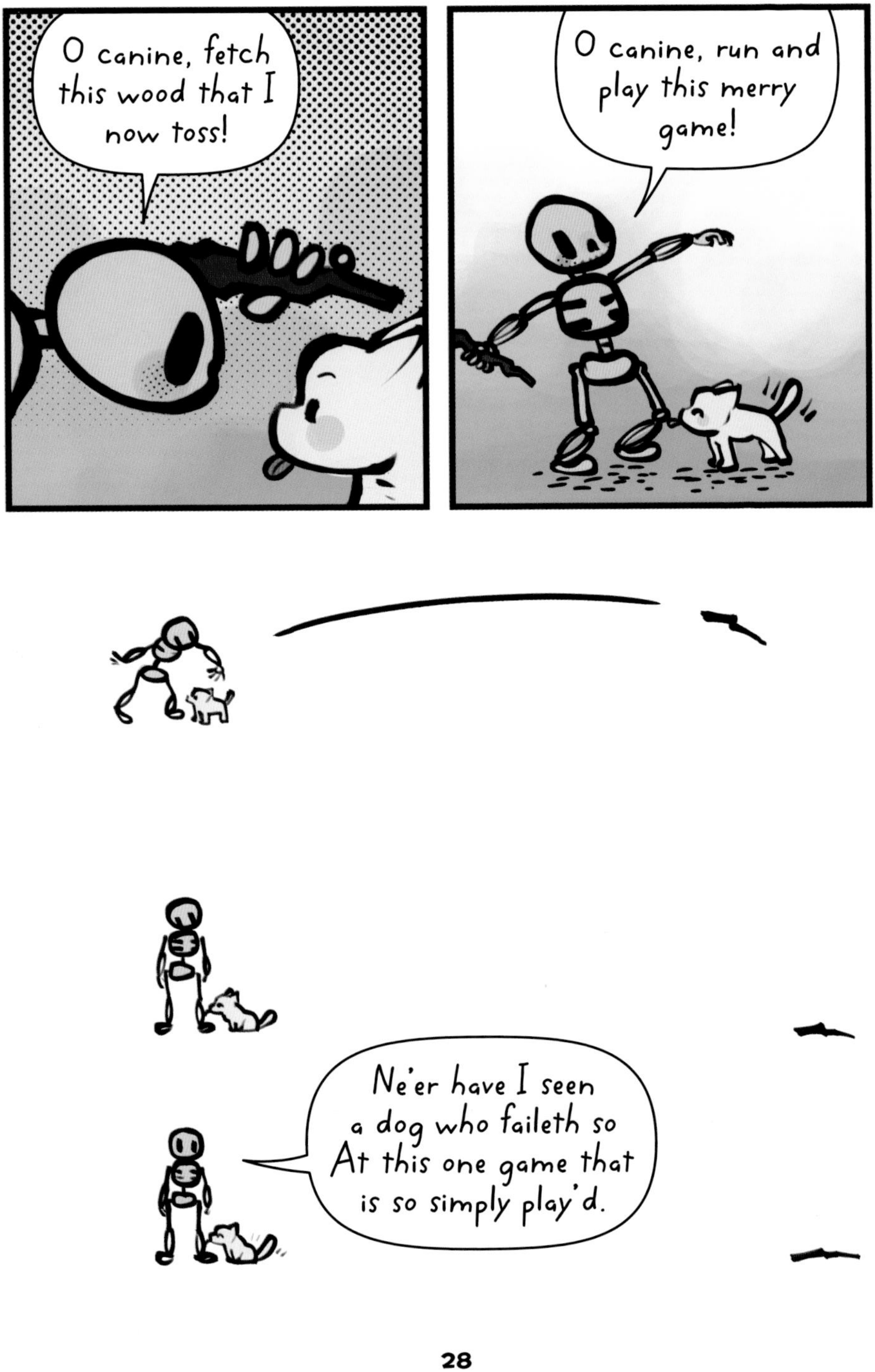
O canine, fetch this wood that I now toss!
O canine, run and play this merry game!
Ne'er have I seen a dog who faileth so At this one game that is so simply play'd.

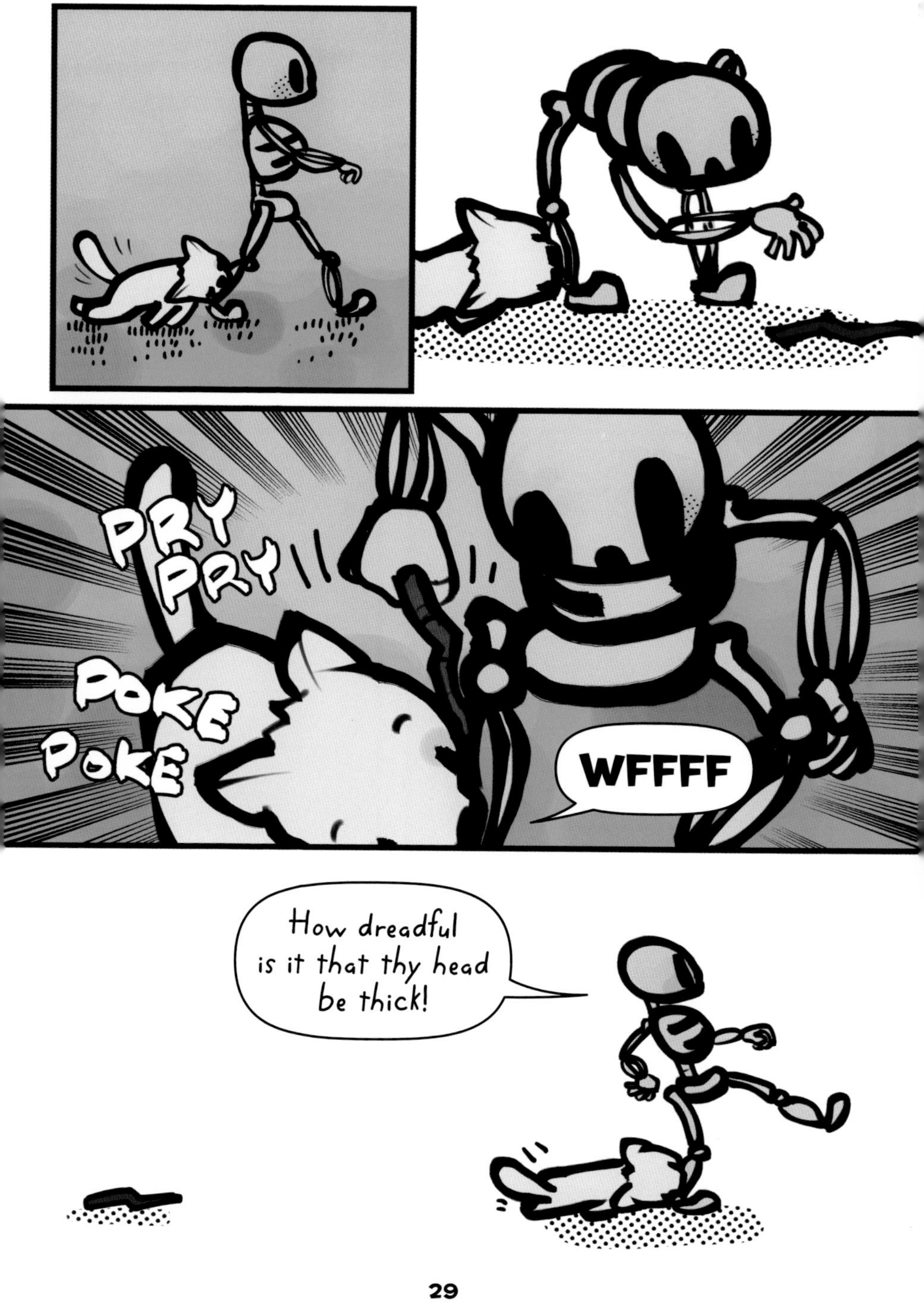
PRY PRY
POKE POKE
WFFFF
How dreadful is it that thy head be thick!

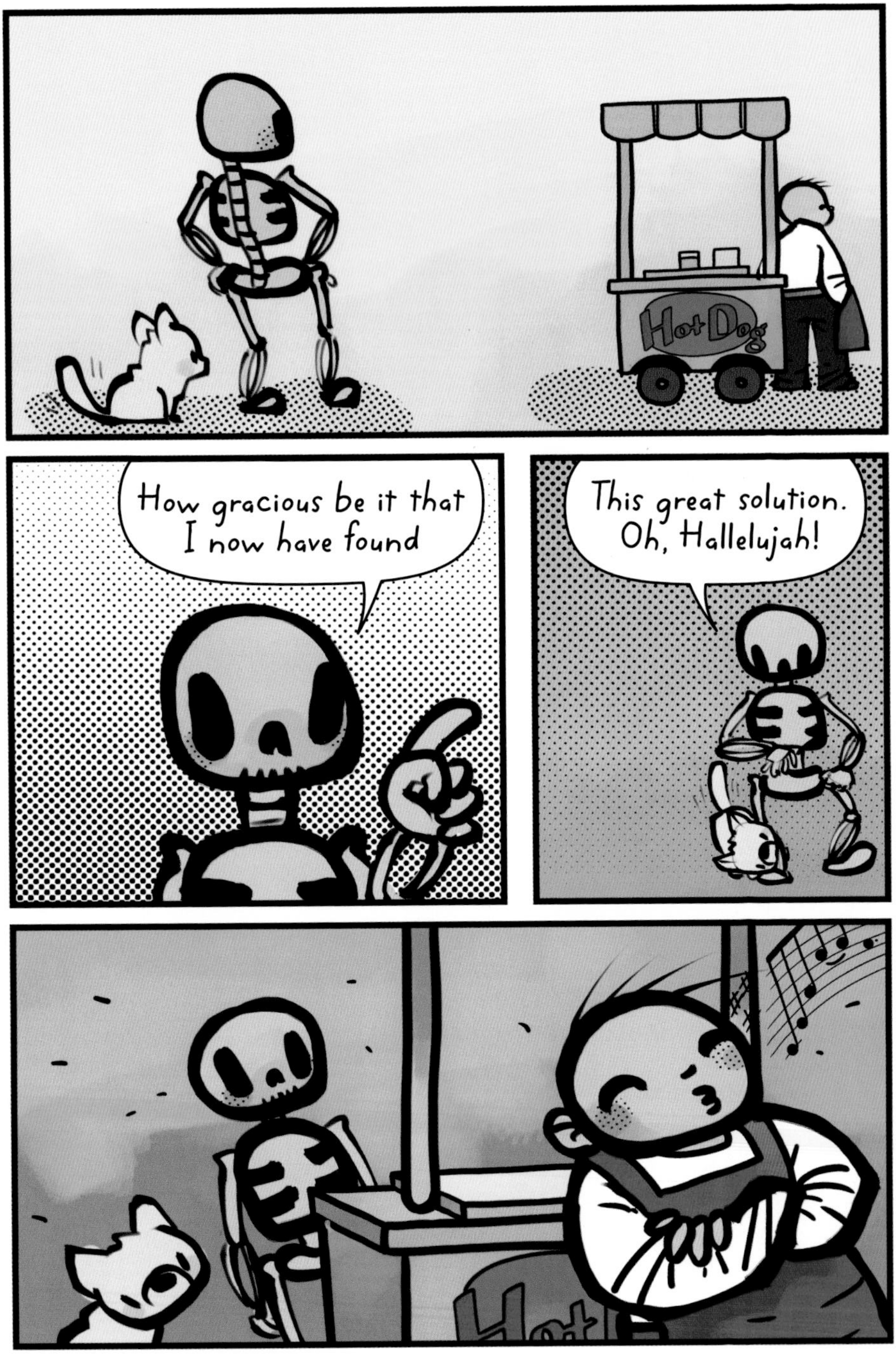
Hot Dog
How gracious be it that I now have found
This great solution. Oh, Hallelujah!

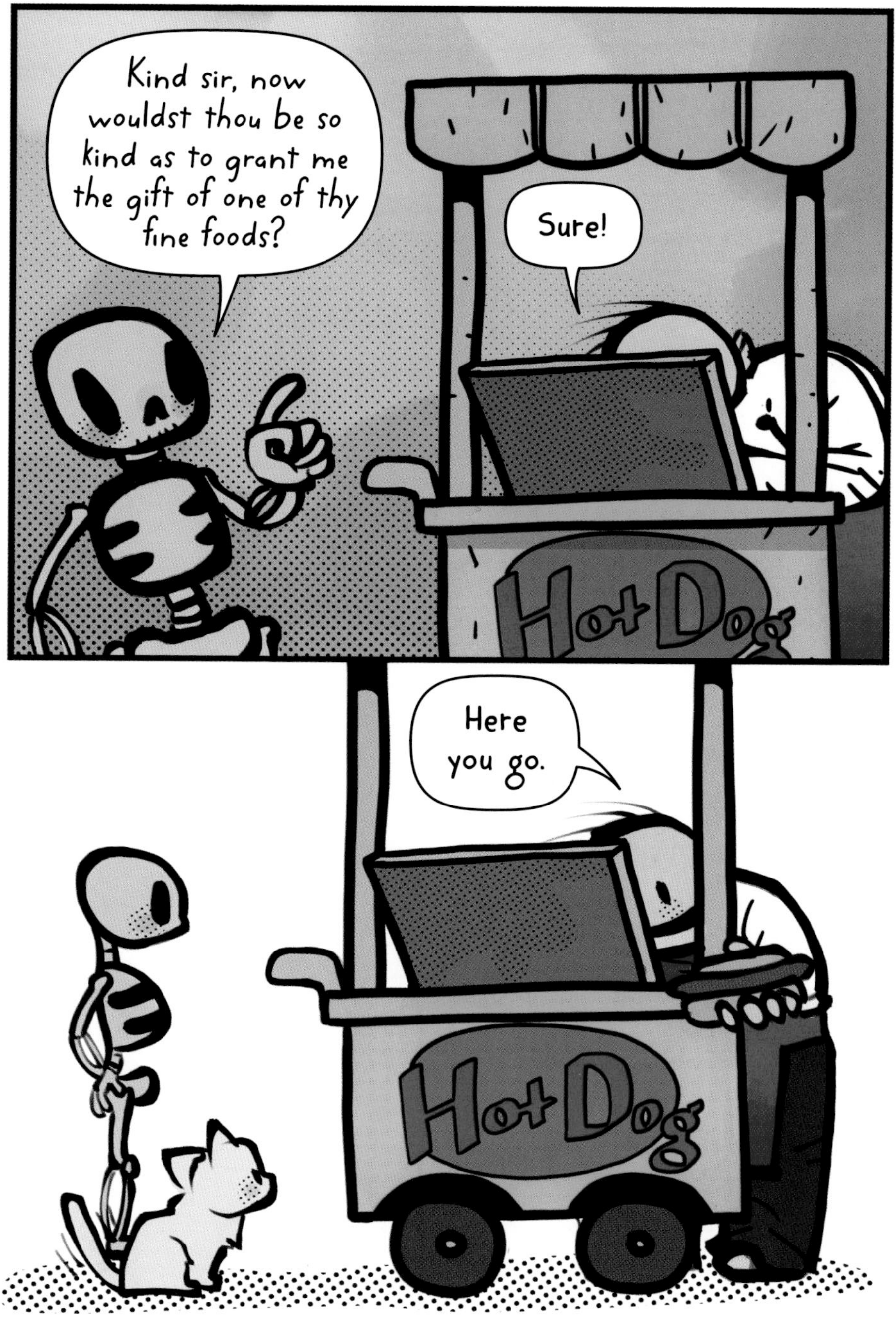

Kind sir, now wouldst thou be so kind as to grant me the gift of one of thy fine foods?
Sure!
Hot Dog
Here you go.
Hot Dog

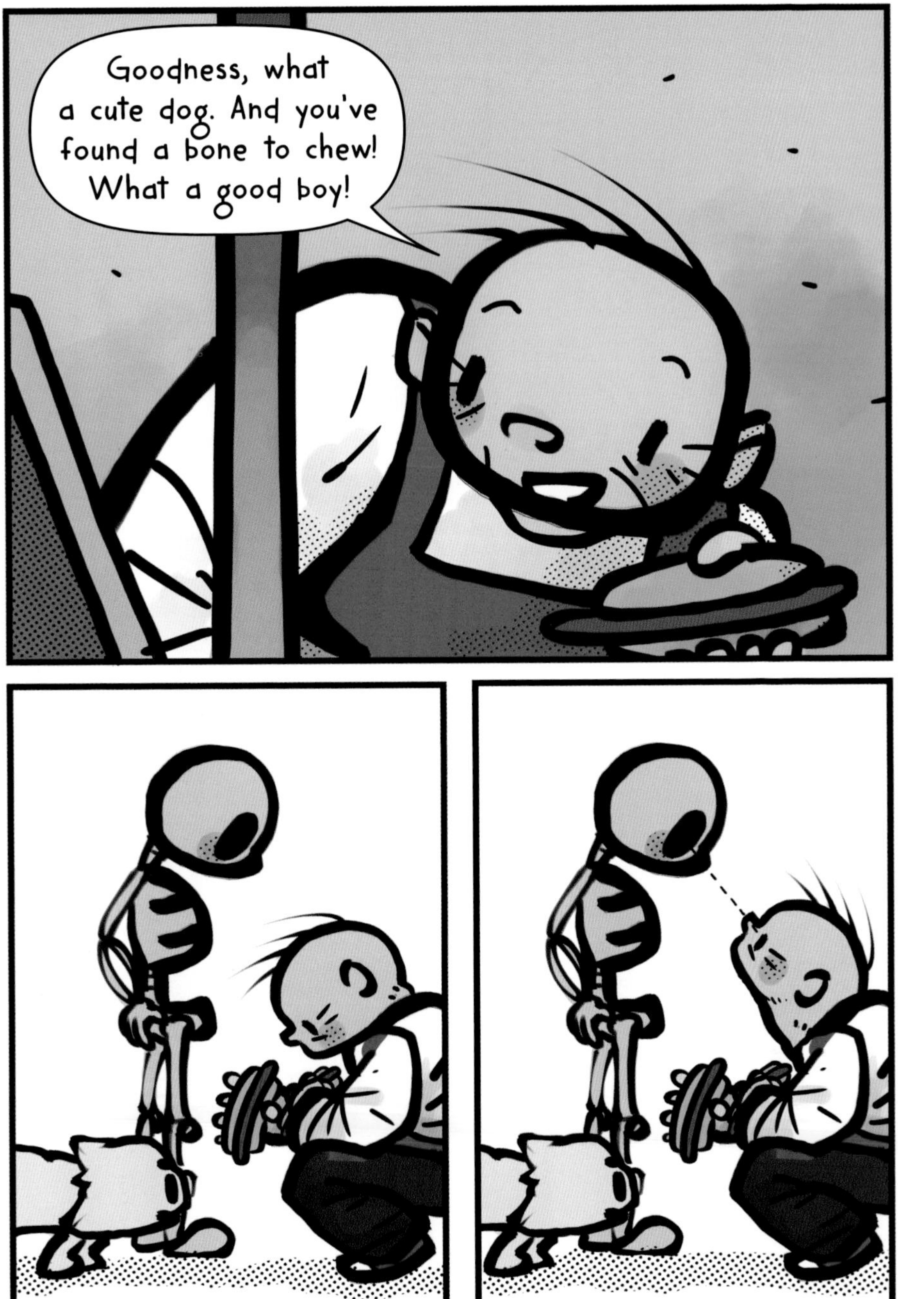
Goodness, what a cute dog. And you've found a bone to chew! What a good boy!

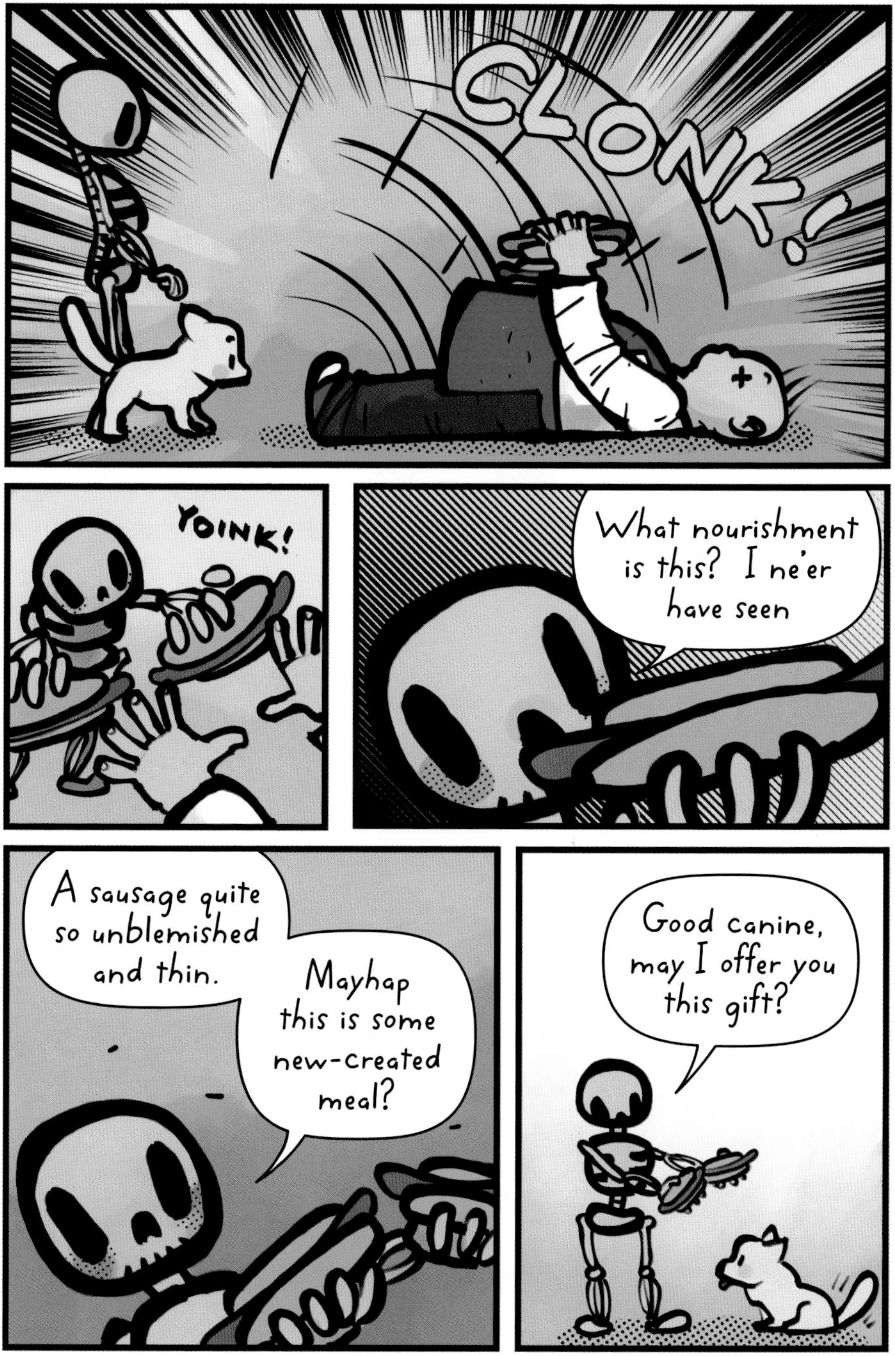
CLONK!
YOINK!
What nourishment is this? I ne'er have seen
A sausage quite so unblemished and thin.
Mayhap this is some new-created meal?
Good canine, may I offer you this gift?

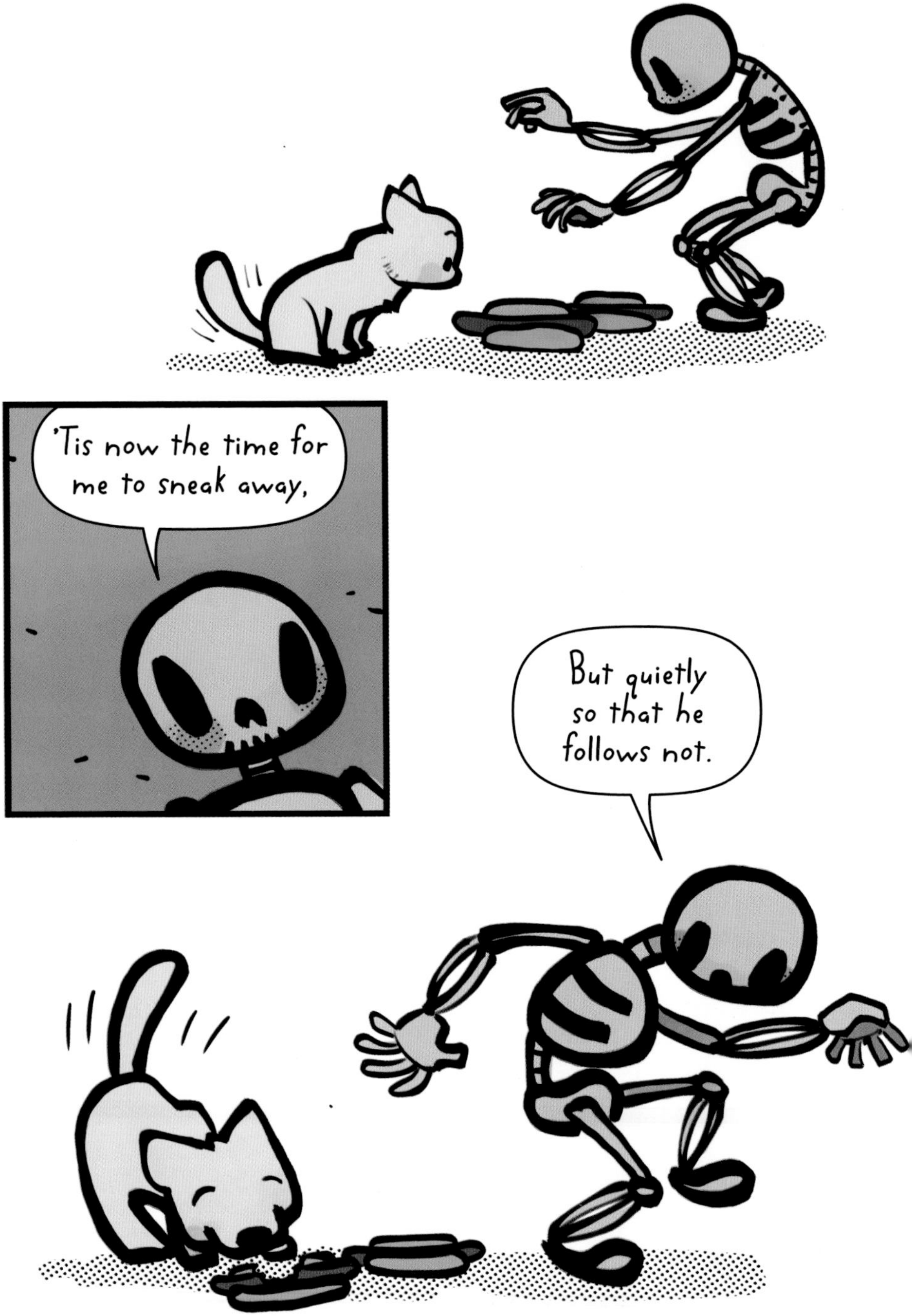
'Tis now the time for me to sneak away,
But quietly so that he follows not.

nom nom nom

sneak sneak sneak

'Tis time my pace of sneaking should increase.

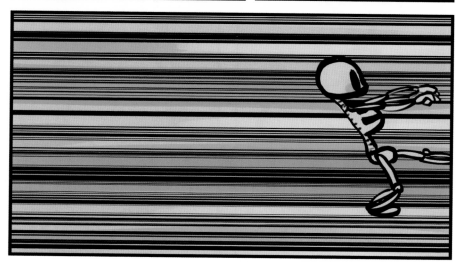

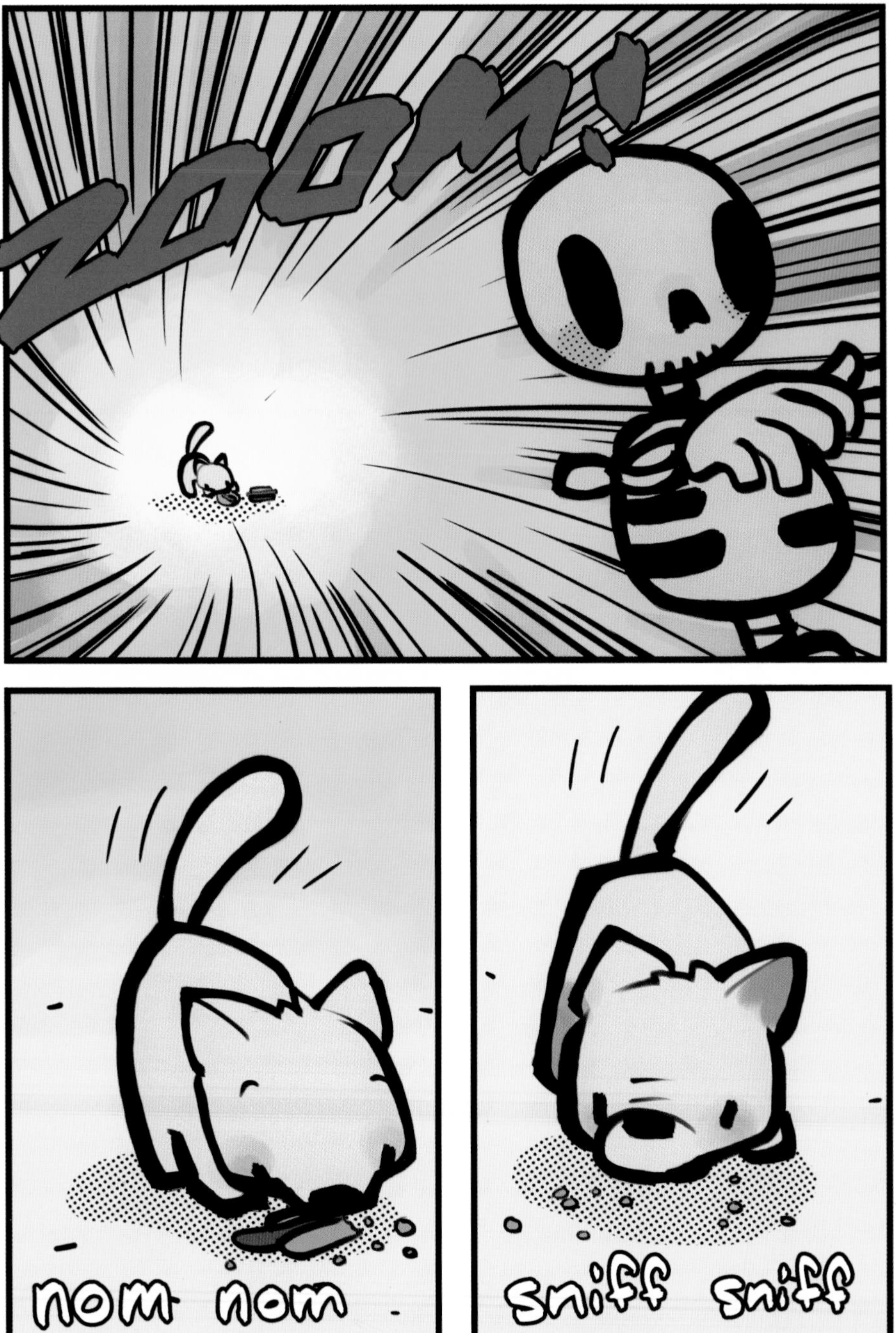
ZOOM!
nom nom
sniff sniff

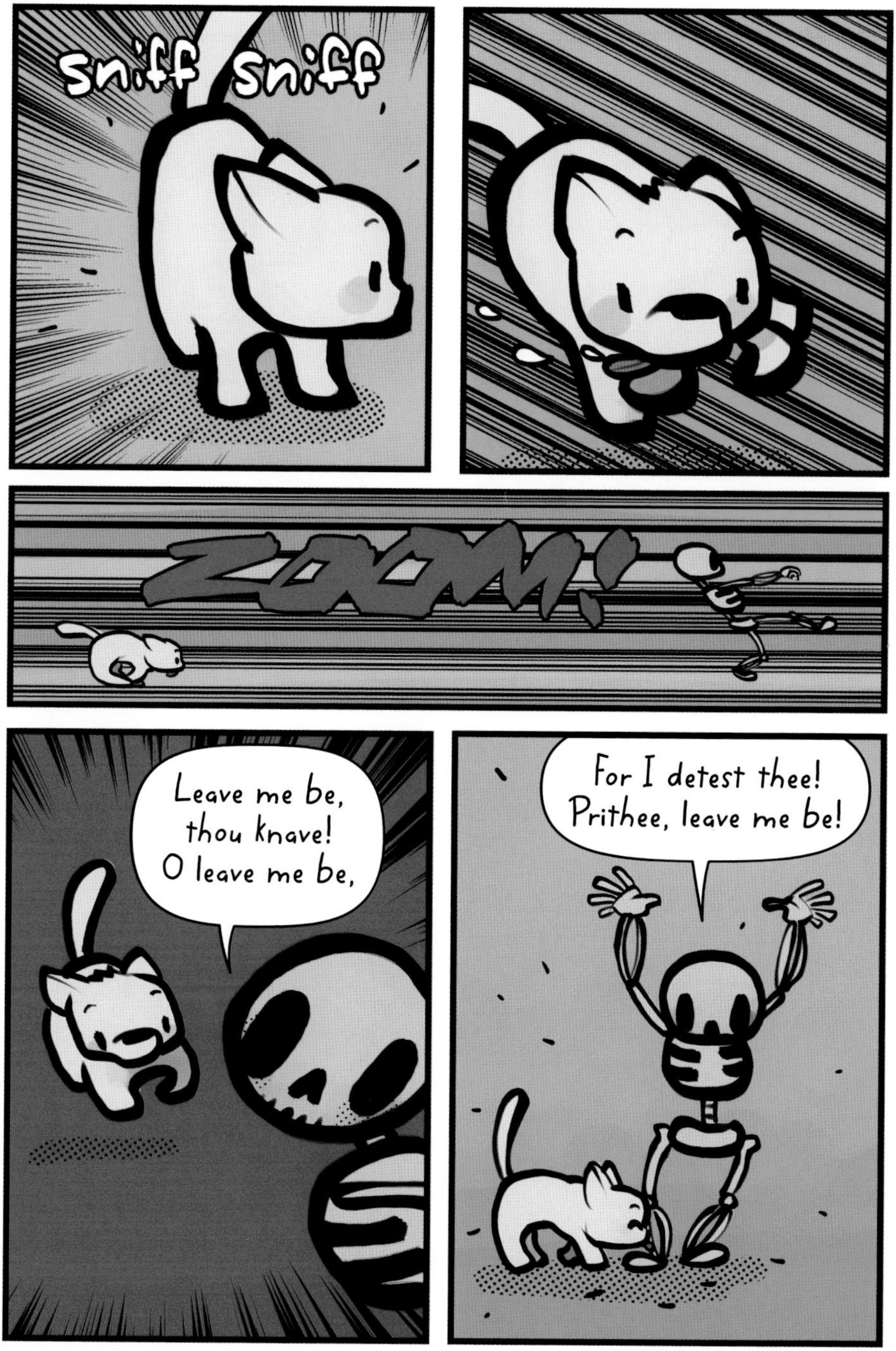
sniff sniff
ZOOM!
Leave me be,
thou knave!
O leave me be,
For I detest thee!
Prithee, leave me be!

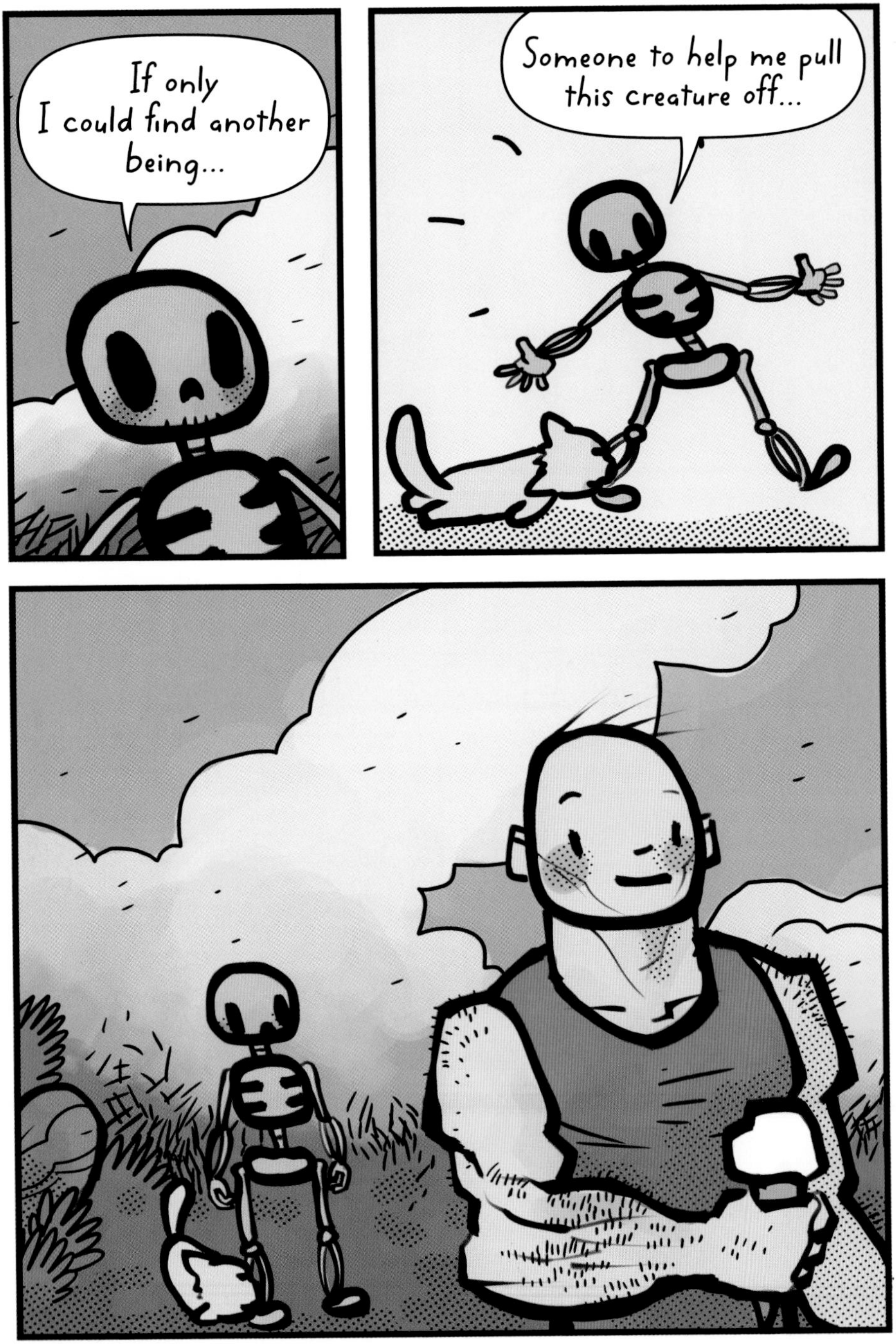
If only
I could find another
being...
Someone to help me pull
this creature off...

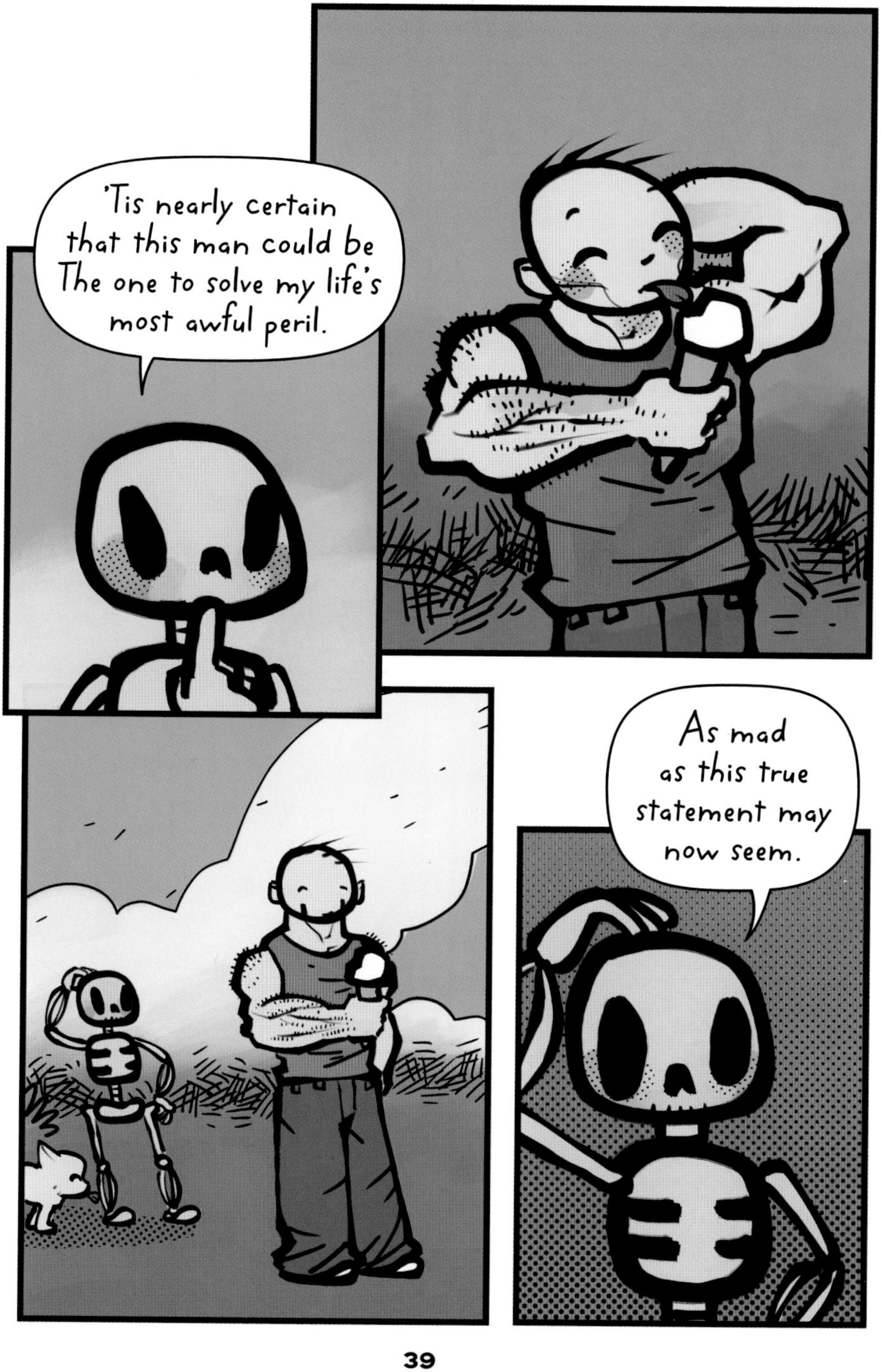
'Tis nearly certain that this man could be The one to solve my life's most awful peril.
As mad as this true statement may now seem.

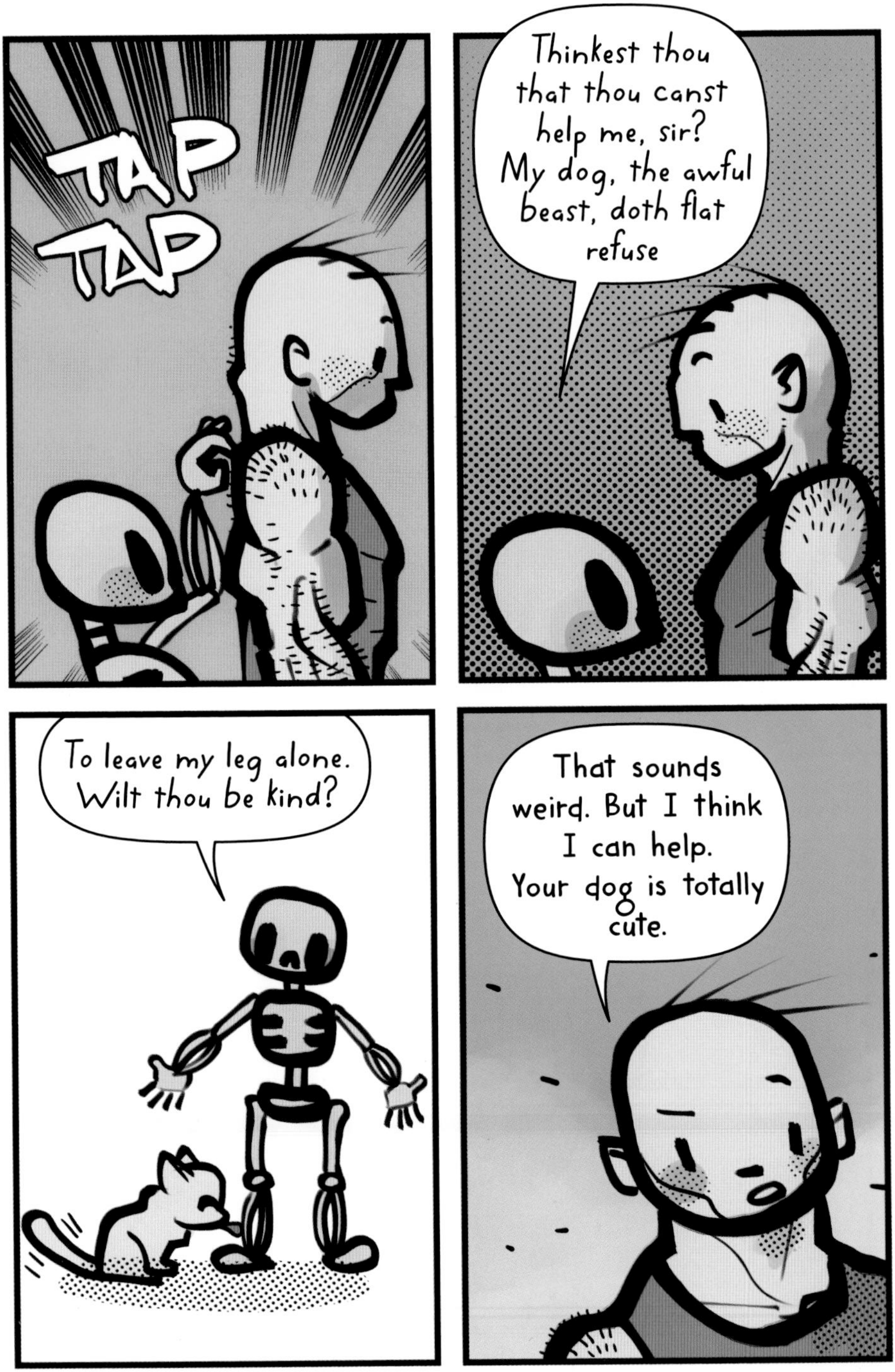
TAP TAP
Thinkest thou that thou canst help me, sir? My dog, the awful beast, doth flat refuse
To leave my leg alone. Wilt thou be kind?
That sounds weird. But I think I can help. Your dog is totally cute.

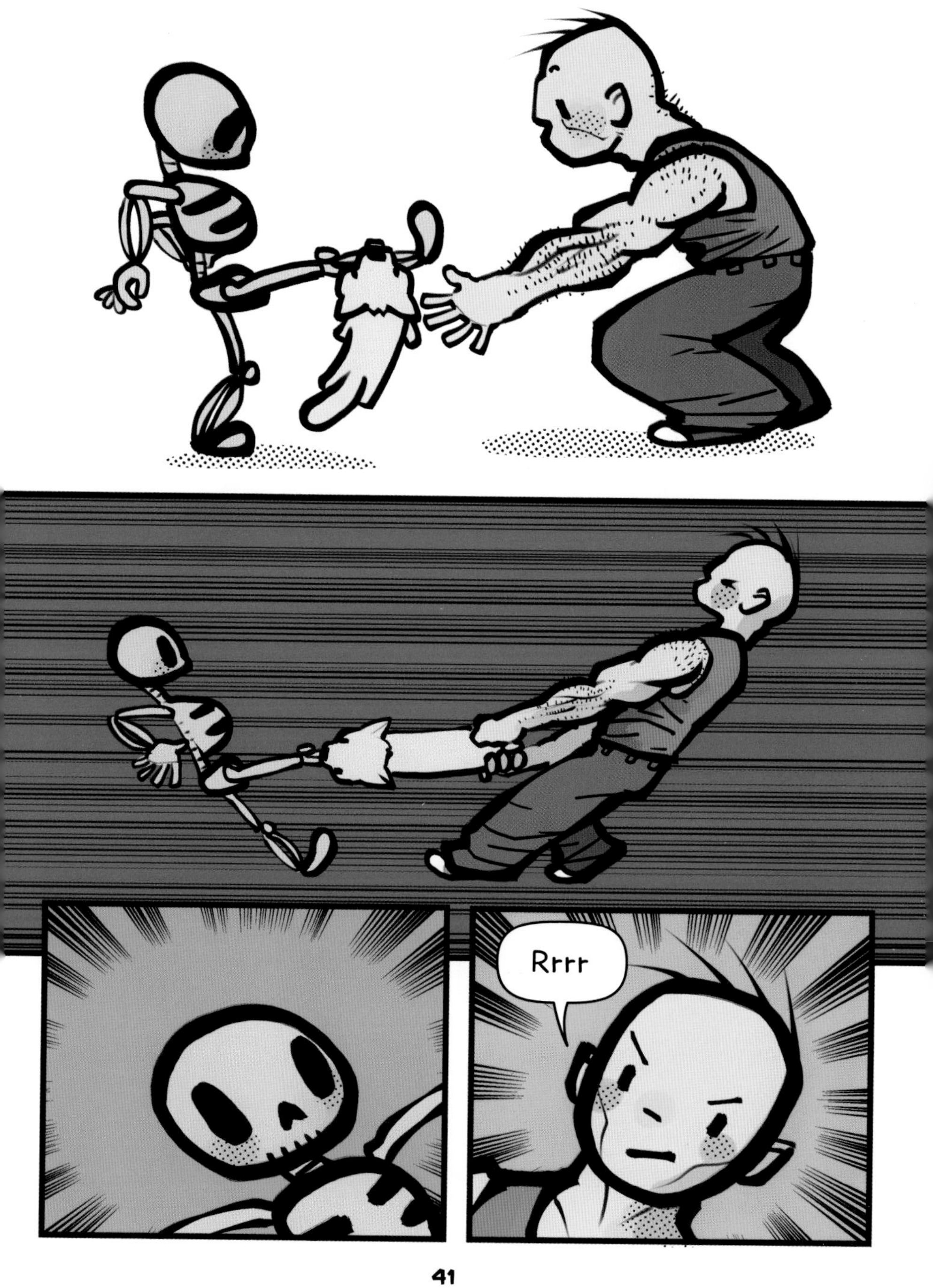
Rrrr

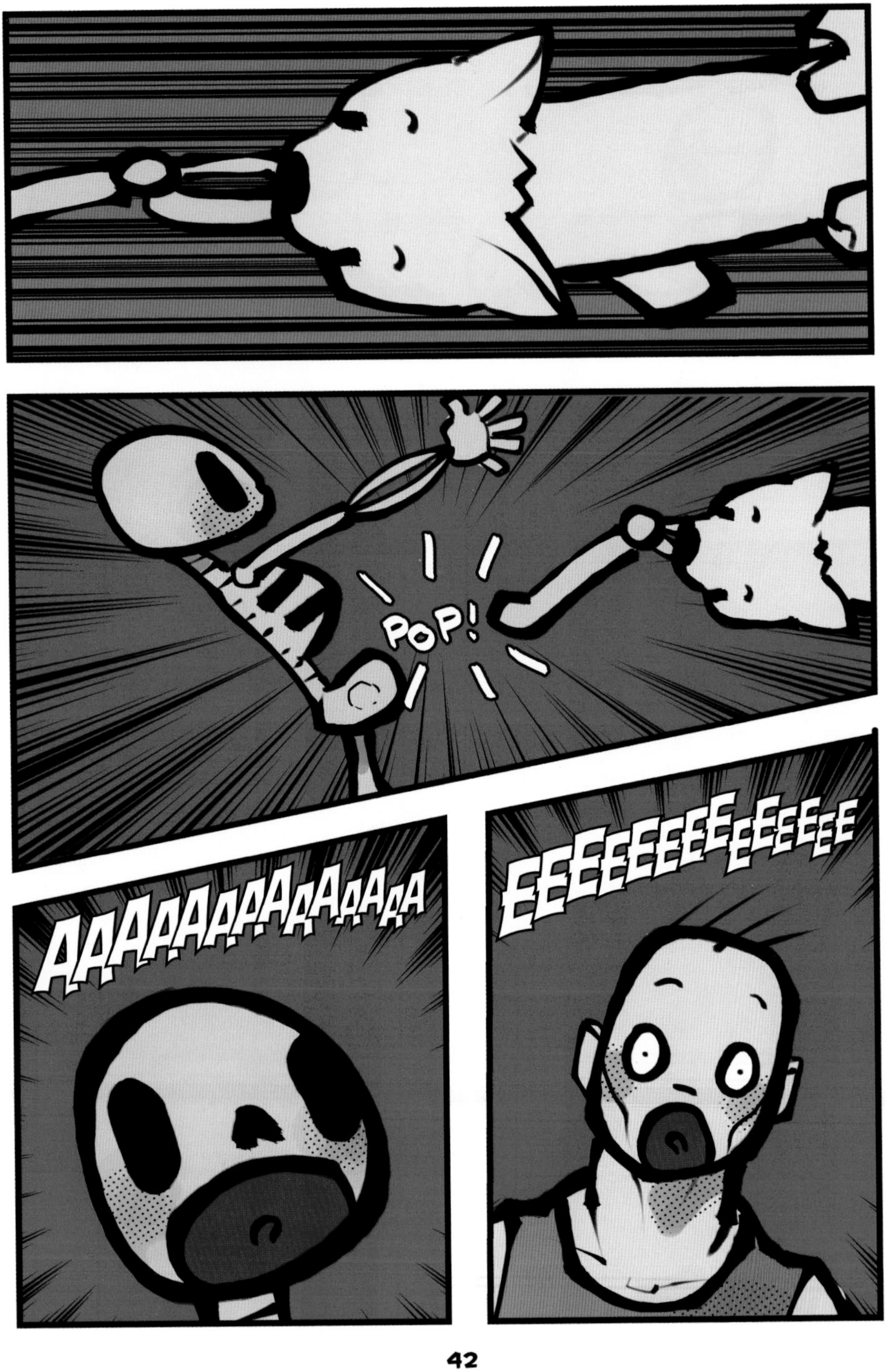
POP!
AAAAAAAAAAAAA
EEEEEEEEEEEEEEE

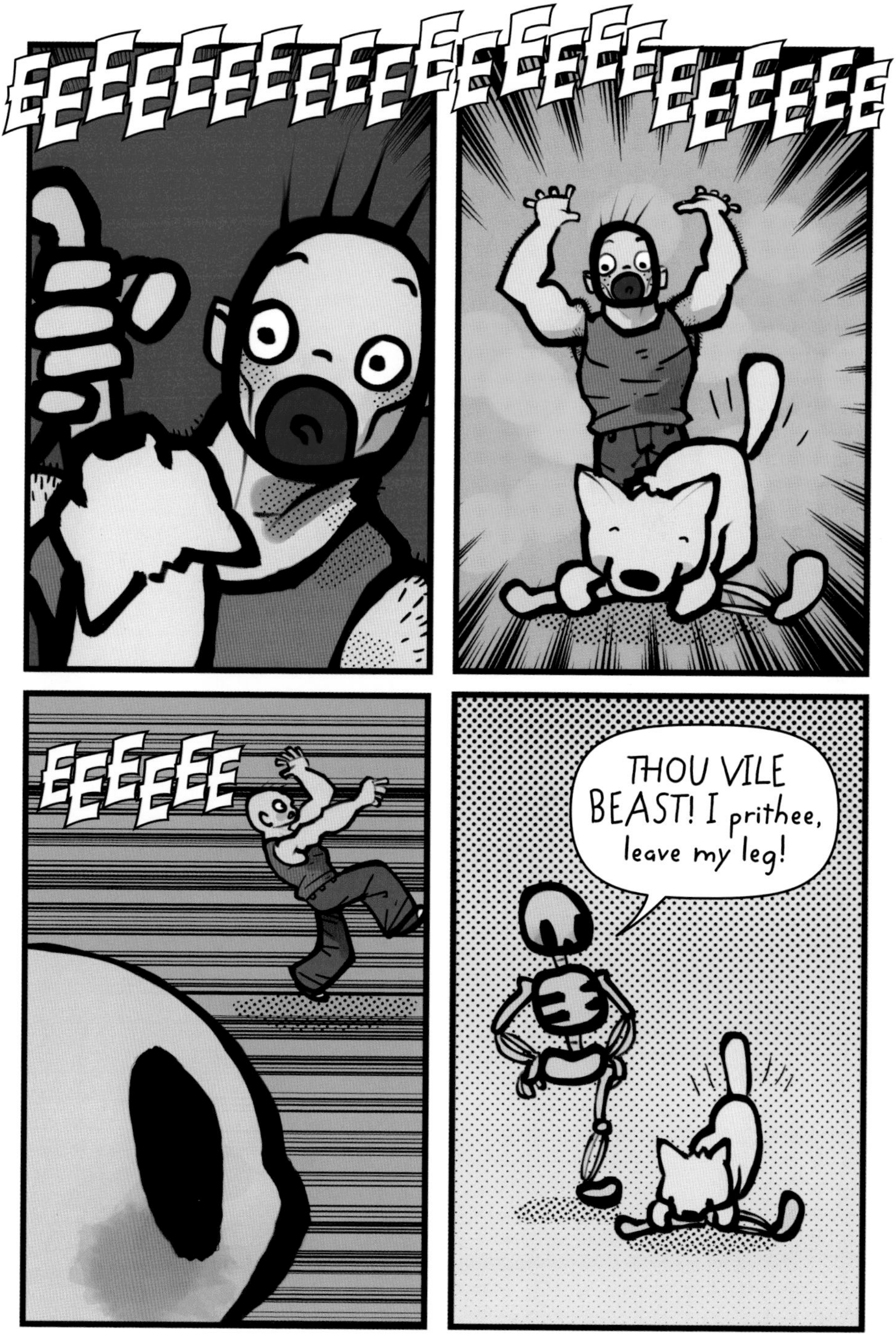
EEEEEEEEEEEEEEEEEEEEEEEE
EEEEEE
THOU VILE BEAST! I prithee, leave my leg!

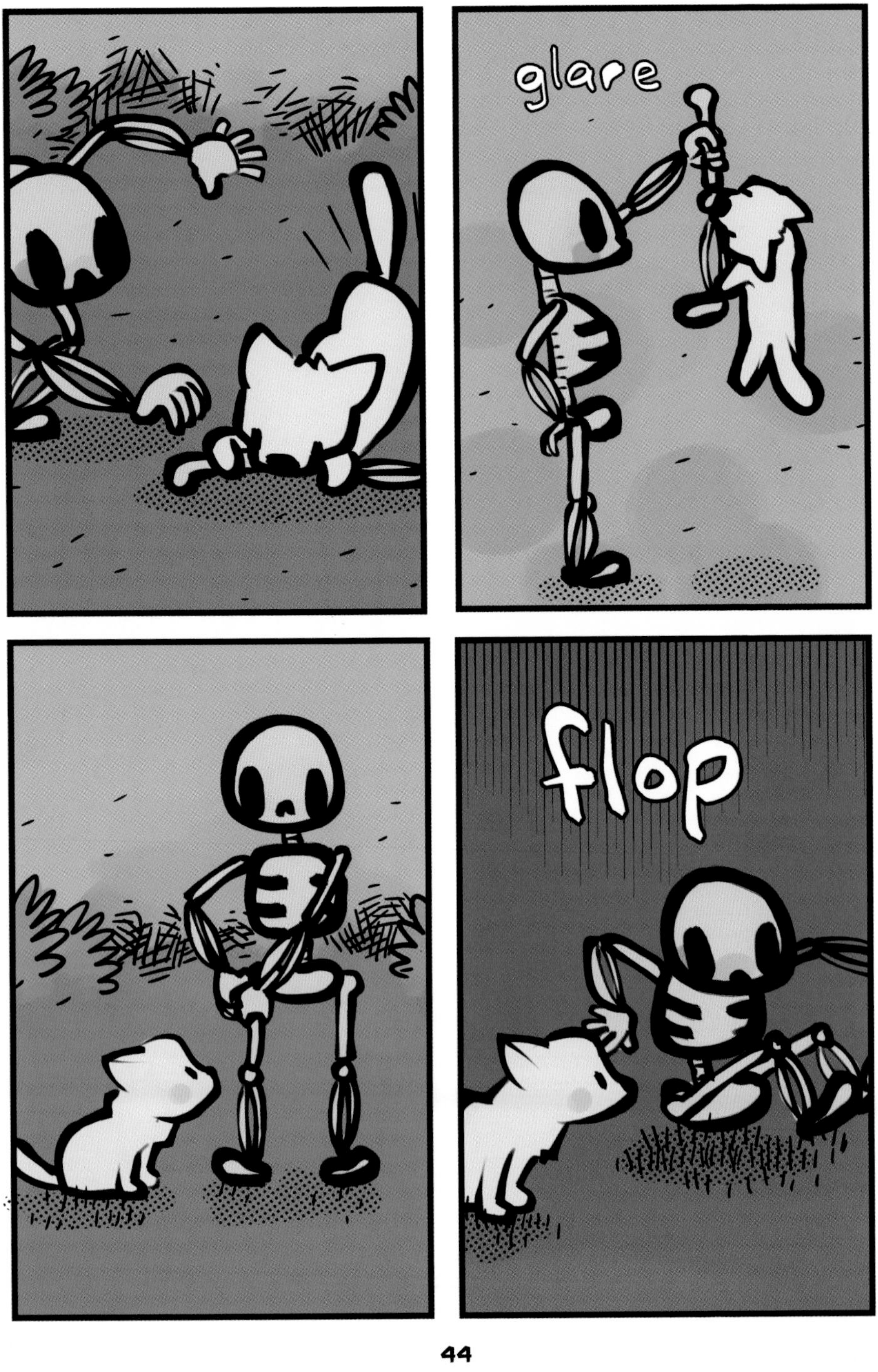
glare
flop

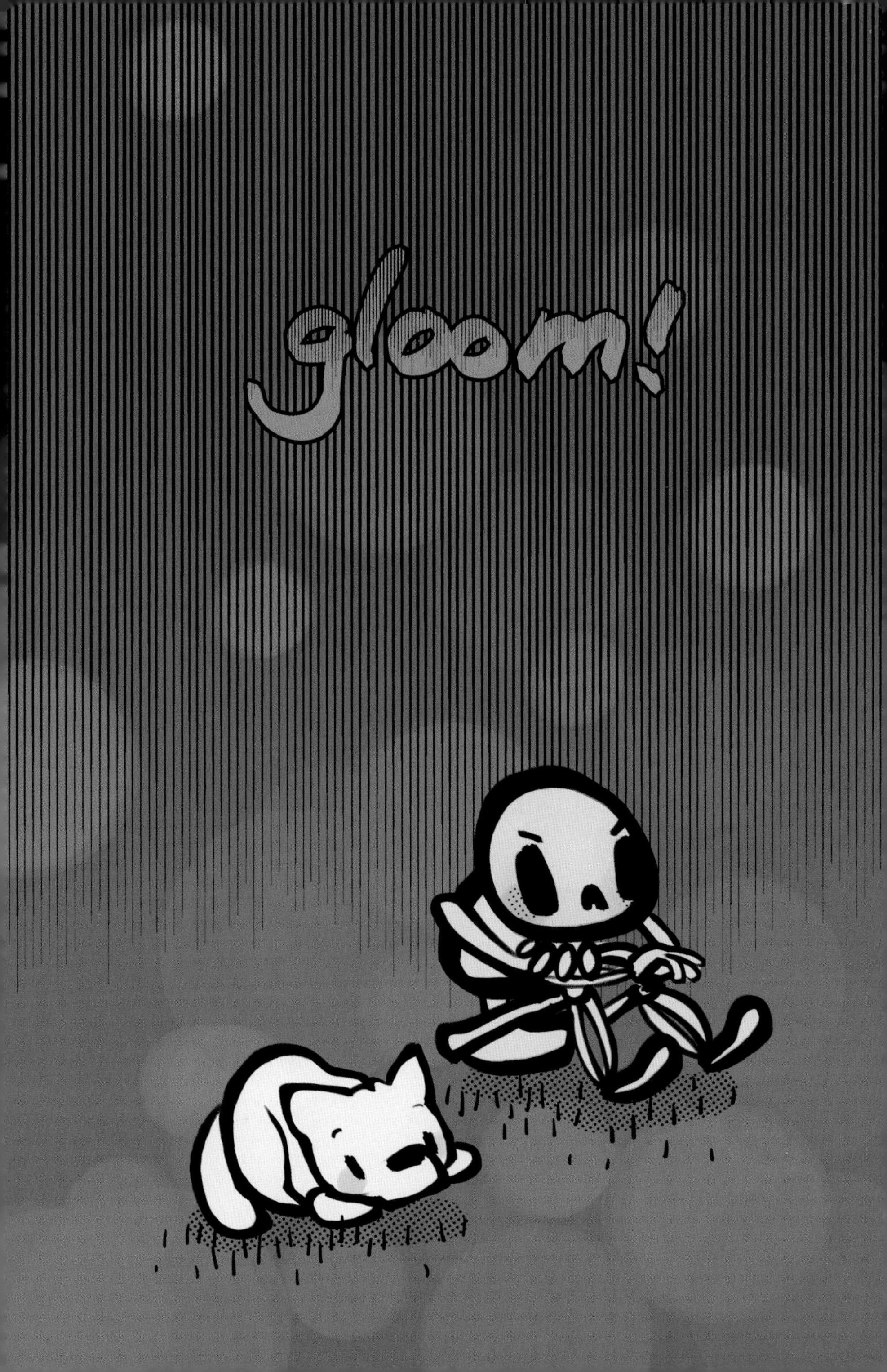
gloom!

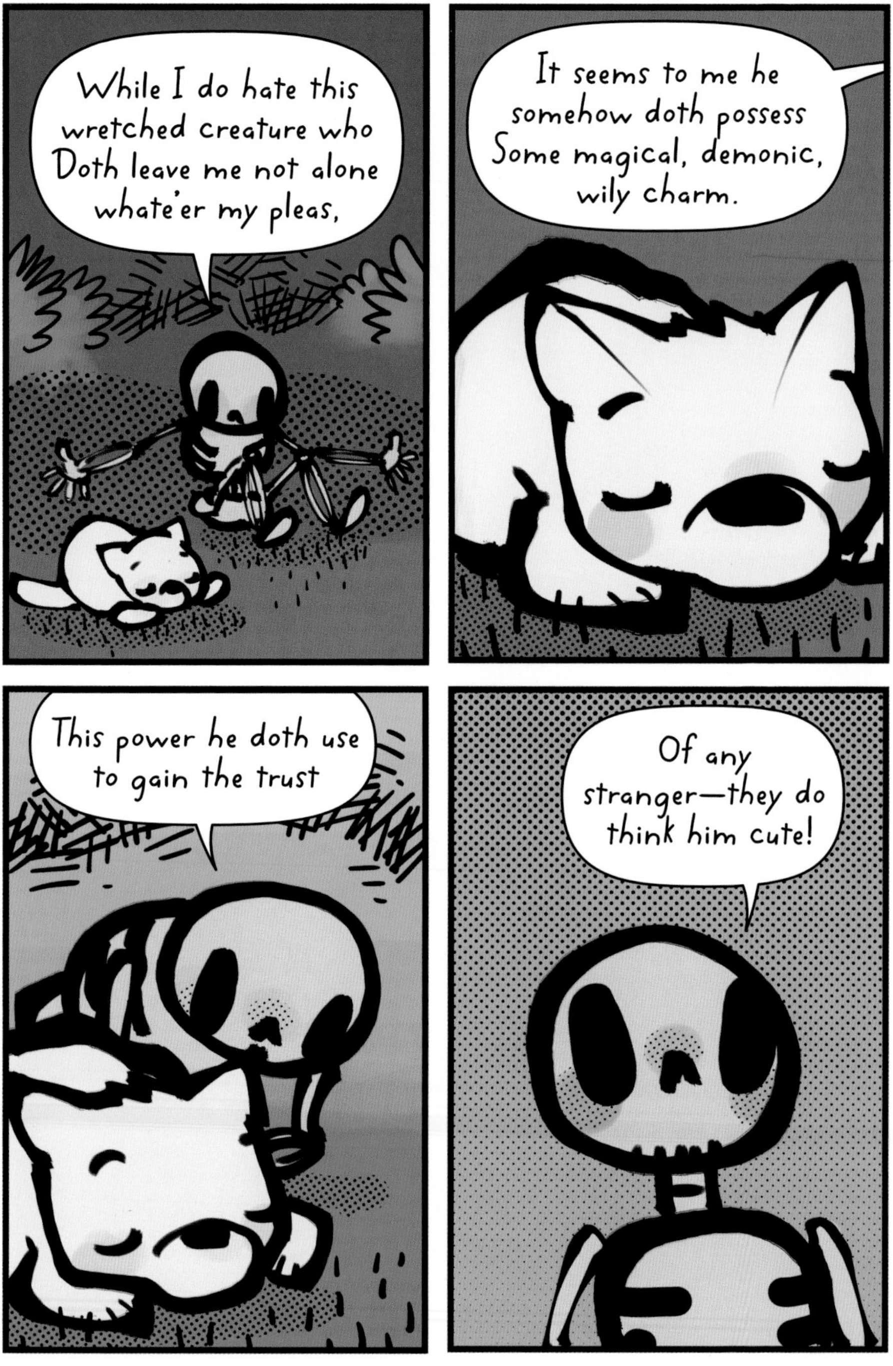
While I do hate this wretched creature who Doth leave me not alone whate'er my pleas,
It seems to me he somehow doth possess Some magical, demonic, wily charm.
This power he doth use to gain the trust
Of any stranger—they do think him cute!

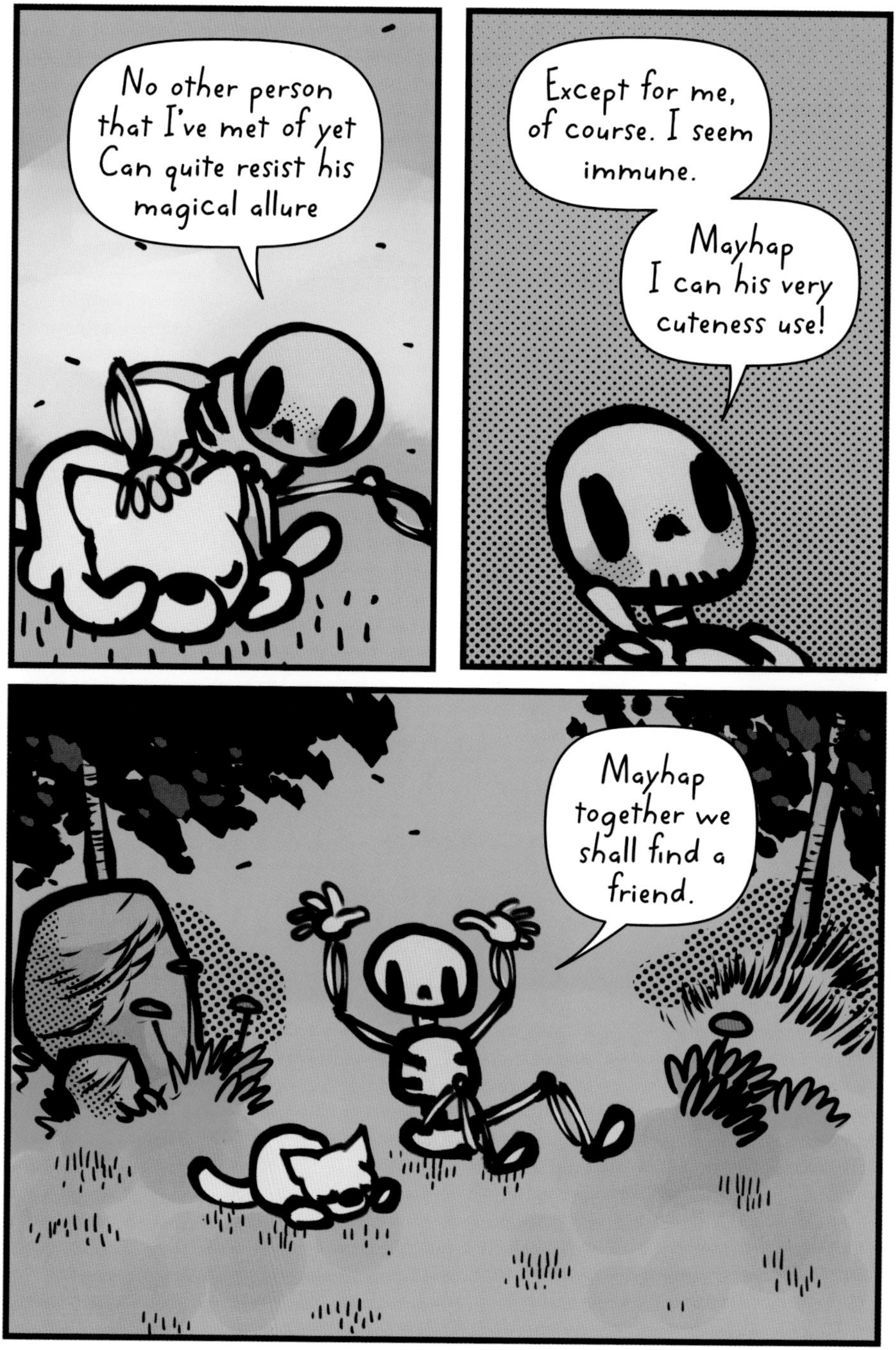
No other person that I've met of yet Can quite resist his magical allure
Except for me, of course. I seem immune.
Mayhap I can his very cuteness use!
Mayhap together we shall find a friend.

ACT TWO:

MAN'S PEST FRIEND

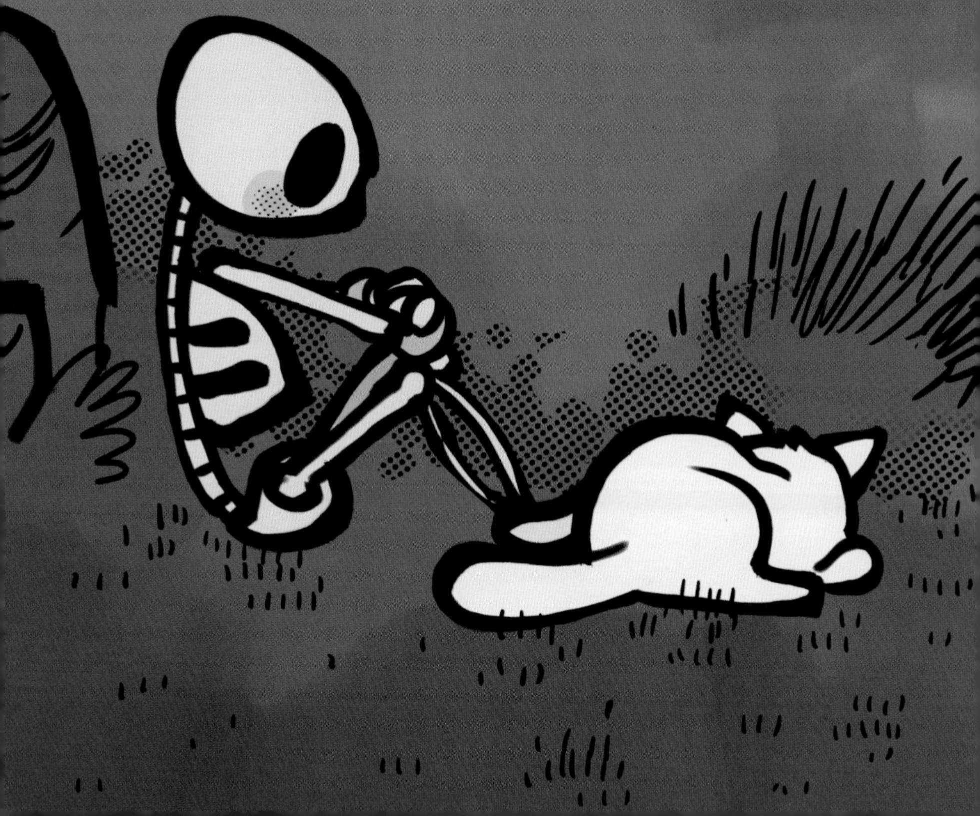

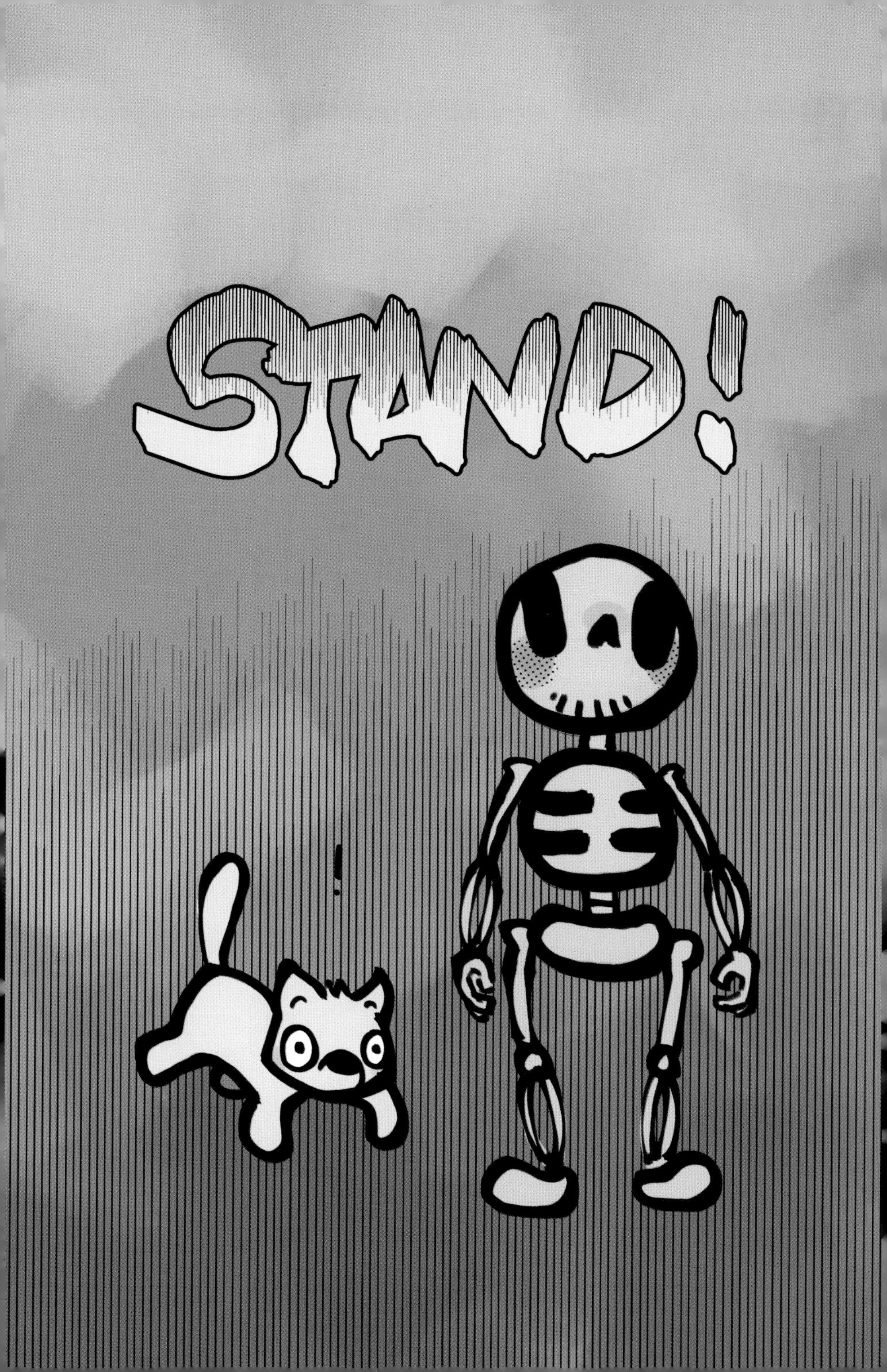
STAND!
!

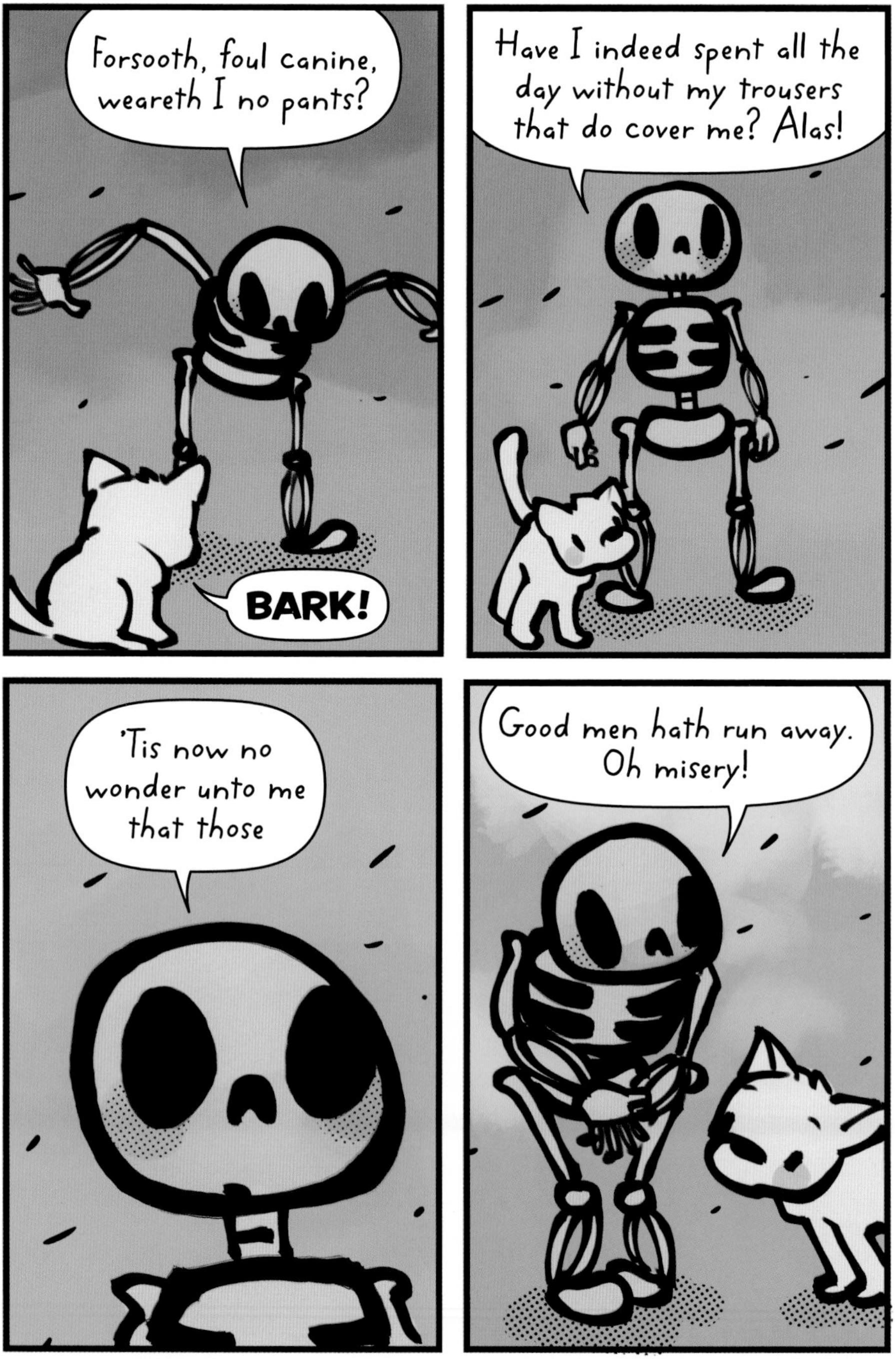
Forsooth, foul canine, weareth I no pants?
BARK!
Have I indeed spent all the day without my trousers that do cover me? Alas!
'Tis now no wonder unto me that those
Good men hath run away. Oh misery!

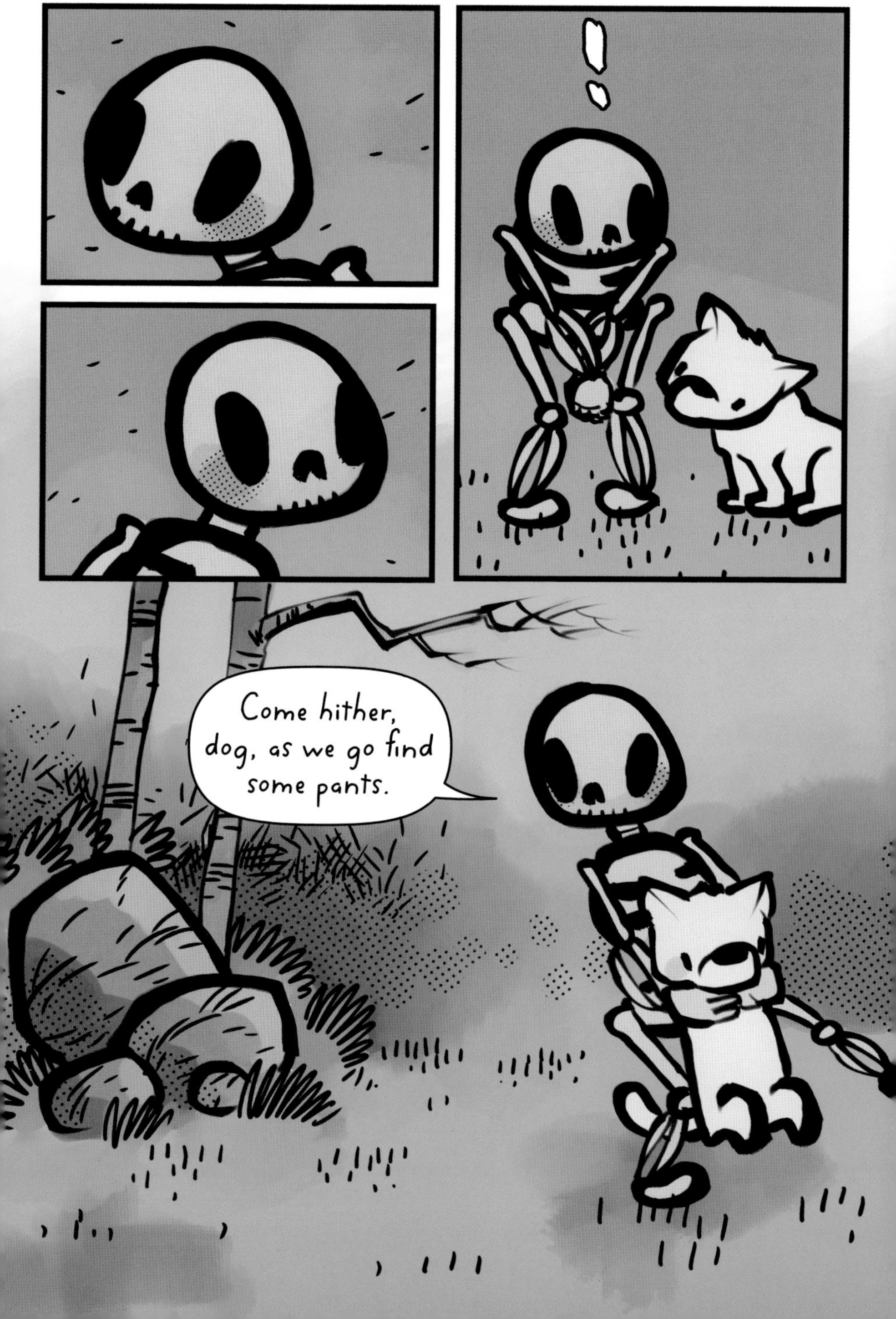
!
Come hither, dog, as we go find some pants.

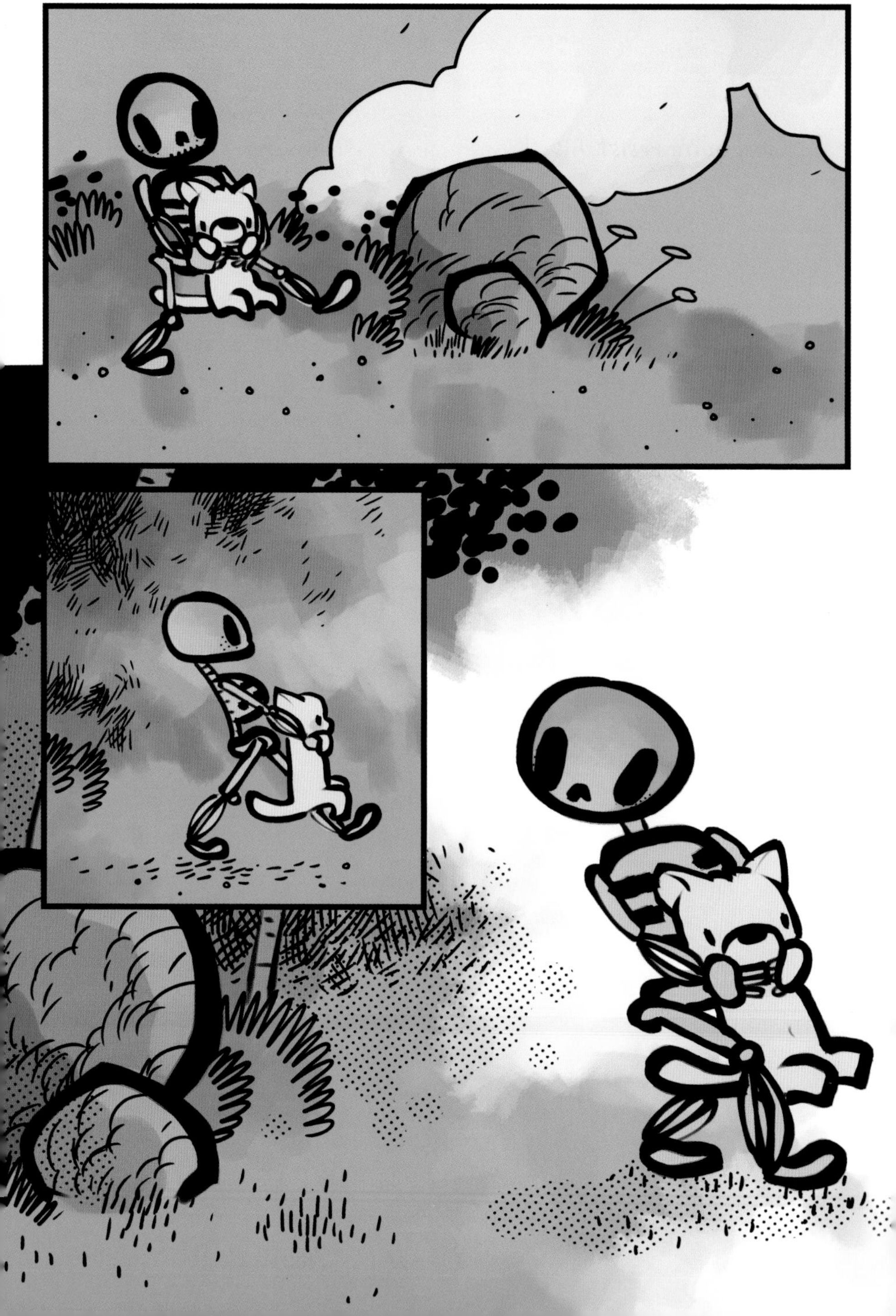

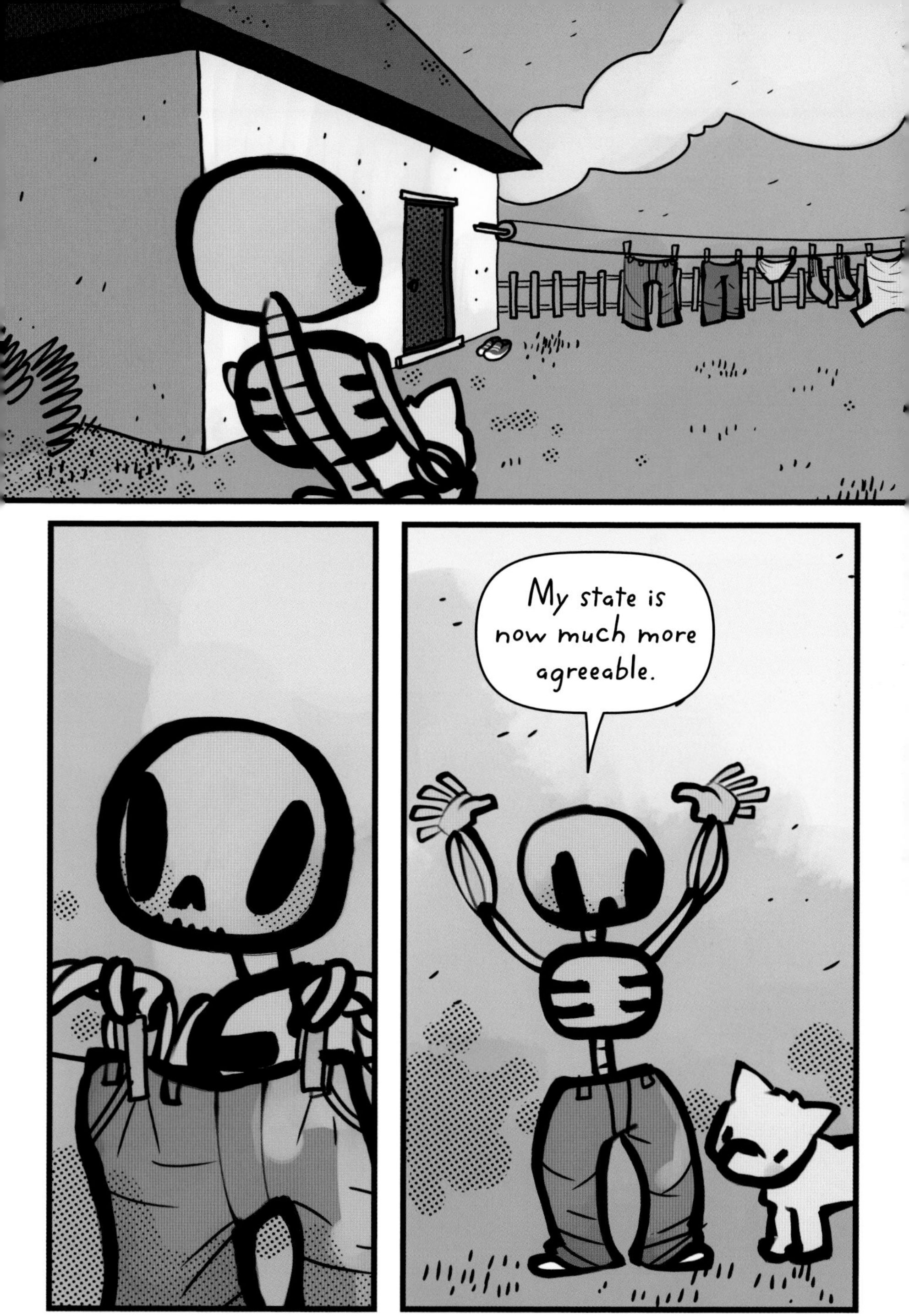
My state is now much more agreeable.

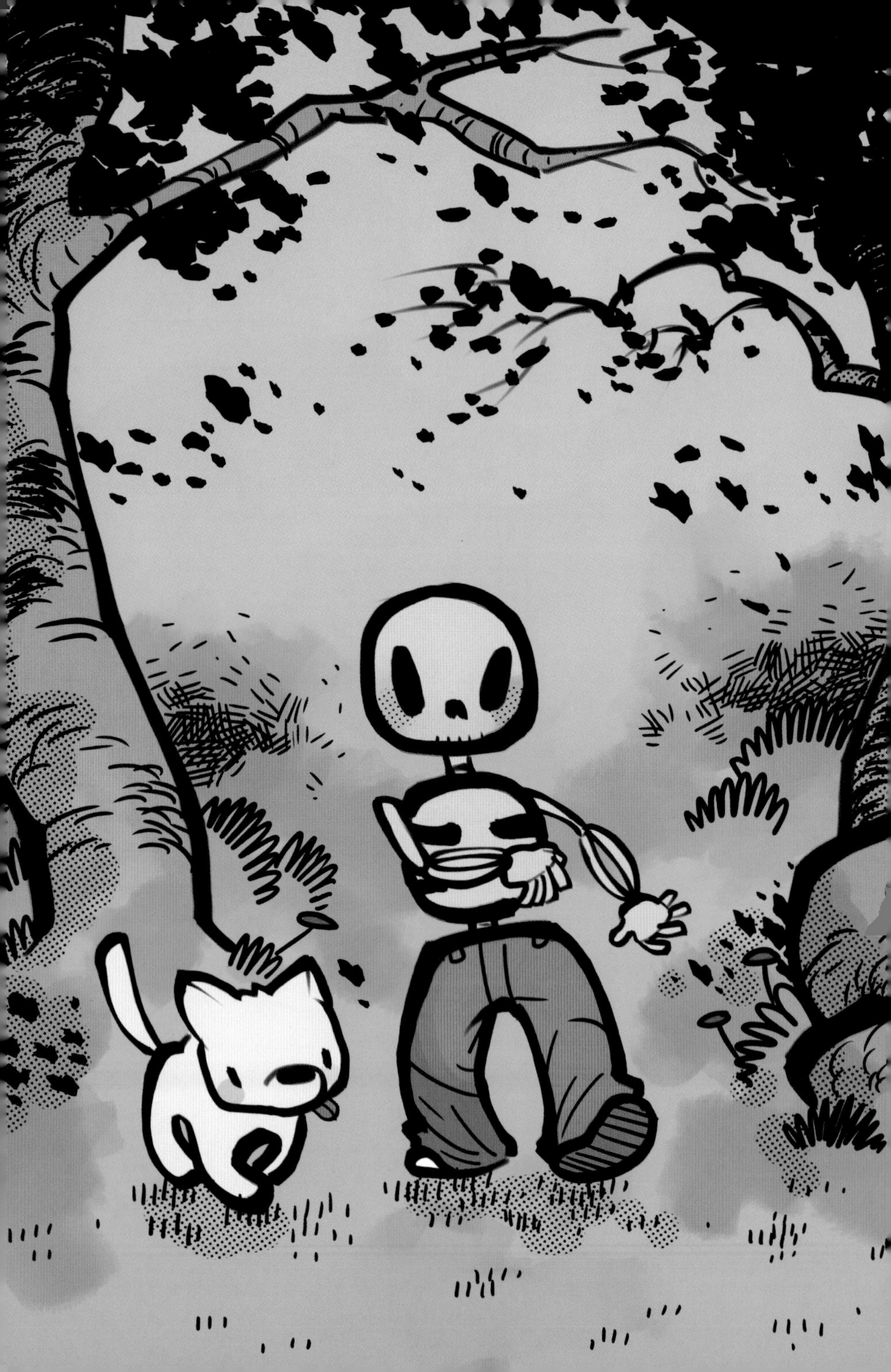

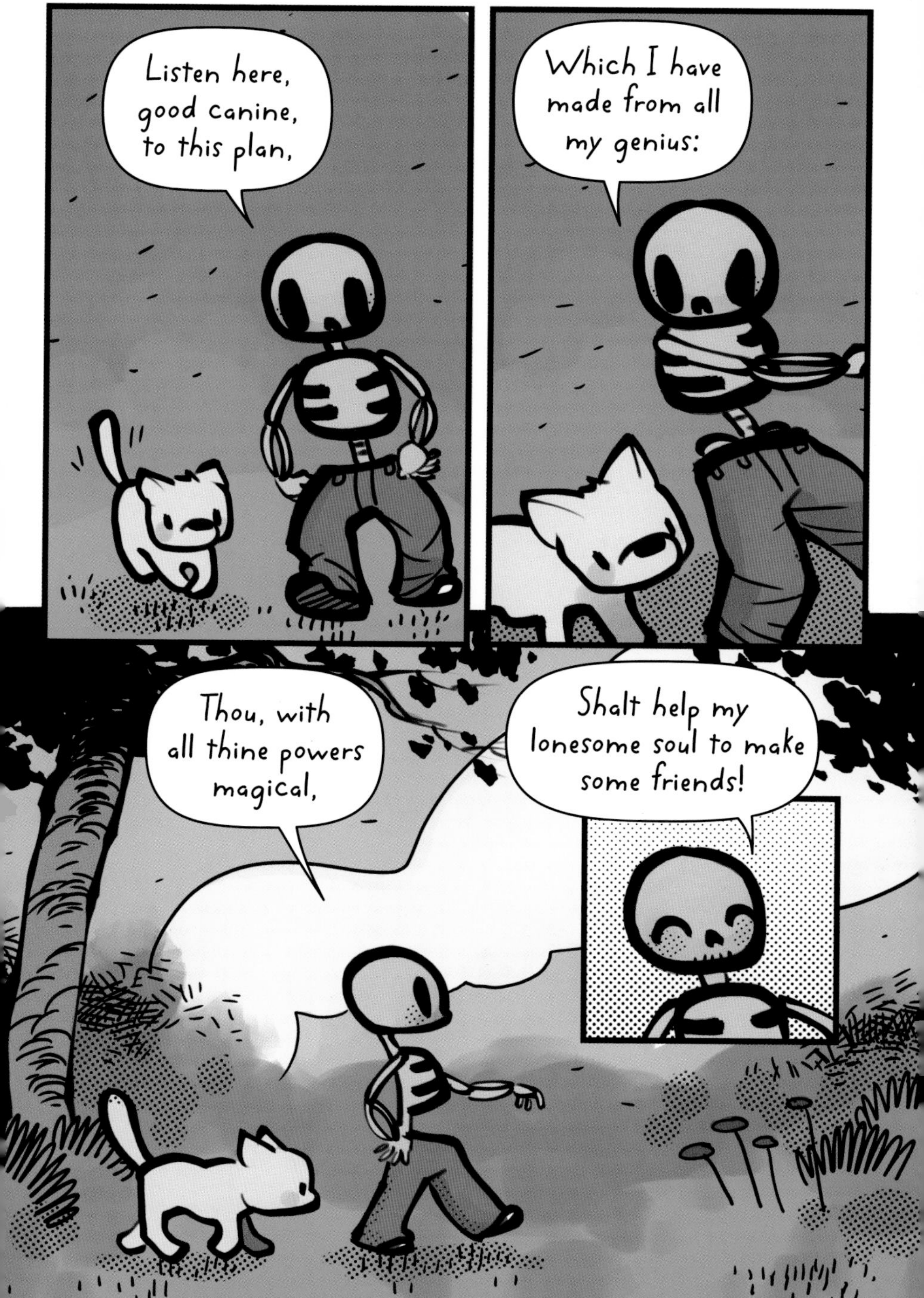
Listen here, good canine, to this plan,
Which I have made from all my genius:
Thou, with all thine powers magical,
Shalt help my lonesome soul to make some friends!

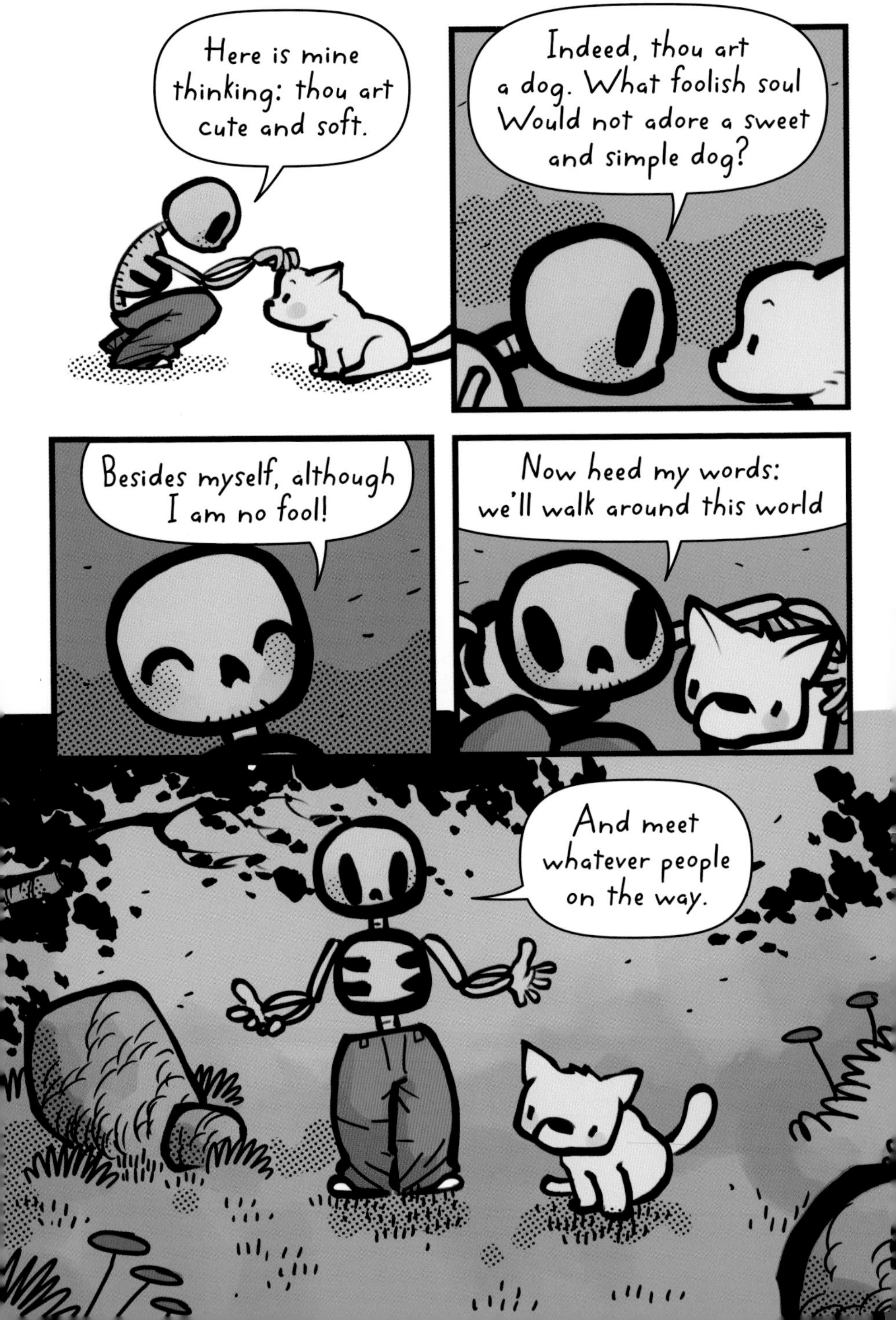
Here is mine thinking: thou art cute and soft.
Indeed, thou art a dog. What foolish soul Would not adore a sweet and simple dog?
Besides myself, although I am no fool!
Now heed my words: we'll walk around this world
And meet whatever people on the way.

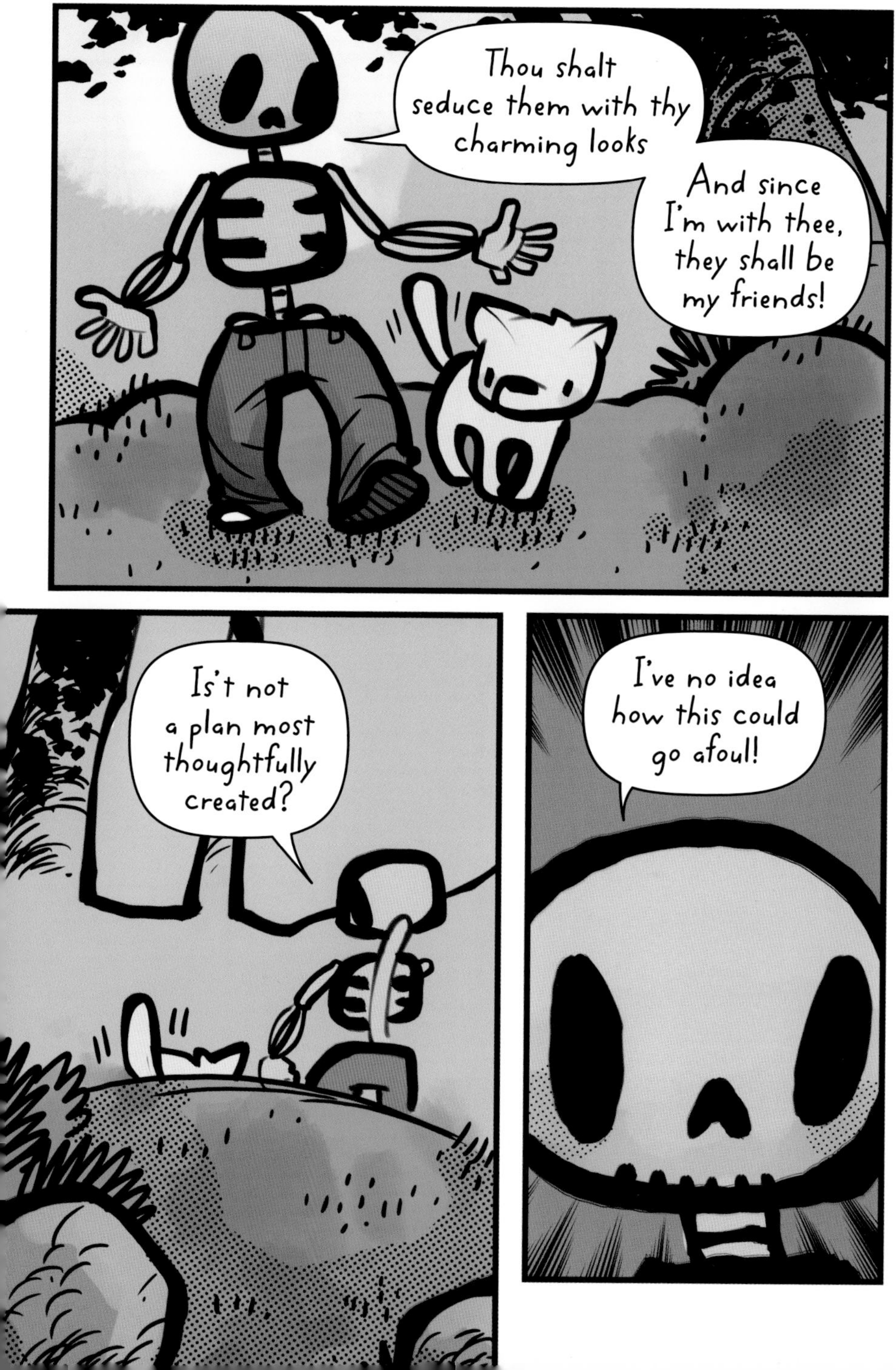
Thou shalt seduce them with thy charming looks
And since I'm with thee, they shall be my friends!
Is't not a plan most thoughtfully created?
I've no idea how this could go afoul!

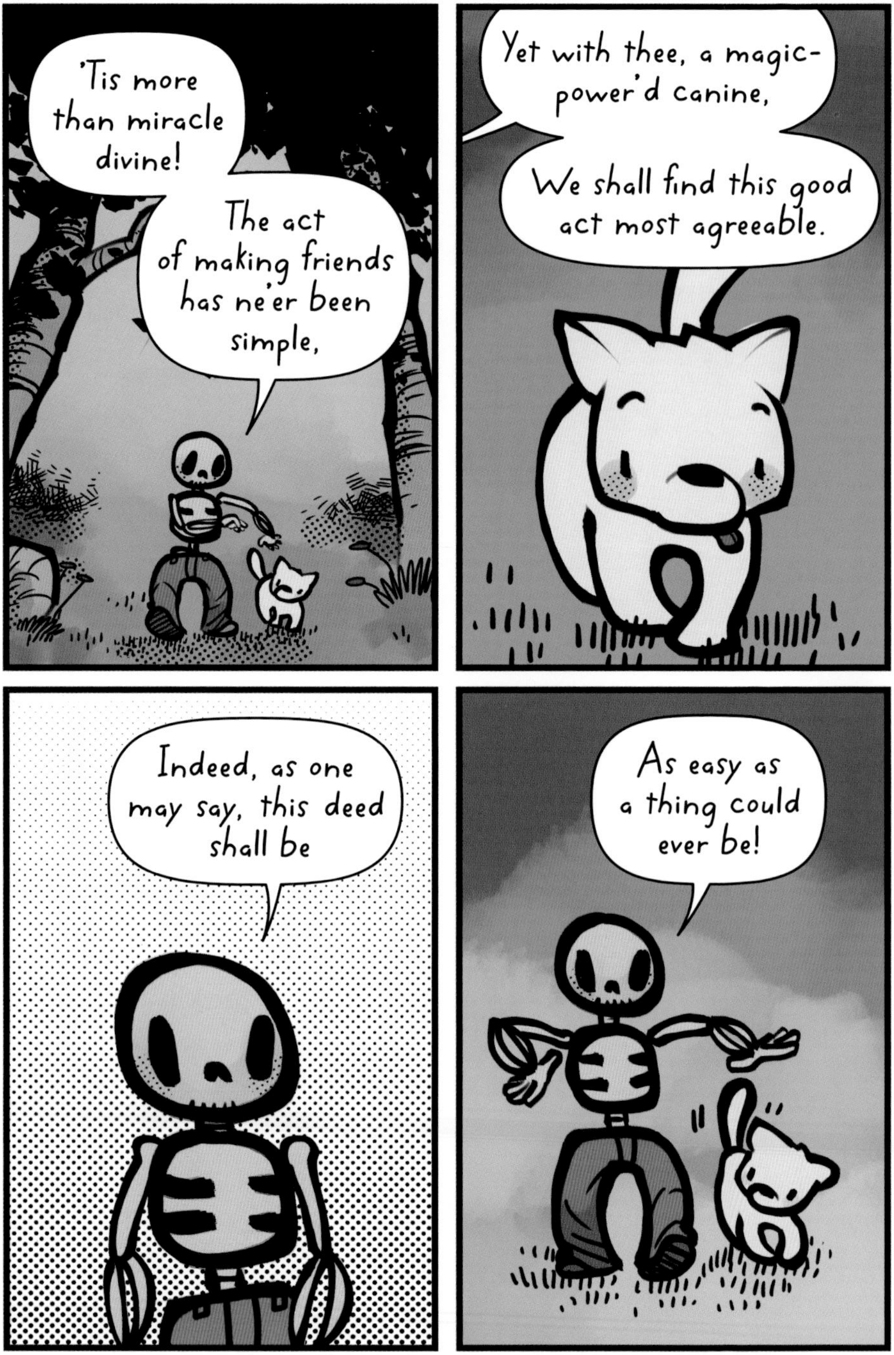
'Tis more than miracle divine!
The act of making friends has ne'er been simple,
Yet with thee, a magic-power'd canine,
We shall find this good act most agreeable.
Indeed, as one may say, this deed shall be
As easy as a thing could ever be!

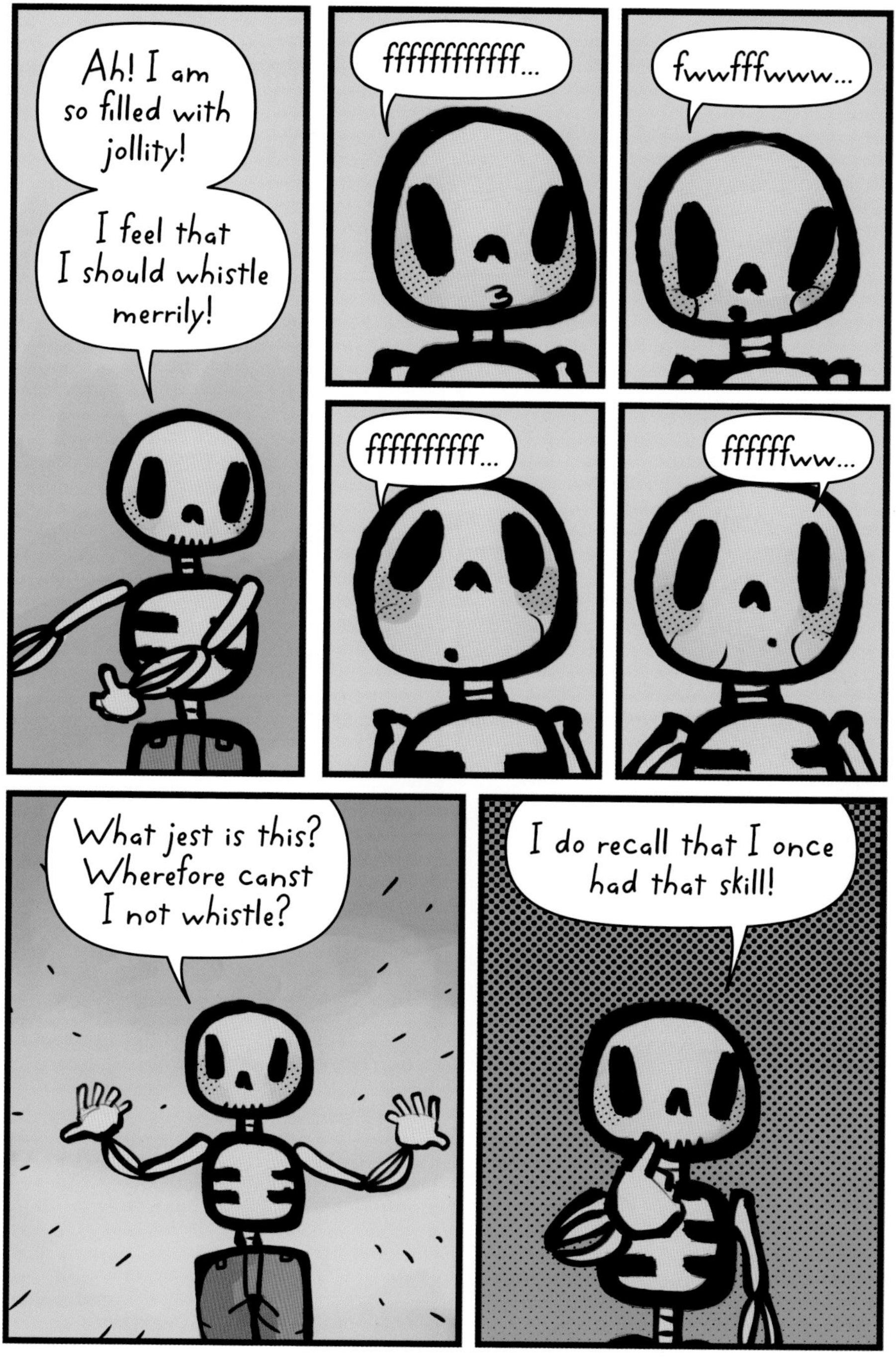
Ah! I am so filled with jollity!
I feel that I should whistle merrily!
ffffffffffff...
fwwfffwww...
ffffffffff...
ffffffww...
What jest is this? Wherefore canst I not whistle?
I do recall that I once had that skill!

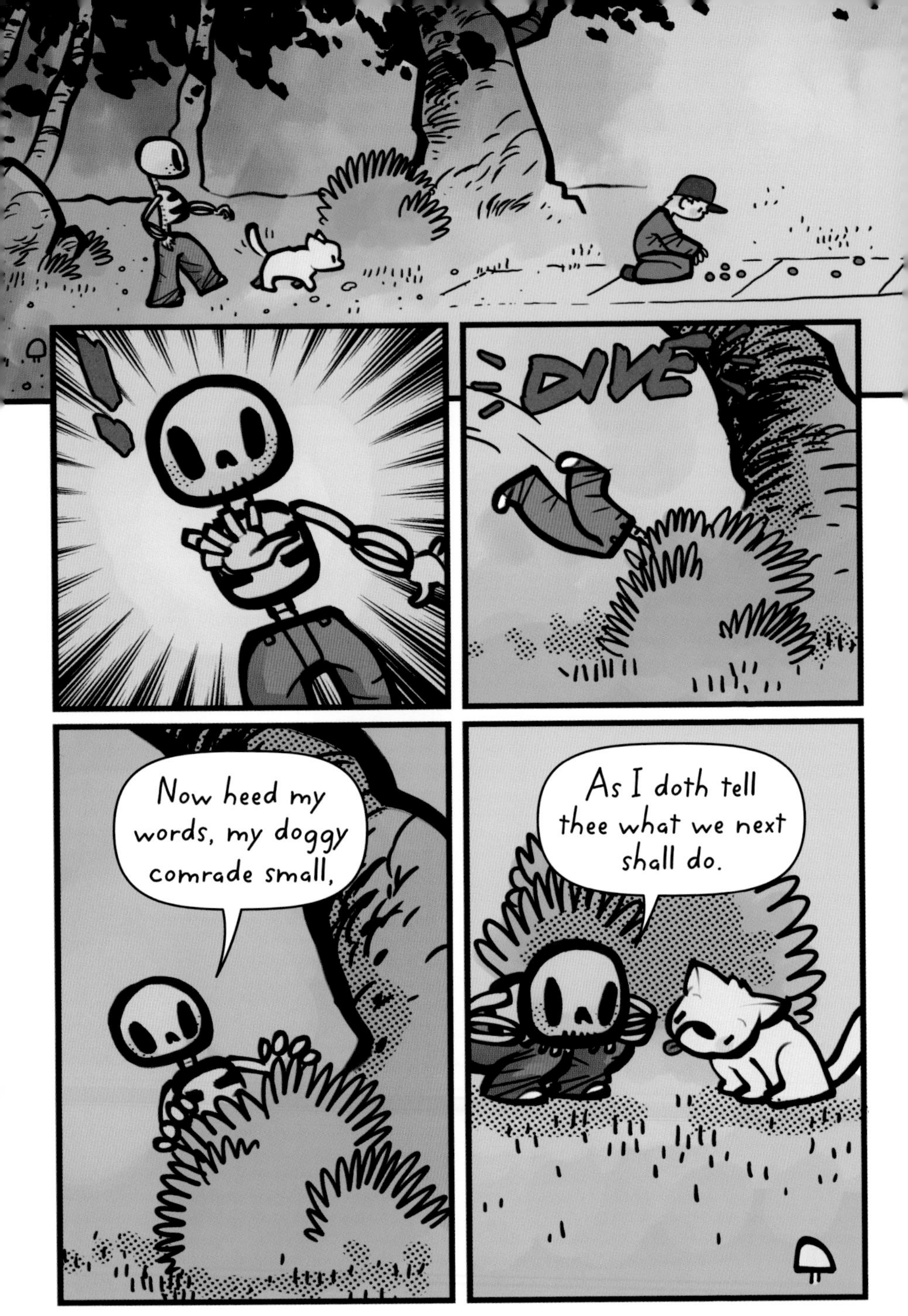
DIVE
Now heed my words, my doggy comrade small,
As I doth tell thee what we next shall do.

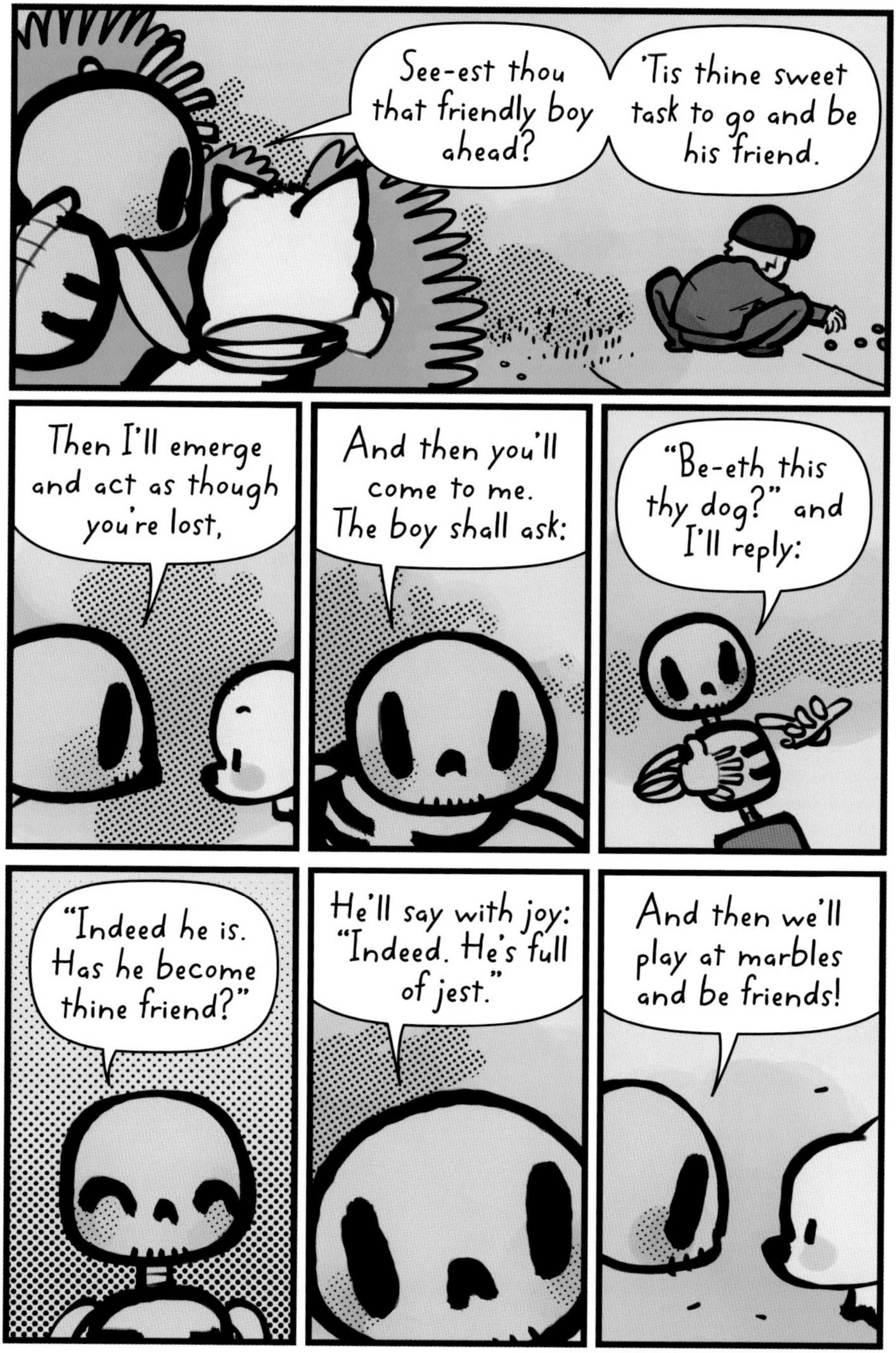
See-est thou that friendly boy ahead?
'Tis thine sweet task to go and be his friend.
Then I'll emerge and act as though you're lost,
And then you'll come to me. The boy shall ask:
"Be-eth this thy dog?" and I'll reply:
"Indeed he is. Has he become thine friend?"
He'll say with joy: "Indeed. He's full of jest."
And then we'll play at marbles and be friends!

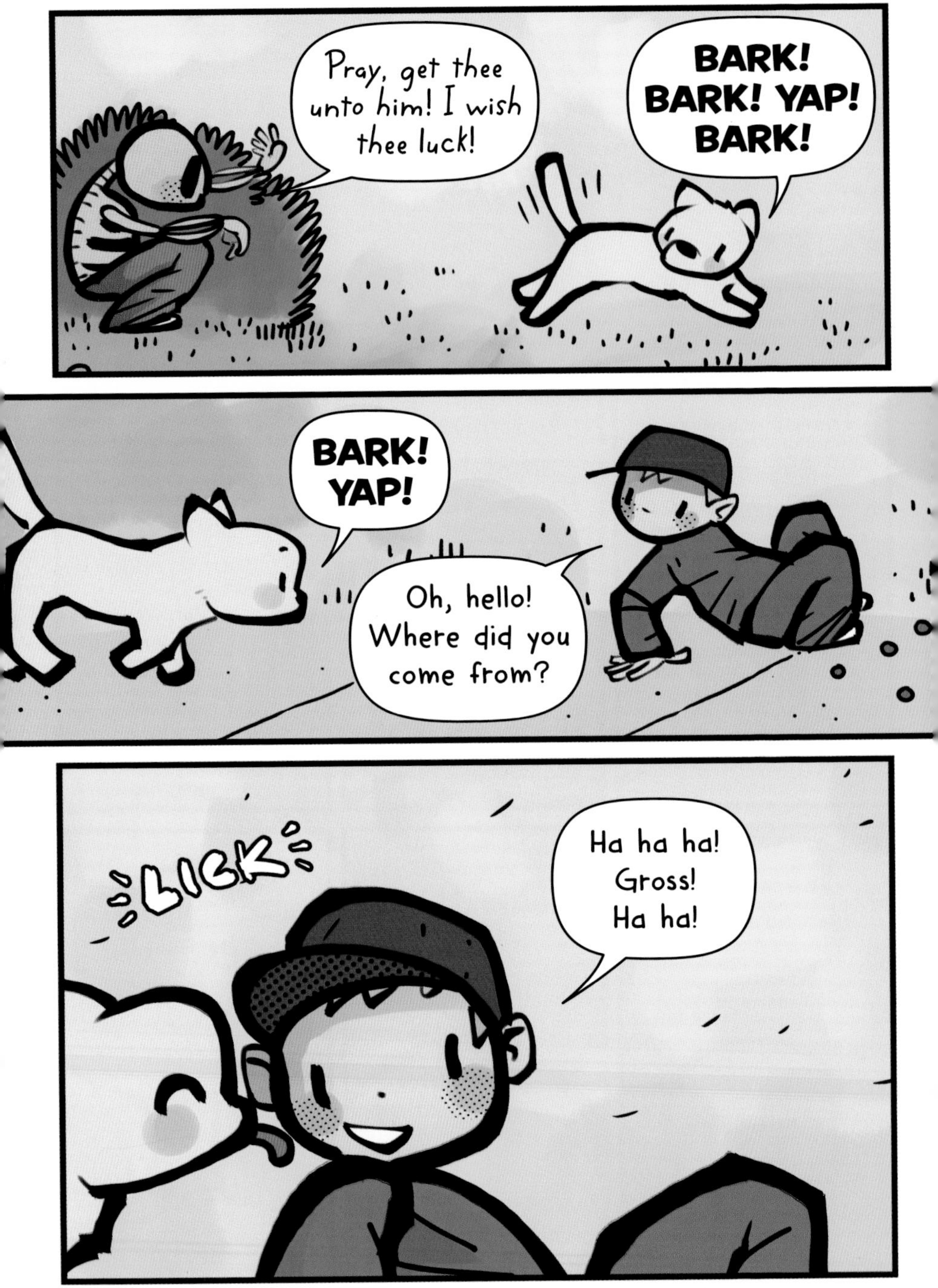
Pray, get thee unto him! I wish thee luck!
BARK! BARK! YAP! BARK!
BARK! YAP!
Oh, hello! Where did you come from?
LICK
Ha ha ha! Gross! Ha ha!

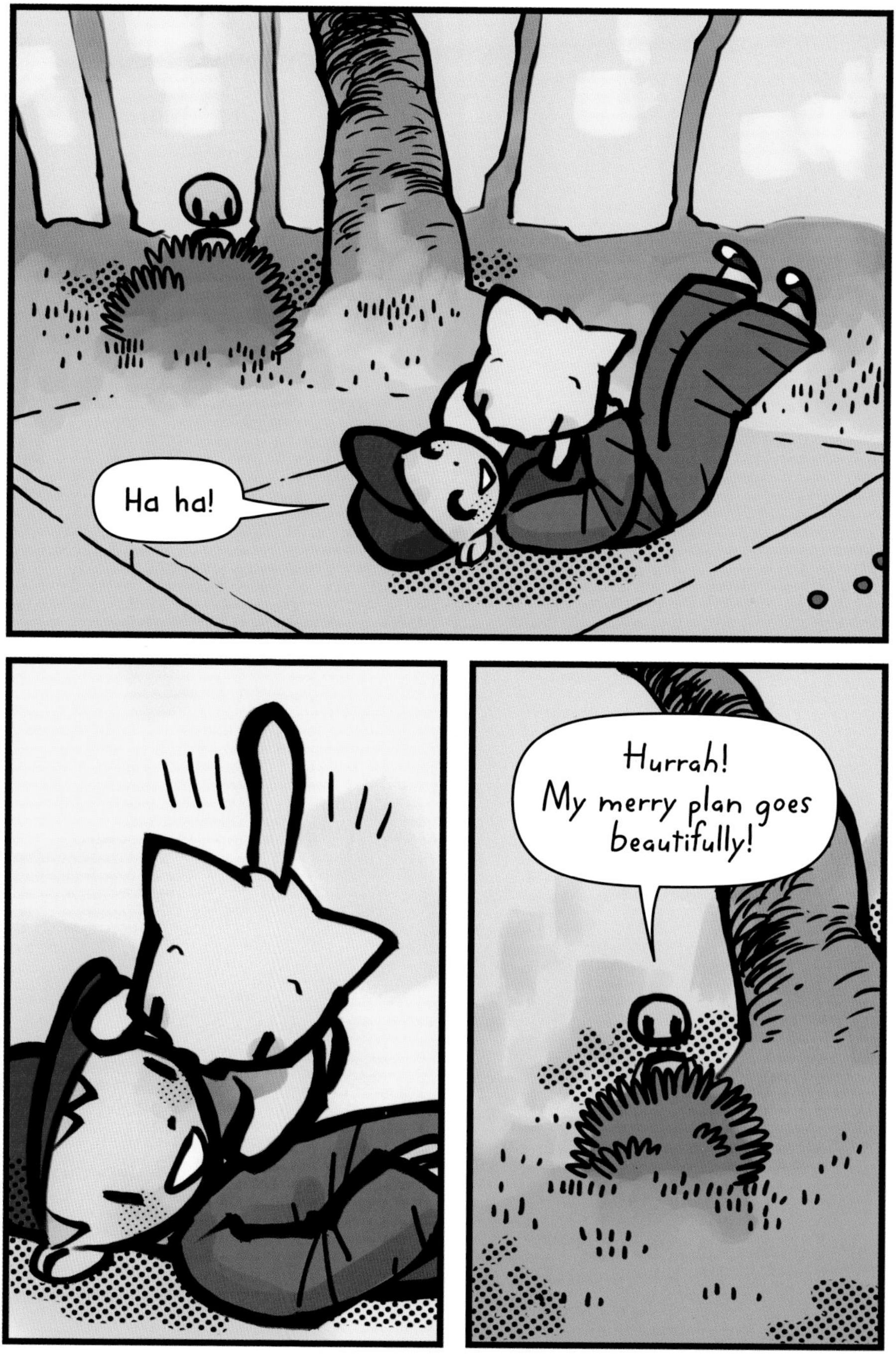
Ha ha!
Hurrah! My merry plan goes beautifully!

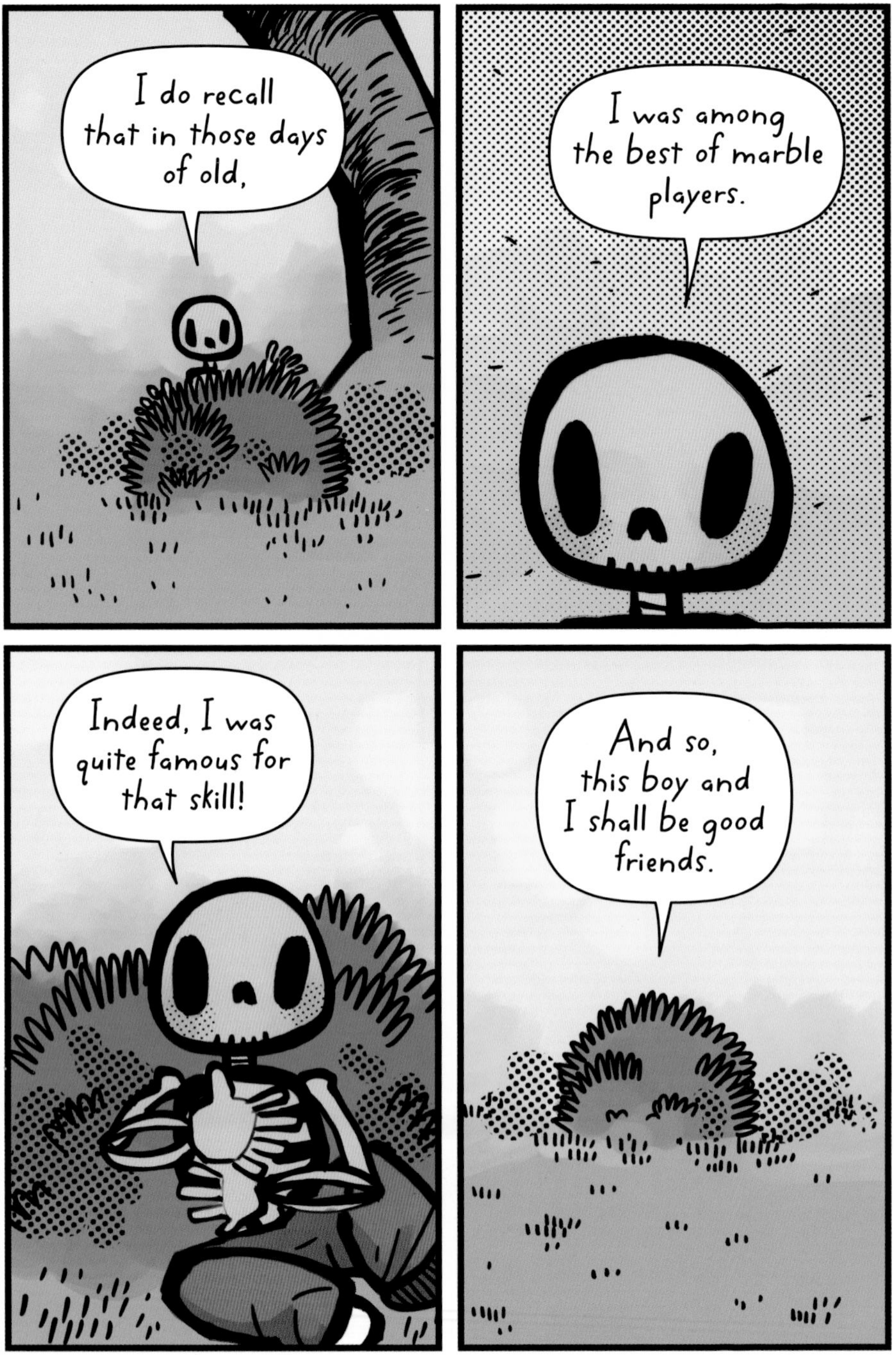
I do recall that in those days of old,
I was among the best of marble players.
Indeed, I was quite famous for that skill!
And so, this boy and I shall be good friends.

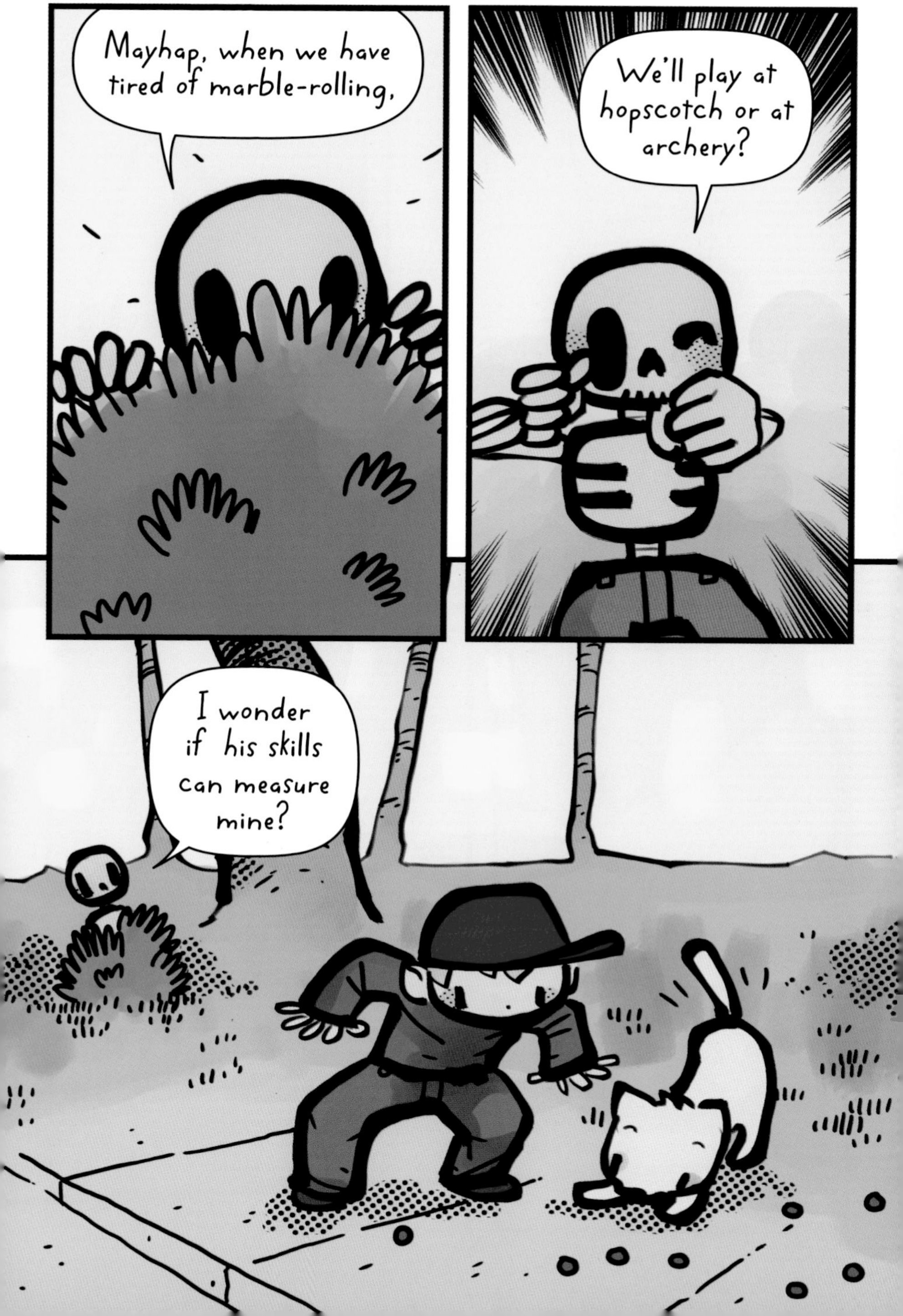
Mayhap, when we have tired of marble-rolling,
We'll play at hopscotch or at archery?
I wonder if his skills can measure mine?

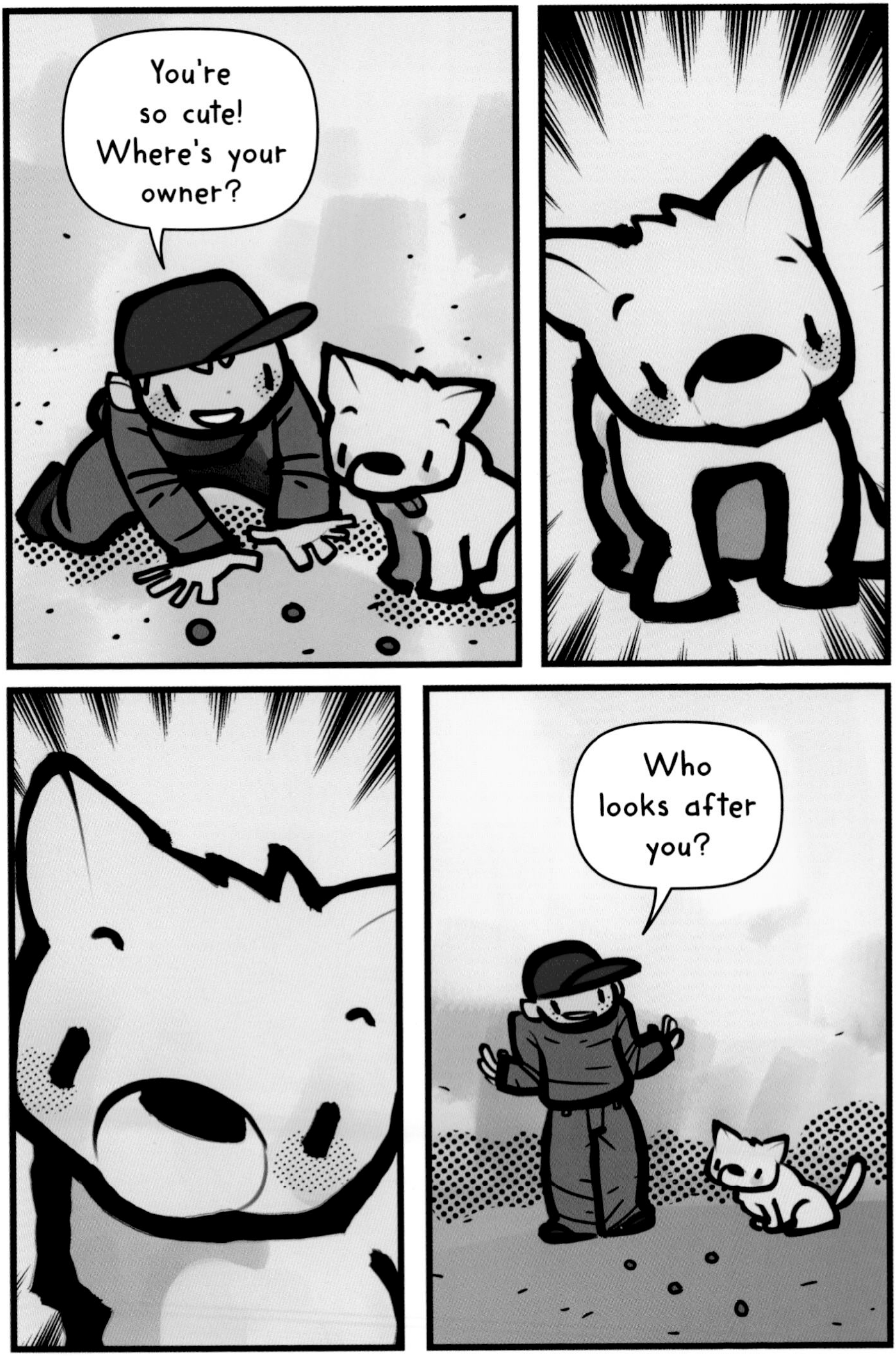
You're so cute! Where's your owner?
Who looks after you?

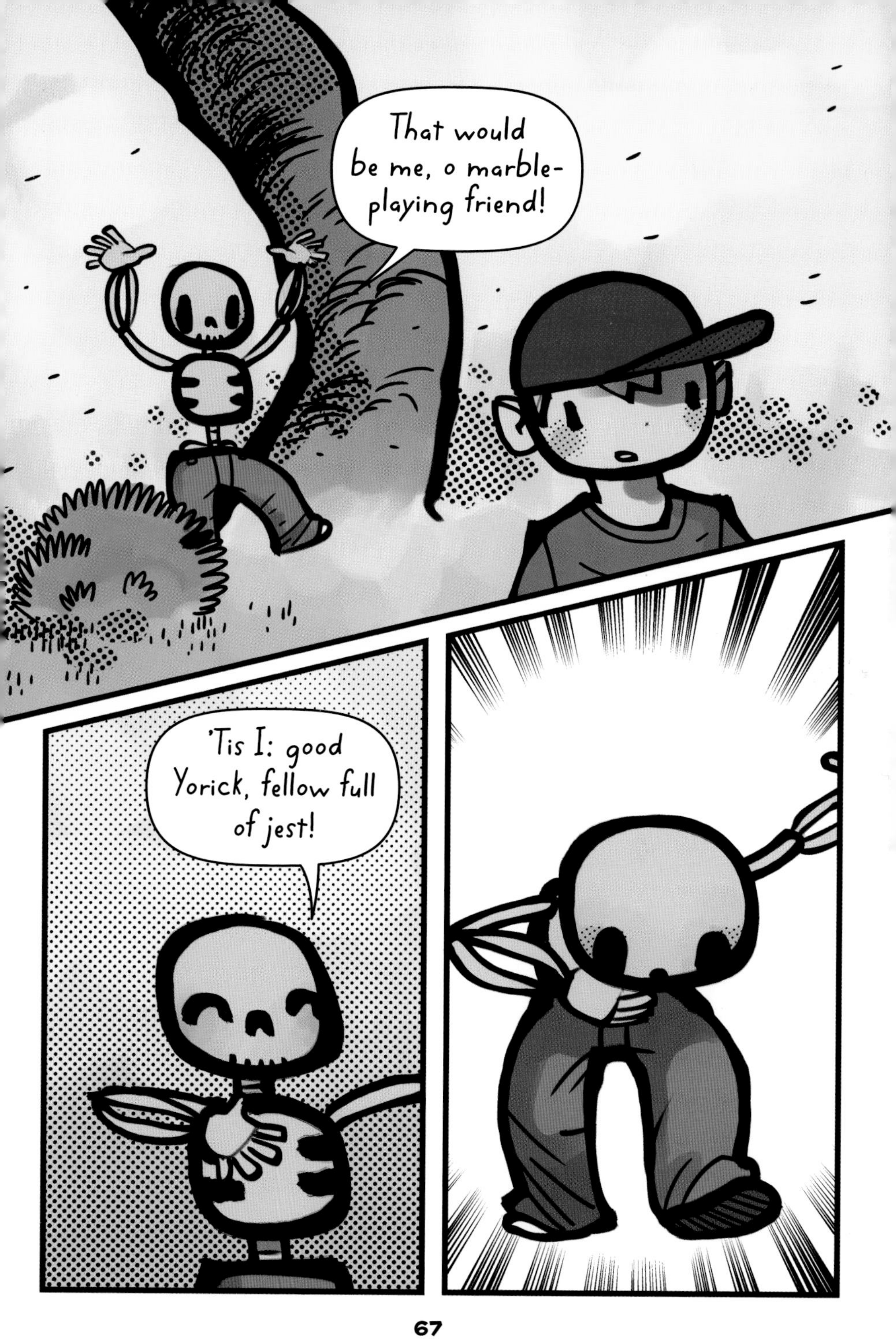
That would be me, o marble-playing friend!
'Tis I: good Yorick, fellow full of jest!

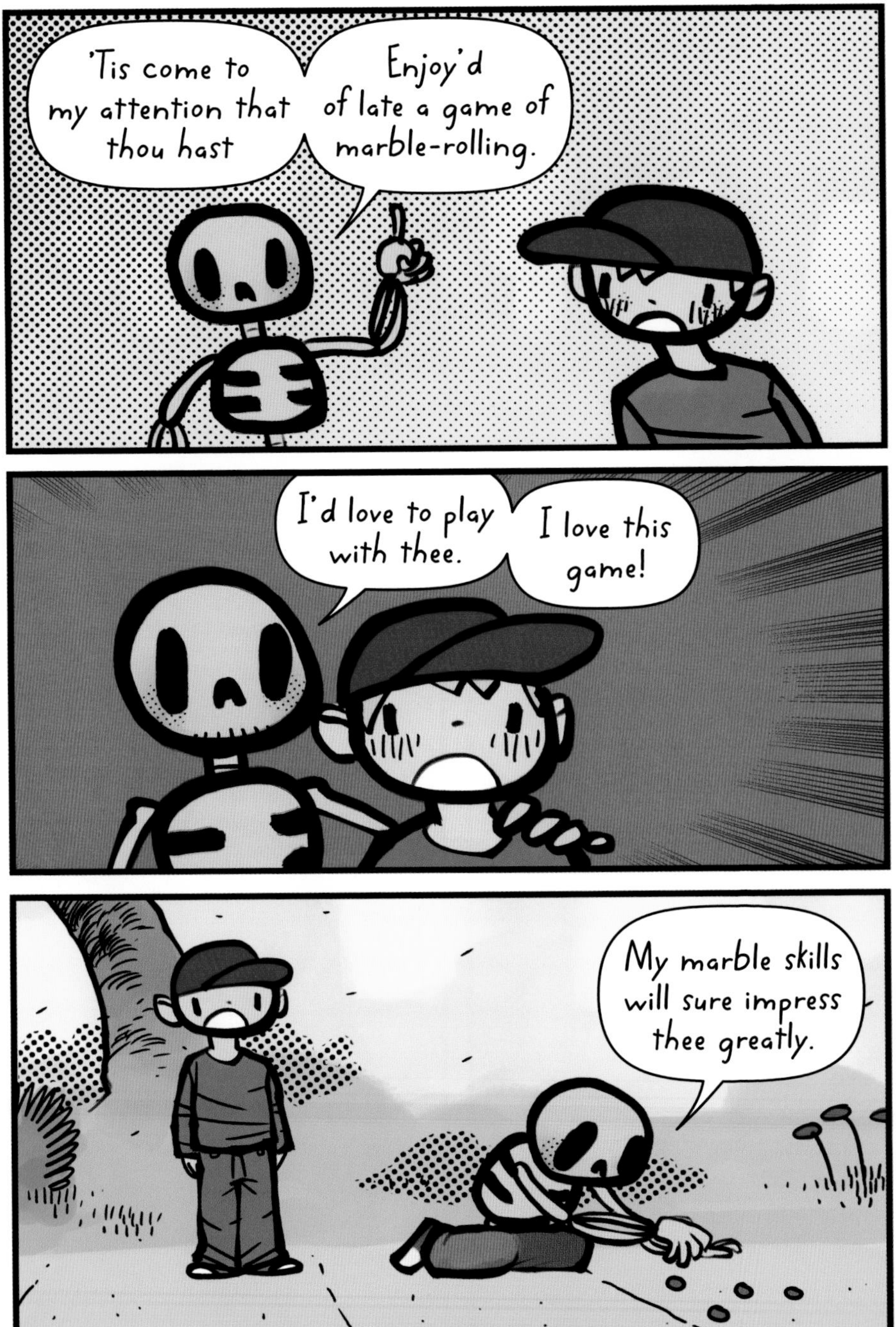
'Tis come to my attention that thou hast
Enjoy'd of late a game of marble-rolling.
I'd love to play with thee.
I love this game!
My marble skills will sure impress thee greatly.

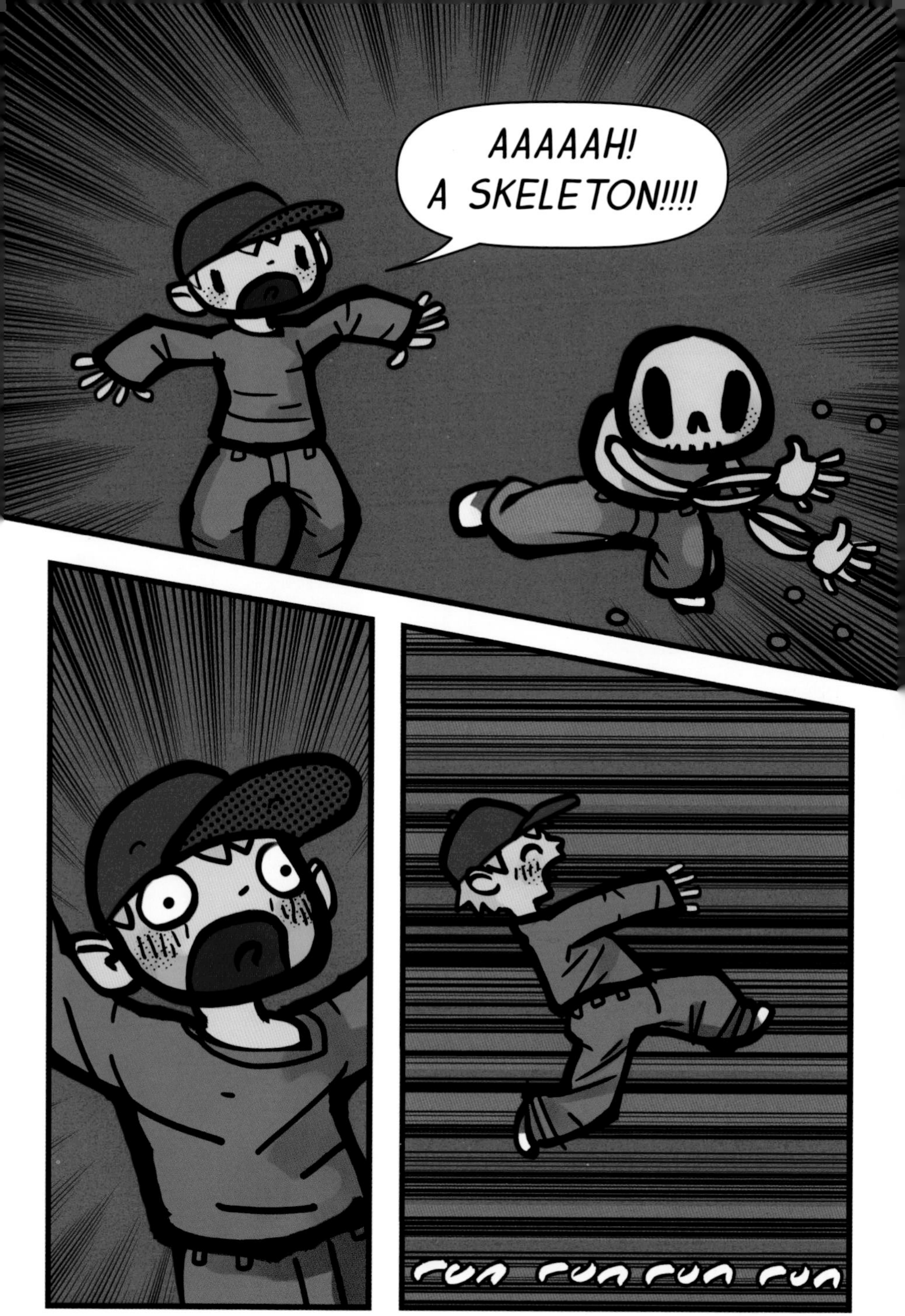
AAAAAH!
A SKELETON!!!!!
RUN RUN RUN RUN

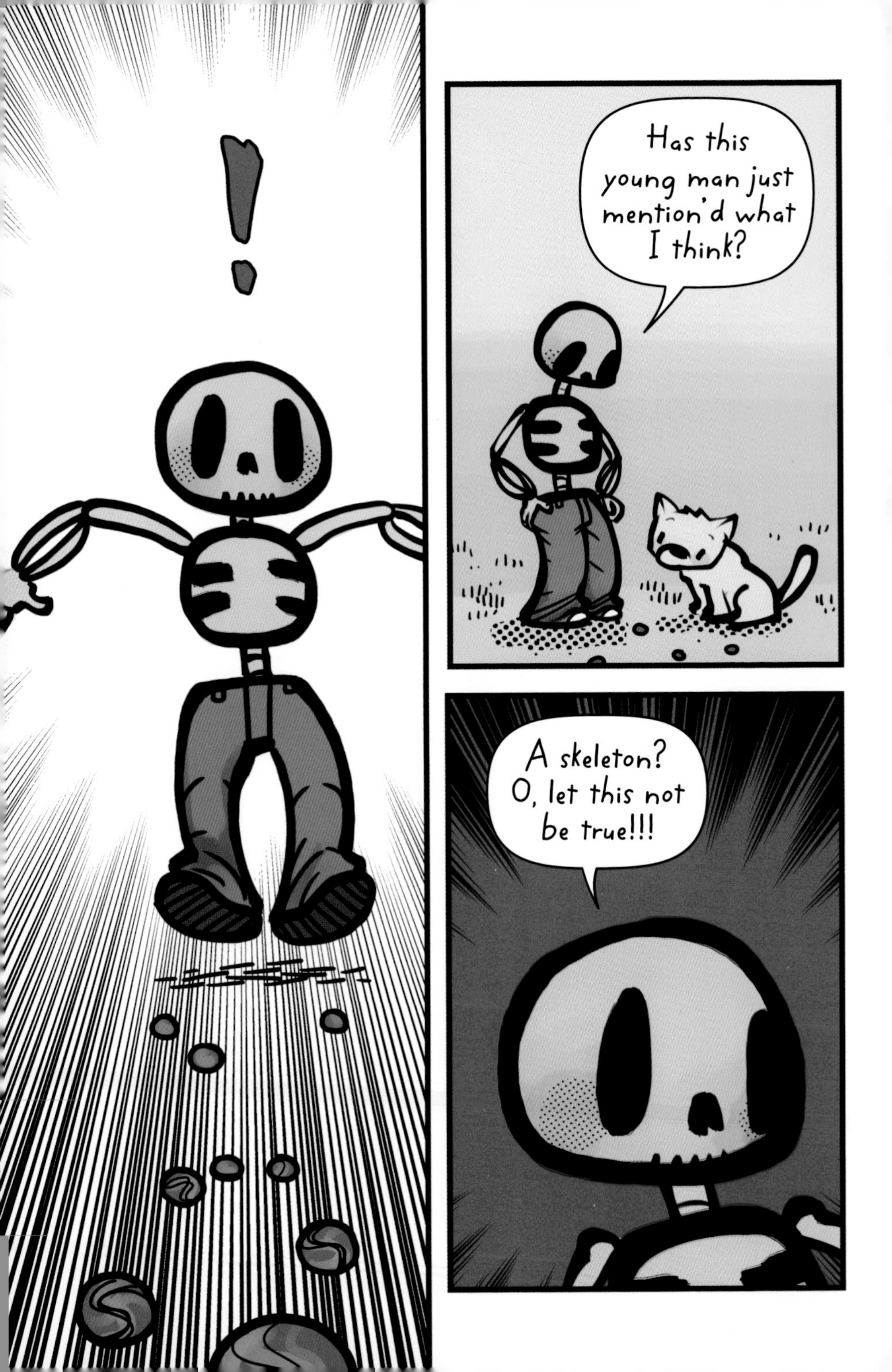
!
Has this young man just mention'd what I think?
A skeleton? O, let this not be true!!!

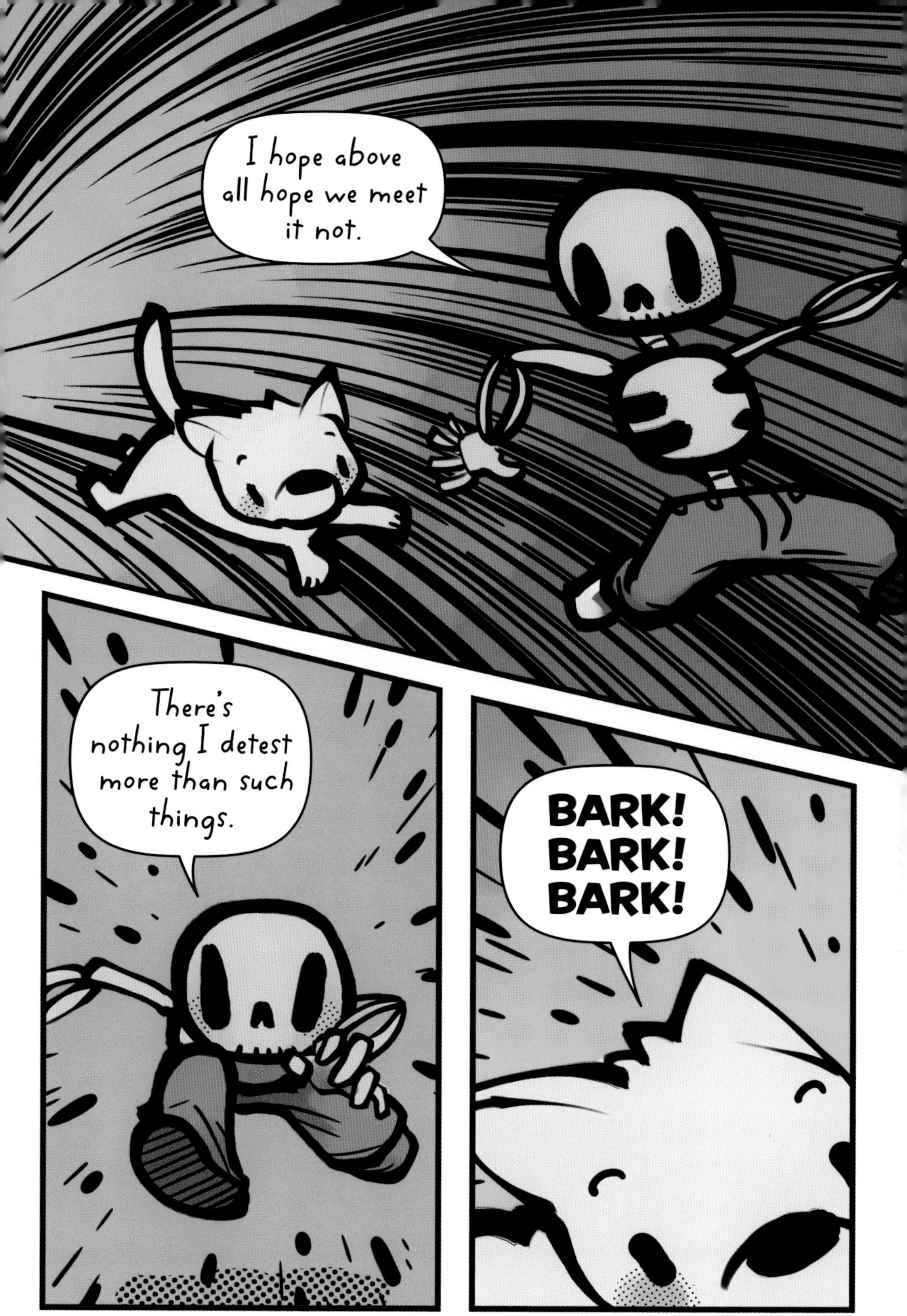
I hope above all hope we meet it not.
There's nothing I detest more than such things.
BARK! BARK! BARK!

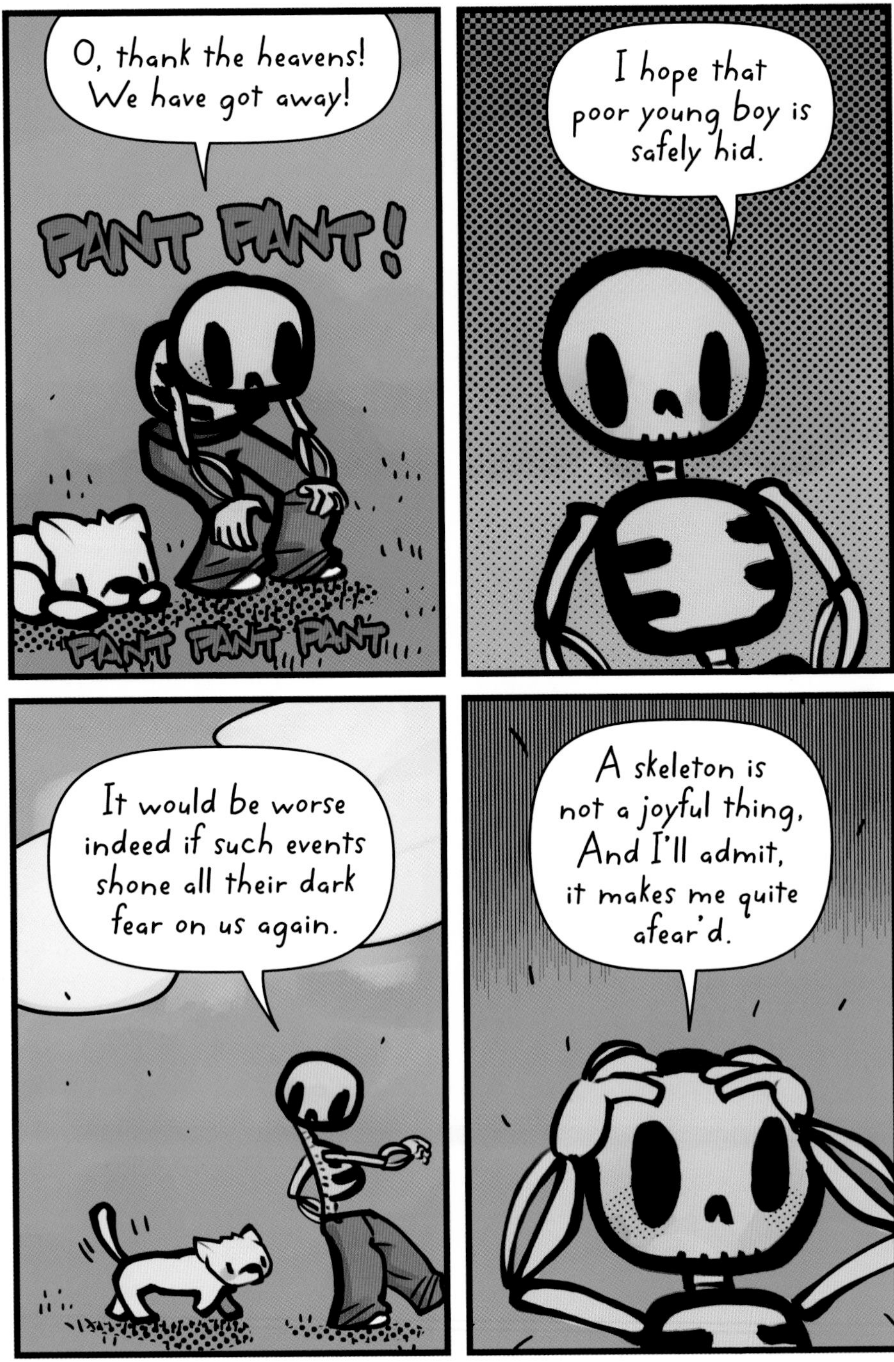
O, thank the heavens! We have got away!
PANT PANT!
PANT PANT PANT
I hope that poor young boy is safely hid.
It would be worse indeed if such events shone all their dark fear on us again.
A skeleton is not a joyful thing, And I'll admit, it makes me quite afear'd.

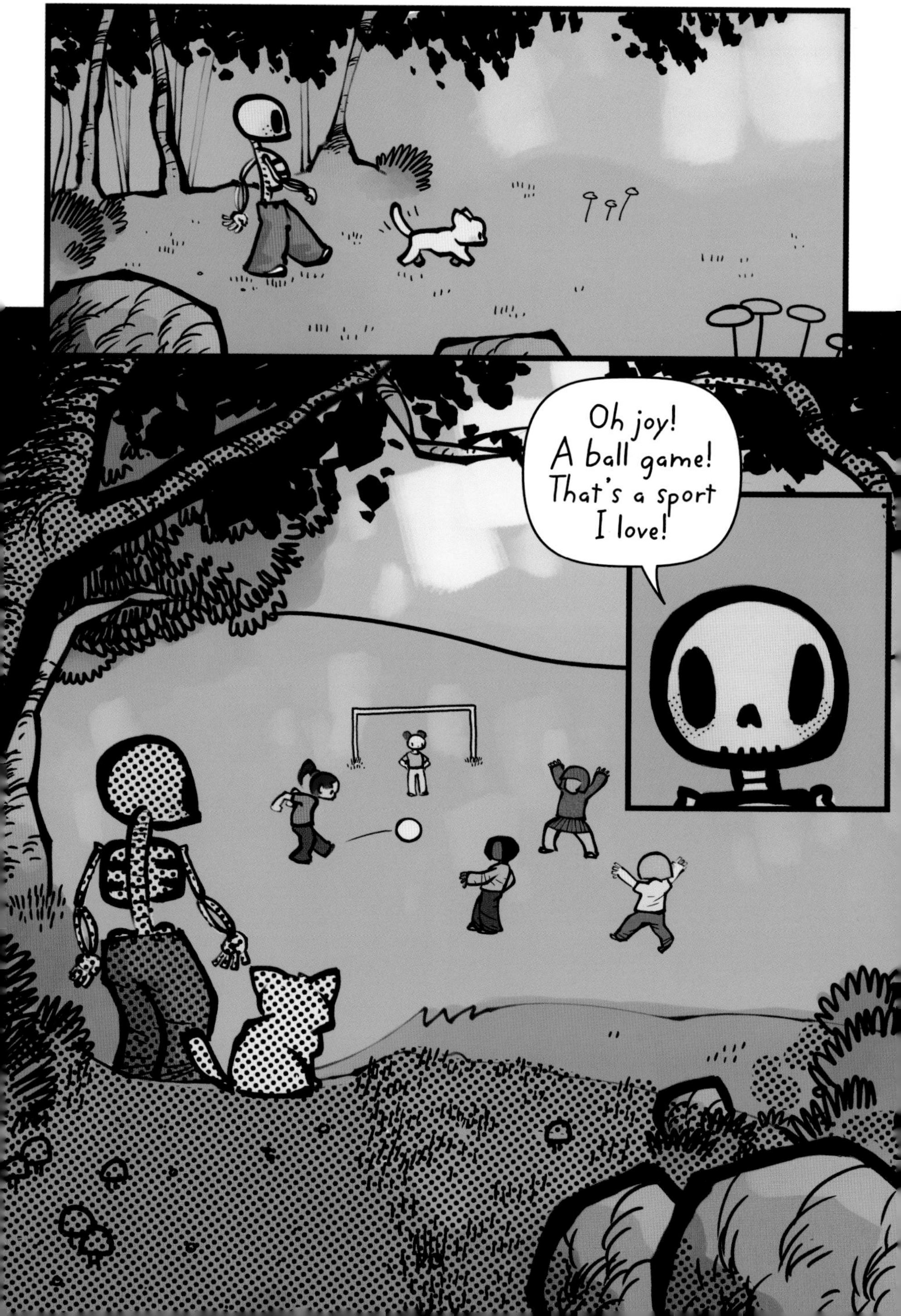
Oh joy! A ball game! That's a sport I love!

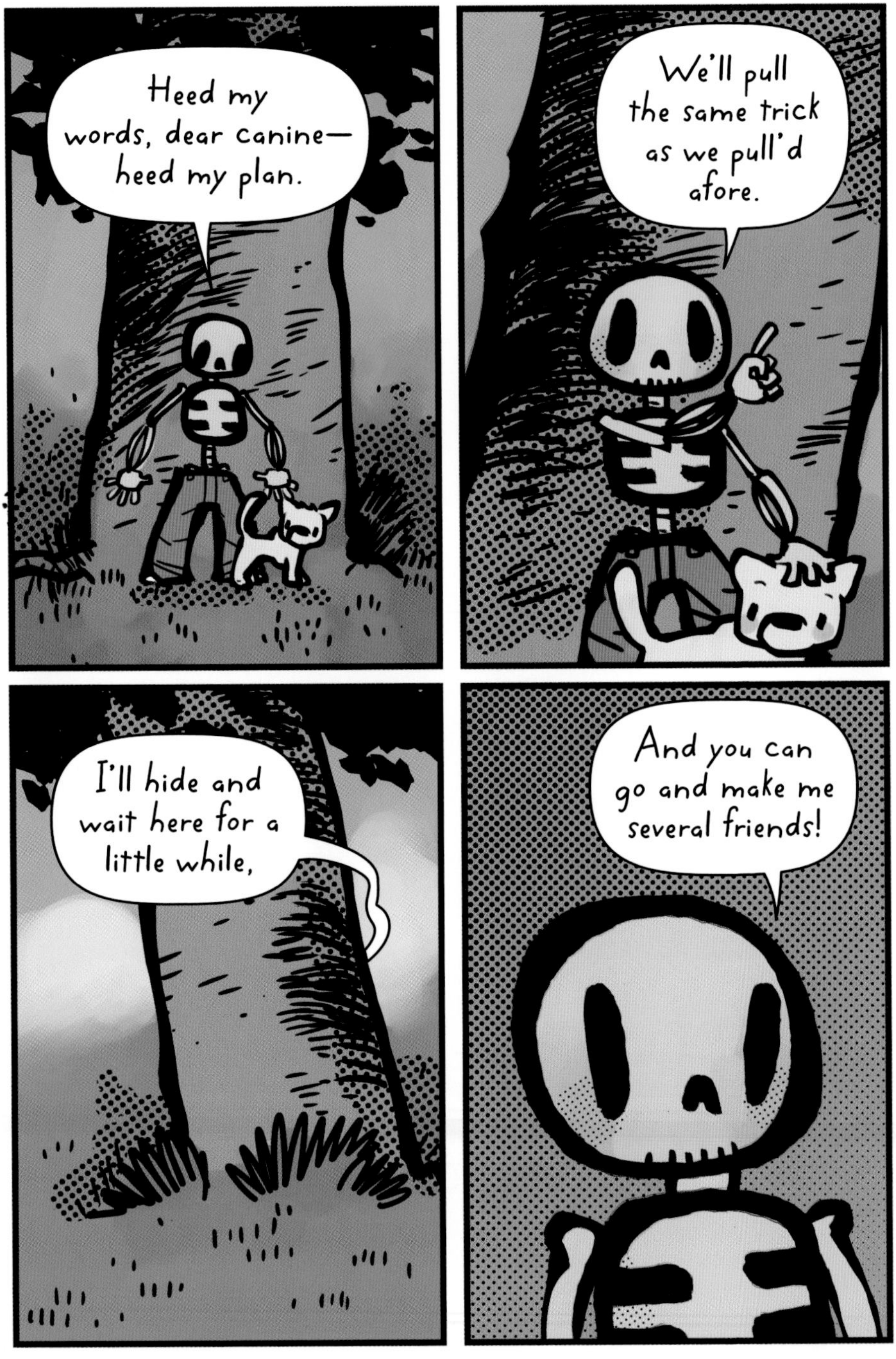

Heed my words, dear canine—heed my plan.
We'll pull the same trick as we pull'd afore.
I'll hide and wait here for a little while,
And you can go and make me several friends!

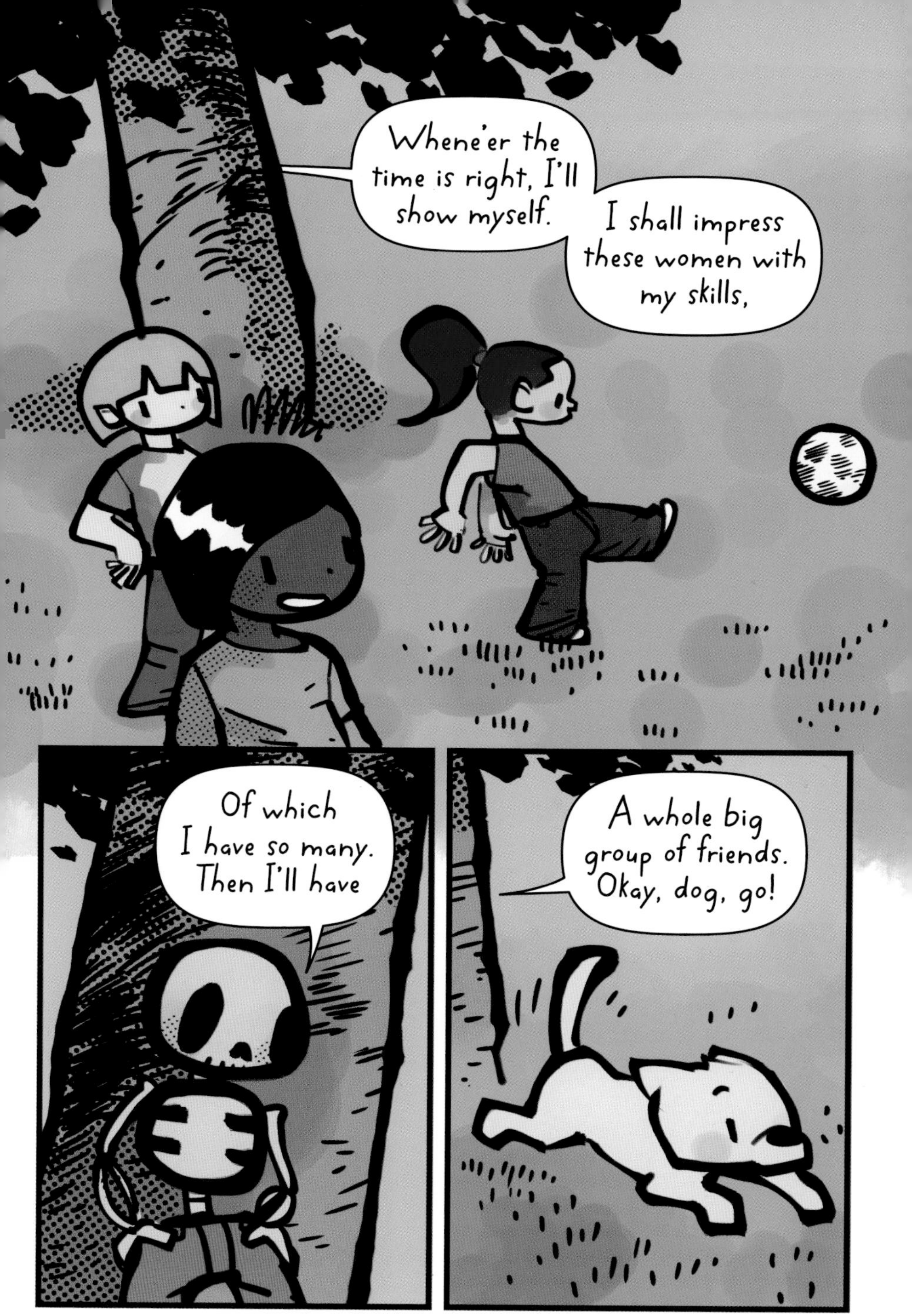
Whene'er the time is right, I'll show myself.
I shall impress these women with my skills,
Of which I have so many. Then I'll have
A whole big group of friends. Okay, dog, go!

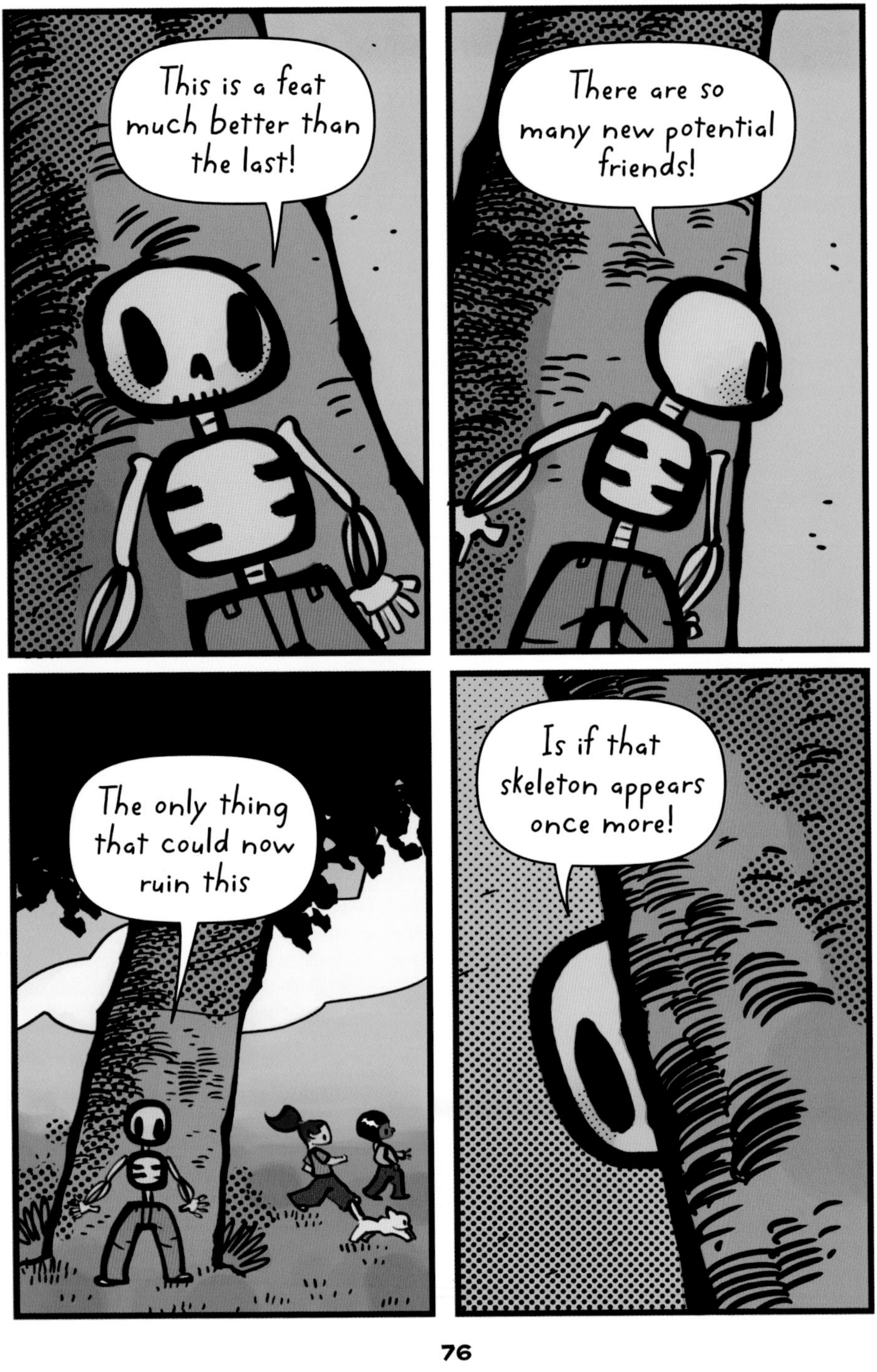
This is a feat much better than the last!
There are so many new potential friends!
The only thing that could now ruin this
Is if that skeleton appears once more!

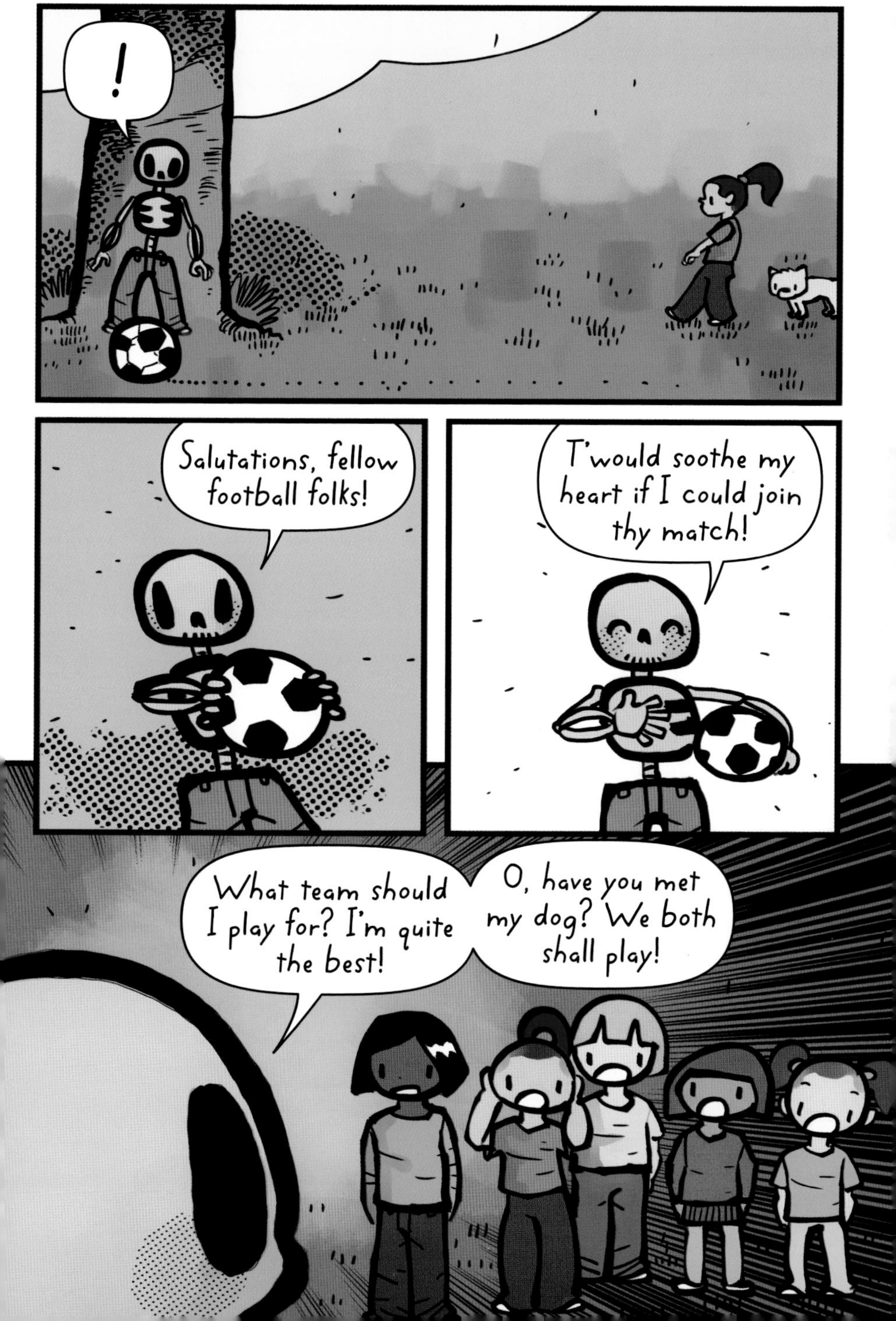
!
Salutations, fellow football folks!
T'would soothe my heart if I could join thy match!
What team should I play for? I'm quite the best!
O, have you met my dog? We both shall play!

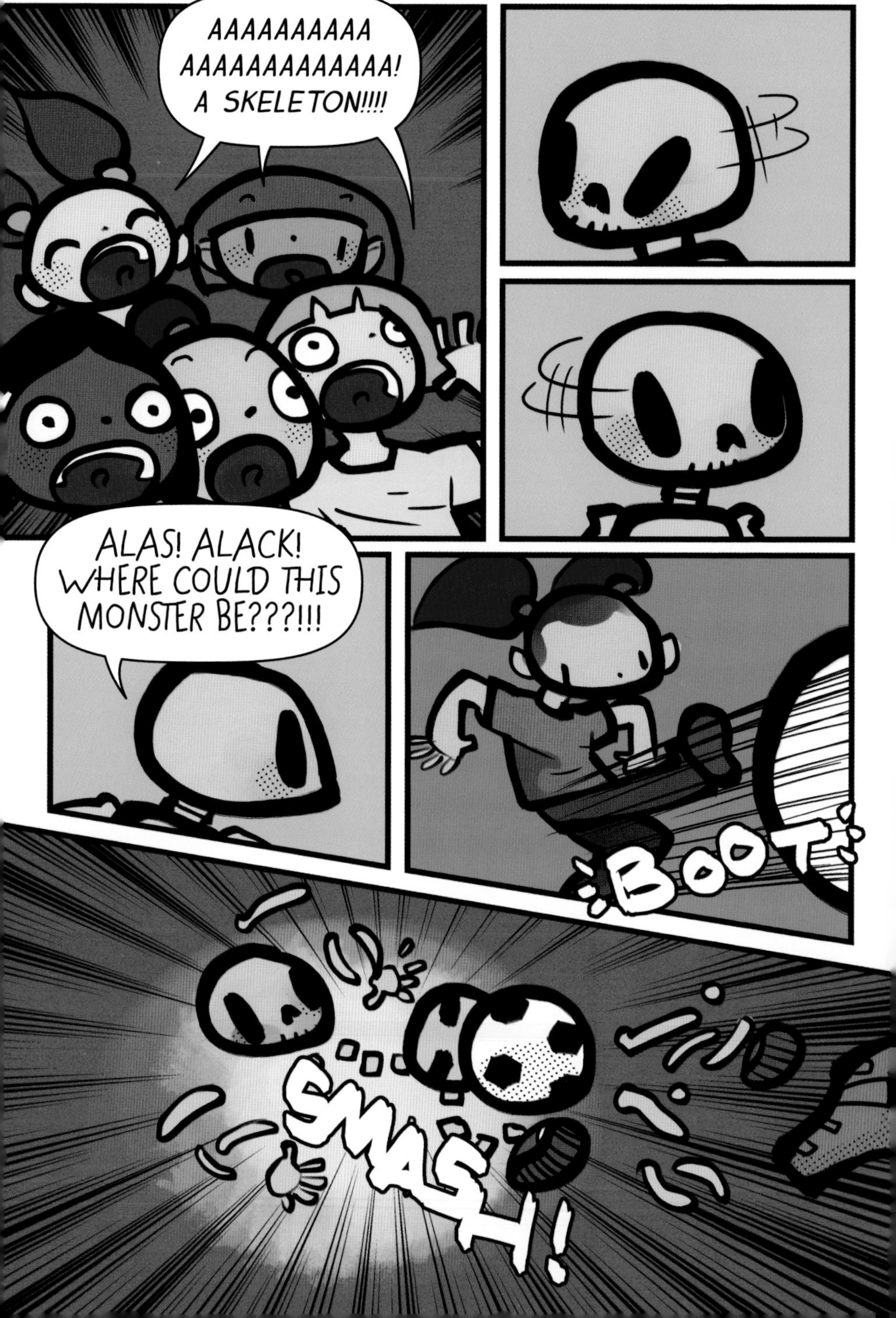
AAAAAAAAAAA AAAAAAAAAAAAAA! A SKELETON!!!!
ALAS! ALACK! WHERE COULD THIS MONSTER BE???!!!
BOOT
SMASH!

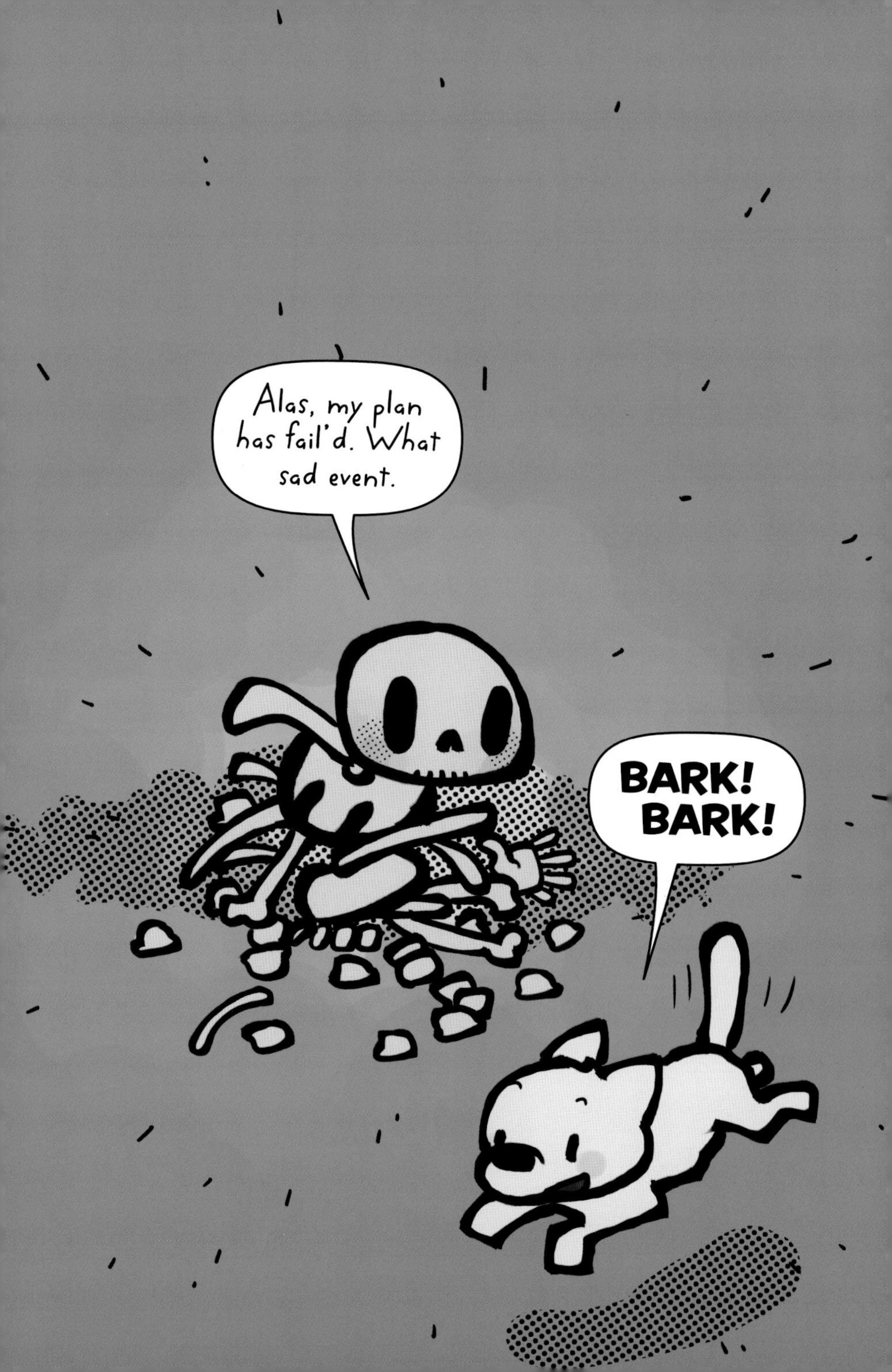
Alas, my plan has fail'd. What sad event.
BARK! BARK!

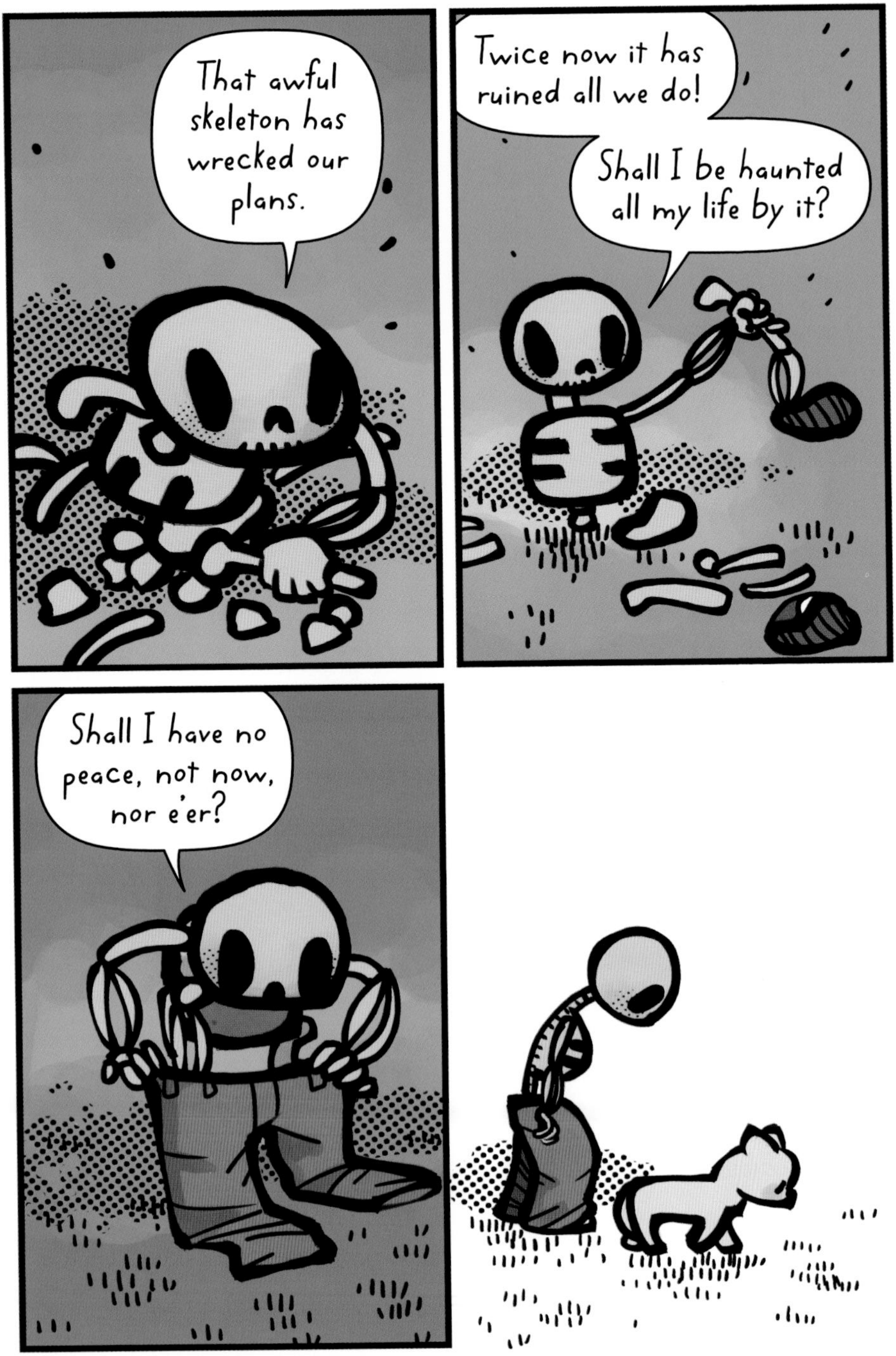
That awful skeleton has wrecked our plans.
Twice now it has ruined all we do!
Shall I be haunted all my life by it?
Shall I have no peace, not now, nor e'er?

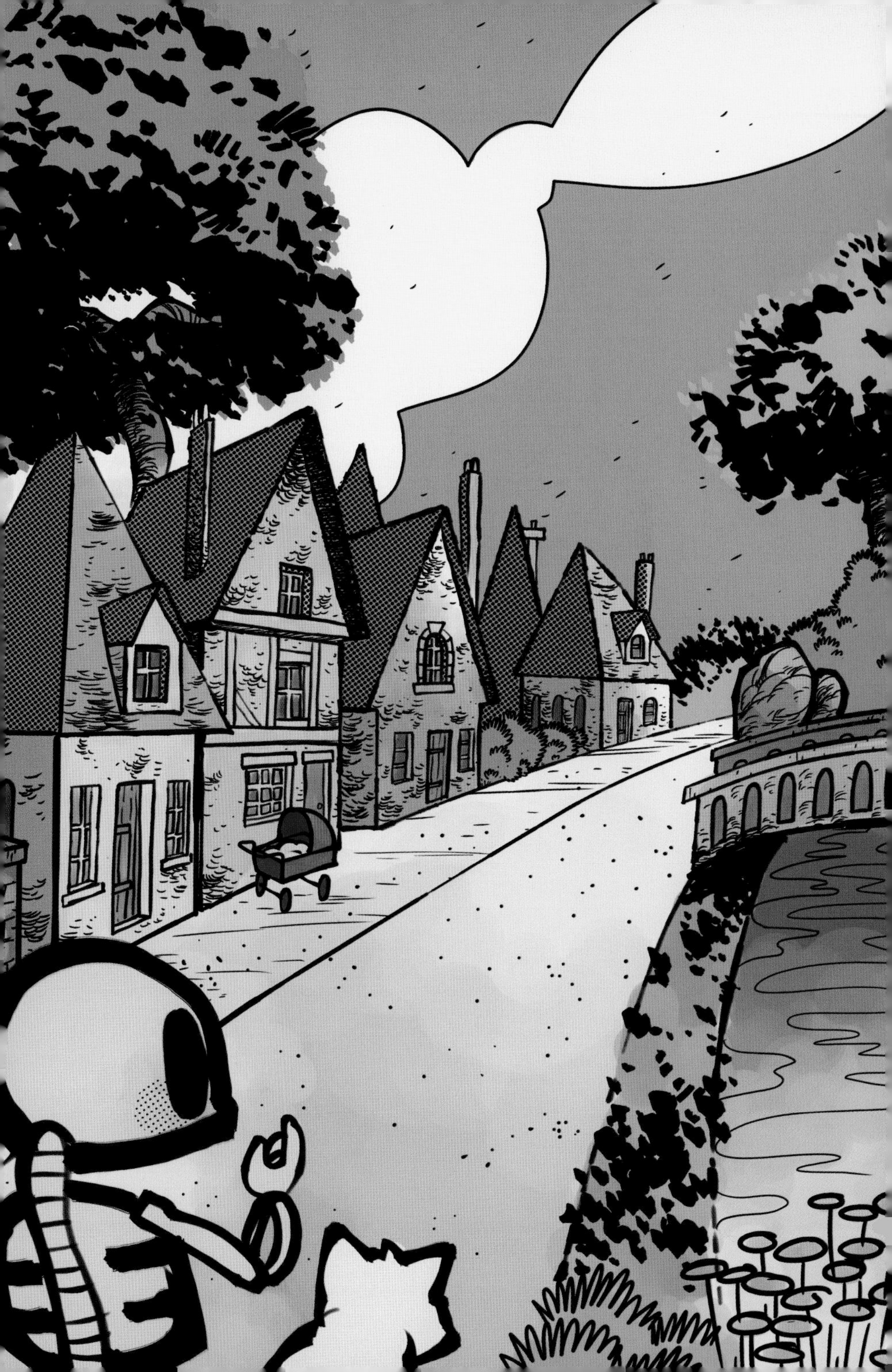

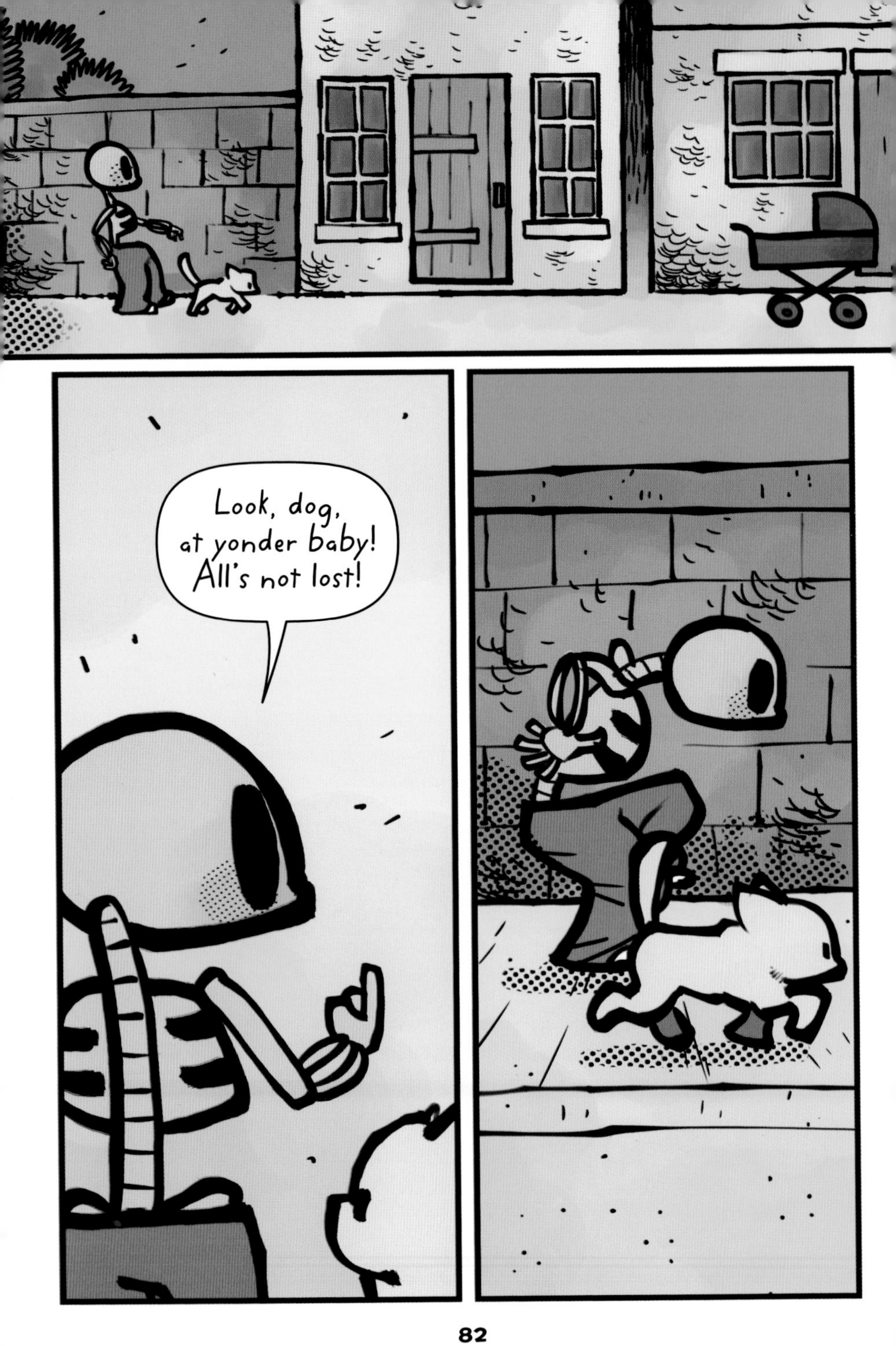
Look, dog, at yonder baby! All's not lost!

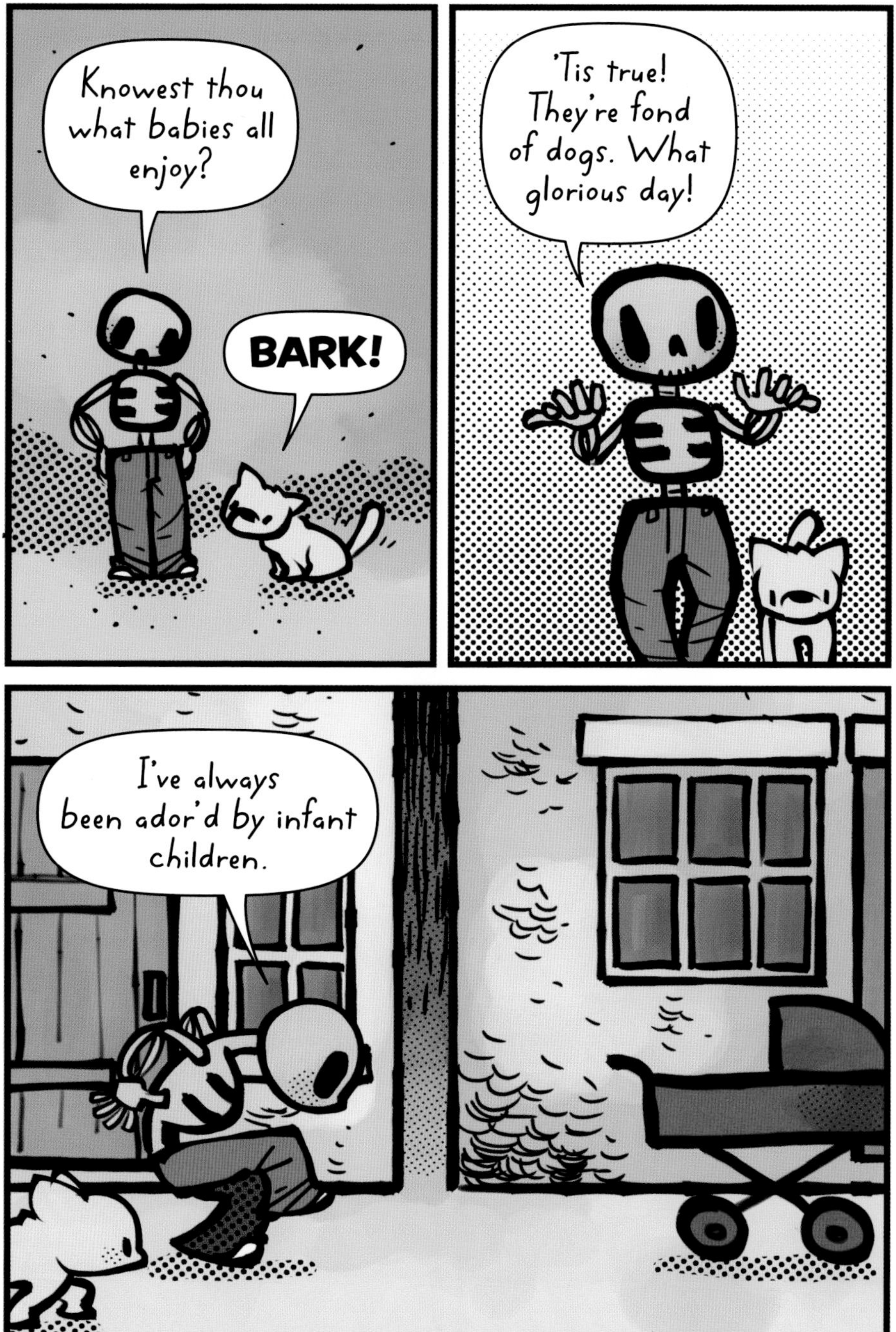
Knowest thou what babies all enjoy?
BARK!
'Tis true! They're fond of dogs. What glorious day!
I've always been ador'd by infant children.

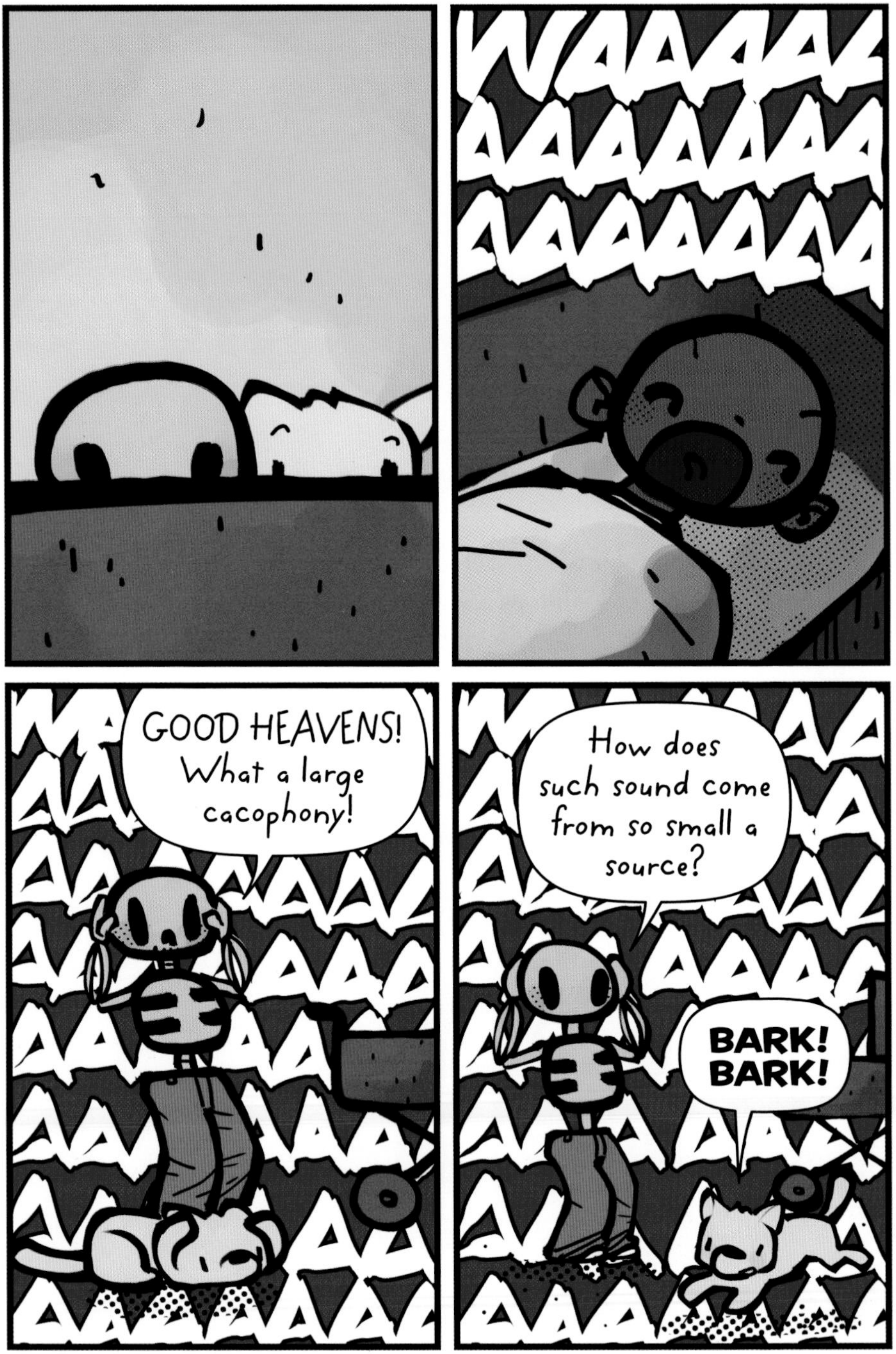
WAAAAAAAAAAAAAAAAAA
GOOD HEAVENS! What a large cacophony!
How does such sound come from so small a source?
BARK! BARK!

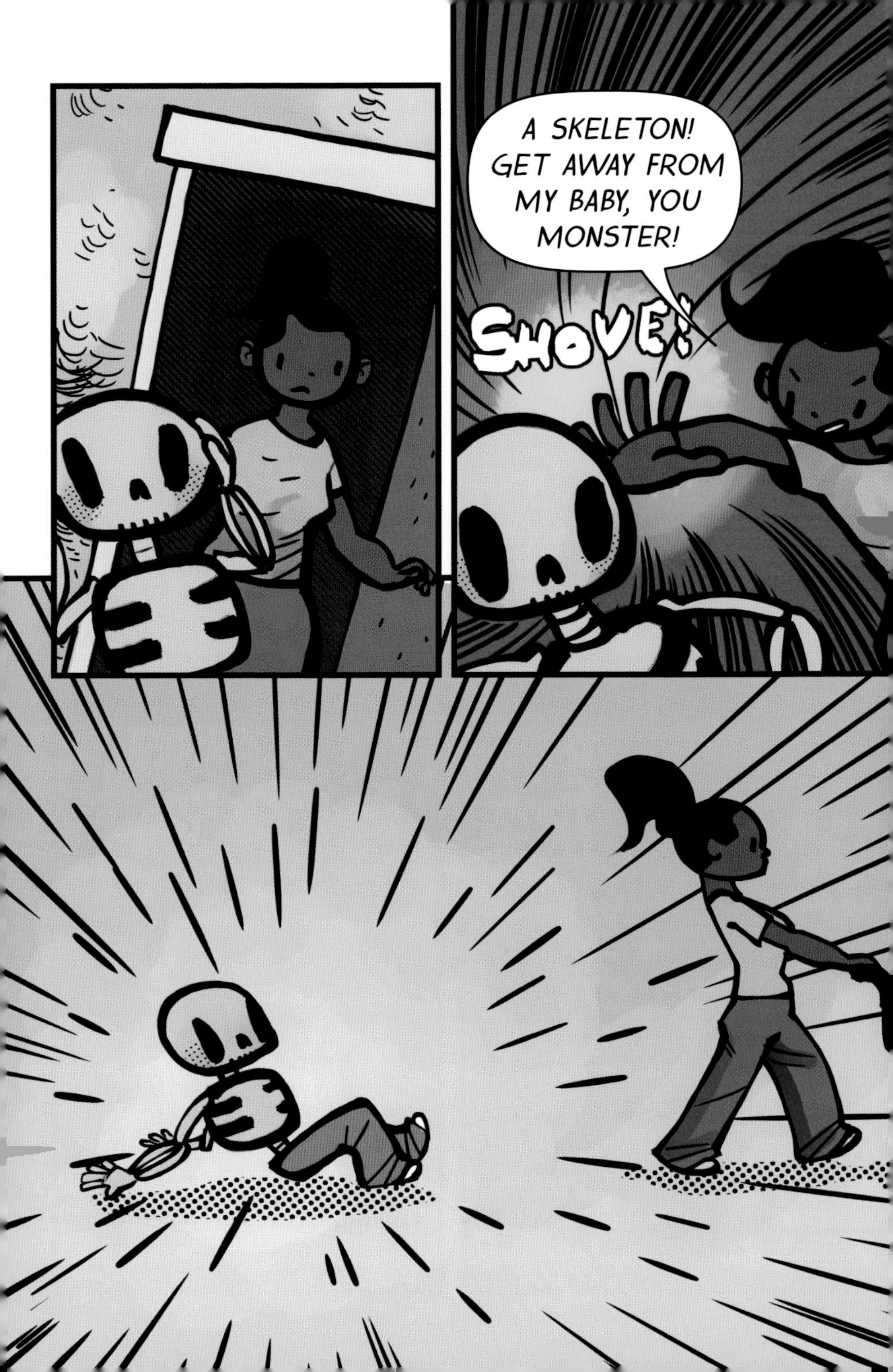
A SKELETON! GET AWAY FROM MY BABY, YOU MONSTER!
SHOVE!

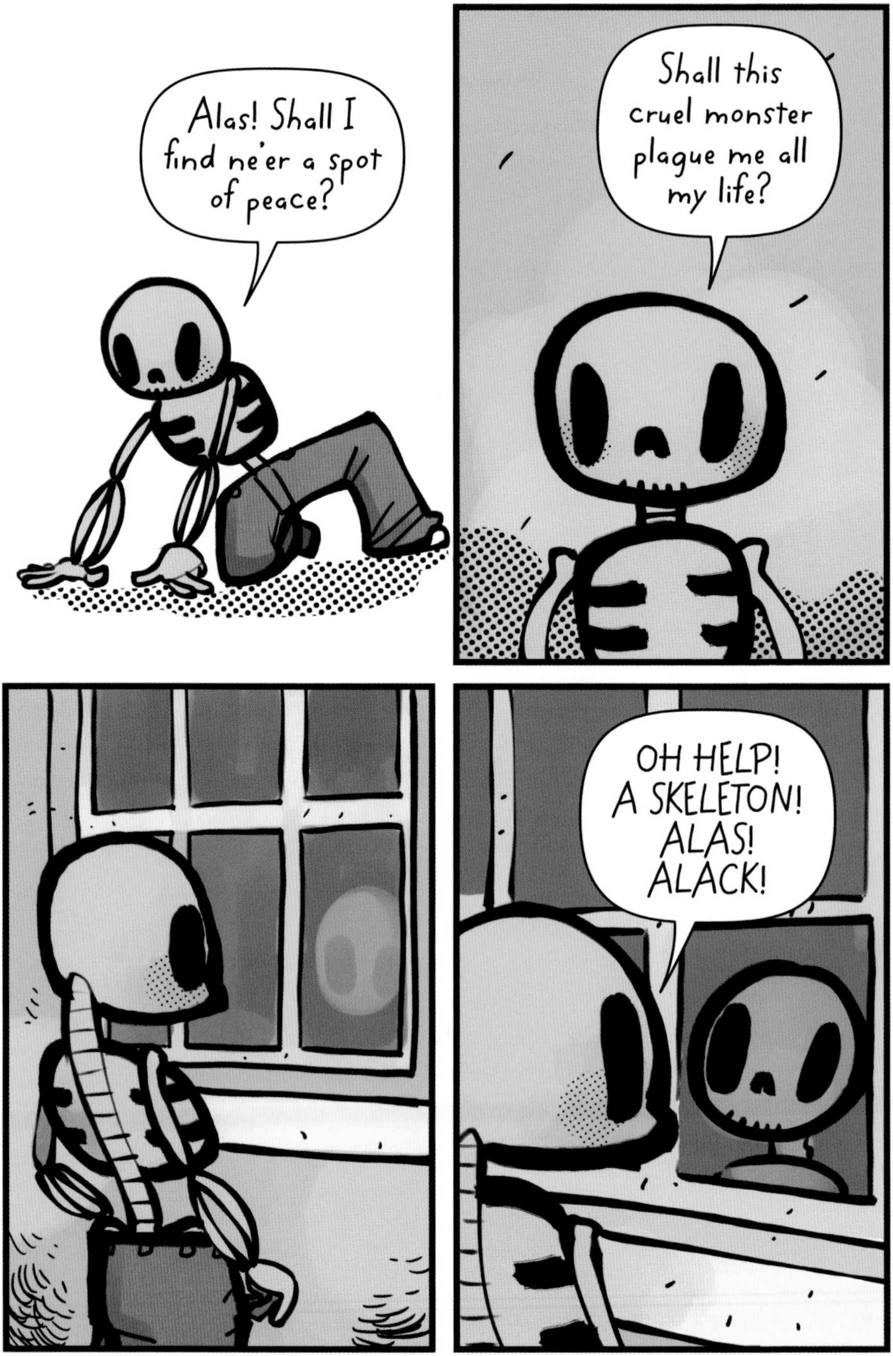
Alas! Shall I find ne'er a spot of peace?
Shall this cruel monster plague me all my life?
OH HELP! A SKELETON! ALAS! ALACK!

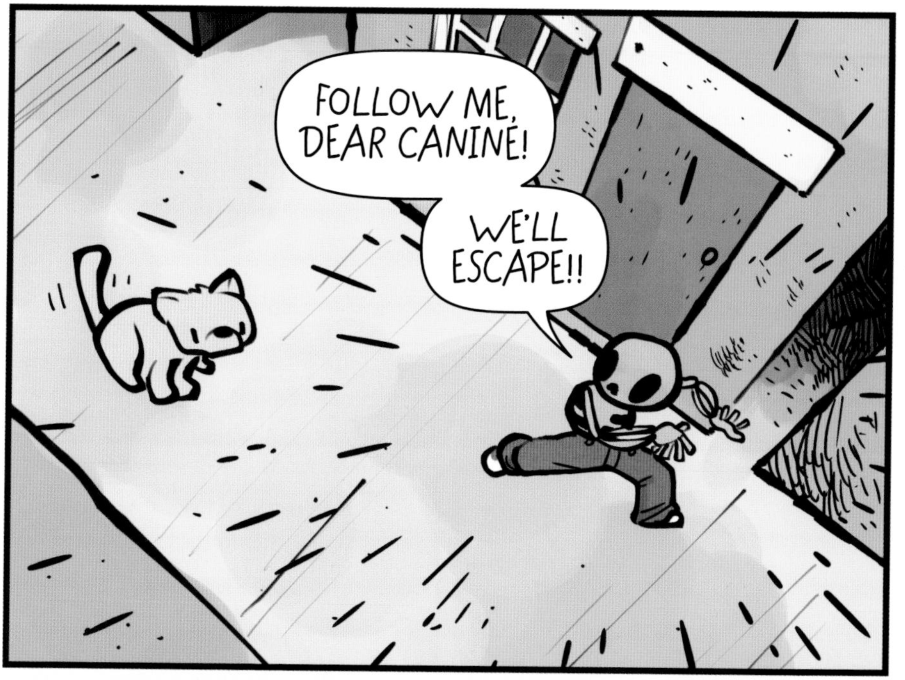
FOLLOW ME, DEAR CANINE!
WE'LL ESCAPE!!

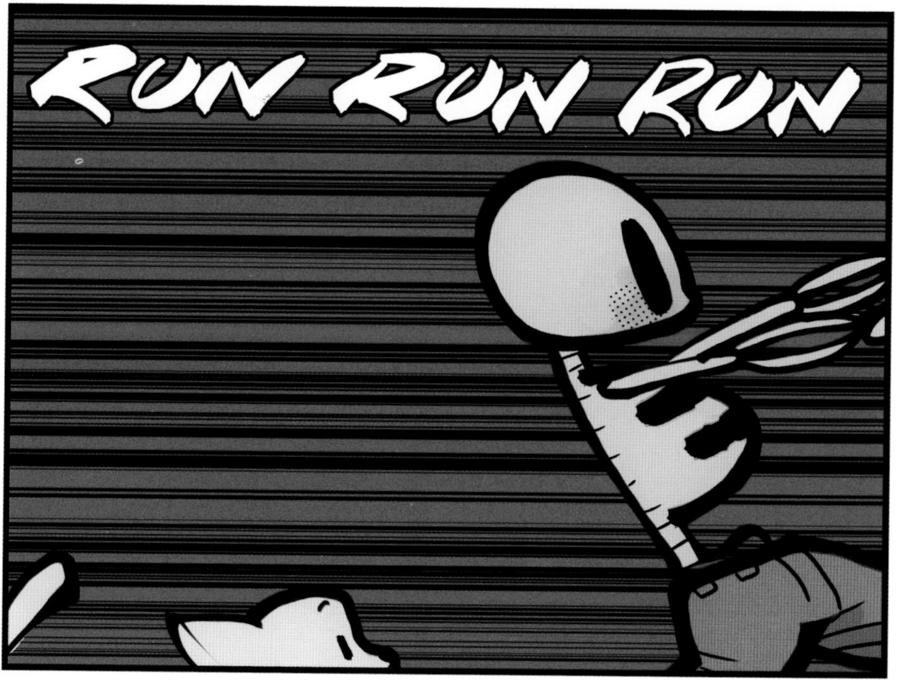
RUN RUN RUN

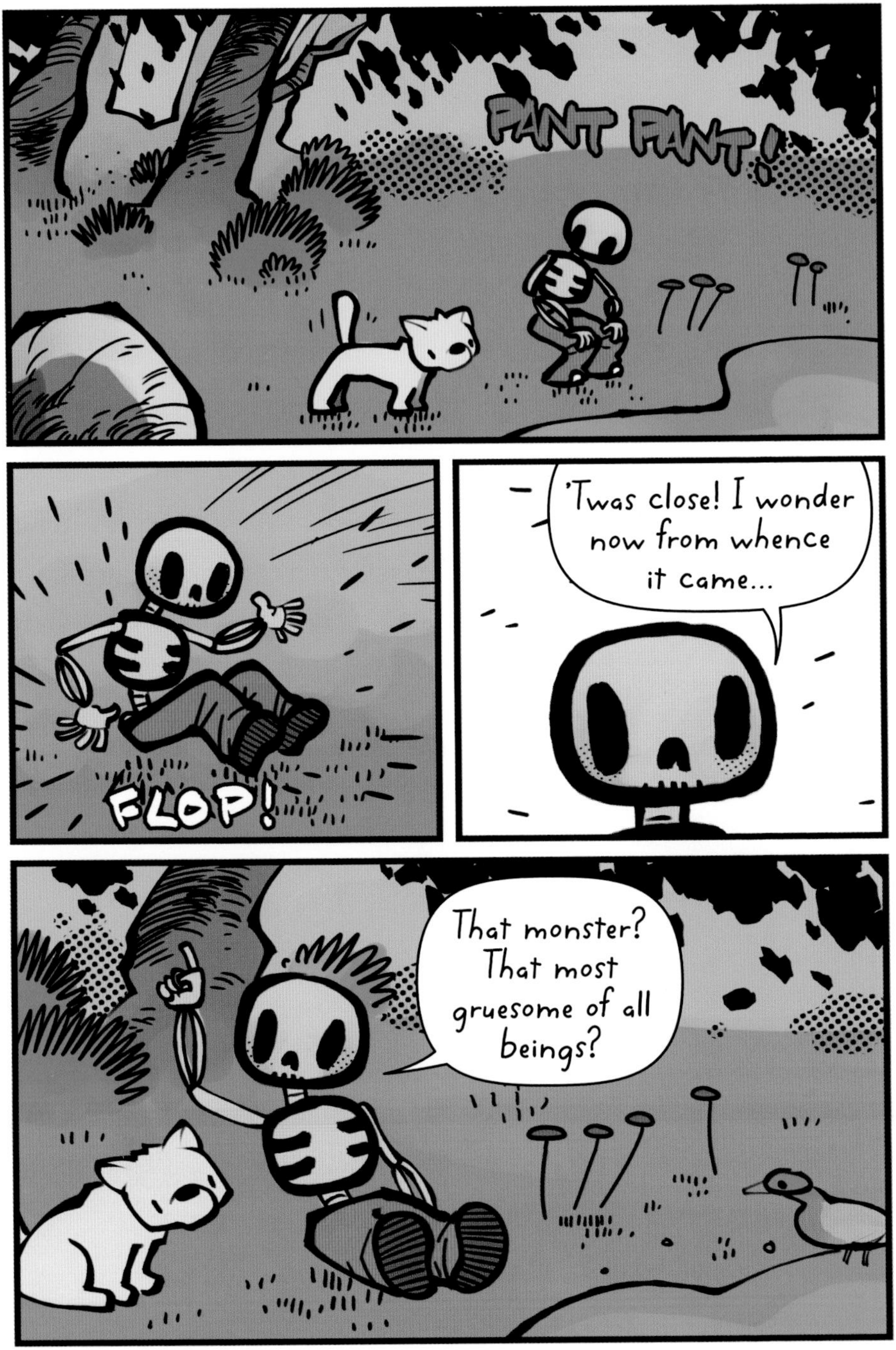
PANT PANT!
FLOP!
'Twas close! I wonder now from whence it came...
That monster? That most gruesome of all beings?

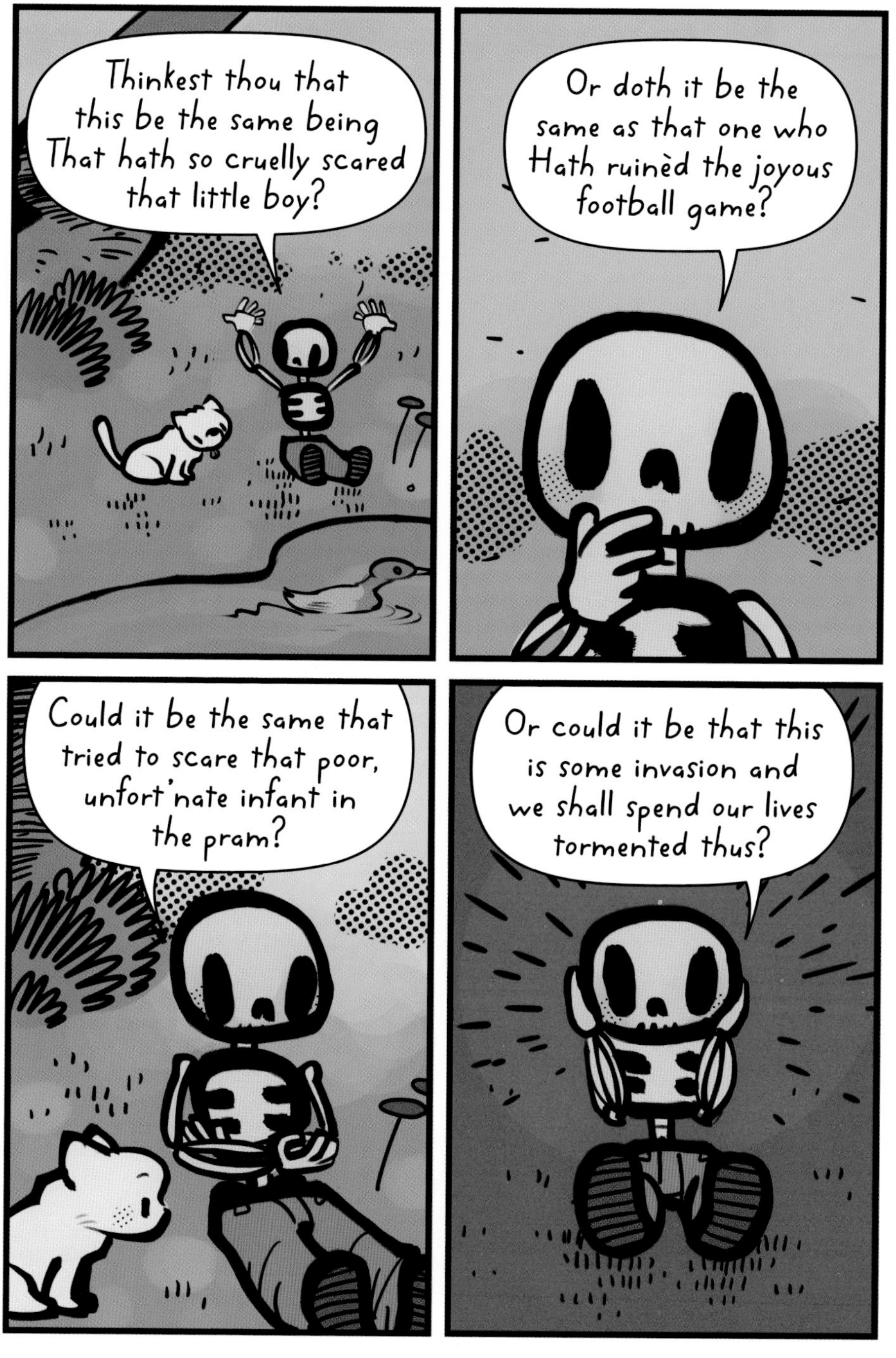

Thinkest thou that this be the same being That hath so cruelly scared that little boy?
Or doth it be the same as that one who Hath ruinèd the joyous football game?
Could it be the same that tried to scare that poor, unfort'nate infant in the pram?
Or could it be that this is some invasion and we shall spend our lives tormented thus?

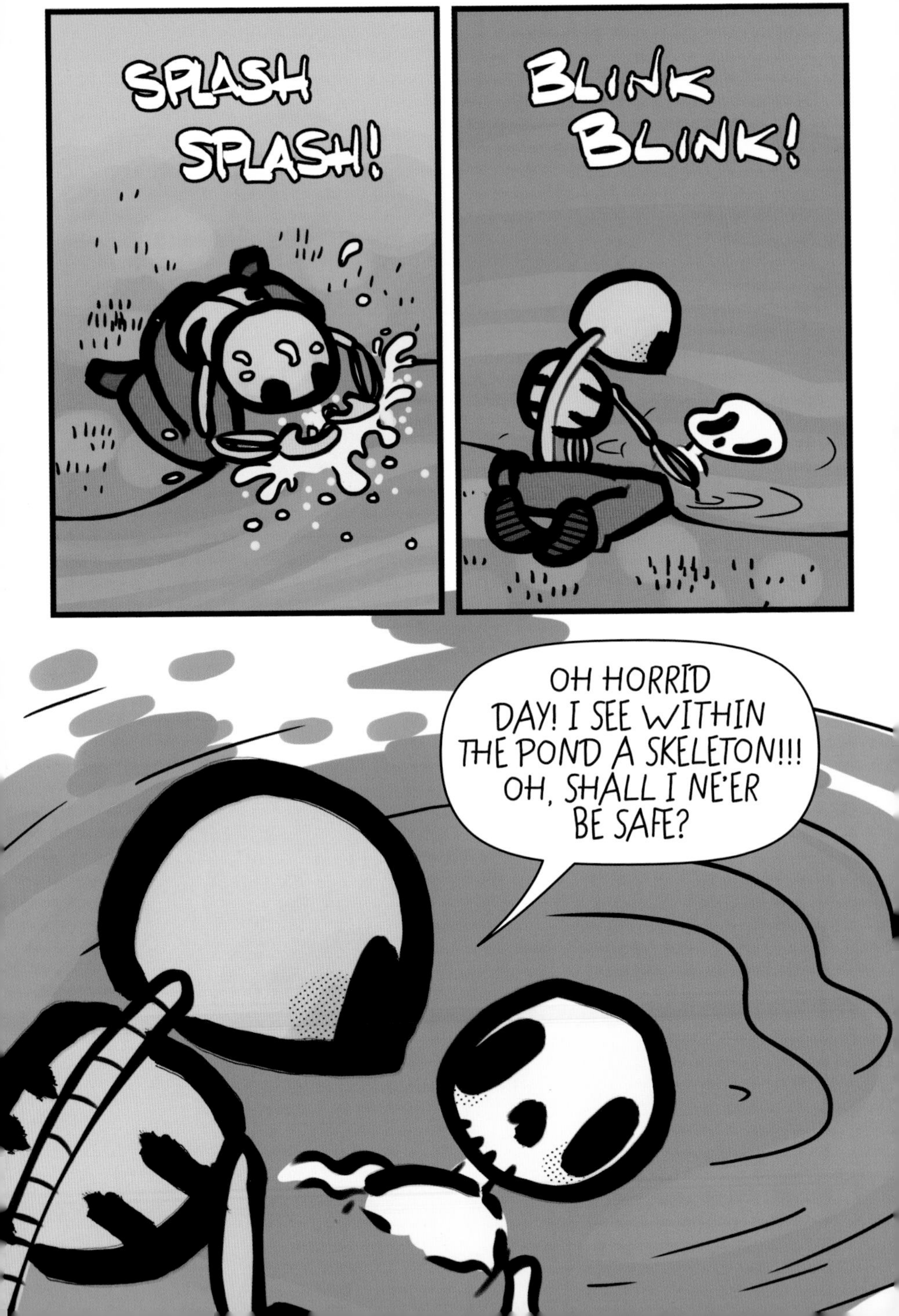
SPLASH SPLASH!
BLINK BLINK!
OH HORRID DAY! I SEE WITHIN THE POND A SKELETON!!! OH, SHALL I NE'ER BE SAFE?

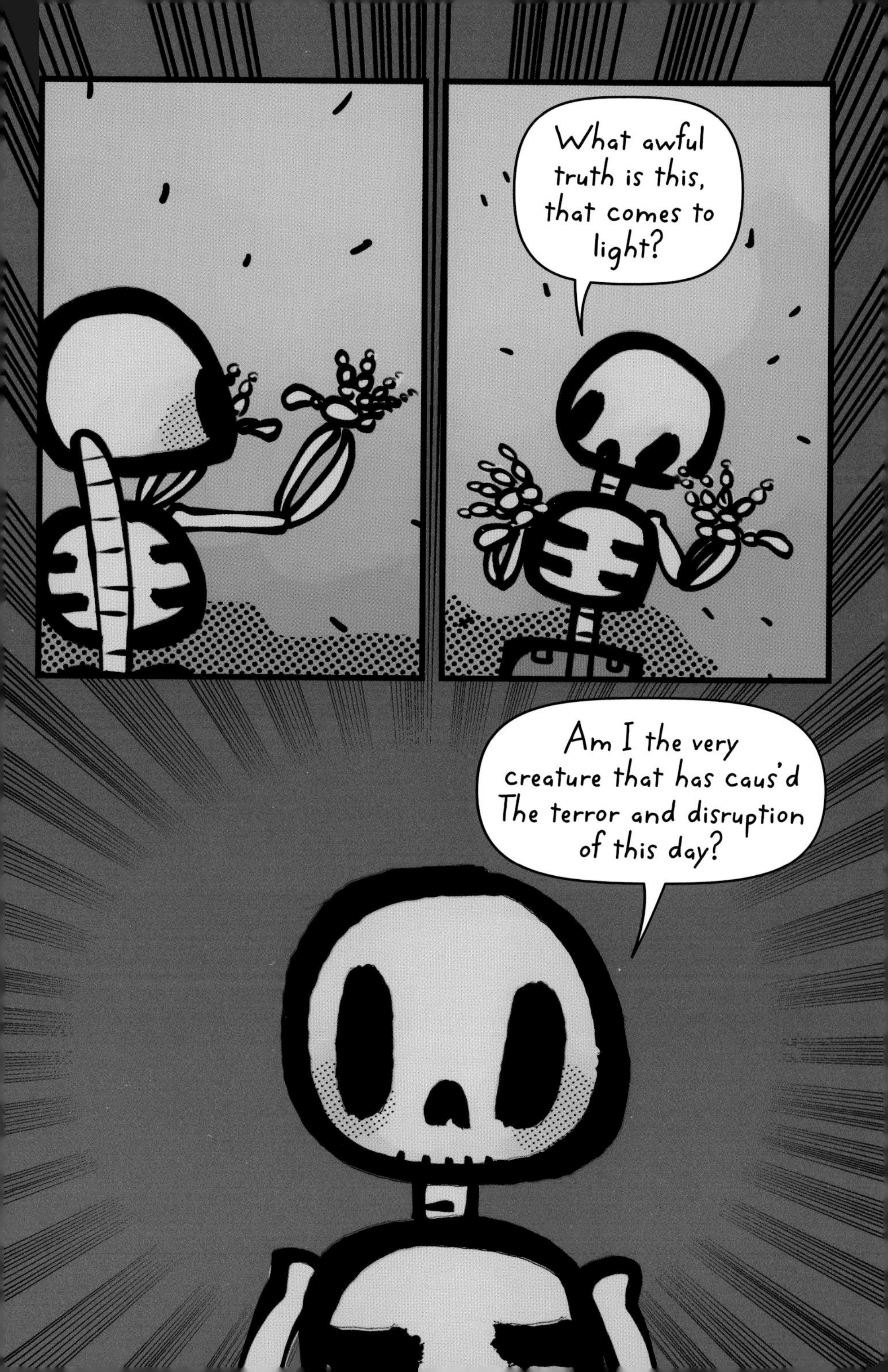
What awful truth is this, that comes to light?
Am I the very creature that has caus'd The terror and disruption of this day?

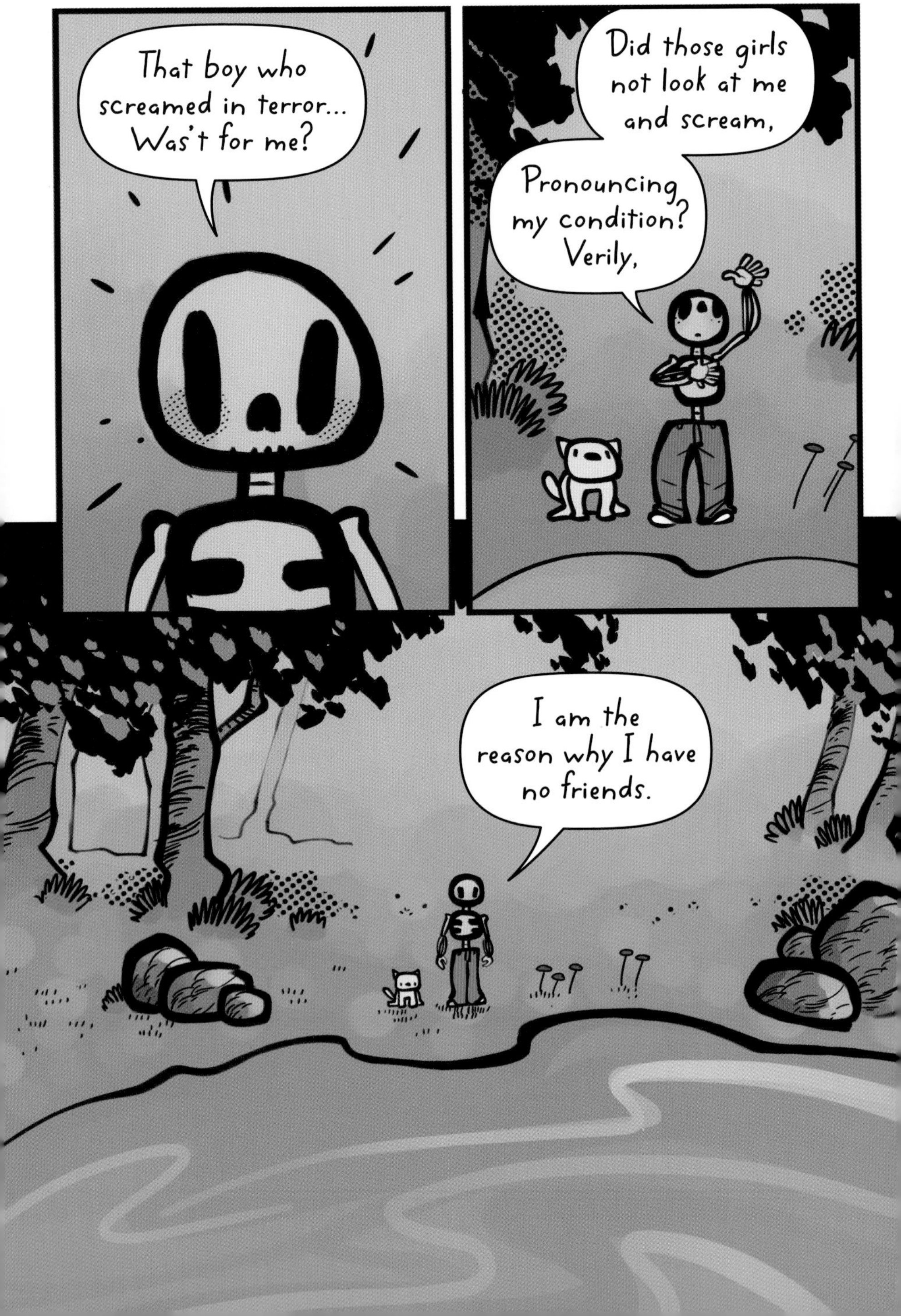
That boy who screamed in terror... Was't for me?
Did those girls not look at me and scream,
Pronouncing my condition? Verily,
I am the reason why I have no friends.

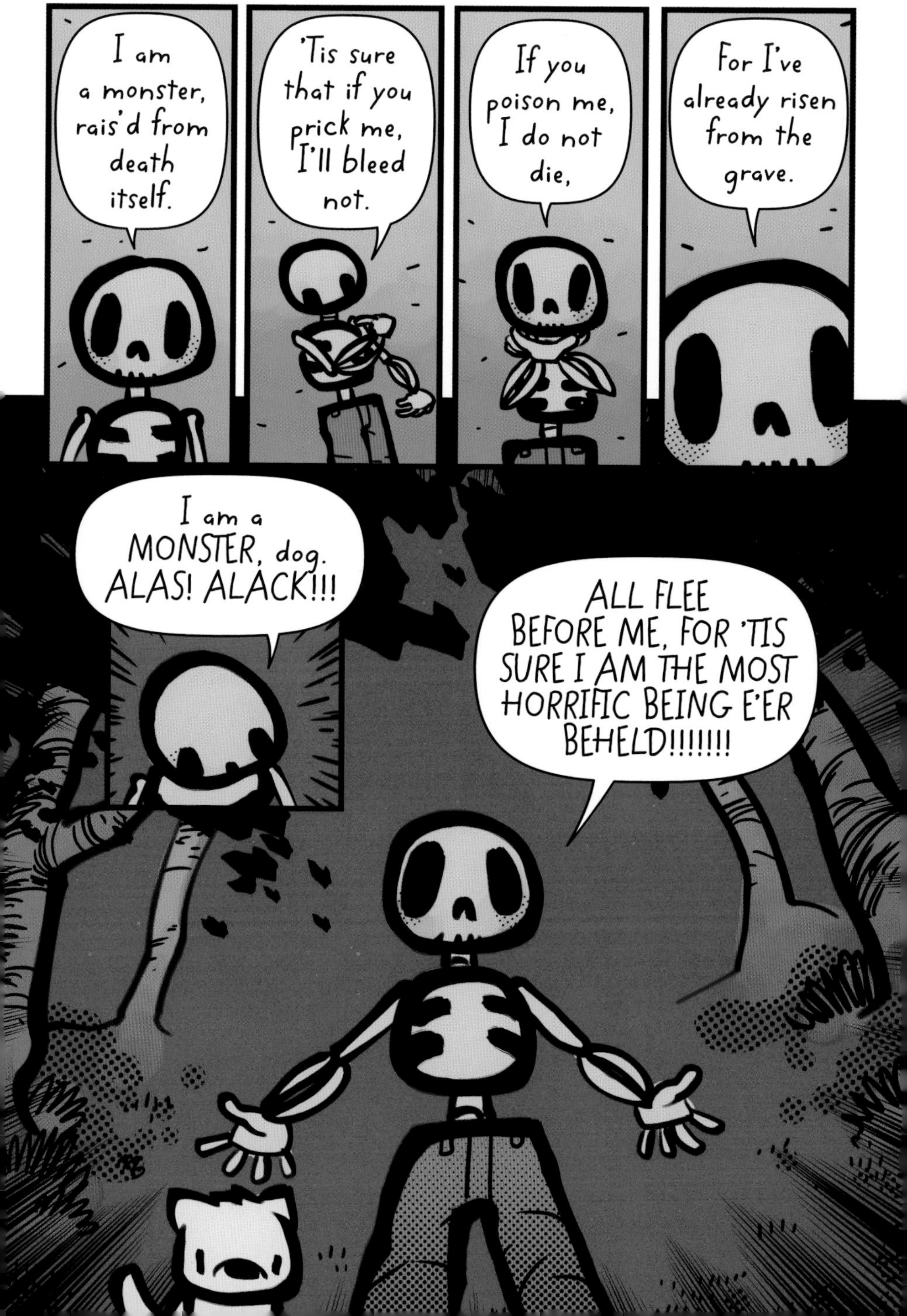
I am a monster, rais'd from death itself.
'Tis sure that if you prick me, I'll bleed not.
If you poison me, I do not die,
For I've already risen from the grave.
I am a MONSTER, dog. ALAS! ALACK!!!
ALL FLEE BEFORE ME, FOR 'TIS SURE I AM THE MOST HORRIFIC BEING E'ER BEHELD!!!!!!!

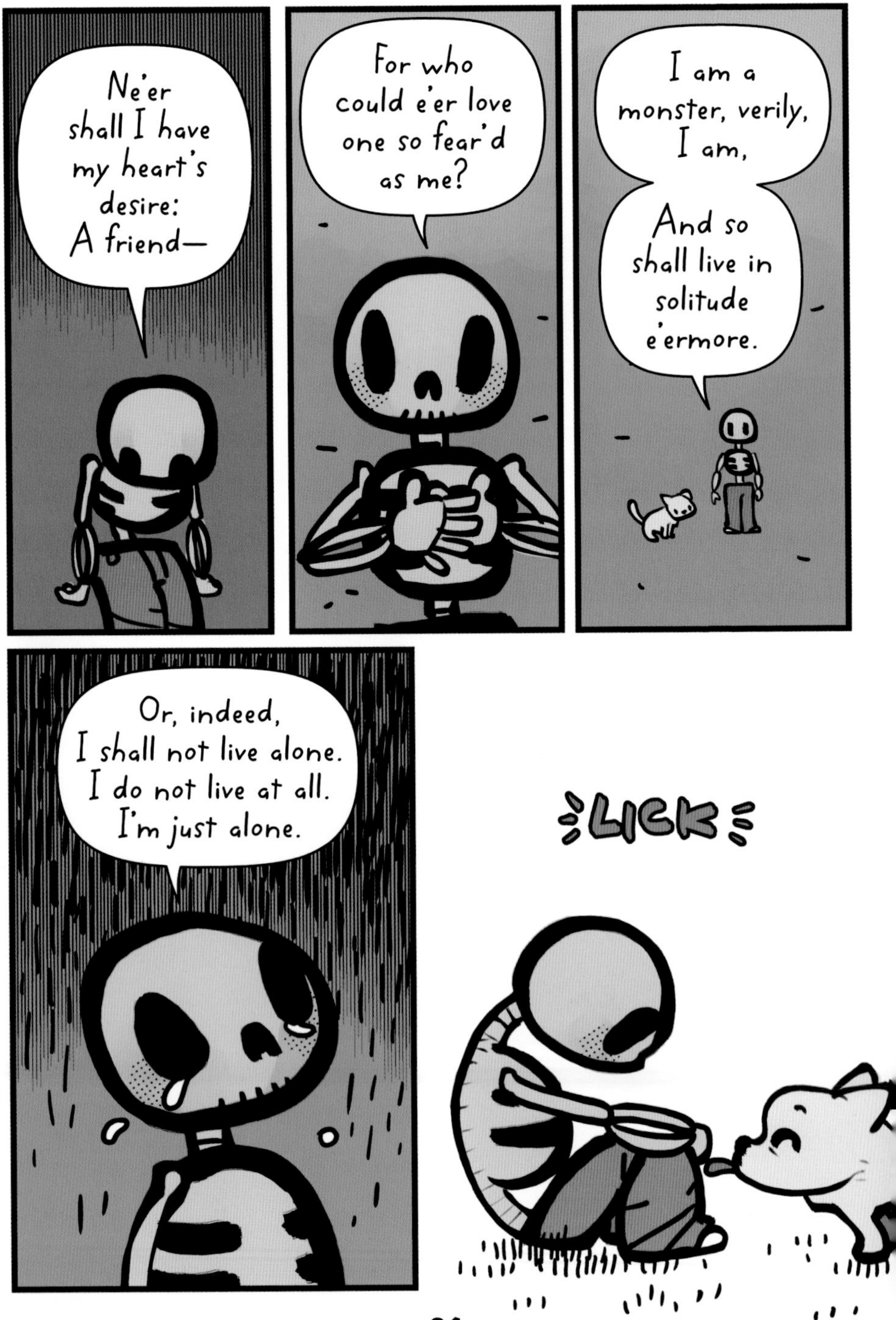

Ne'er shall I have my heart's desire: A friend—
For who could e'er love one so fear'd as me?
I am a monster, verily, I am,
And so shall live in solitude e'ermore.
Or, indeed, I shall not live alone. I do not live at all. I'm just alone.
LICK

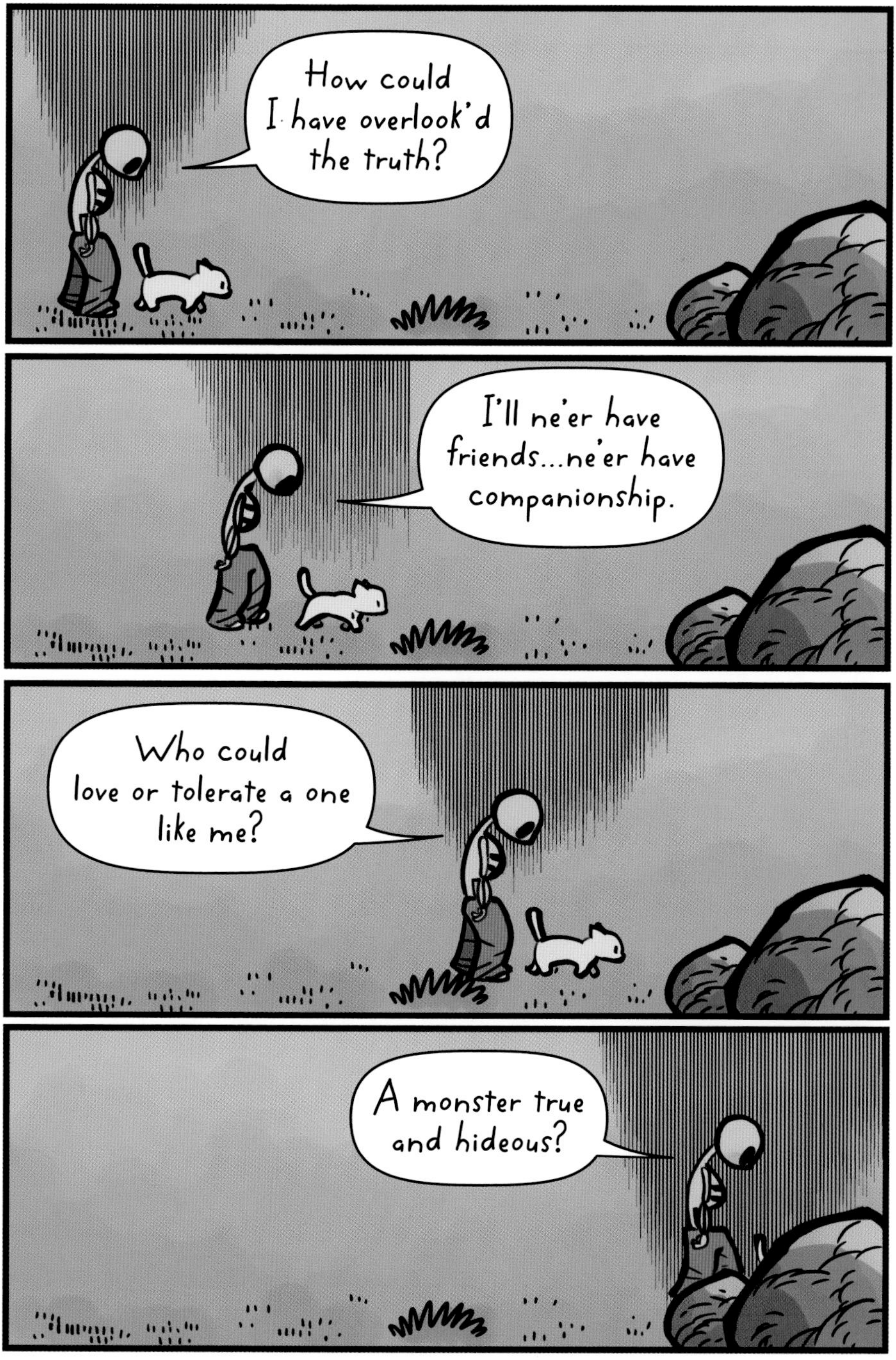
How could I have overlook'd the truth?
I'll ne'er have friends...ne'er have companionship.
Who could love or tolerate a one like me?
A monster true and hideous?

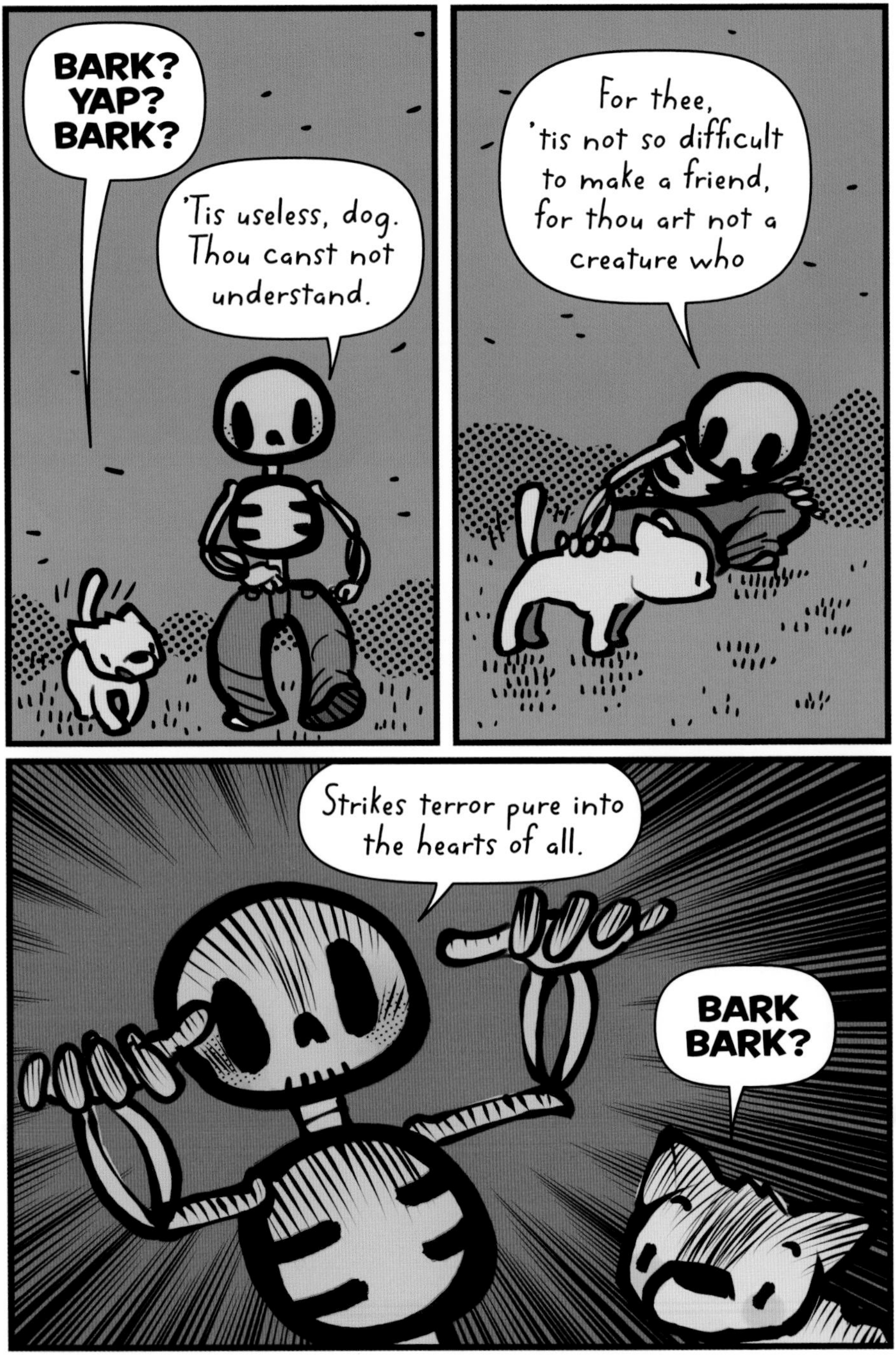
BARK? YAP? BARK?
'Tis useless, dog. Thou canst not understand.
For thee, 'tis not so difficult to make a friend, for thou art not a creature who
Strikes terror pure into the hearts of all.
BARK BARK?

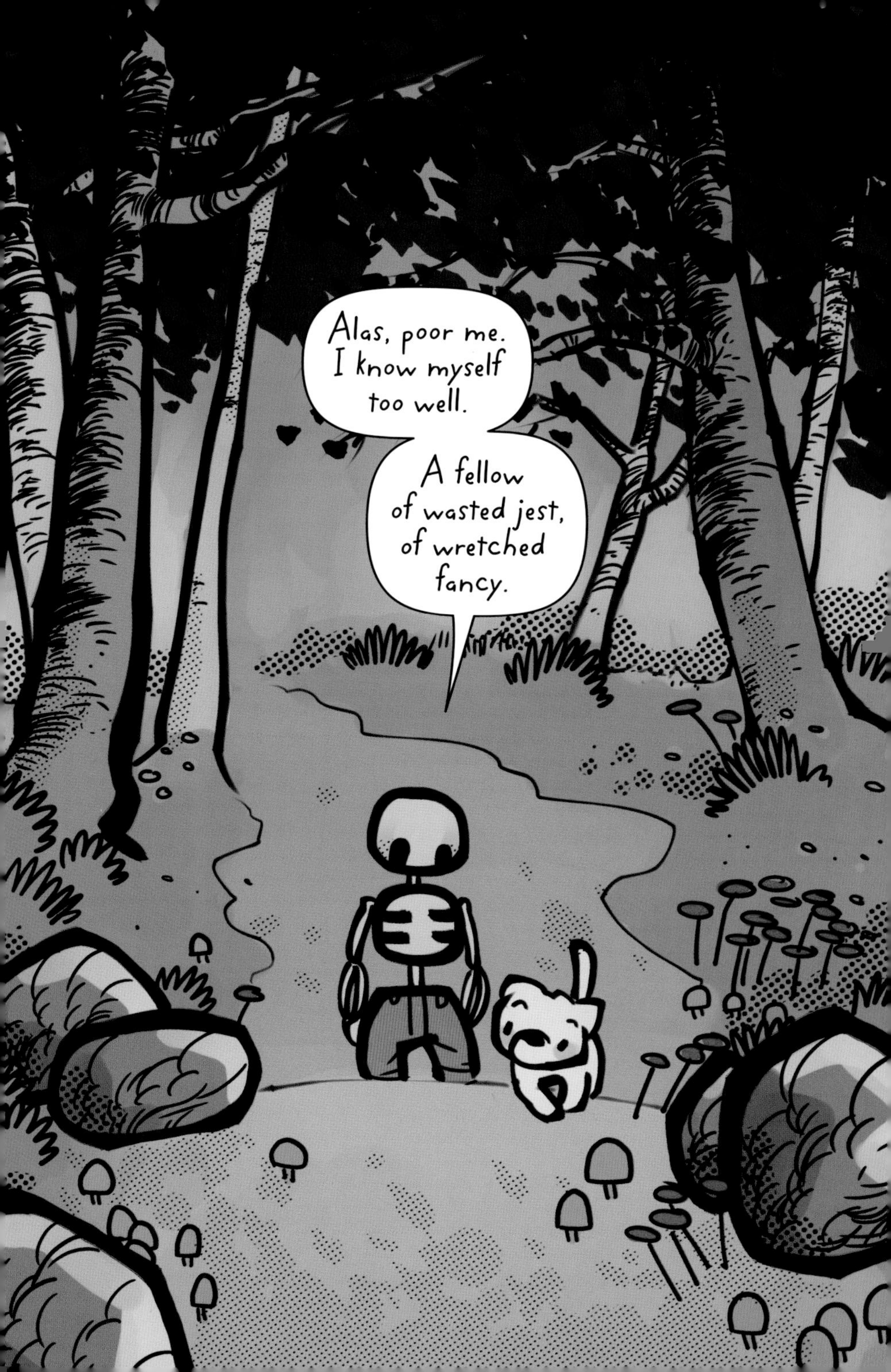
Alas, poor me. I know myself too well.
A fellow of wasted jest, of wretched fancy.

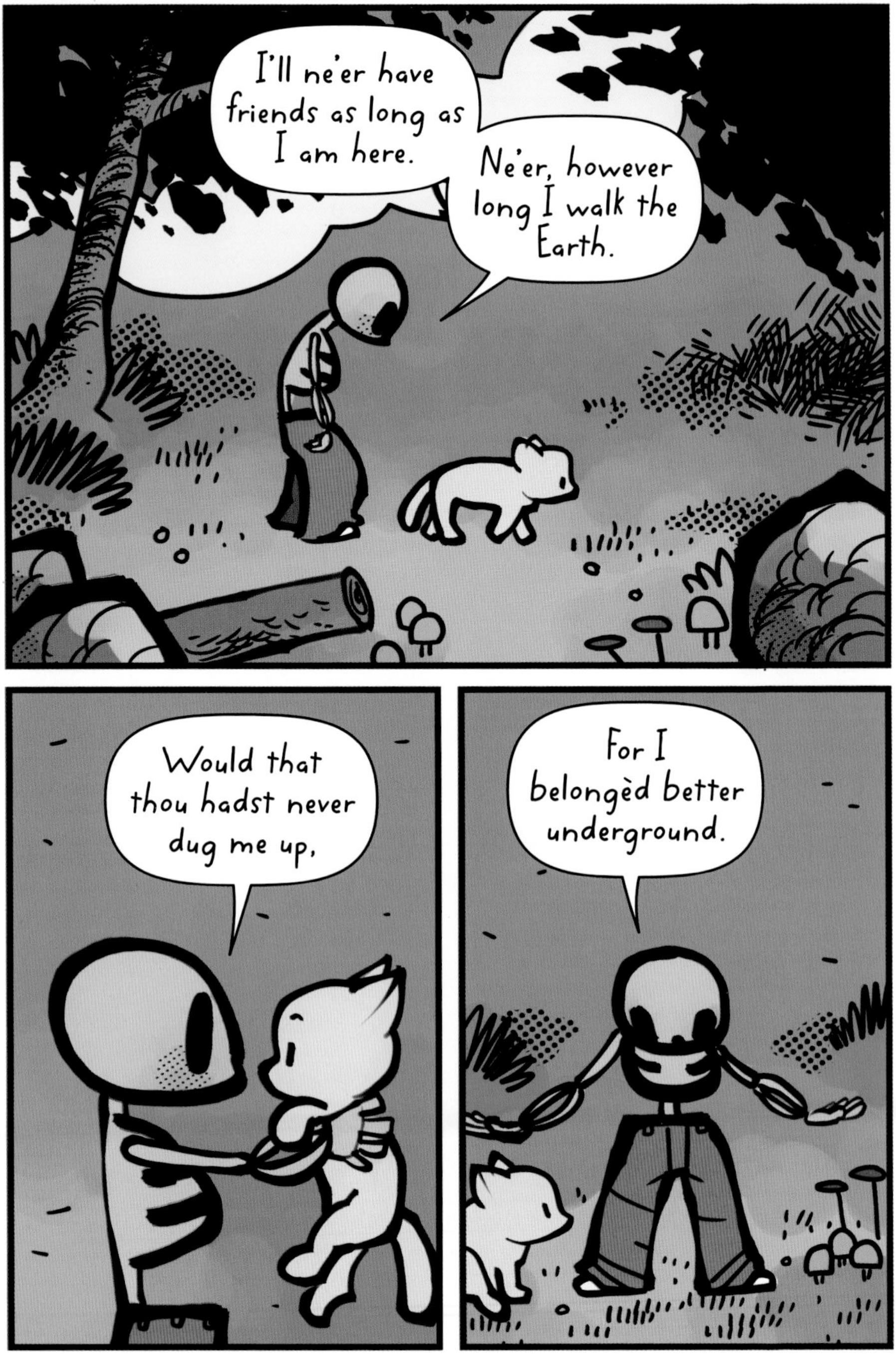
I'll ne'er have friends as long as I am here.
Ne'er, however long I walk the Earth.
Would that thou hadst never dug me up,
For I belongèd better underground.

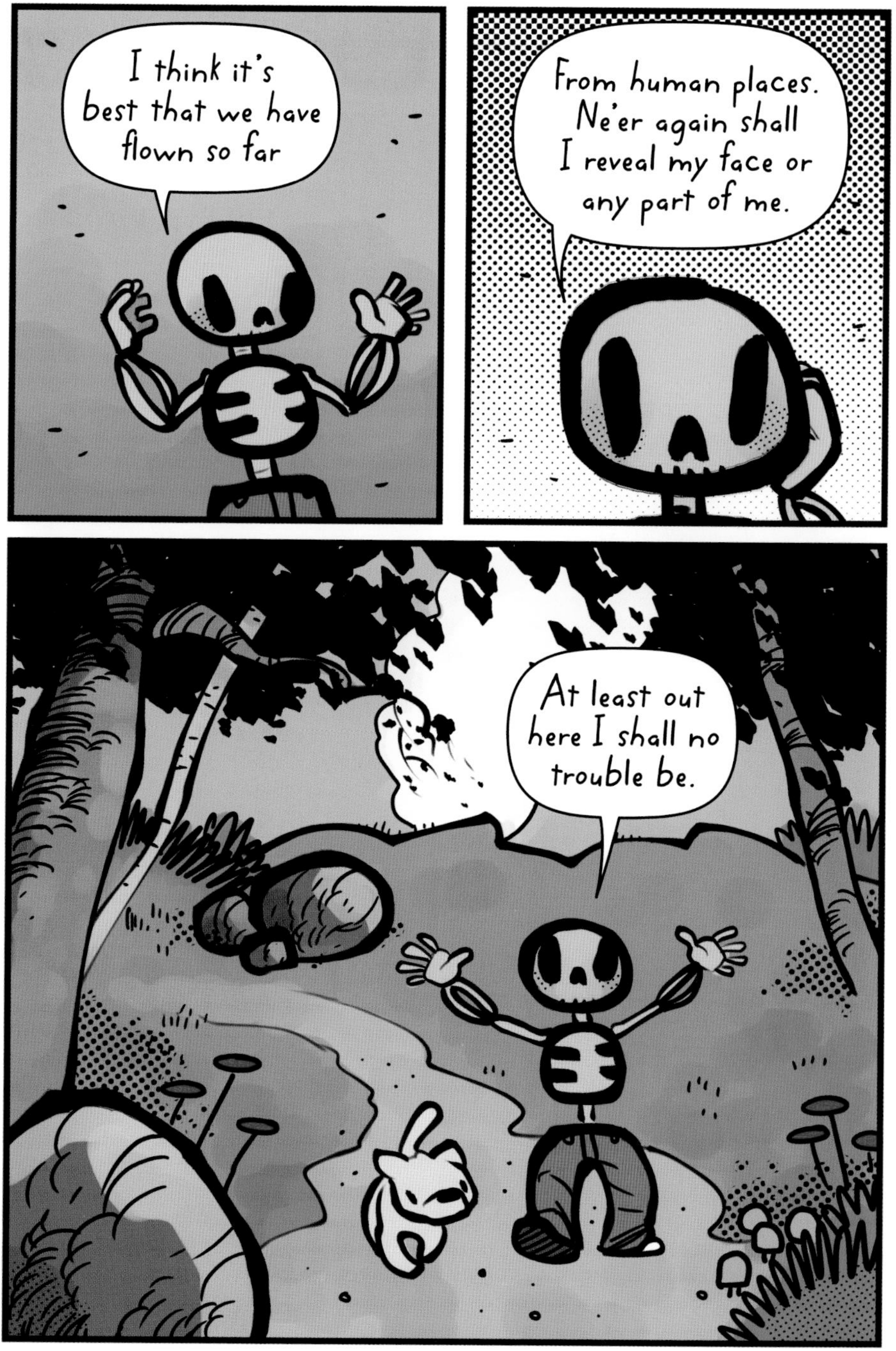
I think it's best that we have flown so far
From human places. Ne'er again shall I reveal my face or any part of me.
At least out here I shall no trouble be.

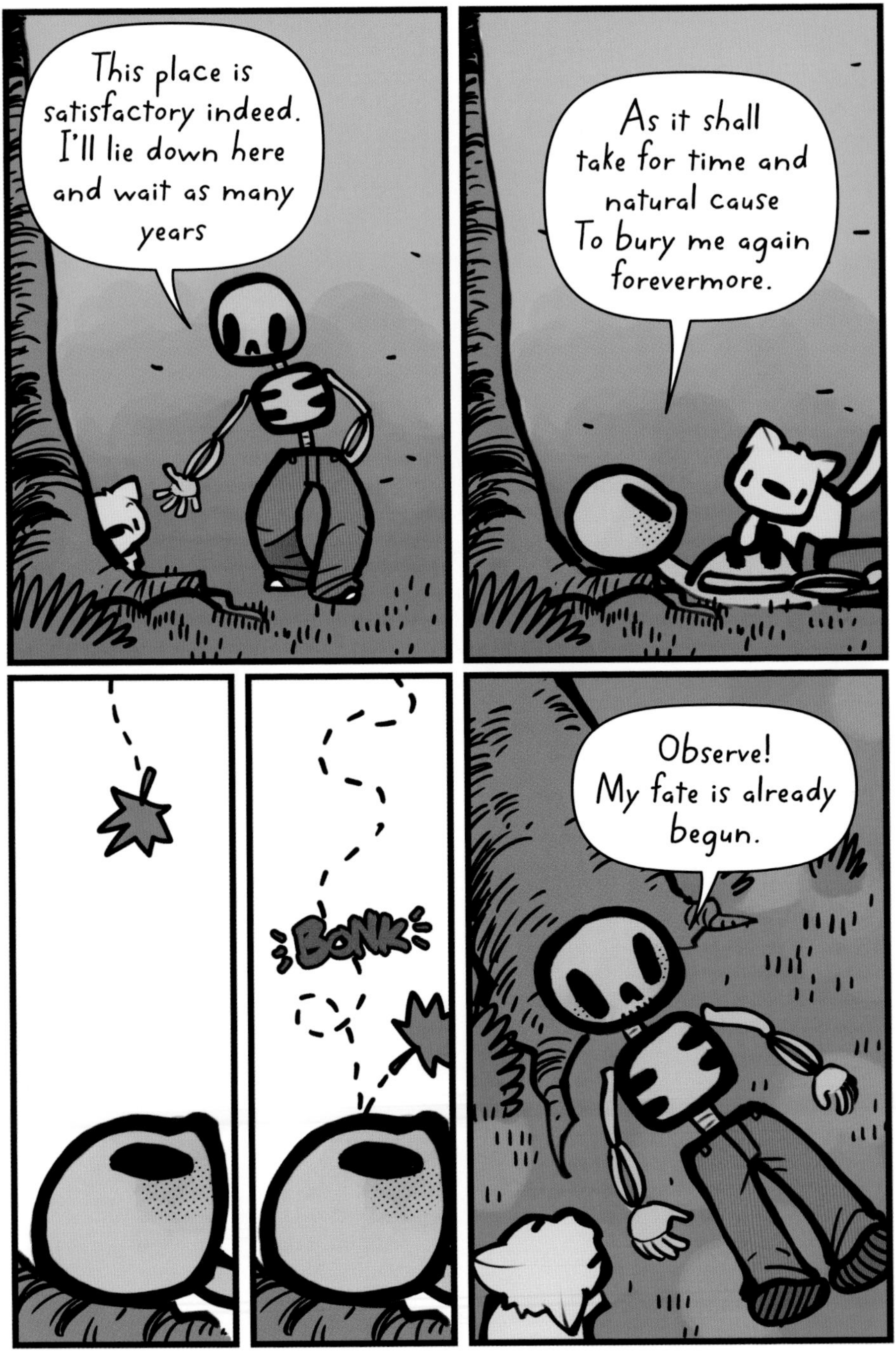
This place is satisfactory indeed. I'll lie down here and wait as many years
As it shall take for time and natural cause To bury me again forevermore.
BONK
Observe! My fate is already begun.

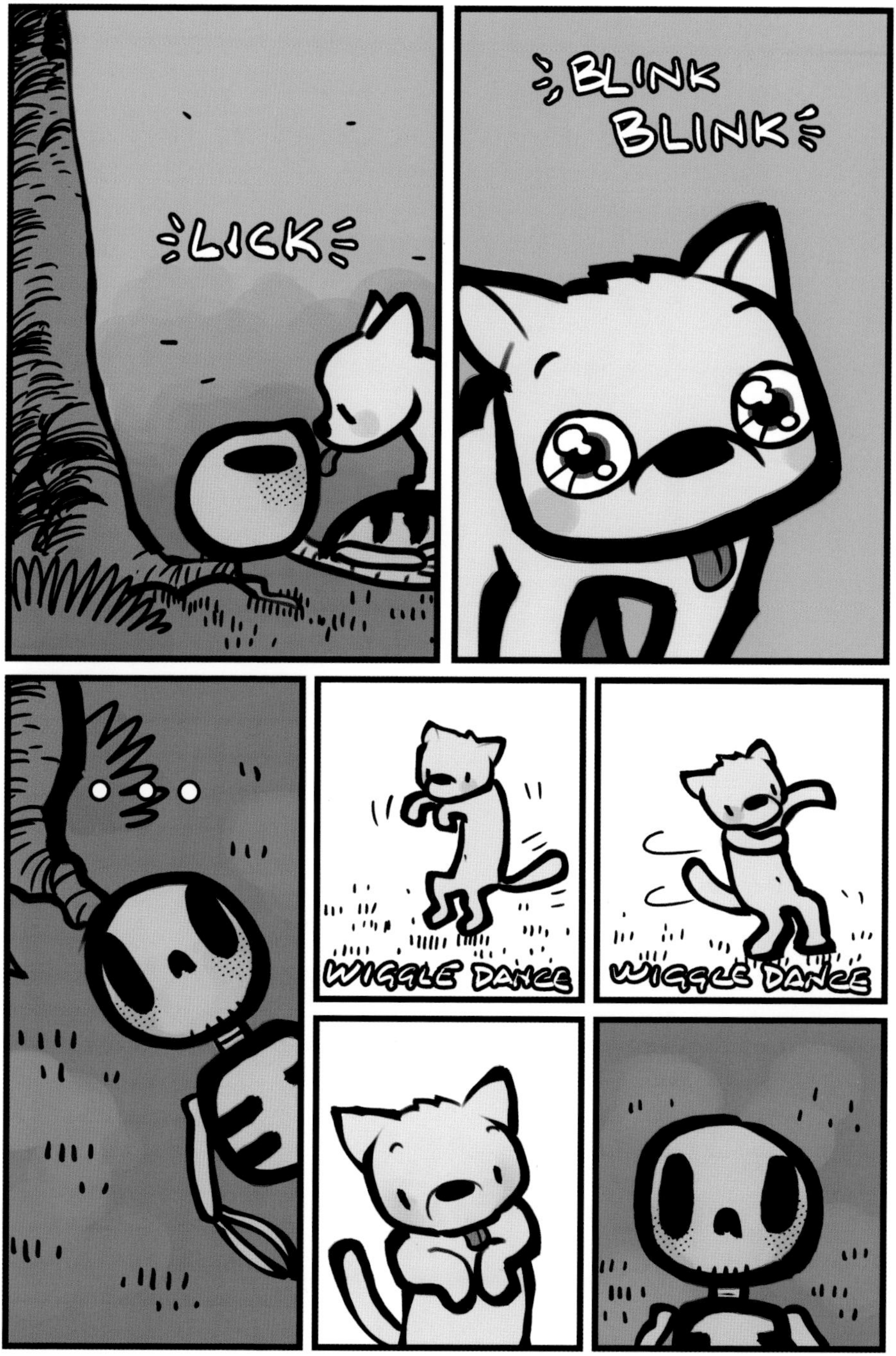
LICK
BLINK
BLINK
...
WIGGLE DANCE
WIGGLE DANCE

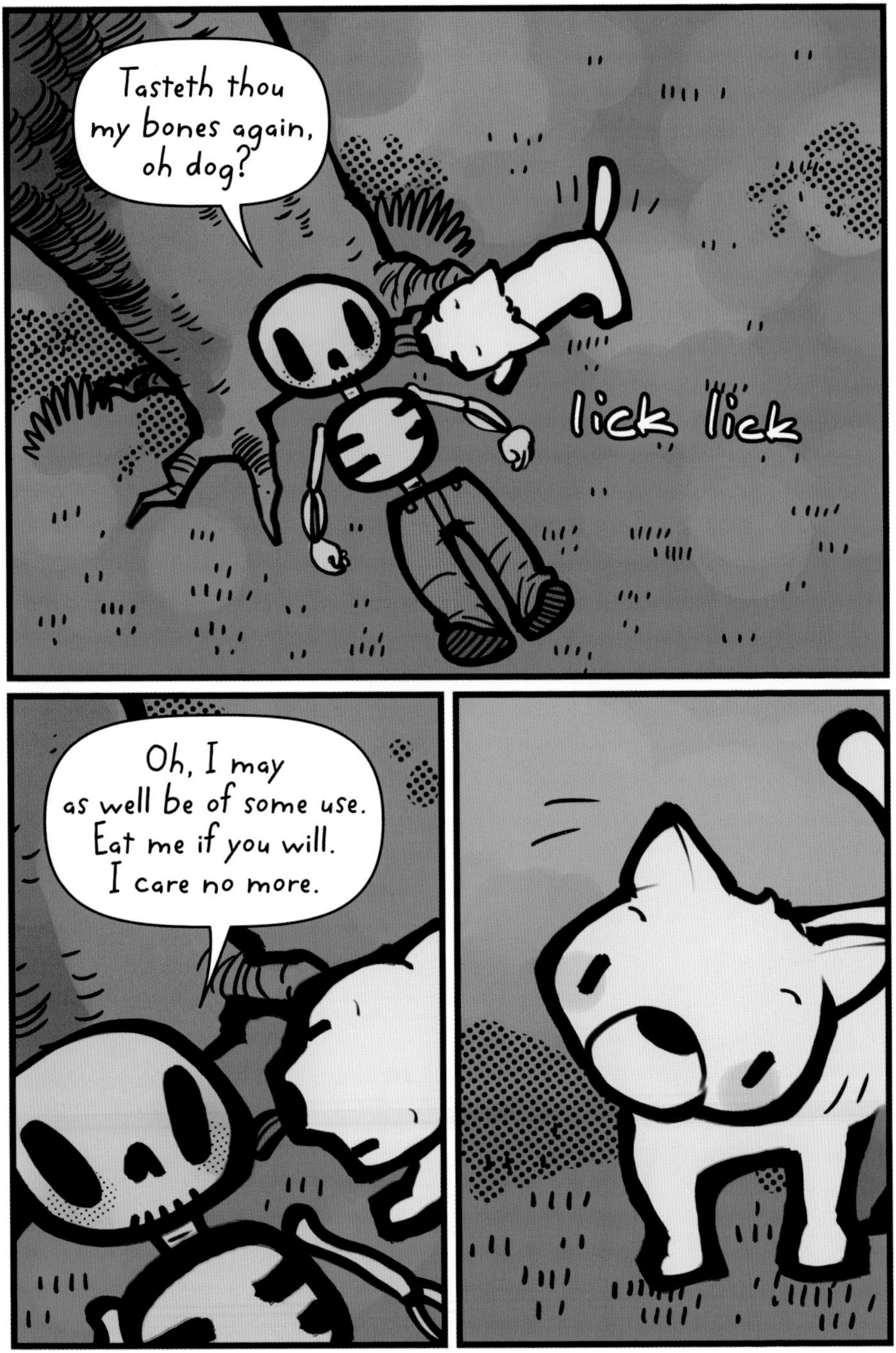
Tasteth thou my bones again, oh dog?
lick lick
Oh, I may as well be of some use. Eat me if you will. I care no more.

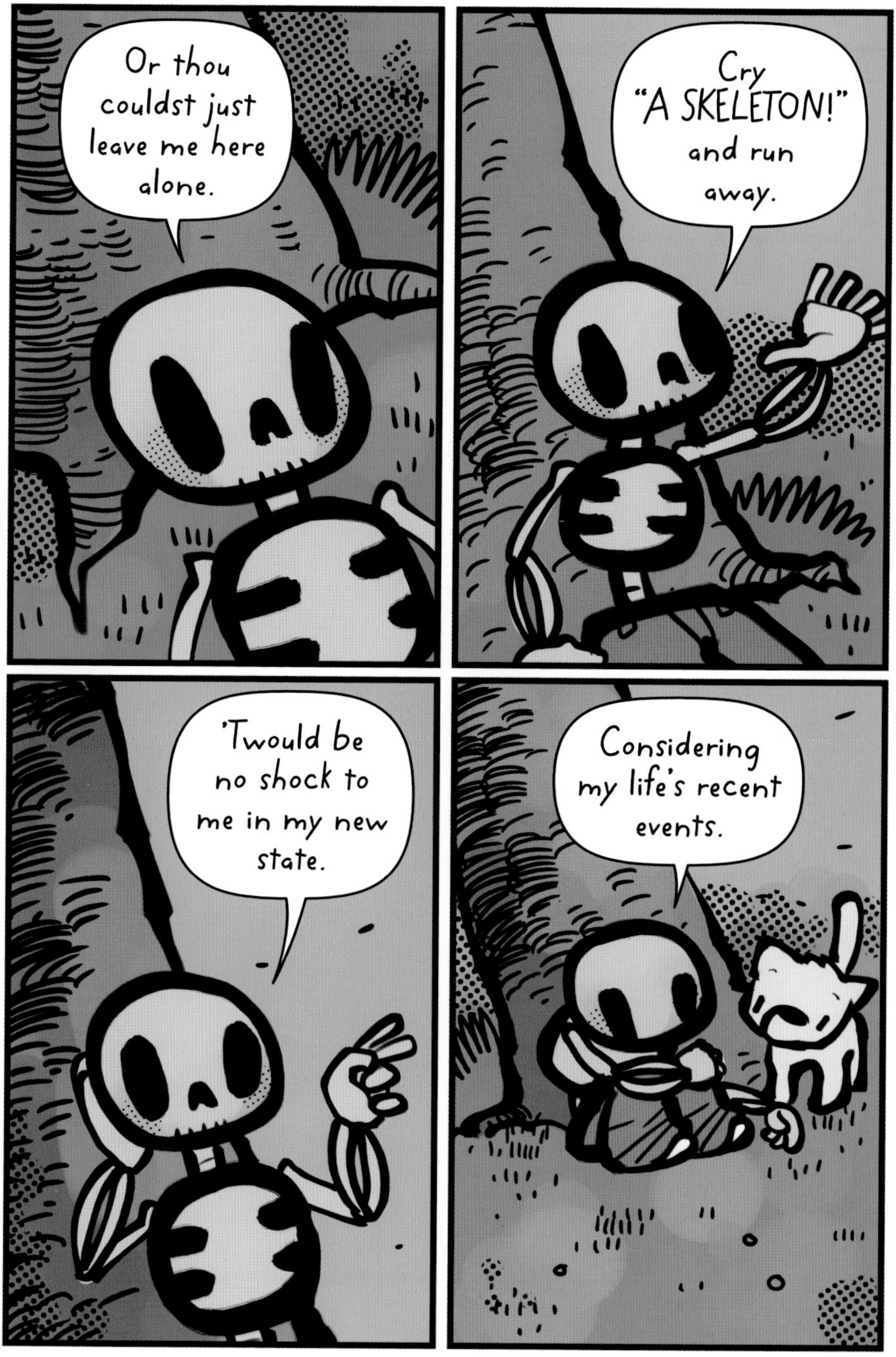
Or thou couldst just leave me here alone.
Cry "A SKELETON!" and run away.
'Twould be no shock to me in my new state.
Considering my life's recent events.

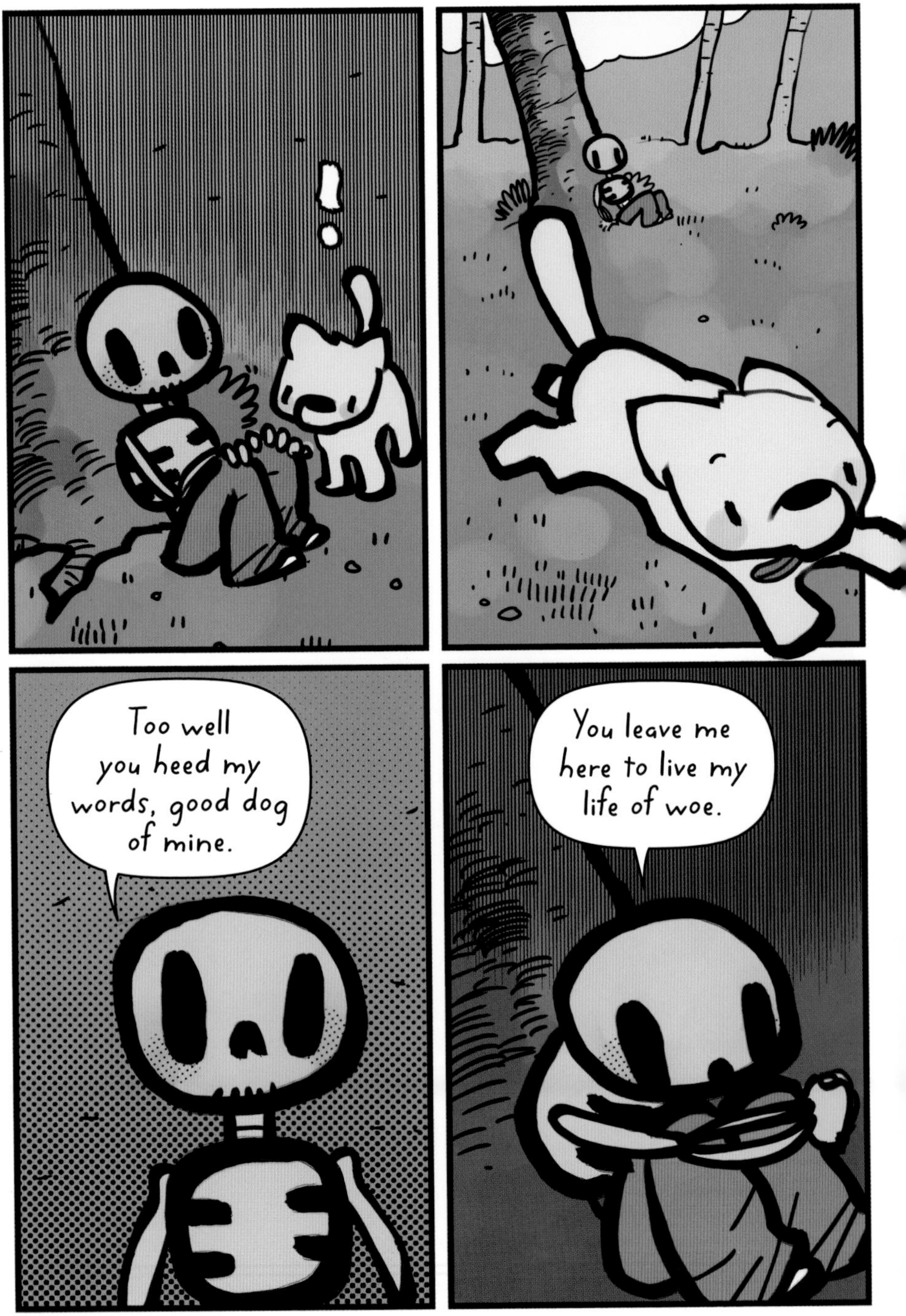
!
Too well you heed my words, good dog of mine.
You leave me here to live my life of woe.

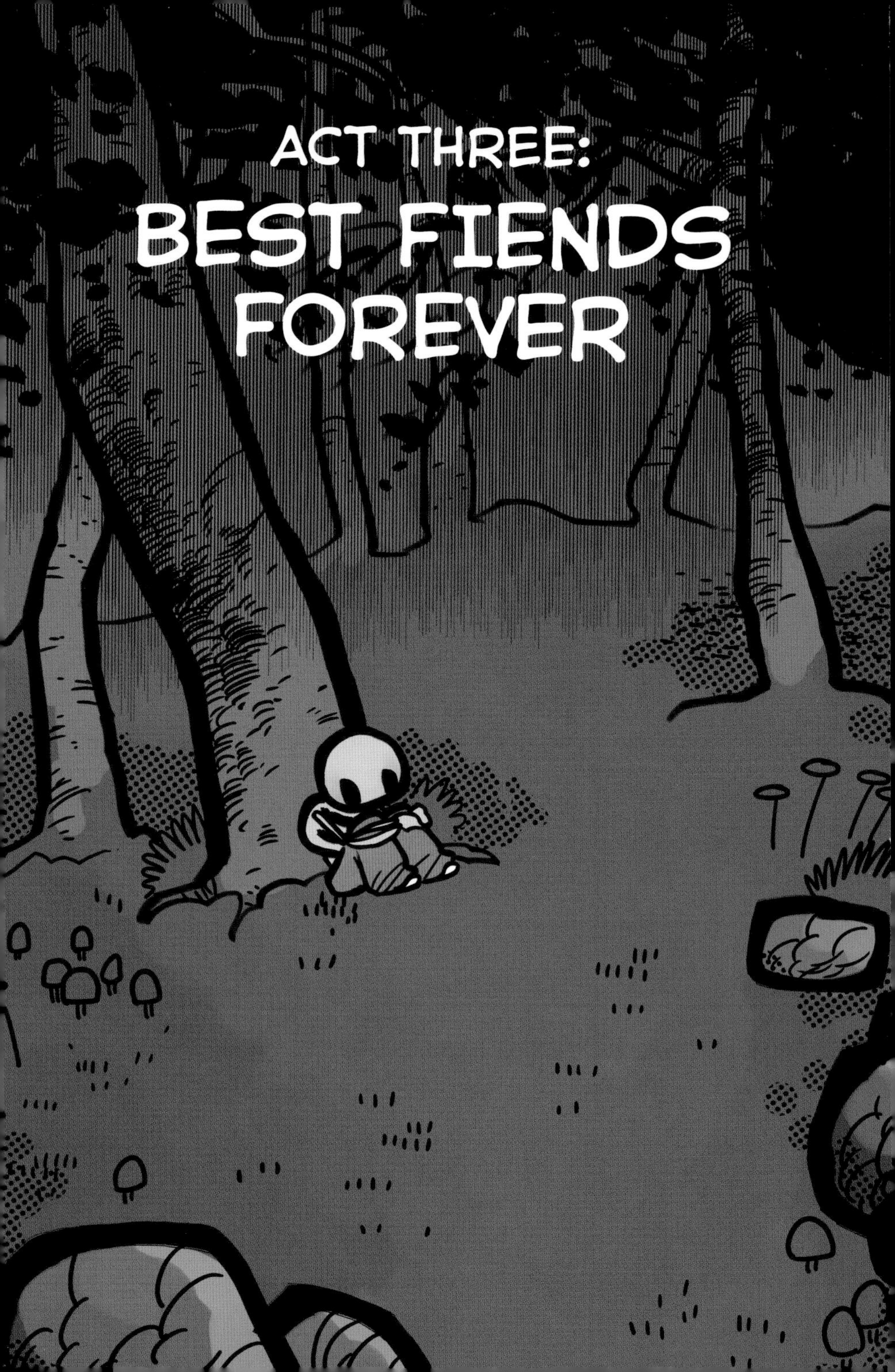
ACT THREE:
BEST FIENDS
FOREVER

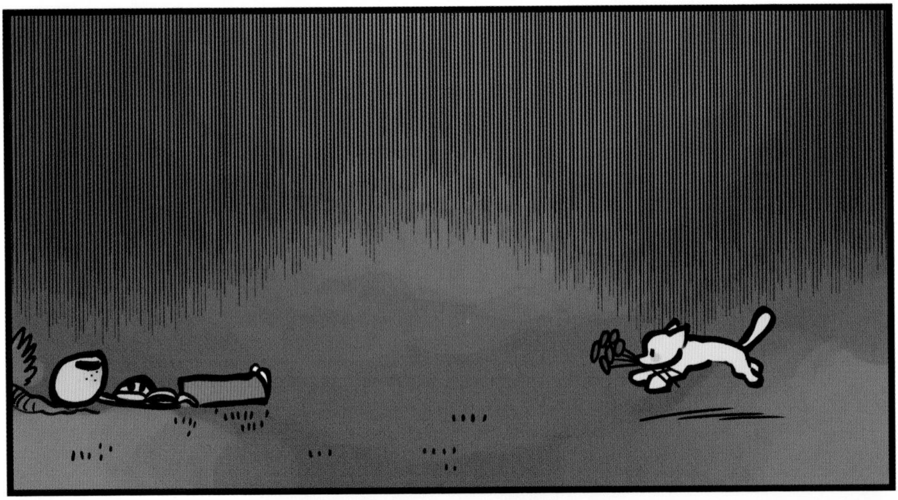

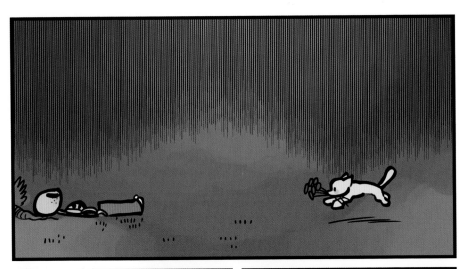

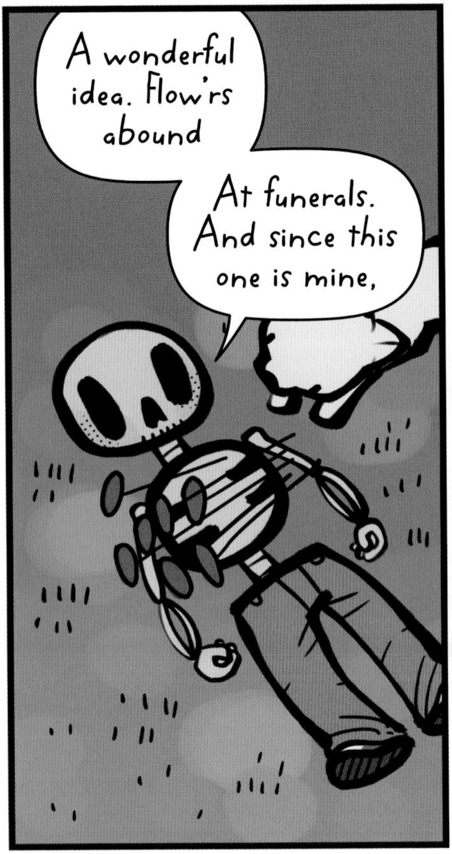
A wonderful idea. Flow'rs abound
At funerals. And since this one is mine,

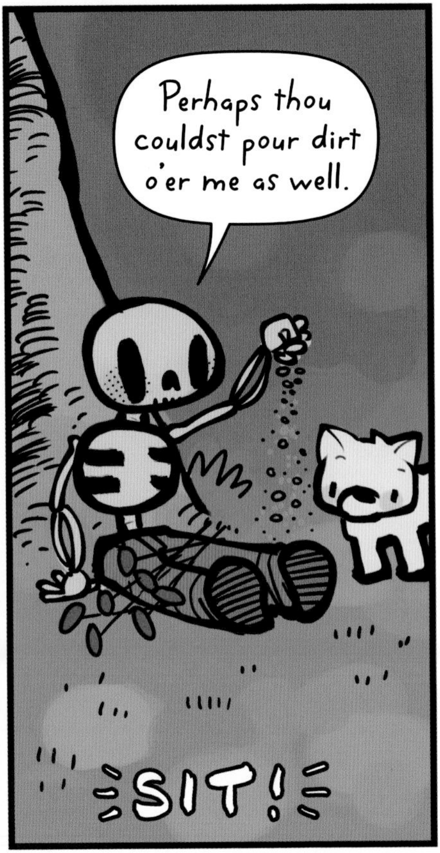
Perhaps thou couldst pour dirt o'er me as well.
SIT!

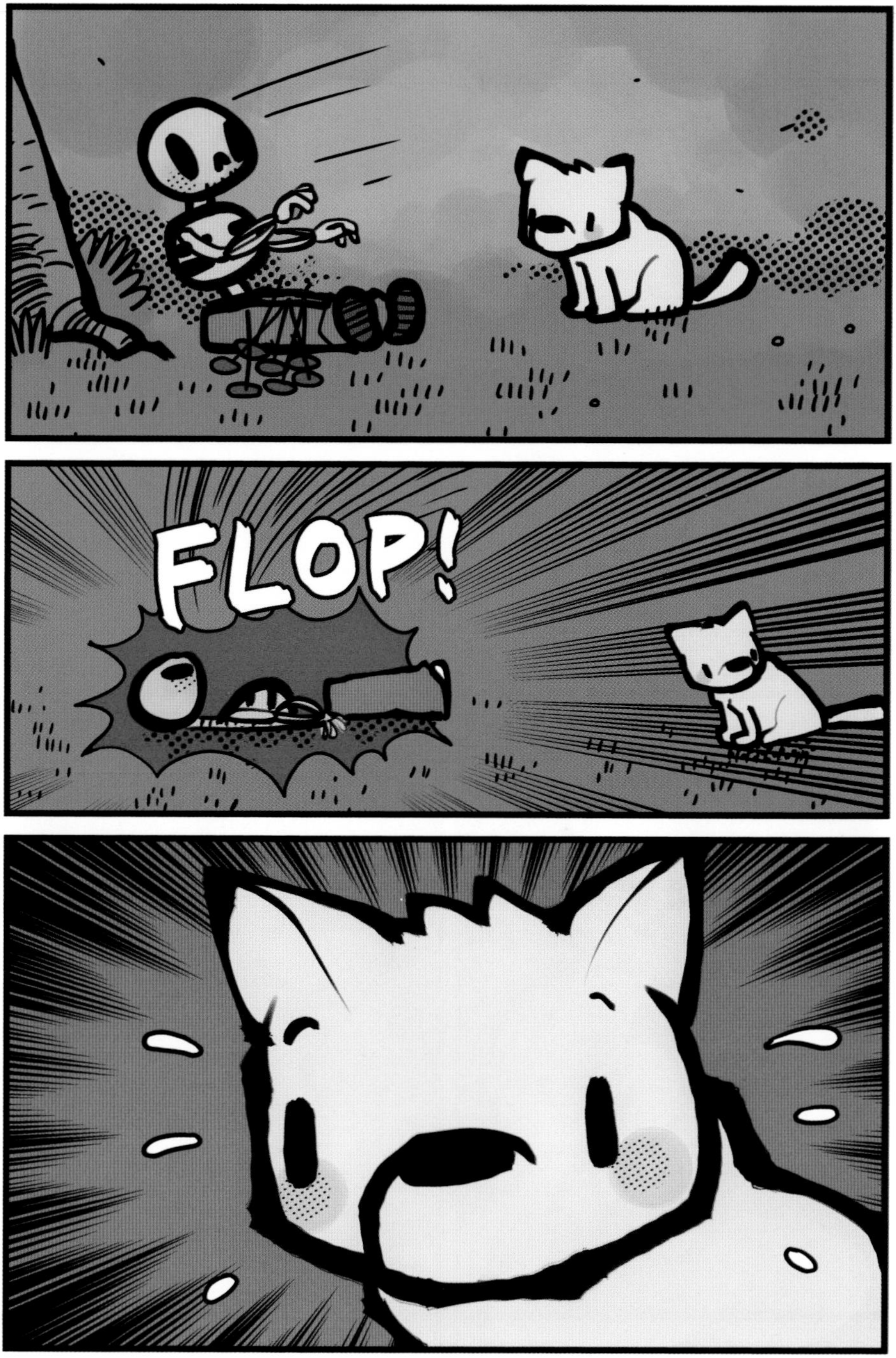
FLOP!

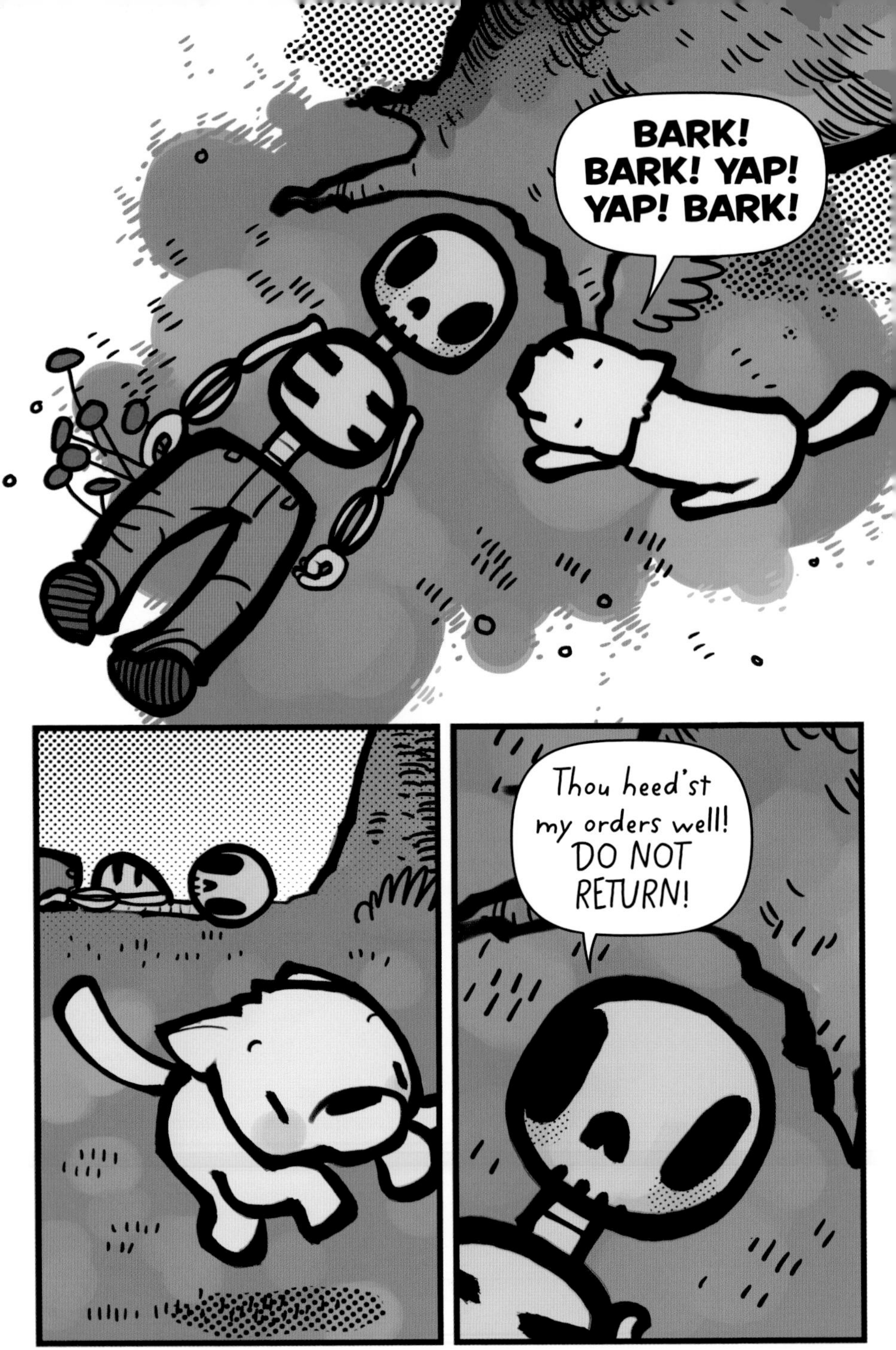
BARK! BARK! YAP! YAP! BARK!
Thou heed'st my orders well! DO NOT RETURN!

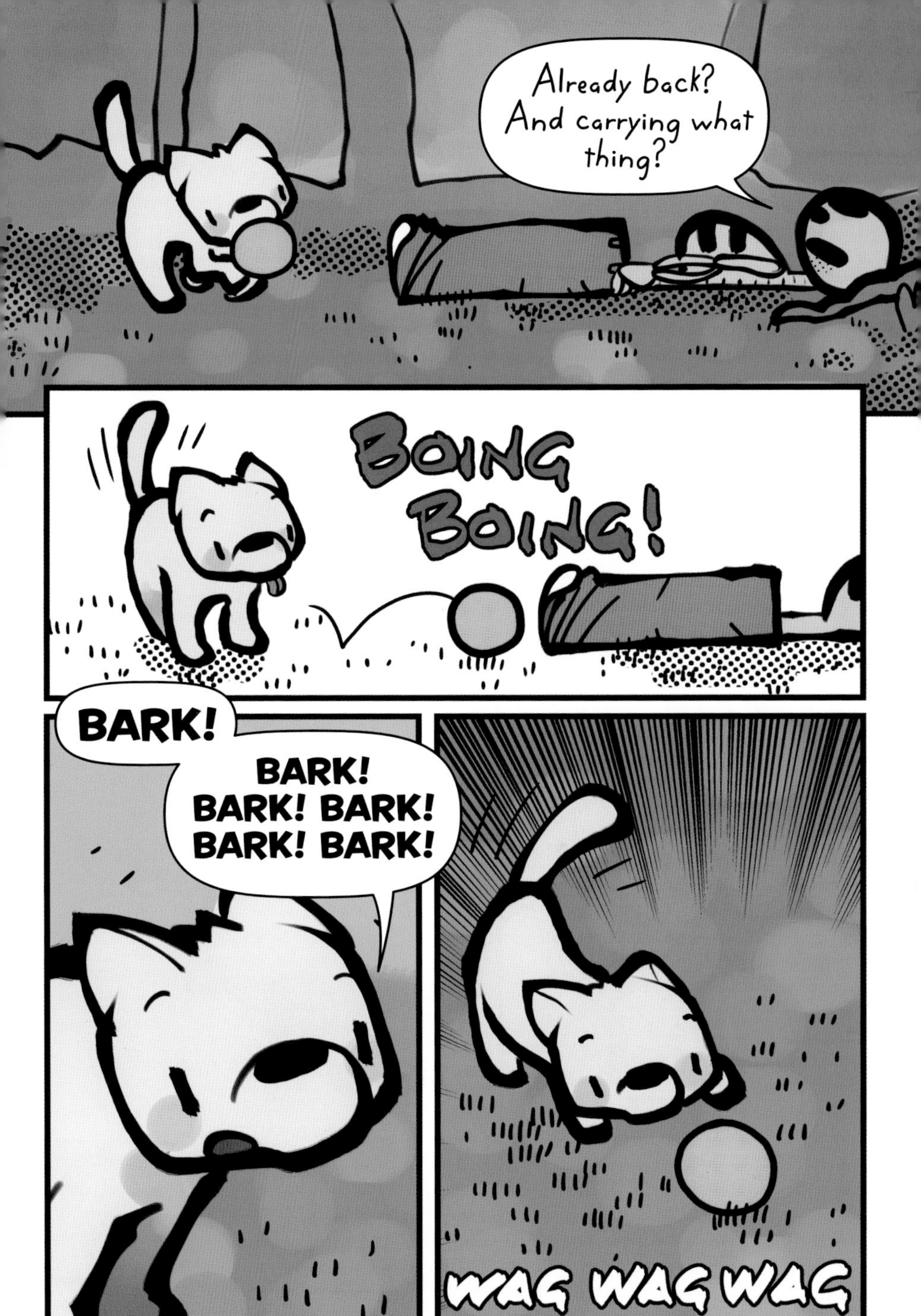
Already back? And carrying what thing?
BOING BOING!
BARK!
BARK! BARK! BARK! BARK! BARK!
WAG WAG WAG

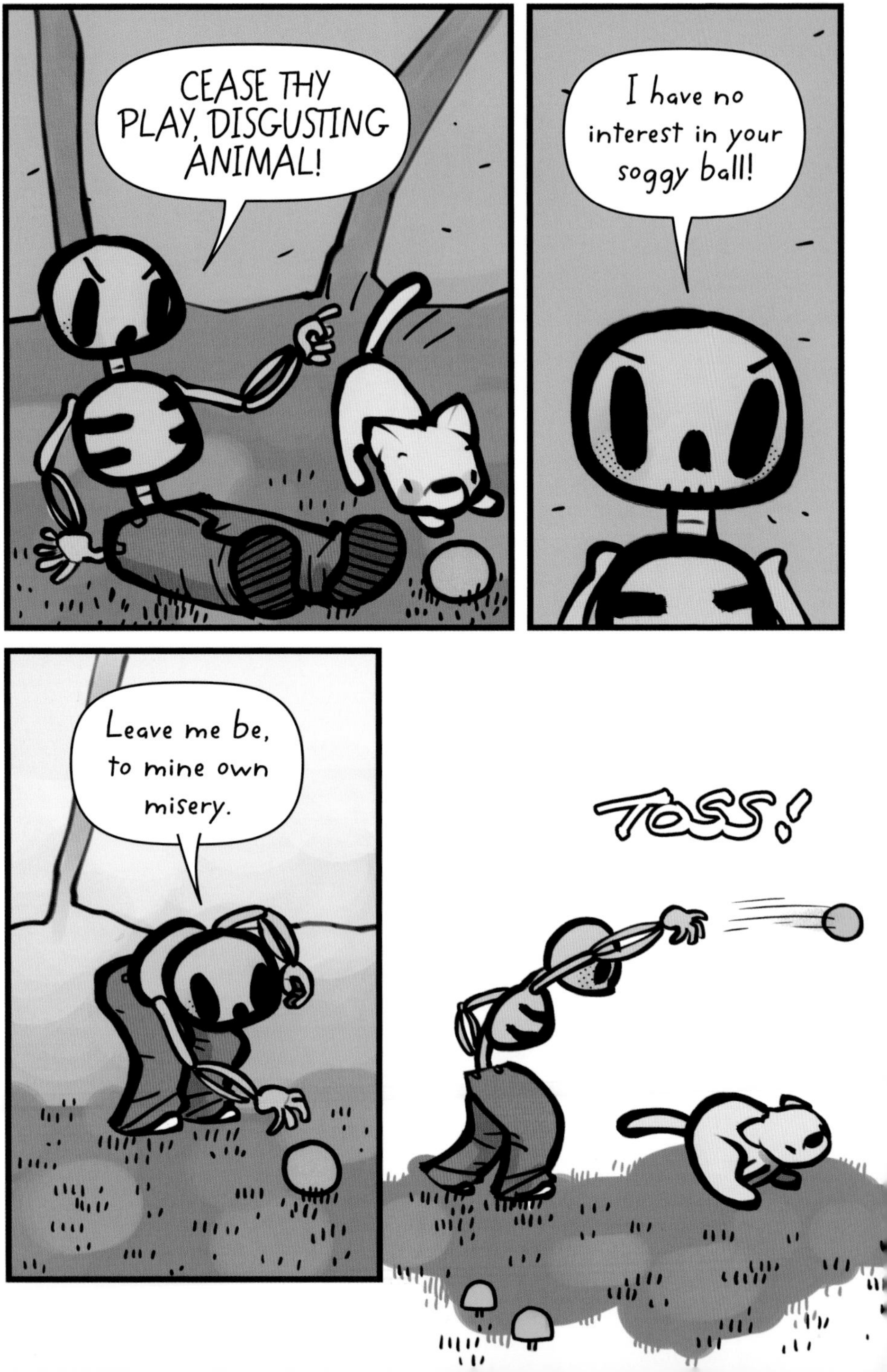
CEASE THY PLAY, DISGUSTING ANIMAL!
I have no interest in your soggy ball!
Leave me be, to mine own misery.
TOSS!

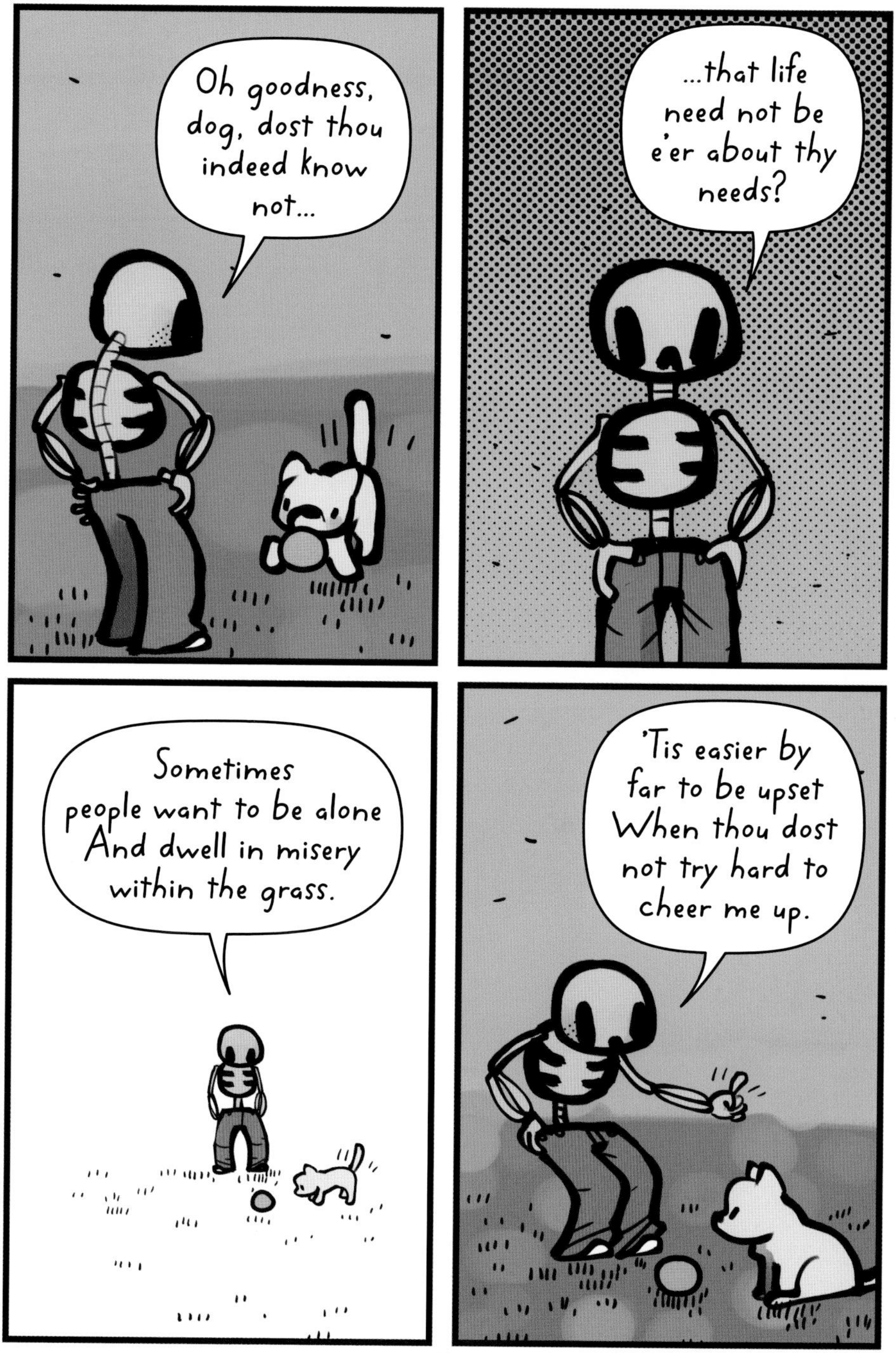
Oh goodness, dog, dost thou indeed know not...
...that life need not be e'er about thy needs?
Sometimes people want to be alone And dwell in misery within the grass.
'Tis easier by far to be upset When thou dost not try hard to cheer me up.

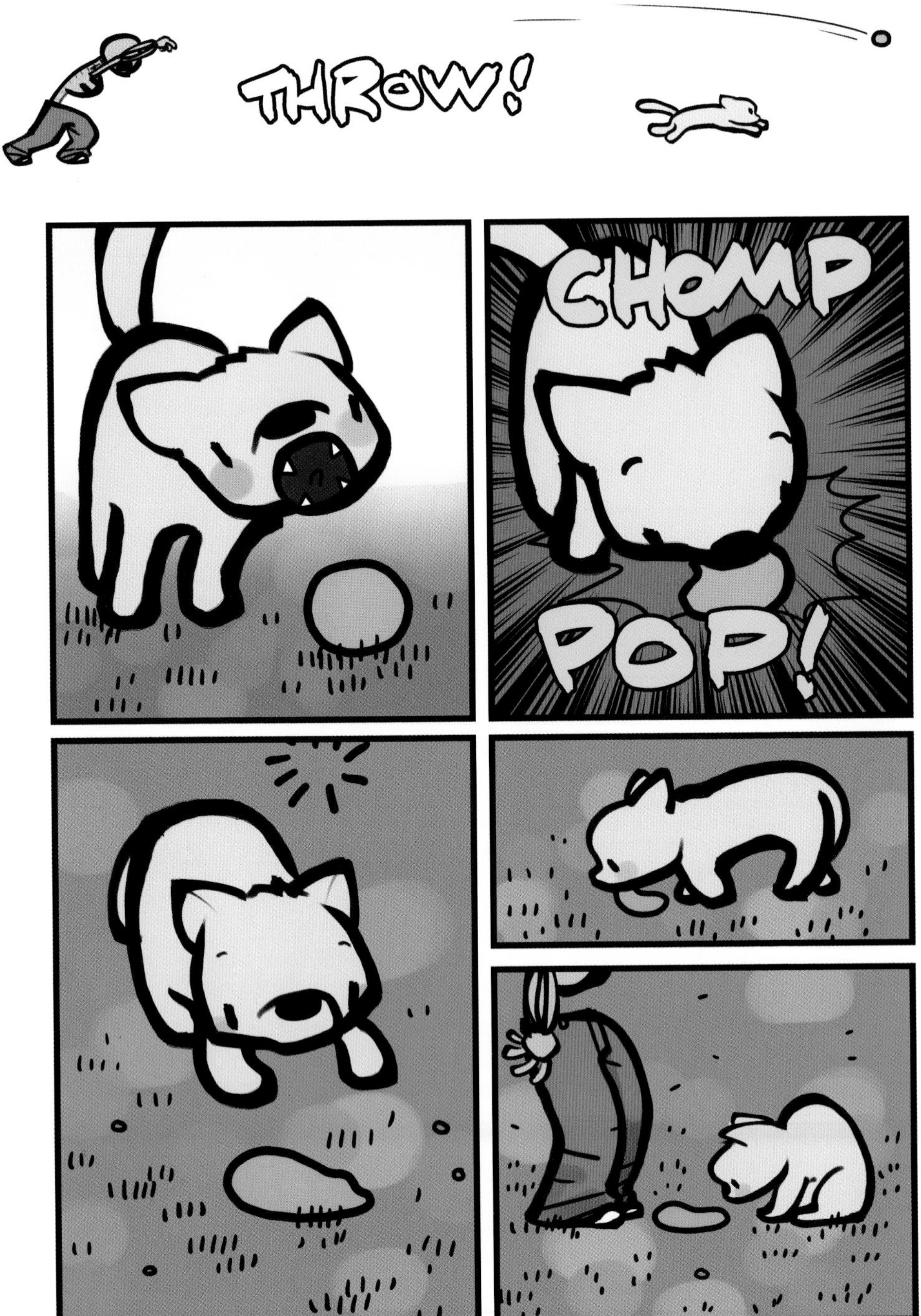
THROW!
CHOMP
POP!

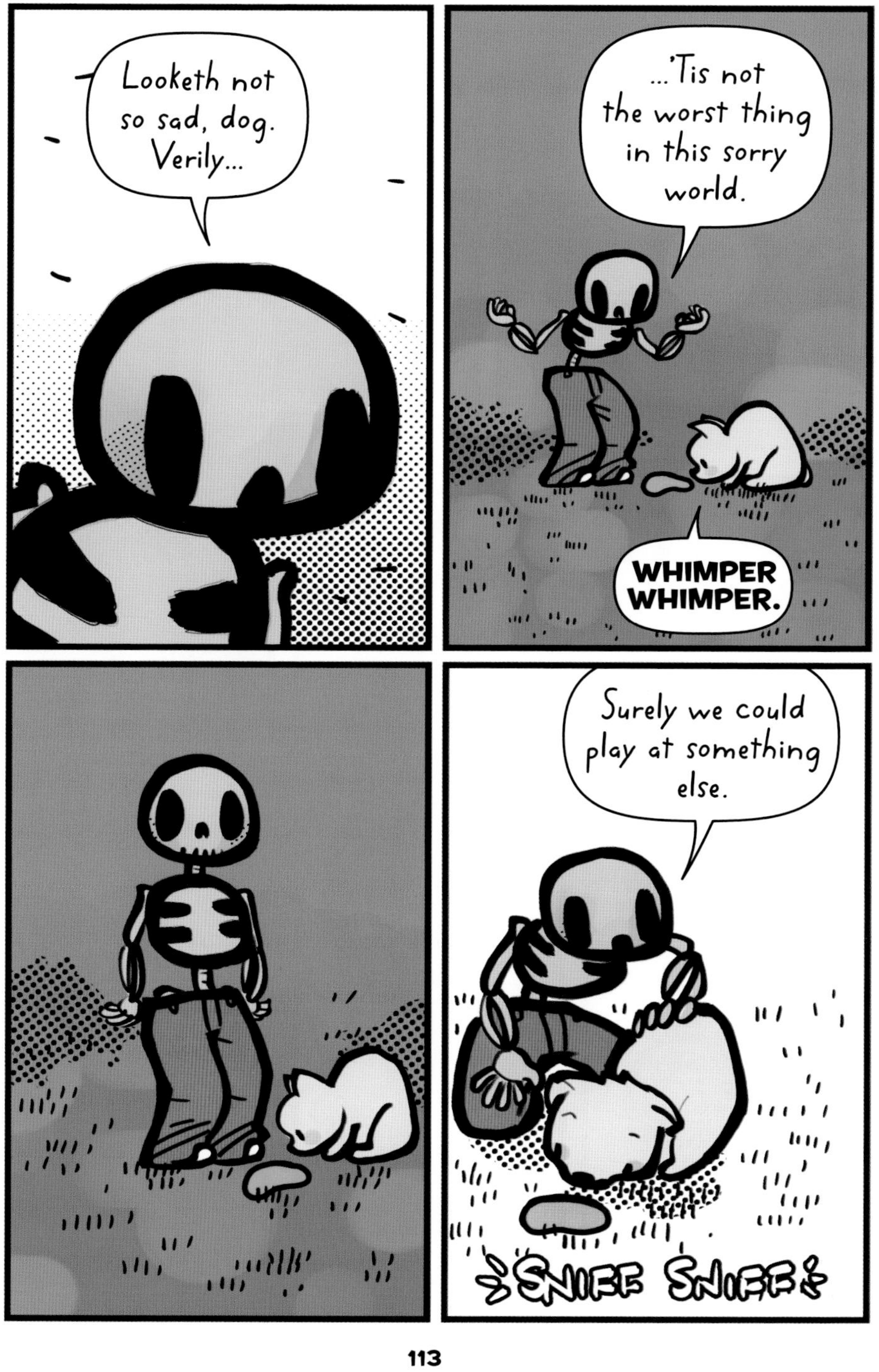

Looketh not so sad, dog. Verily...
...'Tis not the worst thing in this sorry world.
WHIMPER WHIMPER.
Surely we could play at something else.
SNIFF SNIFF

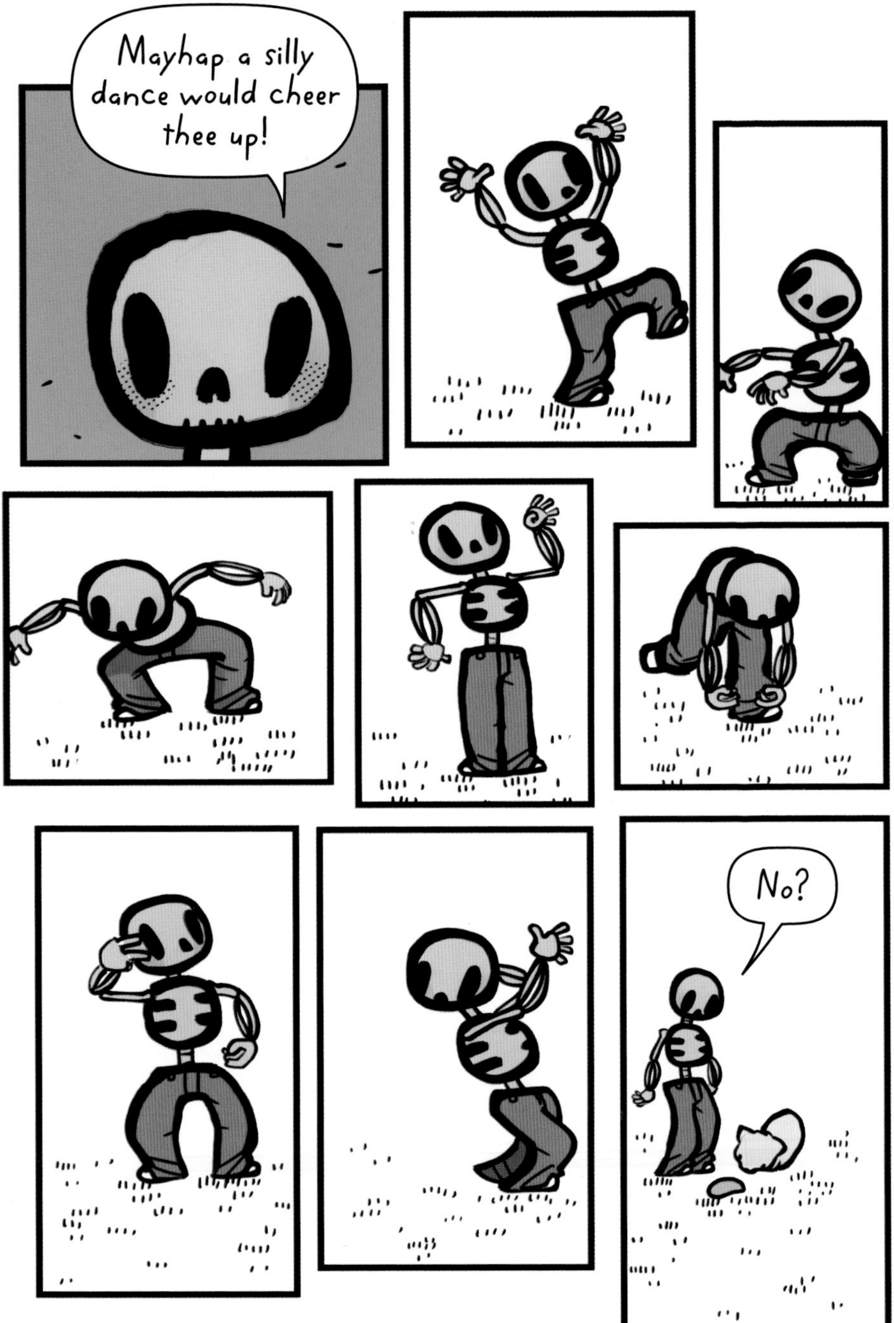
Mayhap a silly dance would cheer thee up!
No?

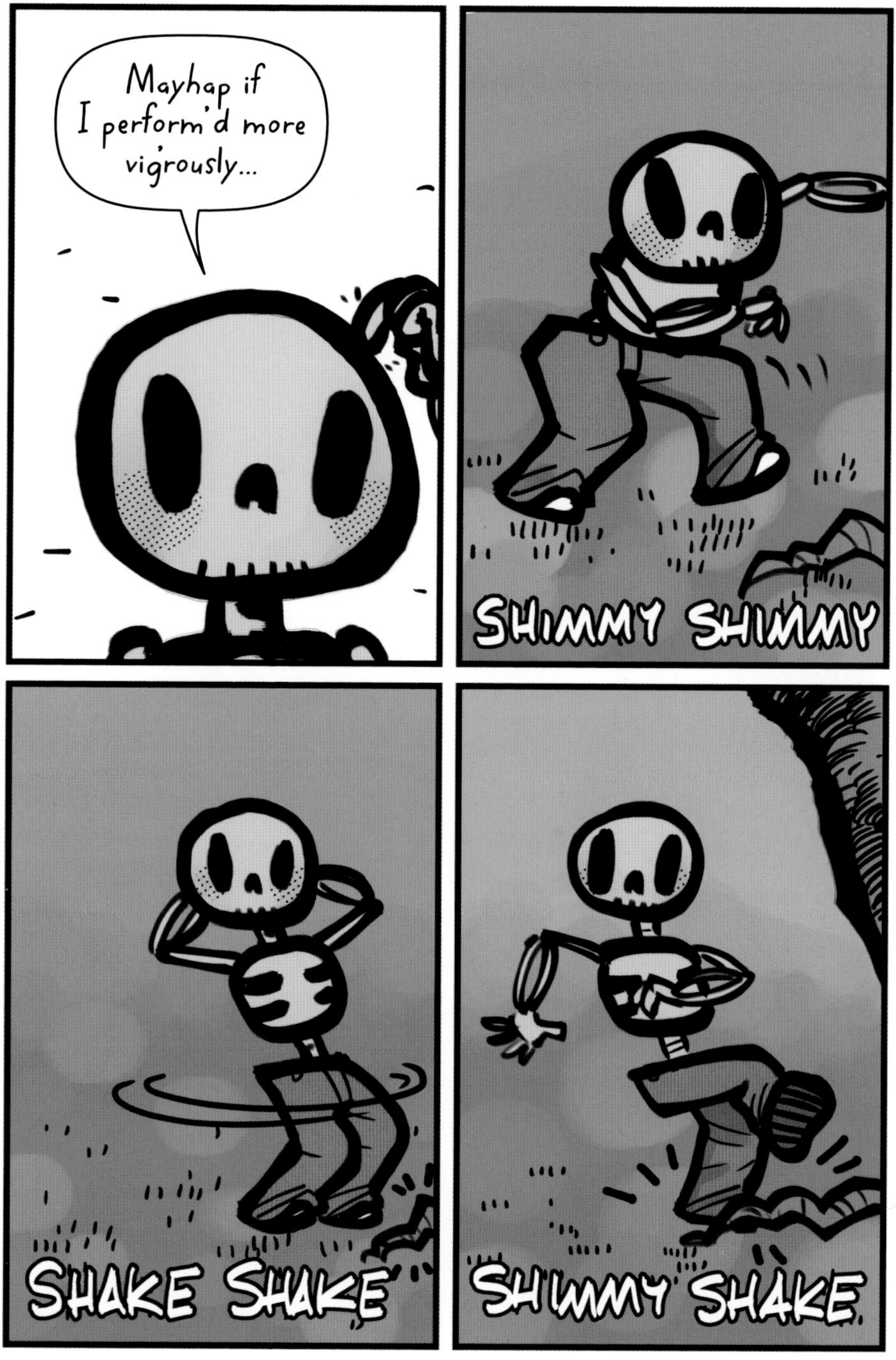
Mayhap if I perform'd more vigrously...
SHIMMY SHIMMY
SHAKE SHAKE
SHIMMY SHAKE

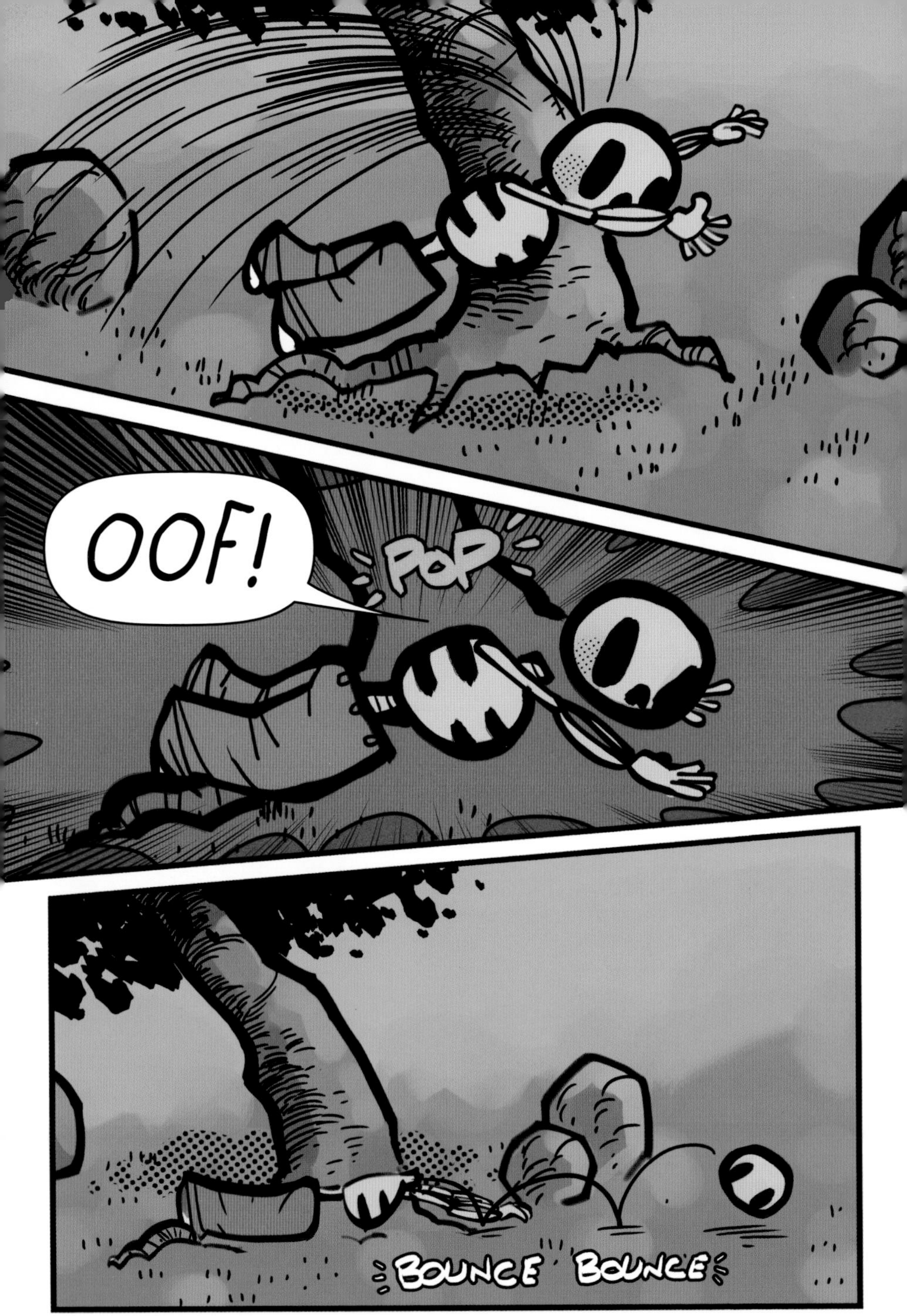
OOF!
POP
BOUNCE BOUNCE

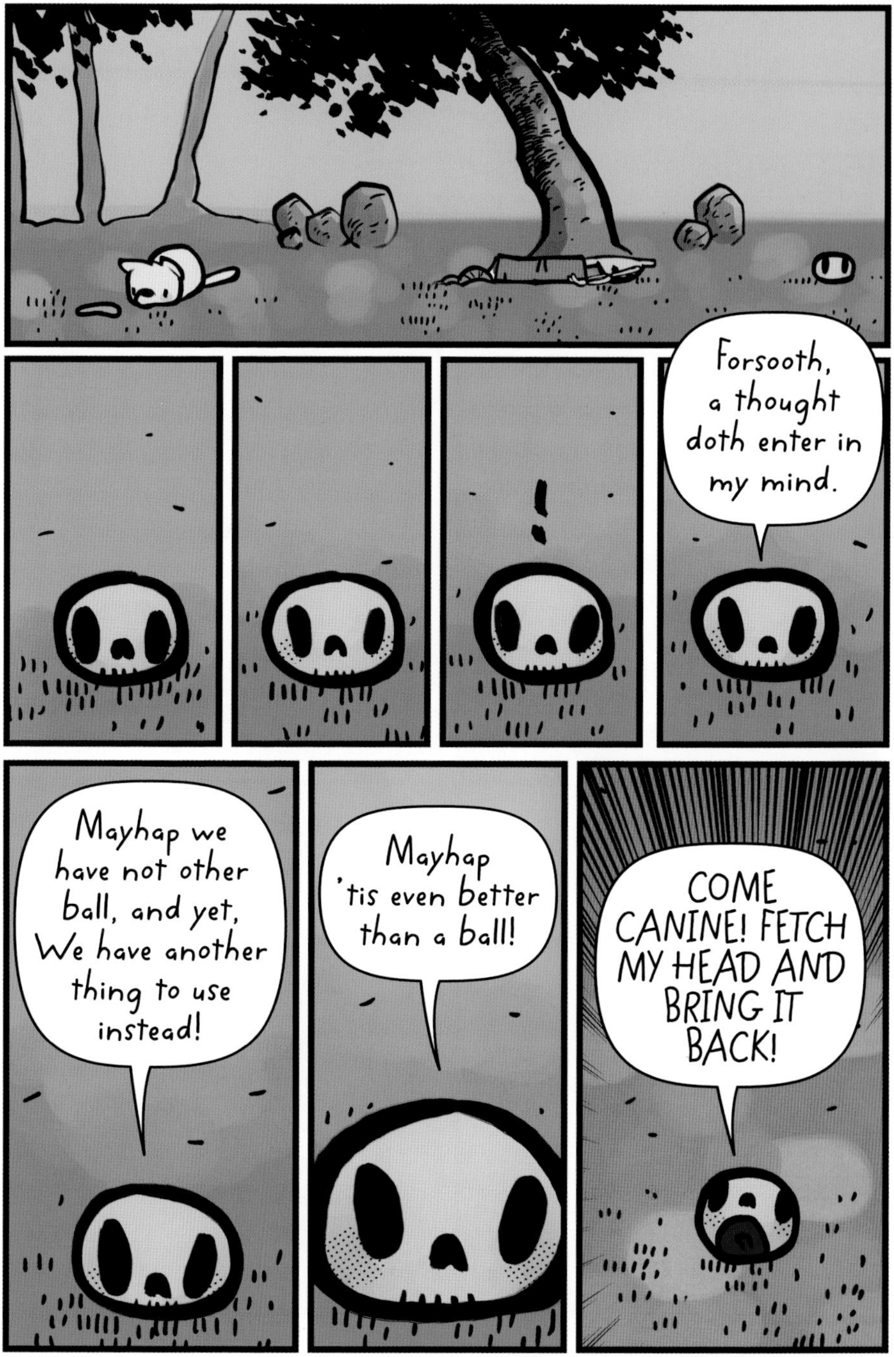

Forsooth, a thought doth enter in my mind.
Mayhap we have not other ball, and yet, We have another thing to use instead!
Mayhap 'tis even better than a ball!
COME CANINE! FETCH MY HEAD AND BRING IT BACK!

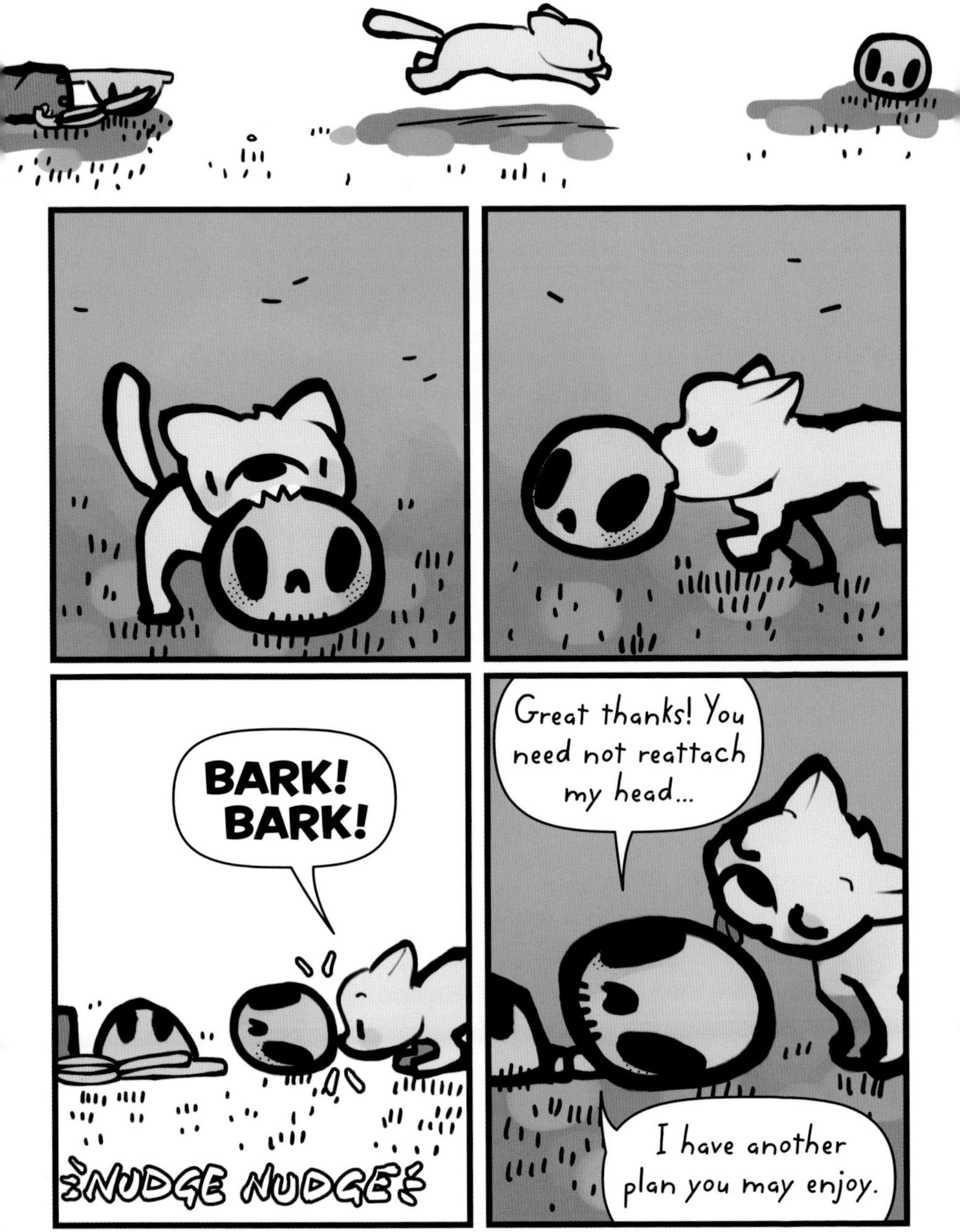
BARK! BARK!
NUDGE NUDGE
Great thanks! You need not reattach my head...
I have another plan you may enjoy.

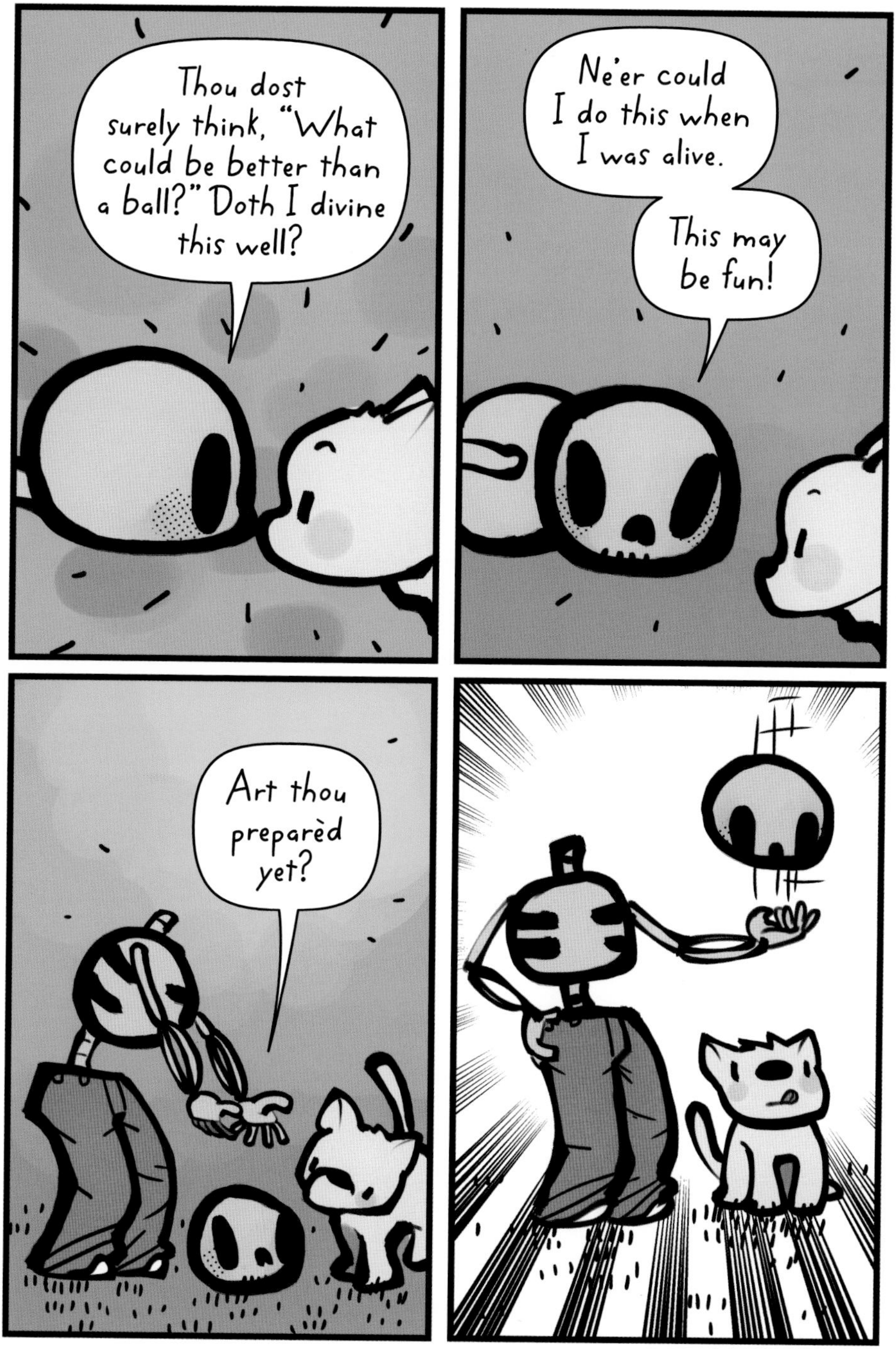
Thou dost surely think, "What could be better than a ball?" Doth I divine this well?
Ne'er could I do this when I was alive.
This may be fun!
Art thou preparèd yet?

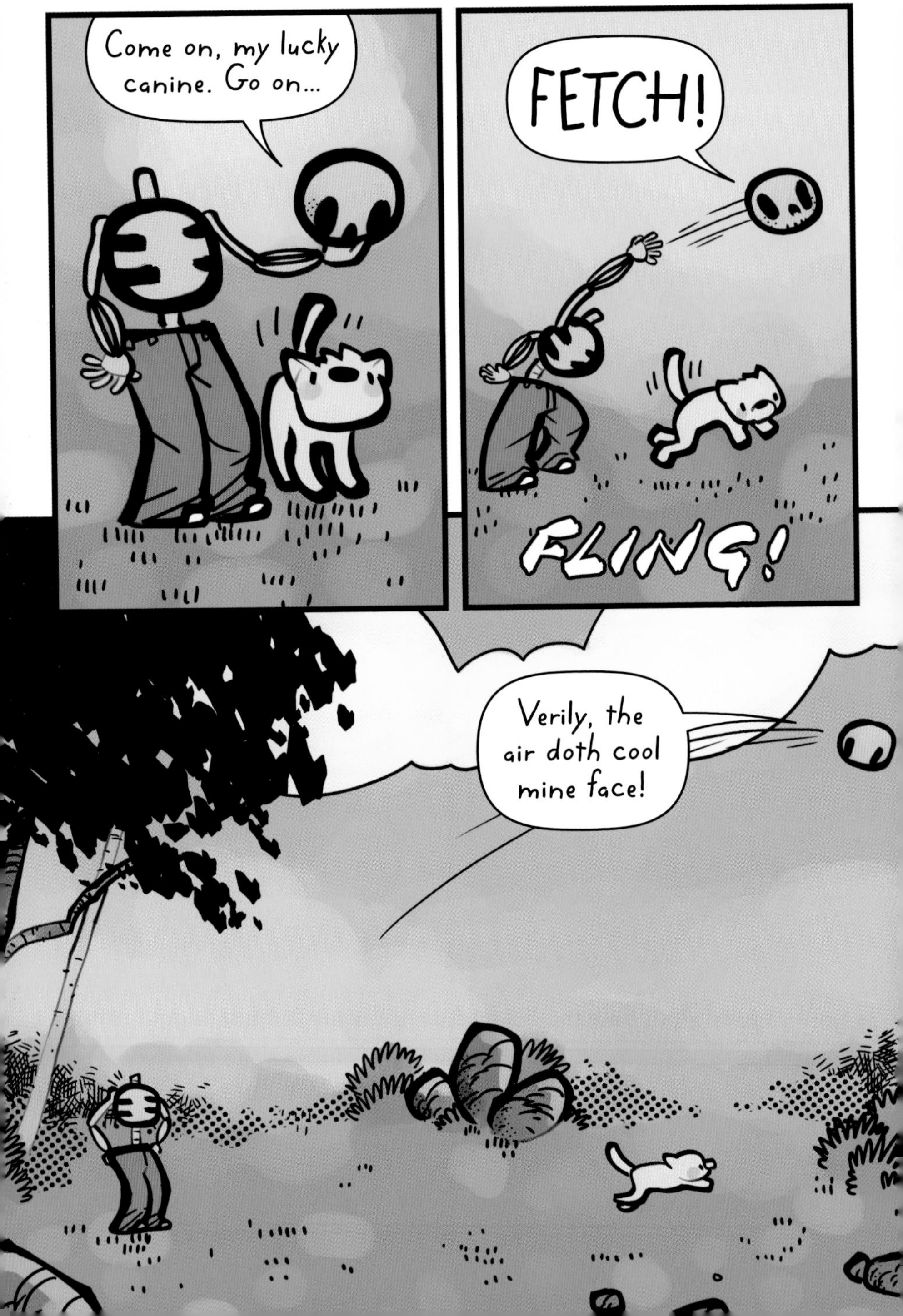
Come on, my lucky canine. Go on...
FETCH!
FLING!
Verily, the air doth cool mine face!

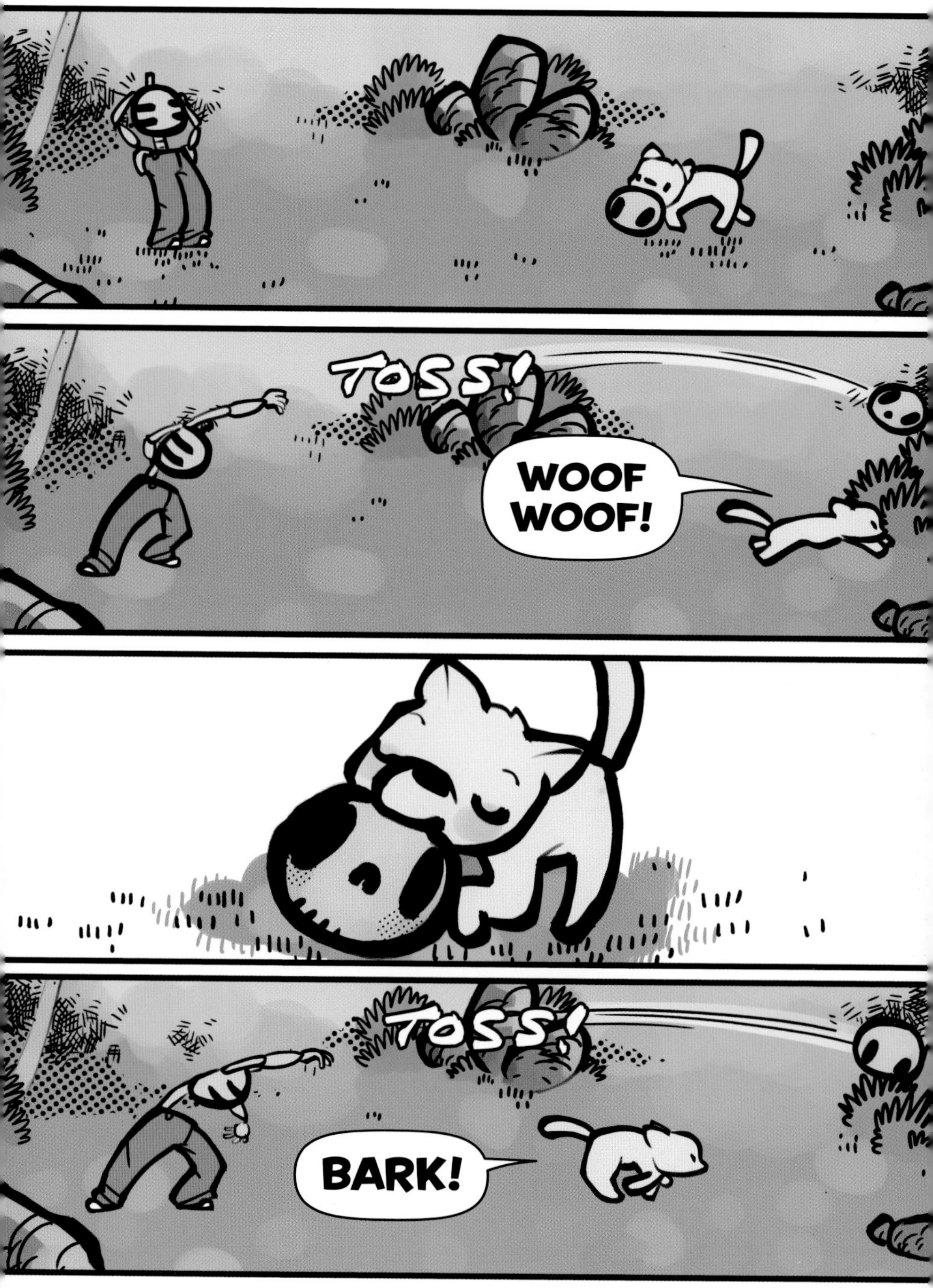
TOSS!
WOOF WOOF!
TOSS!
BARK!

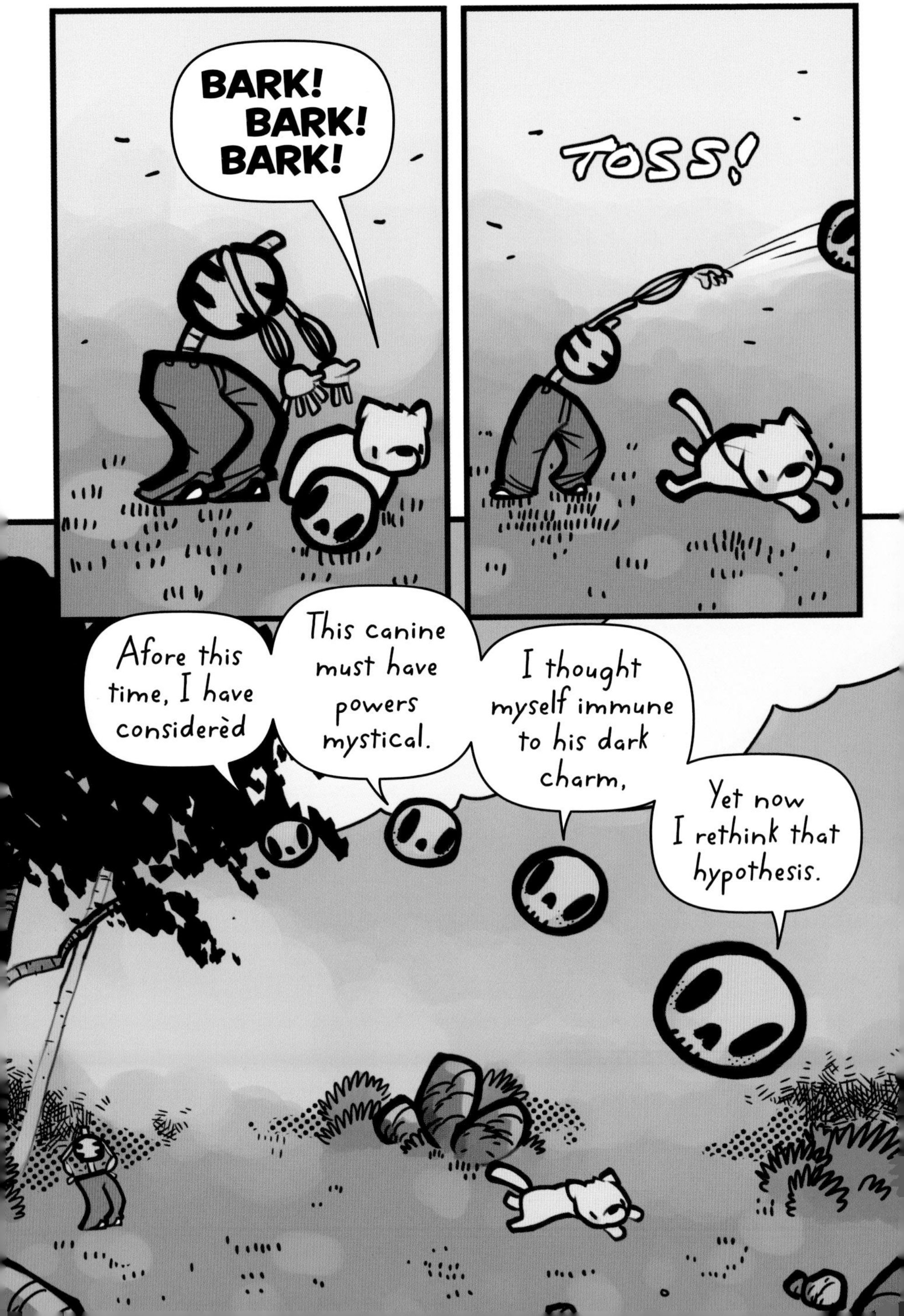
BARK! BARK! BARK!
TOSS!
Afore this time, I have considerèd
This canine must have powers mystical.
I thought myself immune to his dark charm,
Yet now I rethink that hypothesis.

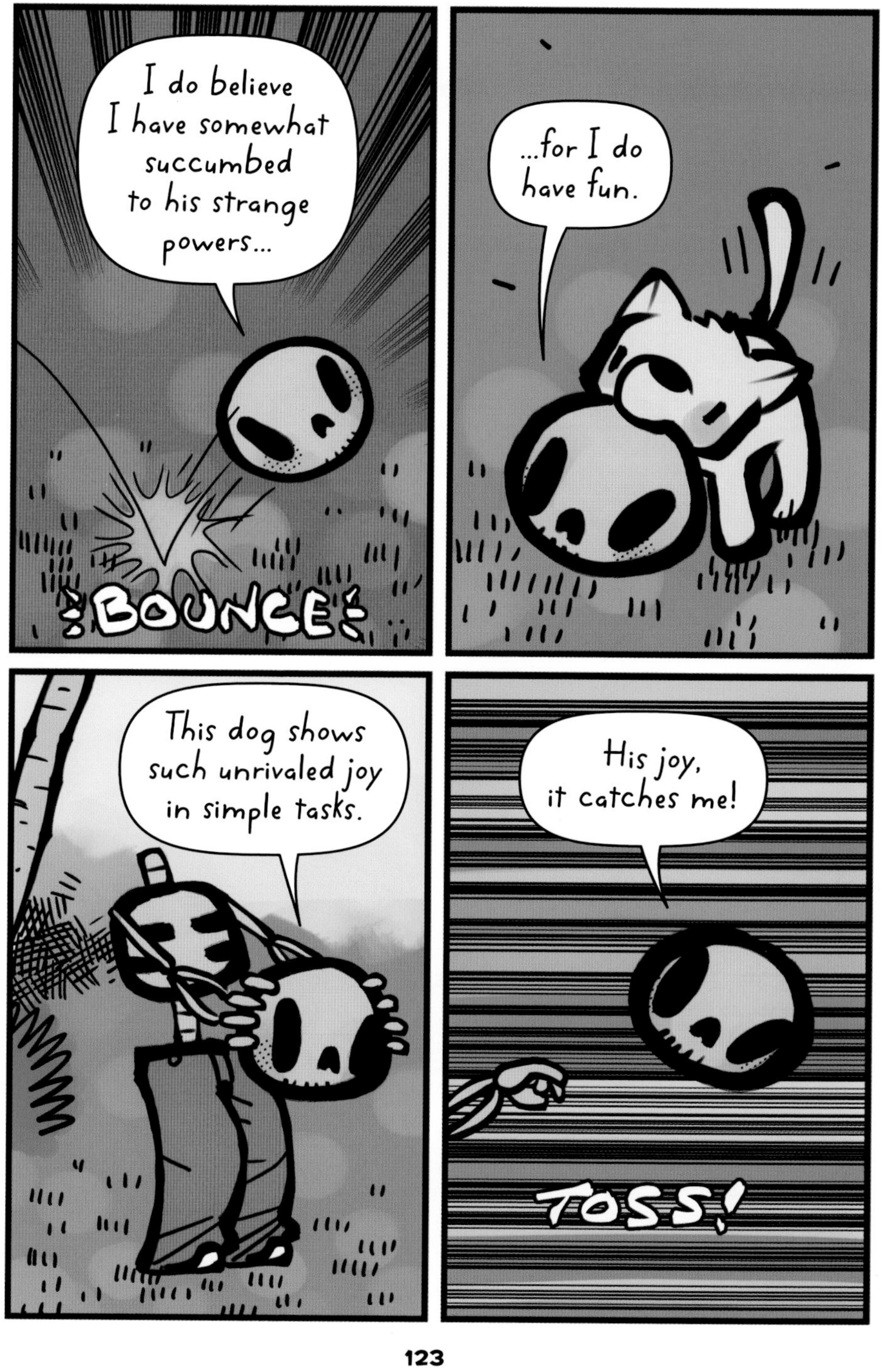
I do believe I have somewhat succumbed to his strange powers...
BOUNCE!
...for I do have fun.
This dog shows such unrivaled joy in simple tasks.
His joy, it catches me!
TOSS!

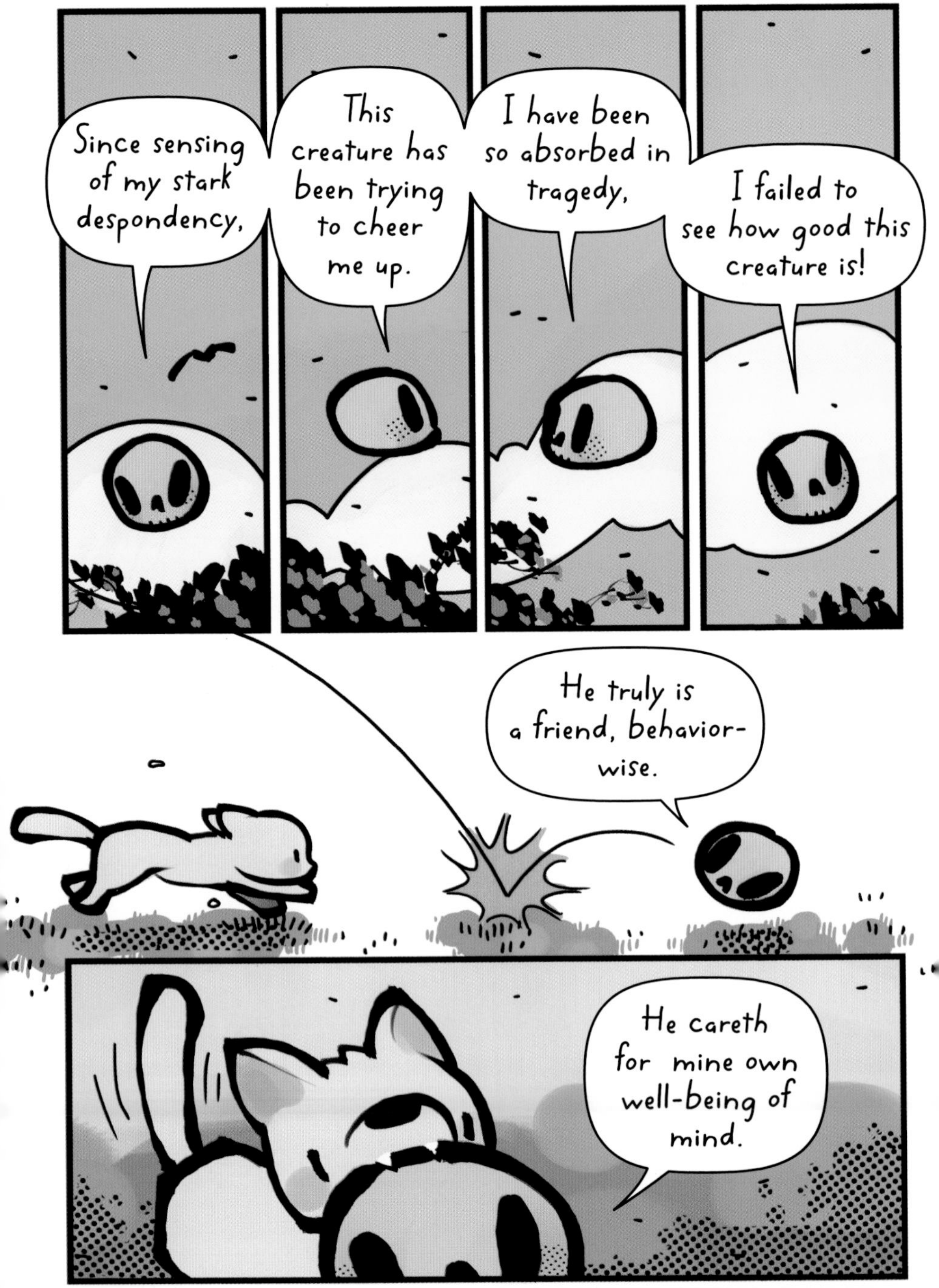
Since sensing of my stark despondency,
This creature has been trying to cheer me up.
I have been so absorbed in tragedy,
I failed to see how good this creature is!
He truly is a friend, behavior-wise.
He careth for mine own well-being of mind.

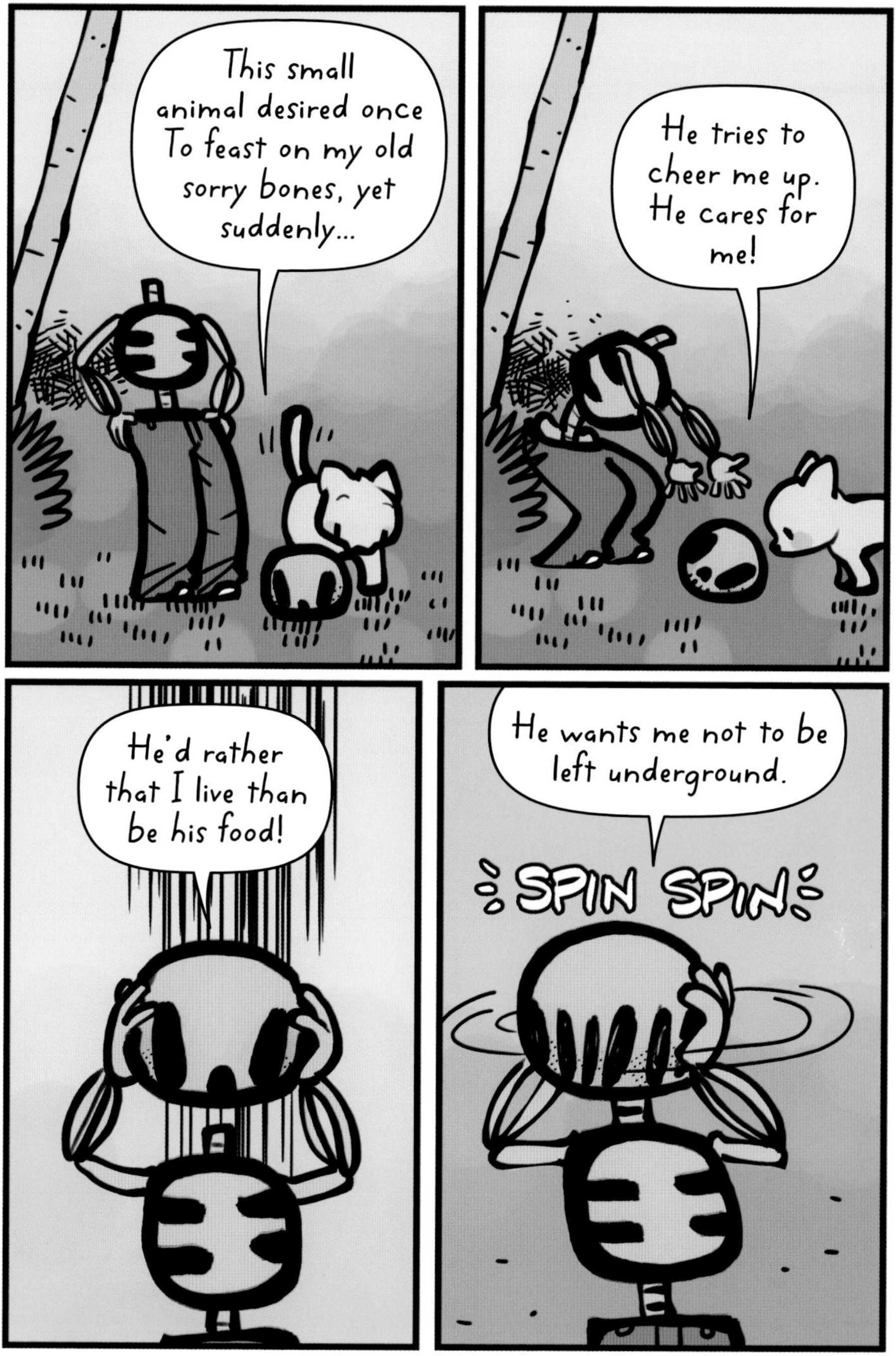
This small animal desired once To feast on my old sorry bones, yet suddenly...
He tries to cheer me up. He cares for me!
He'd rather that I live than be his food!
He wants me not to be left underground.
SPIN SPIN

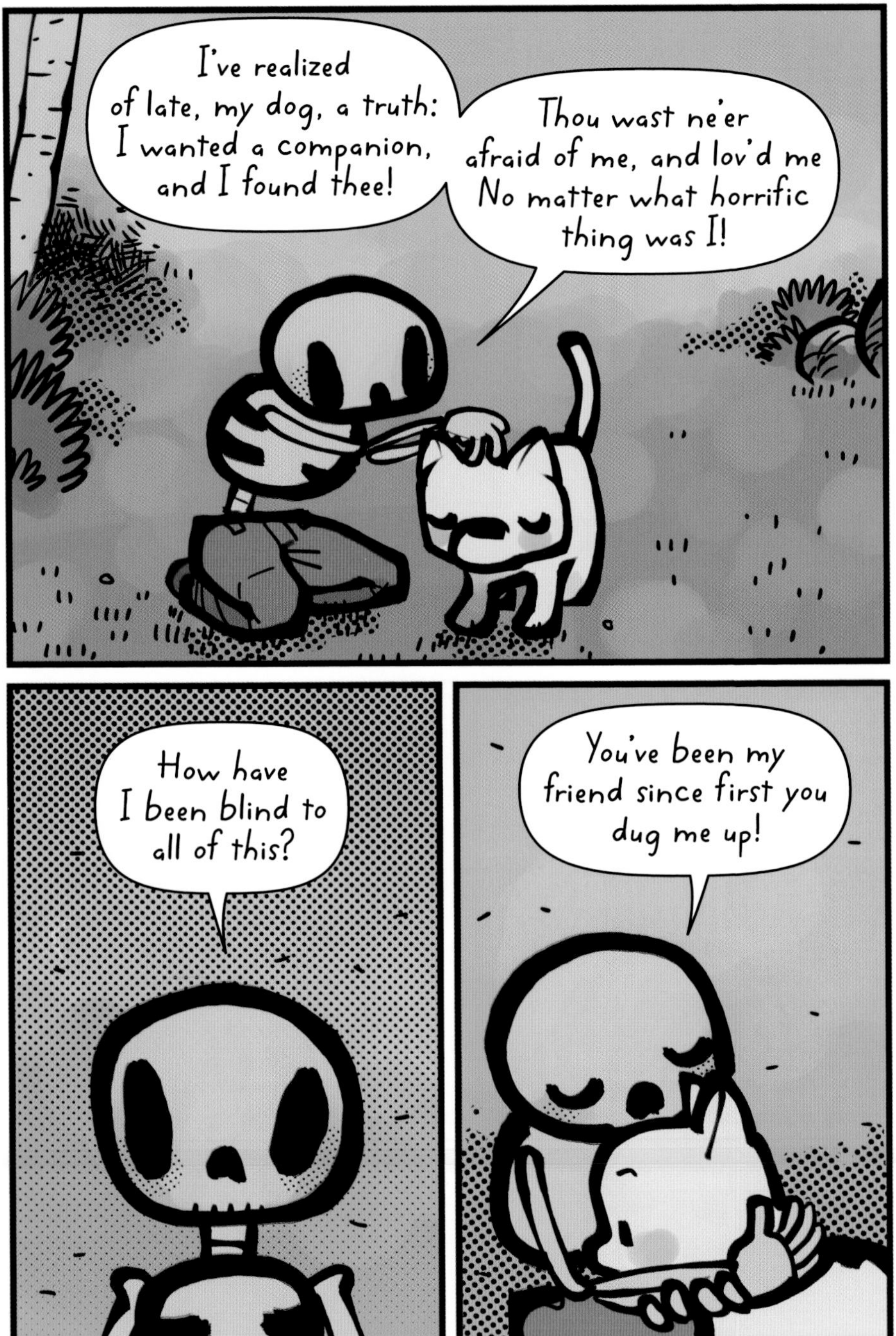
I've realized of late, my dog, a truth: I wanted a companion, and I found thee!
Thou wast ne'er afraid of me, and lov'd me No matter what horrific thing was I!
How have I been blind to all of this?
You've been my friend since first you dug me up!

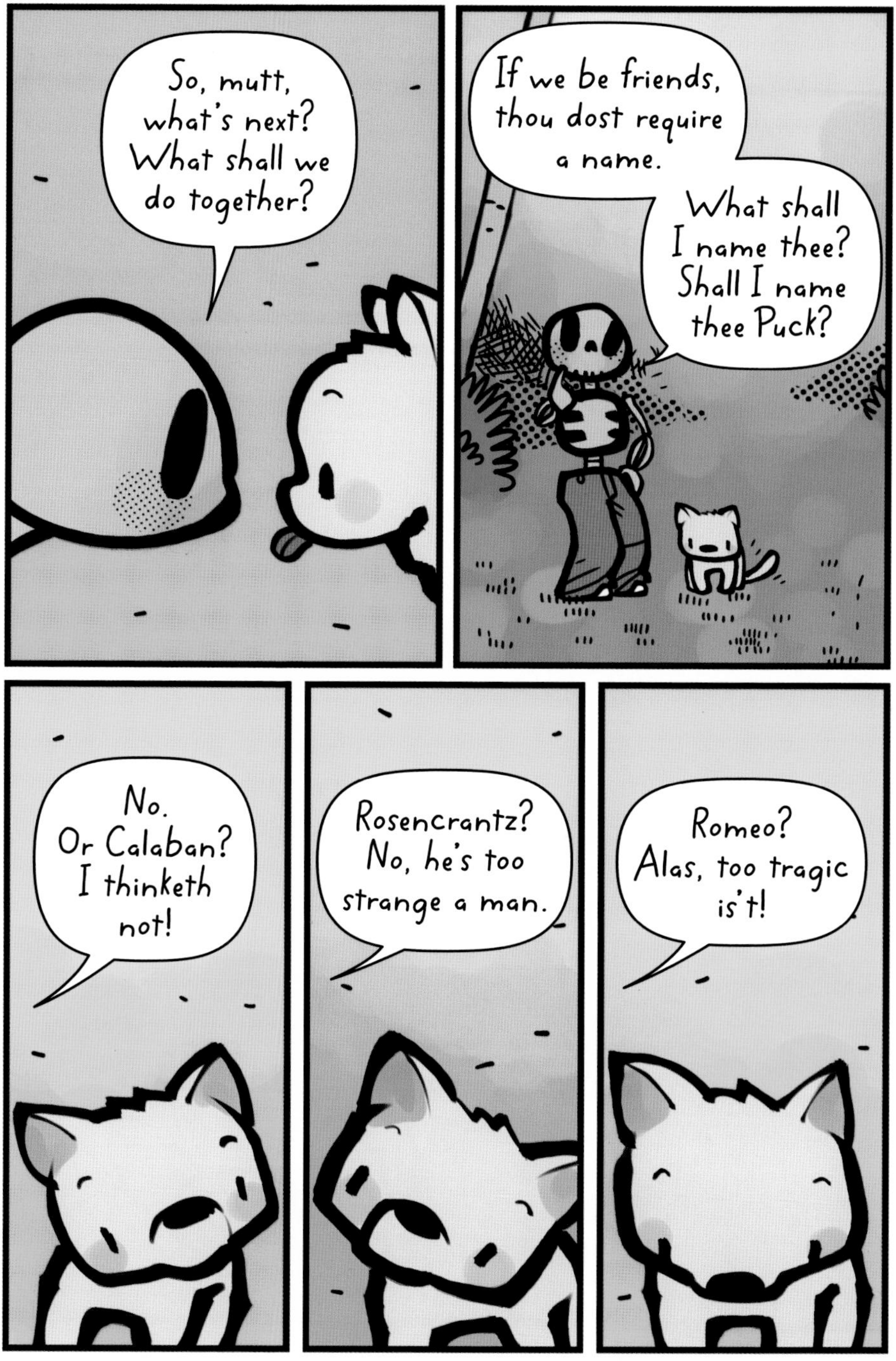
So, mutt, what's next? What shall we do together?
If we be friends, thou dost require a name.
What shall I name thee? Shall I name thee Puck?
No. Or Calaban? I thinketh not!
Rosencrantz? No, he's too strange a man.
Romeo? Alas, too tragic is't!

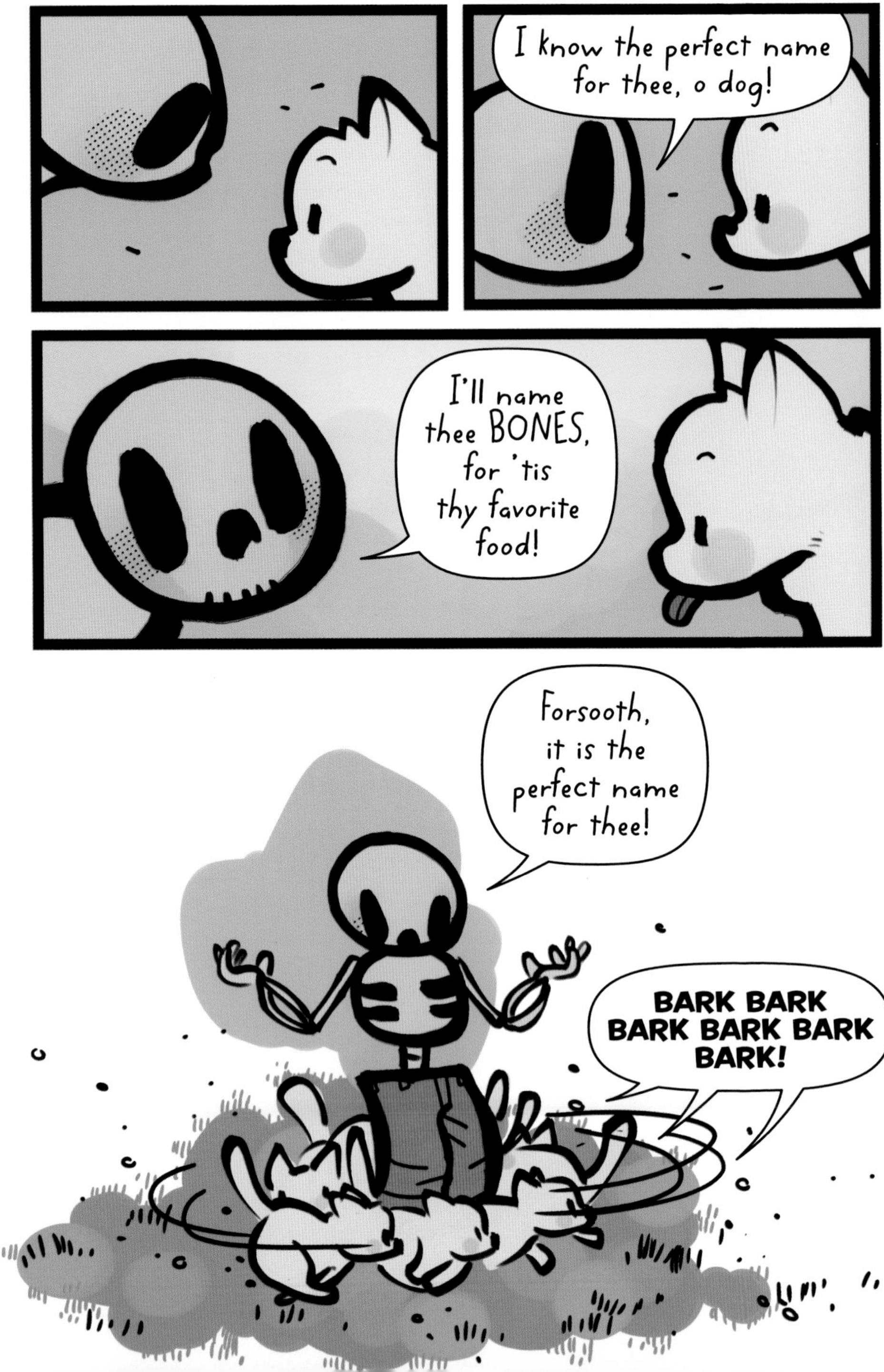
I know the perfect name for thee, o dog!
I'll name thee BONES, for 'tis thy favorite food!
Forsooth, it is the perfect name for thee!
BARK BARK BARK BARK BARK BARK!

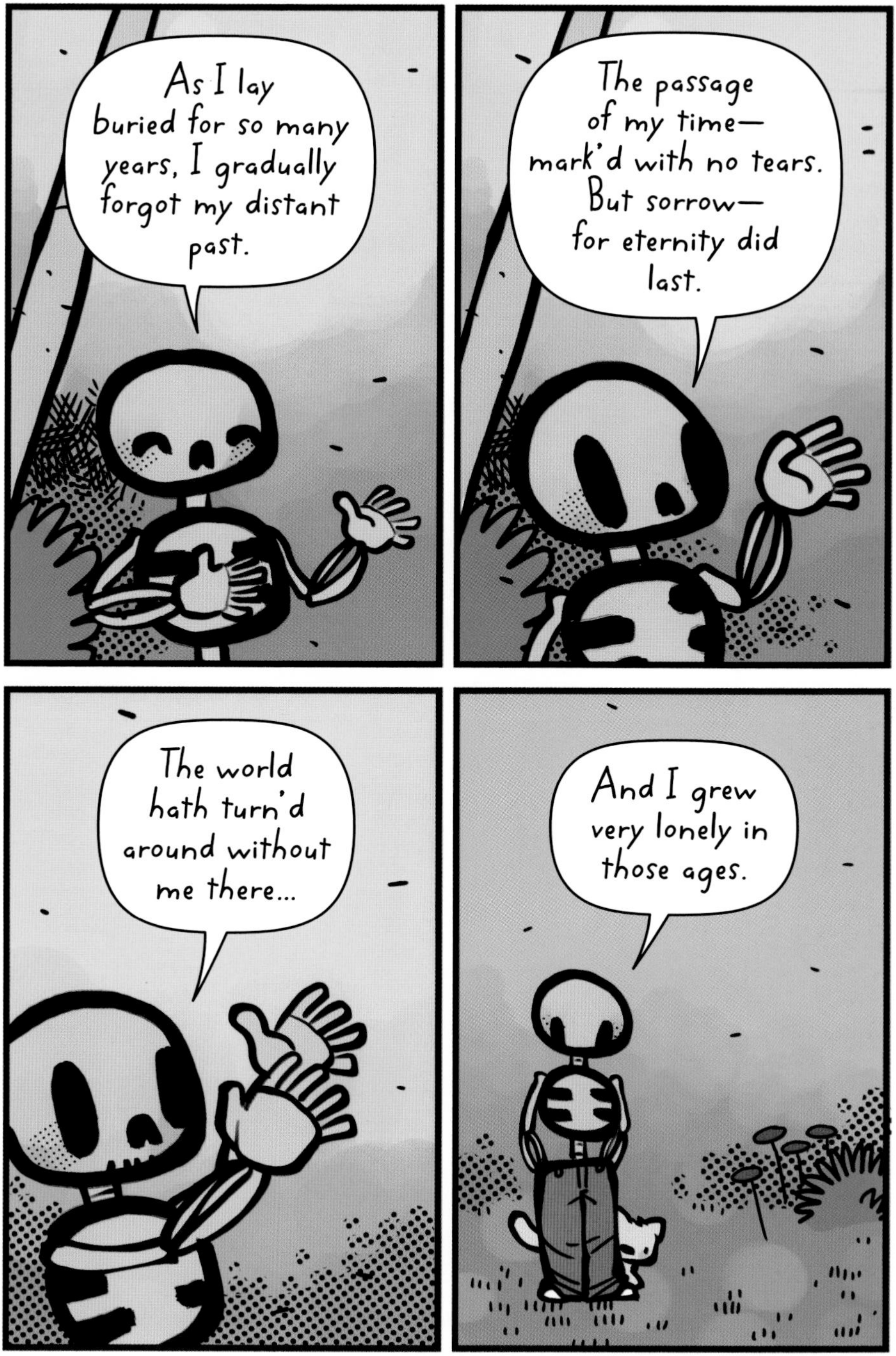
As I lay buried for so many years, I gradually forgot my distant past.
The passage of my time— mark'd with no tears. But sorrow— for eternity did last.
The world hath turn'd around without me there...
And I grew very lonely in those ages.

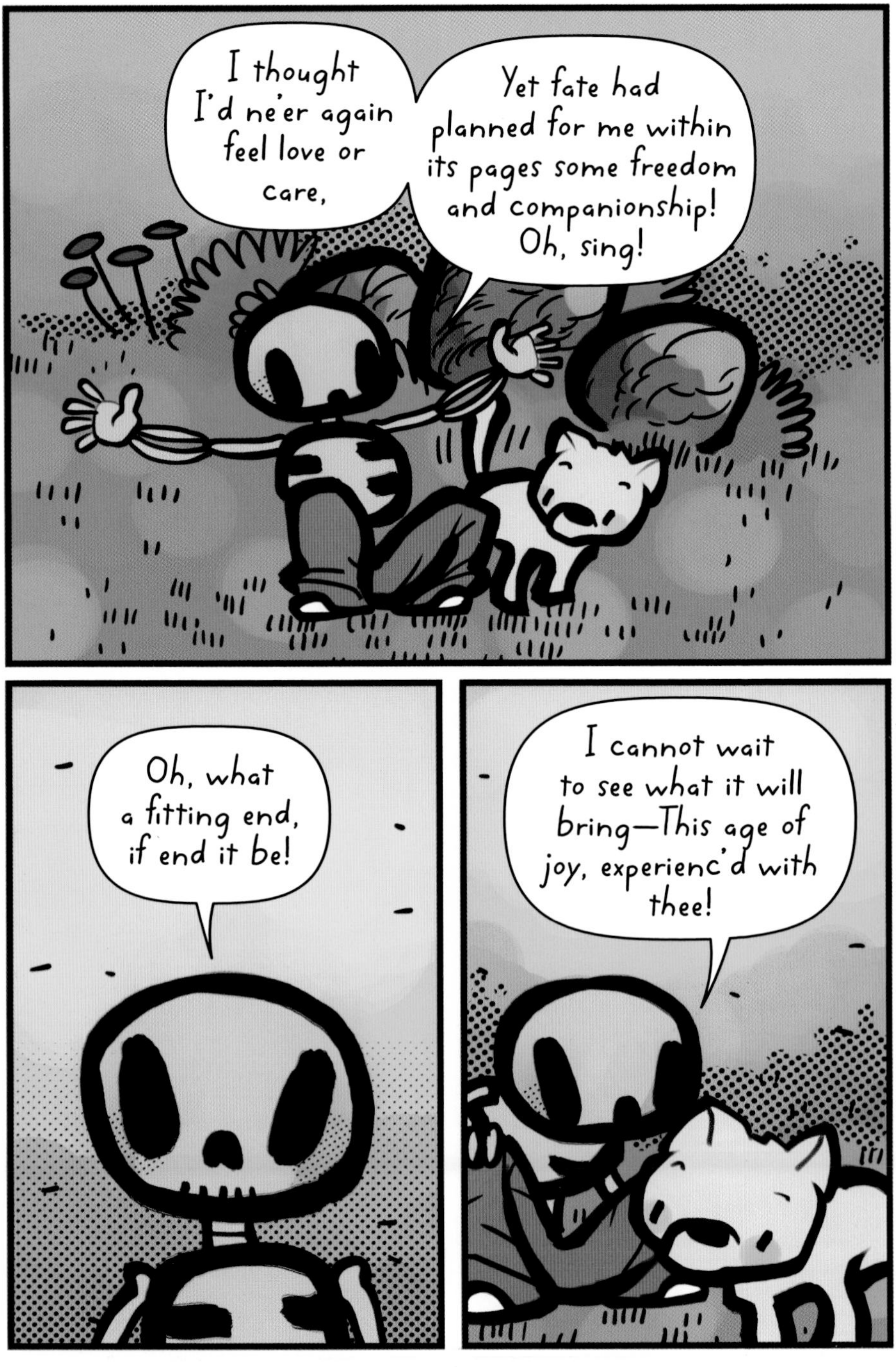
I thought I'd ne'er again feel love or care,
Yet fate had planned for me within its pages some freedom and companionship! Oh, sing!
Oh, what a fitting end, if end it be!
I cannot wait to see what it will bring—This age of joy, experienc'd with thee!

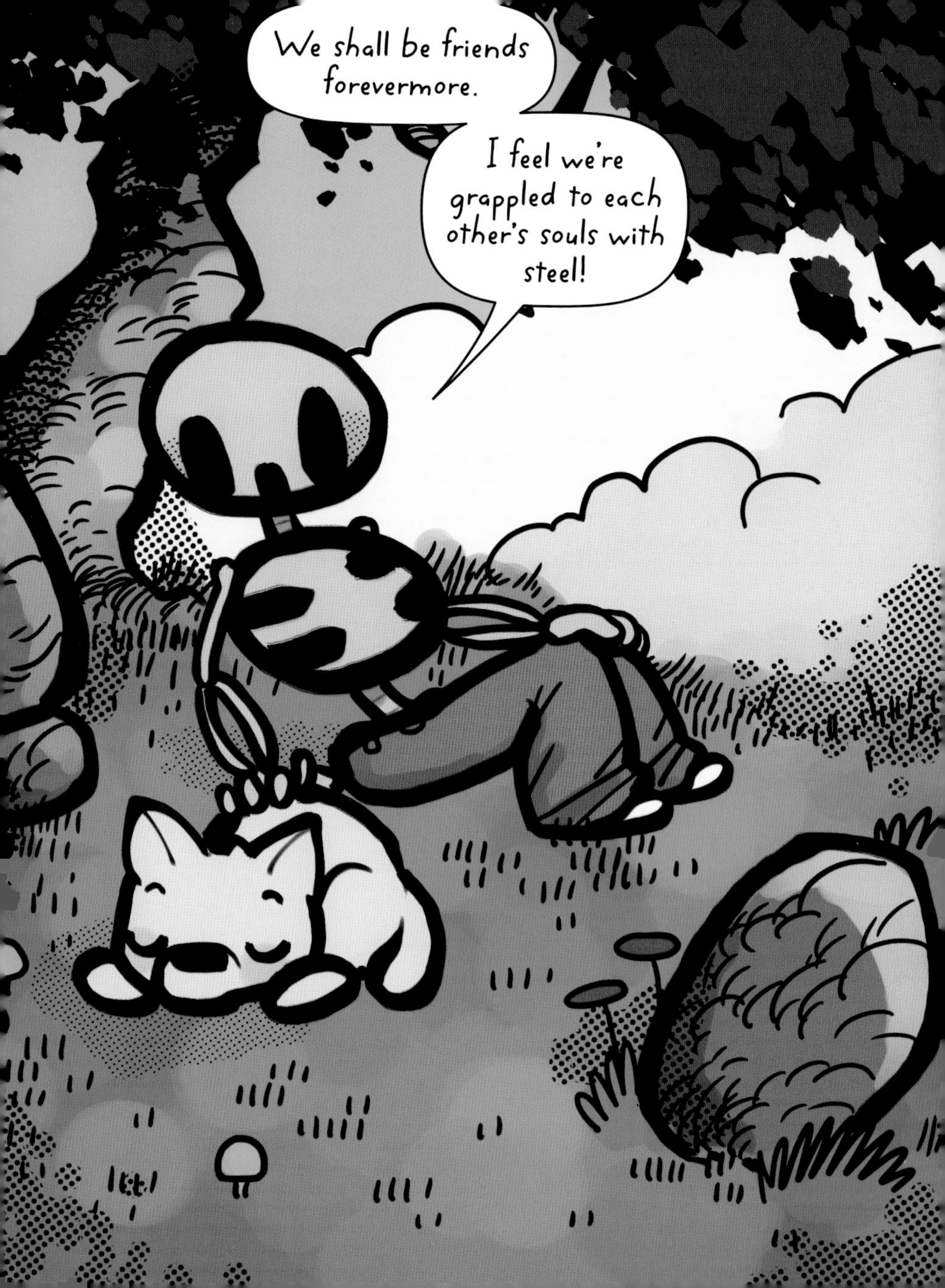
We shall be friends forevermore.
I feel we're grappled to each other's souls with steel!

Acknowledgments

Jeremy

This book has been the recipient of much love in its almost nine-year creation. It actually began life when I was seven years old. I drew a skeleton being terrorized by a small dog who wanted to eat him. Many years later I showed this drawing to some children during a school visit and suddenly realized there was a story to tell here! I came home and began writing and drawing a picture book. This picture book eventually became the graphic novel you now hold in your hands. It could not have made it to this point without a LOT of help. I especially wish to thank my agent, Holly McGhee, who, after years of reading my rewrites, suggested I hand the project over to Hermione, then only fifteen years old, and see what she could do with it. Holly had read a short Shakespearean script that Hermione had written and saw a spark of something amazing. The resulting script, along with some sample art, wound up in the hands of Andrew Eliopulos, who edited everything you just read and helped me hone this story into a real live book. I also owe a debt of gratitude to Erin Fitzsimmons and David Curtis for their expert art direction and design, and to everyone at HarperCollins Children's Books for getting behind this unique project. And, most important, to Hermione, for agreeing to take a stab at translating her dad's script into Shakespearean iambic pentameter, thus giving voice to Yorick. What an extraordinary partner to collaborate with! There's also my good friend Pat Sarell, who has been an enthusiastic supporter and encourager and sounding board. And finally, I must thank my wife, Heather, and my son, Theo, for their enthusiasm and encouragement for all my books. And, of course, you, dear reader, for coming along for the ride. Thank you.

Hermione

I am so grateful to my dad, the creator of this project, for letting me tag along on something that he's been working on for so long! This truly has been a journey, however, and so I feel that I should put my acknowledgments in chronological order. I would like to first thank my mom, without whom there would be no me. Jumping ahead a few years, I would like to thank Susanne and Paul Moniz de Sà, who directed the theater program I was in. They have taught me so much about theater and about life, and I believe it was Paul who first taught me about the rhythmic structure of Shakespeare's plays. So, thank you to Paul and Susanne. Next, I would like to thank Holly McGhee for looking at one of my creative projects, a rewrite of my dad's *Grumpy*

Bird in iambic pentameter, and encouraging me to use this weird skill! Thank you, of course, to Andrew Eliopulos for the amazing feedback and editing and pointing out of things that I would not have otherwise considered, and to everyone at HarperCollins. You really made this book what it is! Thank you, of course, to my dad for letting me be a part of his work. I have admired my dad's books since *Grumpy Bird* came out, and it is such an honor to be able to collaborate with him on this. Thank you to Ian Doescher, Adam Long, Daniel Singer, and Jess Winfield—some fellow writers/Shakespeare nerds who are a huge inspiration to me. Thank you endlessly to my mom, Heather, my brother, Theo, and all my wonderful friends for being so amazing and supportive and just honestly the best. And finally, thank you for reading this book! I hope you liked it!

Early Development of *Yorick* and *Bones*

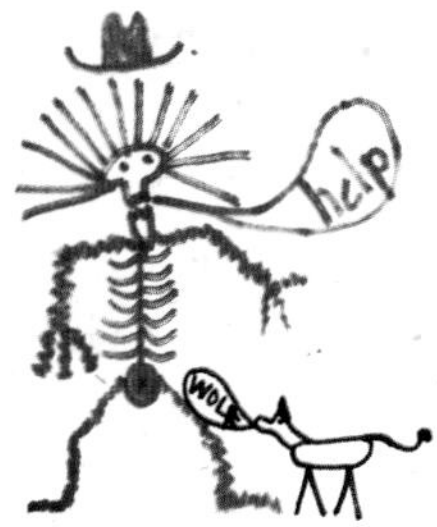
help

I did this drawing when I was seven years old. I spelled "WOOF" wrong.

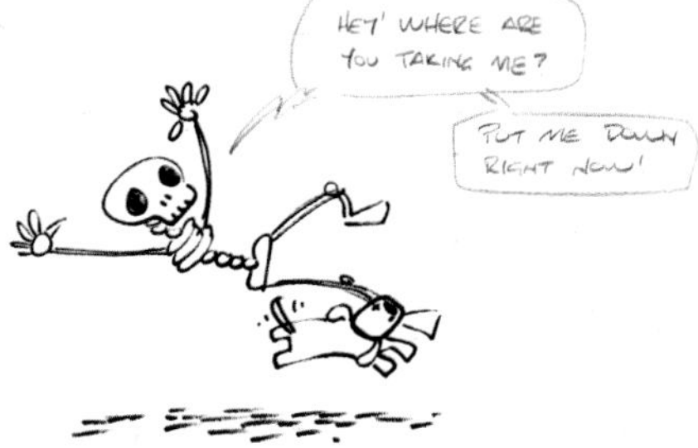
HEY! WHERE ARE YOU TAKING ME?
PUT ME DOWN RIGHT NOW!

As I began work on *Yorick and Bones*, my early design for Yorick was fairly similar to my childhood drawing. I opted to keep adult proportions for Yorick. This changed later in the process because I decided smaller proportions worked better. When Hamlet talks to Yorick's skull in Shakespeare's play, he doesn't make it clear whether Yorick is a grown-up or not. I decided that Yorick was Hamlet's childhood friend.

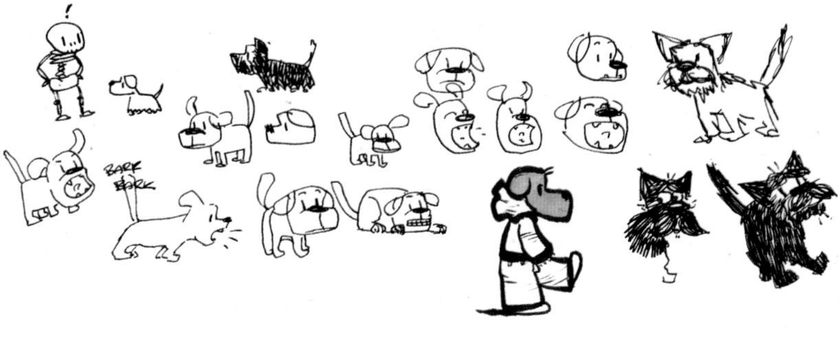
BARK
BARK

Bones provided more challenging design problems than Yorick. What sort of a dog was he going to be? What color? Would he be anthropomorphic, wearing human clothes? All I knew was that I wanted him to be a small dog. And cute.

More drawings of Bones. When I'm uncertain about designs, I often fall back on a more highly rendered style—somewhat more realistic. This helps me see the "real" picture before I begin simplifying toward a final design.

More Yorick drawings. I had originally thought I would draw the whole book with a brush and ink. Some hand/wrist issues necessitated switching to digital tools. While I missed working with ink, I have no regrets. I think the digital art looks fantastic—it's nice and clean.

YORICK
AND
BÖNES